IN HIS
HANDS

ADRIANA
ANDERS

sourcebooks
casablanca

Published by Sourcebooks Casablanca, an imprint of Sourcebooks, Inc.
P.O. Box 4410, Naperville, Illinois 60567–4410
(630) 961–3900
Fax: (630) 961–2168
www.sourcebooks.com

Printed and bound in Canada.
MBP 10 9 8 7 6 5 4 3 2 1

To big A: You are my real life hero. I'll love you, always.

To little A: You are my heart.

THE CHAIN-LINK FENCE WAS THE ONLY THING STANDING between Abby Merkley and freedom.

She picked up the bolt cutters with trembling hands and hacked away at the metal. Judging from the way the sun cleaved through the bare trees, casting long skeletons of shadow, it was close to noon.

Which meant she had to hurry.

Peeling back the chain link wasn't easy the way she was shaking, but she managed to do it without cutting herself. Thank the Lord, else Isaiah would wonder what she'd gotten into and send someone after her.

In order to get through the hole, Abby had to remove her wool coat and carefully avoid the gleaming edges of fresh-cut metal. She paused, out of breath. For some reason she couldn't explain, she undid the ties at her chin and shoved her bonnet back through the hole before standing up.

"Good heavens," she whispered, shocked by how close everything looked without the chain link's honeycomb filter—how clear and bright and full of possibility.

She clutched at the metal behind her, needing it to counteract this dizzying wave of hope.

After a moment, she set off through the vines, gazing at row upon row of bare branches. Would Grape Man have work for her without grapes on his plants?

He had to. He *had* to.

What if he wasn't here? He could easily have left in the half hour it took her to walk here from the Center. The thought had her racing messily between the army of dry, brittle-looking plants, crucified on the mountainside.

The smell of woodsmoke was the first sign that he wasn't far. He was home, at least, thank goodness.

Past a woodshed and through the open picket gate she went. She climbed the three porch steps, breathless, sopping hem hugging her calves uncomfortably. Before she had time to stop herself—because if she stopped, if she thought this through, she wouldn't do it—her knuckles rapped the door.

Out of breath, face prickly hot and the rest of her body chilled, Abby waited.

Nothing. No shuffling, no footsteps, no sound at all besides the creaking floorboards beneath her feet. *I've made it this far*, she told herself. *Keep going. Keep going.*

She turned and scanned the buildings: the henhouse with its little yard full of chickens, two older sheds, and that big, refurbished barn to crown it all. Was he all the way up there?

Abby tromped back down the sagging steps with a renewed sense of purpose, ignoring the chafe of shoes that had seen better days—shoes that weren't made for running.

Ladies aren't meant to run, Hamish used to say. She

swallowed back the memory. He'd been gone for weeks now. And a good thing, too. Nobody deserved the pain he'd endured in those last days.

Nerves buzzing, she circled the cabin—which looked a lot worse up close—went through the back gate, and up the steep slope to the barn. Everything felt strangely off, like stepping through a mirror and seeing things the wrong way around.

The barn, it appeared, was the only building Grape Man had worked on since taking over—the only thing, besides the vines, that he seemed to care about. It was enormous and built right into the boulders that crowned the mountain, with fresh boards and a perfectly straight door that hung slightly ajar. Tentatively, Abby knocked on the thick wood. Too quiet. He wouldn't hear a thing from inside, but she felt hesitant, weighted. *What if he doesn't give me a job?*

Just a few months ago, while Hamish was dying, the place had been a hive of activity. She'd barely had time to glance outside, much less spy on the neighbor.

This place, so silent now that she desperately needed help, intimidated her. But nothing would be worse than going back without accomplishing her goal.

"Hello?" She hated how small she sounded.

"Anyone here? Mr…" Halfway through the door, she stopped. Mr. Grape Man, she'd been about to say, but that would be strange, wouldn't it? It was time to adjust to the way people spoke outside. "Hello?" she called louder, urging herself to move farther in. One step, then a second brought her through a dark vestibule hung with metal equipment. Tall boots lined one wall, and across from her stood a door, which proved to be locked.

This roadblock gave the turmoil in her belly nothing to do, nowhere to go. Weighted by hopelessness, she turned and walked back outside.

All the while, precious time passed. When would they send someone after her? Not for a couple hours at least.

From this height, everything splayed out beneath her looked like toys. The cabin reminded her of something she'd played with as a child, the chickens as artificial as the squat, happy animals from that same foldaway barnyard. *Oh, gracious*, there he was. She stood frozen for a few seconds, eyes fixed on the man who looked nothing like the plastic farmer from that long-ago toy. *I'm doing this. This is real. He's real.*

Her stomach twisted as she finally forced herself to move and scrambled down the rocky slope, half-excited, half-nervous.

She was close when the man finally noticed her. Close enough to feel tiny in comparison to his towering, long-limbed frame. Close enough to see how graceful his movements were, despite his imposing size. Close enough to see his eyes widen in surprise and his high forehead crease into a scowl. From the top of his unruly hair and unshaven face, over faded work clothes—which strained immodestly on his shoulders and arms—to the tip of his muddy boots, everything about this man loomed as darkly foreboding as the mountain.

She took him in for a beat or two, waiting for some sign of welcome from this man whose size did nothing to allay the fears she'd plowed through to get here. The hope she'd depended on to counter the many, many risks.

He offered no kindness at all, no neighborly hello

or hand raised in greeting. Abby almost stepped back, intimidated. But there was no choice. There'd be no leaving here without a job. Judging from the entrenched look of his frown, she'd have bet those immobile lips hadn't twisted into anything resembling a smile in years. As she forced herself to step forward into his shadow, the lines around his eyes deepened. *Make that decades.*

"Good morning, sir," she forced in her friendliest voice. Surely he'd hear the cracks beneath the surface, that edge of desperation. He opened his mouth, but before he had a chance to say a word, she soldiered right through. "My apologies for disturbing you on this…" She glanced at the lowering clouds, as broody and gray as his frigid eyes, and blubbered on. "I'm Abigail Merkley. Abby, I mean. *Abby* Merkley. I'm looking for work, sir."

He squinted at her outstretched hand in a way that was decidedly unfriendly, and for a good few seconds, it appeared he might not accept. Her first handshake ever, rebuffed.

Breathe, Abby. Breathe.

He relented after a bit, carefully setting down the tool he used to prune the vines and sliding his palm against hers.

She remembered the fish man at the market, the way he shook hands with his best customers. He'd told her it meant something. A connection, a promise. A *covenant*. Setting out this morning on the half-hour walk to the fence line, she'd planned this shake. Firm, businesslike. Secure. *Confident.*

The reality was nothing of the sort. It was… Well, goodness, the handshake wasn't a meeting of equals, the way she'd pictured it. It was consumption, one hand swallowed by the other. And it did things to her. Made her feel the difference in stature quite keenly. There was also the matter of how alone she was out here on this mountain. No one knew where she was—not a solitary soul—and here she'd gone and put her hand into an ogre's. Walked right up to him and offered it up.

He didn't scare her nearly as much as what lay on the other side of the fence, though. He should have, but... what was it about his face? Not the unexpected translucence of those eyes nor their chilly distance. He didn't trust this, she could tell. He was angry, maybe, at her intrusion, but there was something else. Something sad or hopeless, apparent in the purposeful squaring of those wide shoulders—an effort, she thought.

"Work?" He uttered his first word as his other hand rose to hers, chafing it in a way she'd have bet was subconscious. The word sounded off, chewed away at the *r*. His voice, deep and growling, was not what she'd expected. It made her want to clear her throat for him. "What work?"

She was ready for this question. She'd watched him, after all. Cutting and moving, cutting and moving. She'd watched and imagined a different sort of life. "I could help out here," she said brightly.

"Here?" He dropped her hand like a burning coal and shifted away.

"I've seen you pruning. Last year, you hired people. I figured—"

"I do it myself," he cut in. This time, she heard it: an accent. Not that thick, but different from any she knew. The words stayed close to the front of his mouth, pushing his lips out into a pout. As he spoke, she finally understood those deep-cut parentheses framing them.

"Oh." Disappointment tightened her chest, a sense of urgency making it hard to breathe. "I can learn," she said. When his expression didn't budge, she begged. "I'll do it for less than you paid the others."

His eyes lowered before meeting hers. "Where's your coat?"

Why on earth did he sound so accusatory?

"I don't…" She glanced back up the mountain, to where she'd left it in a pile by the fence, and pictured slipping it back on over shoulders bowed by defeat.

He wasn't going to do it, was he? He wasn't going to give her the job that might save Sammy's life. This wasn't the man. It wasn't the day. It wasn't the mountain. Quite possibly not the lifetime. Was there any point?

She ignored him and turned back, taking in the view—different from the one on the other side—Church land, with its westward-facing vista. It was rockier here, steeper and more interesting. The sky in this direction pulled out all the stops, its high-contrast clouds cut off right over the seam of the mountains, saving their drama for these richer folks.

This side had begun to represent a way out, a better life for Sammy. Today, it had lost its glow—soured by anguish and despair and the almost audible ticking of the clock. *Get Sammy out, get him out, get him out*, it chanted in time with the panicked beating of her heart.

Sucking in a big, icy breath, Abby looked right into that unforgiving face and said, "I would do most anything, sir."

She meant it, too.

◇◦◇

Luc Stanek blinked, wondering if he was hallucinating this woman. The wind buffeted her dress, long hair coming loose from her braid, and the crisp winter light hardened her edges. All of it turned her into a statue. Or a painting, stark and stiff, washed with amber like something by one of those Wyeths or Whistler or whoever.

Those words—*I would do most anything*—accompanied by the memory of her hand between his set off a faint prickle that was almost desperate. It moved something inside him. A part of him he hadn't acknowledged in a while.

The woman turned away, shielded her eyes against the sun, and squinted back up the mountain. Toward where she'd clearly come from: that sect with their old-world skirts and aprons and those white things on their heads. Strange, strange people with all that razor wire surrounding their little world. It was like a prison, or one of those military testing facilities you'd sometimes see in American films. Was it fear of discovery that sent her gaze back in that direction?

Her dark-red hair, uncovered, snaked over one shoulder in a single braid, ending at her waist. It looked thick and strong compared to her slender form. He should have known she was real—he'd never have created a redhead for himself.

And *mon Dieu*, she appeared starved. Her cheekbones were painfully sharp, dark bruises etched under her eyes, and the eyes themselves…

Luc's brain stuttered to a halt, caught in their light. They were whiskey brown, too big for her pale, freckled face. Someone needed to feed this woman a big plate of *steak frites*.

He shook himself. *Don't get involved*, his brain told him. But his tongue, so unused to opportunities like this, escaped him. "They sent you?"

She blinked, near-translucent moon-shaped lids covering those eyes before focusing back on him so hard he had to look away.

"Who?"

"Those people. From over there. Your dress and shoes. The Church of the…"

"Apocalyptic Faith," she finished for him. Her brow lowered and her mouth hardened, gossamer softness turning rigid and defensive.

"Did they send you to me?" he asked. He reached back to find a vine, his fingers shifting from cordon to brittle canes—not one of his family's. No, this vine was his alone. With a proprietary stroke, he removed his hand and forced his attention to stay on the woman.

"I need money. I knew you'd hired those men last year and—"

"No. Too many…questions." The workers had been a nightmare. More exhausting than the work itself. He couldn't get around hiring them for harvest and crush, but pruning he would do alone. Leave the big-time personnel management to hot shots like his half brother, Olivier.

"Oh," she said, and he hadn't realized how lively her face had been until her features sank even further. "I could learn," she said again. Her chin lifted with the words, baring a long neck, pale and slender and covered in gooseflesh.

"You need the money to buy a coat?" Where were

these questions coming from? He didn't want to know. Shoving the curiosity down, he turned back to his half-pruned vine. He let his hands lead from spur to spur, snipping before moving on to the next. If he ignored her, maybe she'd leave.

"One of those shiny, puffy ones," she said with a smile he tried hard not to see. "They look real warm."

Was she being serious? He couldn't tell. She sounded too nervous to be joking.

As his body worked and his brain did its best to pretend the woman wasn't there, Luc's mouth continued of its own volition, asking questions without his consent. "Your coats don't warm you?" he asked.

It took a few cuts for the secateurs to become an extension of his arm again, sharing in his warmth, giving it back. He almost never wore gloves for pruning. At least, he hadn't back home. Here in this frigid place, he probably should. But gloves cut him off from his plants, dulled the connection he felt when cutting away each cane. Shaking his arms to relieve them of their numbness, he moved on to the next vine, cradling its trunk with one hand. He ran his fingers up the head, along the closest cordon to the first spur, and snipped, leaving two buds and adding another crisp, dry sound to a crisp, dry day.

Without answering, the woman followed his progress.

He slid one bare finger along the arm to the next spur, small and pitiful. The brittle sound of it succumbing to the secateurs confirmed that it wasn't meant to be. He gave the cane a quick, affectionate squeeze before pulling it out of the wires, throwing it down onto the ground, and moving on. His gaze caught the space on his hand where a ring finger used to be. Even weak, useless appendages deserved respect in their final moments.

"What happened to your finger?" she asked, as if reading his mind.

"Are you all so curious in your…" What was it? Not a village, although it sort of looked like one from afar, with its log cabins and big, ugly central building. And calling it a cult to her face didn't seem right. "Your group?"

"Oh, goodness. I'm sorry." She seemed abashed.

Luc felt a rush of shame at picking on her. This was why he didn't do this conversation thing. He always managed to say the wrong thing.

"I cut it off. With secateurs. Battery-powered ones that my broth—" He stopped himself from telling her the whole story, took in a couple of deep breaths, and blindly trimmed a spur he should have left. *Merde*. He breathed in slowly, out slowly, the way he'd learned to do whenever faced with strangers. "It was a cold day like this. You see? It is too dangerous for you to help."

"You could cut and I could pull the branches out, to save you time and—"

"No!" The word came out sharp and loud enough to echo off the cliff face. It sounded, if possible, angrier in the retelling.

She stiffened, her hand dropping from the canes he'd already cut. She took a step back and, head low, whispered, "Thank you, sir. For your time."

Bordel, he hadn't meant to hurt her. He'd… *Just let her go.*

As she turned and made her way up the row of vines, Luc looked at the shadowy rocks above her. Their faces, normally benevolent as they oversaw his progress, exuded something different today—something forbidding. Ominously biblical shards of sunlight shone through the roiling clouds. None of this was good. She needed to leave him alone to his work and go back to her side of the mountain, but he didn't like this dirty feeling the encounter had put in his gut, like a film that needed rinsing.

He called out to her, "Good luck," hating how badly he wished she'd turn back for one final glimpse.

When she didn't respond, irritation rose up in a childish burst.

Why the hell had those cult people sent her to him? What kind of maneuver was this? And if they hadn't sent her and she was…escaping, or whatever it was, she should just leave. The woman was old enough to know better. If a person didn't want to be part of a religion, she should take off. Simple.

He'd learned from experience that if you wanted it badly enough, you could rip your roots from any soil, no matter how deep they'd grown.

Or how much it hurt.

෨൦

As she crawled back through the fence, jobless, Abby's head was bowed, nerves and excitement replaced by the weight of failure. How would she find help for Sammy now?

Her dress snagged on the sharp edges, adding one more item to the pile of mending she'd ignored since Hamish had passed. Everything, from her back to her hips to the space behind her eyes, ached with defeat.

It was time to walk the fence. A ridiculous job created just for her, since she couldn't be trusted with anything else—too restless to work in the kitchen, too friendly to work with outsiders. The day Isaiah'd taken her off market duty, she'd lost some faith. Just a tiny bit, but enough to chip away at the steadfastness inside her.

There'd been other things since, her late husband's suffering high among them, and now Sammy. Poor Sammy. They'd come back to the Church once he was cured.

I have to get him out first, don't I?

Her shoes cut a noisy path through the yellow grass, skirting the chain link that separated the Church from the rest of the miserable world. She tried not to think of Grape Man's face. How badly he'd wanted to be rid of her.

It was so different from the encounter she'd imagined. Probably because she'd pictured him like a member of the Church or one of the farmers who sold at the market: soft-spoken and civilized. Instead, he'd been as wild as this mountain, sharp as the craggy rocks above. Those hands, rough and missing a finger. Even his voice had been unpolished enough to prickle her skin, like rubbing an animal hide the wrong way. Uncomfortable.

After two long hours—about half a circuit of the fence line—she headed back toward the empty cabin she called home. Not for long, she knew, since Hamish was gone and some other man would be assigned the place. Possibly even the woman. Her stomach tightened at the notion. Who would she be given to this time? Daniel, whose beady eyes trailed her all the more relentlessly since she'd become a widow? Or James, another old man, even less suited to the duty of getting her with child than Hamish had been? No. There wasn't a single palatable option among them.

I shouldn't be thinking like this, doubting God's will.

Seeing someone suffer would do that to a person, she thought as she skirted around Mama's cabin, where she could usually find a warm meal. But not tonight. Not when she couldn't possibly hide these feelings of betrayal and disillusionment.

So, of course, the door opened and Mama stepped out to call, "You coming? Made chicken pot pie. Pickled beans. Isaiah'll be home soon. Come in and help me set the table."

"Can't tonight, Mama. I'm not—"

"What? You got something more important to do? Someone you gotta see?"

"No, I'm just tired."

"Come on, girl. 'They will greet you and give you two loaves of bread, which you will accept from their hand.' Don't make me ask twice." Knowing she'd made her point, Mama disappeared inside her warm cabin. How could Abby refuse its pull when all that awaited in her own home was the lonely stench of sickness? It was still Hamish's cabin to her mind, no matter how often she'd aired it out over the past weeks.

Giving in to Mama's invitation was easy, although she knew acting normal after what she'd done wouldn't be.

"Wash up and set that table," Mama ordered.

"Yes, ma'am." Abby didn't mind doing as her mama asked. Better to be occupied, she supposed.

They worked in silence for a bit, the smells of pot pie taking her back to a time before she'd been wed to Hamish.

There'd been so much good when she and Mama had arrived at the Church. So much better than life before. As a poor, starving seven-year-old, Abby had gone from having one struggling mother to a whole family, where everyone pitched in for the greater good. All servants of God, preparing for the Day.

But then they'd taken her away from Mama and that… Lord, that had been hard after sleeping tight against her side all Abby's life. No matter that they'd been snuggled in the back of their old station wagon. At least they'd been together.

"Got your head in the clouds again, girl? Always someplace else, aren't you?"

"Just remembering how it used to be. Before we came here."

"Why would you do that?"

Abby shrugged. "Just feeling sad, I suppose."

Regretting the impulse to share, she looked away as her mother straightened her face, taking on that look she got before a lecture.

"Did not God choose the poor of this world to be rich in faith and heirs of the kingdom?" she asked, her earnestness breaking Abby's heart. "Your husband, Hamish, was a Chosen One, honey. You know that. It was his time."

"He didn't have to suffer like that," she whispered. As expected, displeasure stormed across her mother's features, but Abby couldn't help it. Nobody else had nursed Hamish through the worst moments. It had been her duty as wife, and she'd done it gladly. Until he'd begged her to help him. That was when her own faith had begun to flag. That exact moment when Hamish, the most devout man she'd ever met, had turned his eyes from the savior he'd built his entire life on and laid them fervently upon her.

"It was God's will for him to suffer, Abigail. You know that better than anyone." Mama lifted her arm and bared the scar, the Mark of the Chosen. "We suffer for our Lord, and when the day is nigh, he accepts us unto him and we will be saved."

Make it end, Hamish had whispered—the man who'd lived life as her better. The man who'd beaten her when she'd eyed the clothing of a modern teenager covetously. The man who'd done his duty by her in their bedroom without taking an ounce of pleasure from the experience. If God could withdraw from so devout a man in his moment of need, how could *she* hope for understanding?

"Yes, Mama," Abby said, but her mother wasn't done. Those hands, only slightly lined from work, grabbed one of hers and yanked Abby's sleeve back. The act of baring another's skin was shocking, despite it being her own flesh and blood. Abby couldn't remember the last time another human's eyes had landed on any piece of her besides her face. Even Hamish, in his couplings, had ensured she remain modestly covered.

"This, *this* was your suffering. You were chosen, and you endured gladly. Hamish was chosen and gave of his life. Would you not give of yours, Abigail?" Mama asked, so close the spittle rained gently on Abby's face.

Abby hesitated. Her eyes widened, huge and dry, her insides not quite as full of that easy conviction as they'd once been.

Finally, on a shaky breath, she said, "Yes, Mama." It

felt close to a lie. It wasn't her first untruth, and she had the miserable expectation it wouldn't be her last, but she hated it nonetheless. Hated the distance between them. Perhaps hardest of all, she hated her own skepticism. If a true servant such as Hamish had been deserted by God in his moment of need, what of Sammy, who needed help now? And what of Mama, whose belief was steadfast and strong?

She pulled her hand away and shut her eyes hard against the fear such thoughts let in. Only, behind closed lids, she was swamped with shame. *I should trust in Him. I should believe.*

When she'd calmed enough to open her eyes again, she was startled to see Isaiah standing stiffly in the doorway.

"Evening," he said, doffing his hat. As he walked in, he eyed them in a way that made her think he'd heard a goodly part of their conversation. "Smells good."

With a loud inhale, Mama bustled to the wood-fired oven, from which she pulled out a perfectly golden pie before setting it on the table. "Come serve Isaiah, Abigail," she said in that bossy, pious voice.

Wonderful. Just what Abby needed. Their fearless leader delivering another sermon written expressly for her. It wouldn't be the first time, she supposed. Although, in a moment of sadness, she knew that if she managed to get Sammy out, it might well be the last. If only Mama would come with her.

When they sat down to grace, she searched her mother's face and resigned herself to the fact that, as with most things, it was best not to ask.

2

LUC WOULD HAVE FINISHED THE ROW HE WAS ON IF the sky hadn't opened up and pissed down on him, the rain close enough to freezing to be dangerous. It had been on this sort of evening that he'd lopped off his finger. He'd been seventeen when it happened, thanks to the combination of cold and the brand-new battery-powered secateurs his half brother had forced on him. In the name of efficiency, Olivier had claimed. Always more, faster.

Luc had pruned the vine with that thousand-euro tool—and his ring finger along with it. Christ, that wasn't something he felt like doing again. *Grandpère* had been off on a sales trip, and Luc would never forget how he'd had to find the finger and bring it to *Maman* and Olivier. How unmoved they'd been. The trip to the hospital, his hand, his *life*, changed forever. That was the day he'd decided to get the hell out of there, his determination a secret thing he'd nurtured and fed until it *became* him.

The very next day, Luc had gone back out there,

cutting vines the old-fashioned way, electric pruners relegated to the back of the toolshed until some other poor ass decided to give them a whirl. From that day on, he'd had something to work toward. It was brutal, but he'd pushed himself. Worked and learned everything he could, mostly from *Grandpère*. But after the old man died… Well, if Luc couldn't be in charge of the vineyard—if they wouldn't do things his way, the *right* way—he'd leave. And he had, the moment he'd saved up enough money.

As grumpy as the chickens in their coop, he stomped inside and took a quick, hot shower. Once dressed, he grabbed his keys and wallet before heading out to his truck. Since pruning wasn't possible, he'd get his weekly shopping over and done with. It was always better at night, when the store was empty.

As he drove past his last row of vines, he breathed in deeply, resisting the urge to tap the steering wheel twice and kiss his fist. He'd left so much superstitious shit back in France. Things like always pruning from east to west, or the same unwashed beret his grandfather had worn for every one of his sixty-eight harvests.

He headed down the steep part of the drive, through the wooded section, and back out into the open. The crunch and pop of gravel under his tires announced his arrival as he downshifted into the last steep curve before the neighbors' land. *Camp Jesus* they called it in town, although he hadn't seen much actual worship on the other side of this fence.

He took one deep breath in, to prepare for the sight that greeted him here most days—the blood and gore of a… *Merde*, he couldn't remember the word. It was *abattoir* in French, but what the hell was it in English? Weird how some words escaped him in one language or the other. Funny how he felt so French in this place, but in France, he'd been too American.

Today, no carcasses greeted him as he passed their open air…killing shack. What was the stupid word? Nothing there, except—

What the hell? He skidded to a halt, the gravel taking a few seconds longer than the tires to still. In the middle of the drive in front of him stood an animal, its eyes two bright dots in the night. He waited for his lungs to crawl out of his throat and let some oxygen into his brain.

It didn't appear confident enough to be a wolf. Was it a coyote? Did coyotes even live around here? He'd never seen one before, but the way it moved—cautious, low on its haunches—made him think of that. He could picture it feeding off the animal carcasses next door.

After a brief standoff where he thought he'd have to get out and shoo it away, the animal slunk from the fence to disappear into the underbrush and the woods farther beyond. An eerie sound rose up to meet Luc in the quiet.

Ignoring the creature's howl, he lifted his foot from the brake—although not too far, since the three hairpin turns down the mountain kept him from going fast. Once the road straightened out, he gave in to his desire to pick up speed. It was good to let go, get some distance. He accelerated too fast down the last section of drive and fishtailed dangerously at the bottom before skidding to a halt right where gravel met asphalt. One meter beyond the front of his truck, a car sped by, shocking his nerves with a long blast of the horn.

"*Putain*," he cursed. He exhaled hard, his heart trying to push its way out of his chest. "*Bordel de merde*." One inconsequential meter from death. All because he'd been spooked by that animal and those religious weirdos next door. After a good thirty seconds spent getting his breath back, he turned left and made his way sedately toward town.

As he approached downtown Blackwood, Luc squinted at the traffic. What the hell was going on? The place was more crowded than usual. People looked frenetic, and the IGA lot was almost full.

He parked, eyes hopping nervously, that familiar shake to his breath. He should go back. Barely controlling the tremor of his hand, he turned the key in the ignition, put the truck into park, and waited.

No. Don't be an idiot. It's just a few more people than usual. He'd go into the store, grab a few necessities, and get out of there. In and out. He could do this.

Inside the supermarket, his eyes danced around as he watched people buy gallon jugs of water, milk, dozens of eggs, and beer. He pushed through it, gathering the usual: coffee, bread, butter, milk, pasta, the sauce to go along with it, and frozen vegetables.

Beans and soup seemed like a good idea, so he moved to that aisle—only to find a dozen people crowding it. Hell no—he'd do without. Instead, he cut up the next aisle. Beer and wine. He grabbed a six-pack of Stella and made a move to turn back rather than pass in front of the wine. But his path was blocked by a family with one of those extra-long carts for the kids to drive parked diagonally across the entrance. The clown horns squeaked like a herd of deranged geese. He had to get out of here. He headed through the wine, ignoring the itch in the center of his back and the undeniable urge to read the labels. *Don't do it*, his mind screamed as his eyes took in the rows and rows of shitty vintages and—

There it was. His family's name—although not his, which they'd never let him forget: *DeLaurier et fils*, emblazoned on a dozen or so bottles. A small, red-and-yellow flag indicated a sale: $9.99 apiece. Christ. Under ten bucks a bottle? He was tempted to take a picture of it to send to his brother. Instead, in a moment of pathetic pique, he took hold of the bottle beside it—another French sellout—and went to check out, calmer than he'd been on the way in.

The cashier, unfazed by the crazed masses, took in his purchases. "Hear they're calling for a storm?" she asked, voice slow while her hands busily scanned and bagged.

Would this store ever get a self-checkout? he wondered. If there were another store in Blackwood, he'd have gone there just to avoid this weekly exchange.

"No."

"Saying we might get a good icing."

Luc didn't respond, but as usual, his silence had no effect. The woman kept talking.

"You only been here a couple of years, right?" She barely paused, not waiting for a response. "Haven't seen real weather yet. Wouldn't be surprised if you got more up on the mountain than we're gonna get here."

How the hell did everybody in town know where he lived? He still couldn't figure that out. He stared at the belt and willed it to roll his items forward faster.

"Won't make it off the mountain if we get ice," she added.

He finally engaged with her. "We're not going to."

"Weatherman Bob Campbell begs to differ."

"No snow," he said with a farmer's certainty. He knew. He'd feel it in his phantom knuckle if snow were truly coming in.

"Well, I guess you're right, since we're getting *ice*. Not snow." The cashier smirked, wagging one of those chubby, age-speckled fingers at him.

In France, a woman this old would never have to work. Nor would a cashier help with anything, much less try to converse. The cashier would ignore everyone, sullen and irritable. Maybe throw down a few plastic bags if none were brought—and even those had to be paid for. He'd prefer angry silence to this constant, cheerful prattle. It was exhausting.

"Snow's one thing, but when the temps go down and every darn thing gets coated in the clear stuff, you won't be able to leave your place for days. Bet you don't see stuff like that where you're from."

What if she was right? Would there be time to get his vines pruned before it hit? *If* it hit, which he still wasn't convinced it would—at least not in the next twenty-four hours.

"When is it supposed to start?" he asked.

"Talking about tomorrow night, but you never know."

Back outside, the sky was clear, the air cold and crisp in his lungs. No precipitation tonight, at least. The band across Luc's chest loosened as he headed back, ecstatic to finally be on his own.

God, he was a misanthrope. His chickens more than satisfied his need for company. And yet…

An impression of that woman's thin, cold hand

sandwiched between his own rose up with a warm blush. He'd rubbed her hand, hadn't he? Trying to chafe some heat into her flesh, he'd thought, but maybe—just maybe—he'd been trying to leach something from her.

Putain, what an idiot. *Quel con.*

He really should see about getting an Internet connection so he could... What? Develop an online relationship? Connect with some other solitary soul? The idea didn't interest him nearly as much as the memory of that woman's pride. Begging for a job with her back as stiff as a rail. Her hand frail-looking, but the bones firm between his, the skin slightly roughened.

He focused on his own misshapen hands. It was a wonder he'd felt the texture of her skin, given the state of his. He tightened and stretched the left hand—stared at that empty space he'd never quite gotten used to. His bones snipped off and discarded like last year's useless vine. *Polish bones*, his mother always called them. Just another affectionate insult.

And wasn't that the crux of everything? Too big for a Frenchman, too thick and rough for smooth seduction. And certainly too ill at ease with the games involved. He shuddered at the memory of dates gone bad.

Halfway up the mountain, Luc was so distracted that he didn't notice the animal until his truck was nearly on top of it again. *Putain*, it wasn't a coyote. It was a damned dog. Probably one of theirs. On the wrong side of the fence.

Or the right side.

From the warm interior of his truck, he waited for it to scuttle away again, but it stayed in the middle of his path. A face-off.

"*Casses-toi*," he said under his breath, wishing the dog gone. "*Allez, vas-y.*" When it didn't move, he opened his door with a sigh, got out, and stomped toward it. He clicked his teeth in an effort to get it out of the way.

The dog only stood taller, watching him closely. Its ears were plastered to its head, coat hidden beneath a layer of dust and filth.

"*Comment t'es sorti, toi*? *Hein*?" he asked, wondering how the dog had gotten out from behind the fence.

Its ears lifted, head cocked to the side. Listening.

"*T'as faim*?"

Nothing.

"Don't speak French, I guess."

It was apparently hungry enough to take another step closer, before cowering back. Did those nuts beat their animals? Weren't these religious people supposed to be peaceful and kind, with their faith and old-fashioned demeanors? He couldn't picture the woman from today—Abby—hitting a dog.

"*Allez, dégages.* Go, go on." He tried to shoo it one last time, with no luck at all. The dog was a mess. Could it even move?

Its head tilted, ears lifting higher, looking hopeful. For a brief second, Luc recalled the expression on Abby Merkley's face when she'd offered her hand to shake.

"My God," he whispered, and the dog, with that sixth sense these creatures had, moved toward him, its steps halting. On a clean wave of anger, Luc wondered if the creature needed to be put down.

He picked it up. Pure skin and bones. *Just like the woman they'd sent over to him.* What the hell was wrong with those people?

He considered putting it into the truck bed, but something about the animal's frail legs and mangy fur, the way it trembled in his arms, made him shove his bags into the footwell and lay it down carefully on the front seat.

He stopped and cocked his head. What was that? A sound in the deathly quiet? A dip in temperature? A crackling in the cloud-muffled night? Luc sniffed, expecting the smell of smoke, not the stench of death that followed it on the air.

This dog was *theirs*. The neighbors'. He was sure of it. First, they sent a woman to him—looking for work, no less—and now a dog, left out to starve in the middle of winter? Well, he'd had enough. *Enough.*

Flying in the face of every one of *Grandpère*'s expressions about good neighbors, he turned the truck around and accelerated back down the drive toward the neighbors' place, ignoring the itch of premonition that skimmed his nape like an icy finger.

Abby pushed opened the door to Hamish's cabin.

My cabin, she thought with a sudden, futile spasm of ownership.

It was dark inside—the kind of pitch-black she imagined modern women never experienced, with their cell phones glued to their hands and purses probably equipped with flashlights. They were so practical, those women, with their bare heads, jeans, and easy cotton shirts.

She scrabbled on a side table for matches, lit the first lantern, and turned to see a silhouette. She dropped the matchbox with a strangled sound. *Hamish?* The fear and shock quickly morphed into relief as the shape came into focus.

Just Sammy.

"Hi, Abby" came his voice, slow and a bit high.

"Goodness, you almost killed me."

"I did?"

"No. I mean, not really. You just scared me, standing here in the dark, is all."

"You said to come, Abby. I'm sorry." He sounded crestfallen.

She immediately went to him, put one arm around his narrow shoulders, and led him to one of the straight chairs in the kitchen area. "Don't be, Sammy. Don't be. I meant it. I was just… It was just a little fright, but I'm happy that you're here. What's a little fright compared to that, huh?"

"Yeah?" His smile lit up those sweet features, the tiny nose and high forehead that made him different from everyone else and made her love him all the more.

"No room at your parents'?" she asked.

"No. Denny and Angie wanted to be alone. So I went to see Benji and Brigid, but he…he tole me to go, too."

Abby knew exactly why the Cruddups had kicked him out. Well, at least one of the reasons. They might be his birth parents, but his differences made him a failure in their eyes—in the eyes of the Church—and they needed to make up for it by coupling and giving the Almighty more babies, despite their advanced years. It was their responsibility as God-fearing members of the Church, and tonight, apparently, they were fulfilling their spousal duty. It sickened her, the idea that they'd rather do that than care for Sammy, already here and alive. A son who especially needed them.

"Did you get dinner?"

At his shake of the head, she grew angrier still. It didn't matter that he looked different from everyone else or that he'd taken longer to learn to tie his shoes. Denying his needs was simply not Christian.

The familiar wave of frustration welled up, only this time it extended past the people of the Church and the fence line to include the man who'd refused to give her a job today.

She had to consciously loosen her jaw before speaking. "Let's get you something, pumpkin." Knowing how little she'd find, she tried the larder—two jars of pickled beets from last summer; the loaf of bread she'd been rationed this week, already moldy; and the butter in the crock, probably turned sour. This was what happened during the limbo between marriages. She'd practically been a child when Hamish had taken her. Children were fed in the refectory, but adult women were left to their own devices. She cut the mold off the bread, sniffed at the butter, and opened another precious jar.

I'm nothing, exactly like you, she thought, handing Sammy a cobbled-together meal you'd have to be starving to consider eating. And she'd been at her mama's, eating chicken pot pie and beans.

He dug in with relish, and Abby's anger inched up a notch.

"You feeling all right?" she asked, ignoring the urge to reach out and stroke his hair. Physical affection was another no-no. She remembered wanting it from Mama, even from Hamish at first. With a hot blush, she recalled the summer she and Benji had discovered touch. Noticing the look on Sammy's face, she shut it down. "No?"

"Happened again."

She stilled. "Another one of your fits?"

"Yeah." He polished off the bread. Too fast. He needed more to eat and she was running low, and rations weren't passed around for another two days.

"Tell me."

"Out lookin' for parts for Dinwiddy's car. Din't feel so good. Sat on the scraggly rock, you know, over by the old crash where I found that rusted-out bolt that time?" She nodded, knowing exactly where he meant. She and Benji'd done things on that rock. Things that had felt so good and been so wrong and, in the end, led to her marriage to Hamish, among other things. Sammy went there all the time, looking for parts in his constant quest to fix things. "Well, I got it again…that feeling like I was there and not. And then…" He stood abruptly, pushing back his chair so fast that it tilted before landing back on all four legs with a clatter. He came to squat in front of her, tilted his head to the side, and, grabbing her hand, put it to his head.

Oh, heavens, it was matted with blood.

"Sit down," she ordered, rushing to grab the lamp and hold it closer. "You hurt yourself, honey."

"Yeah. Hurts."

"I know, Sammy." She patted his shoulder. "All right. Let's…" She looked around. Another few minutes wouldn't change a thing, she supposed, but worrying him would serve no purpose. "Finish your dinner first. We'll take a look at your cut after."

"'Kay."

It wasn't until she'd gotten him cleaned up and snug in her bed, covered in her patchwork quilt, that Abby considered what would happen next. She folded herself into the chair beside the woodstove.

So much energy and expectation had gone into that man—the one she'd barely let herself think of since she'd crawled back through the hole in the fence—and now…nothing had changed.

Staring into the flames, she racked her brain for some other solution, another way out. But no matter how hard she tried, she came up with nothing.

Nothing besides *him*, the grape farmer with the rolling accent and stern brow, the chilly eyes and hot, hot hands.

That meant one thing, no matter that she didn't like it or that he most certainly wouldn't either: she'd go back to him tomorrow. And this time, she wouldn't leave without a job.

❧

Luc had driven this far up the county road only once, and that had been the day he'd made the offer on the vineyard. As part of his due diligence, he'd investigated the entire area, in search of hidden nuclear power plants the real estate agent might have forgotten to mention. Well, and to scope out the neighbors. As his grandfather had drilled into his brain as a boy, your crop is only as good as your neighbor's.

Turning into the sect's drive, his first impression had been mixed: the sunny-yellow sign such a contrast to its words of imminent apocalypse, paint worn and fraying at the edges. Now, in the dark, his headlights found it.

Just beyond was the gate, closed like so many others in the area—ostensibly to keep livestock in. He'd wondered about these people. Because who the hell needed a two-meter-high chain-link fence around a property this size? Even goats did fine with one meter of chicken wire.

No, that fence was strange. But good neighbors didn't pry. Another one of *Grandpère*'s rules. So after his initial meeting with the group's leader—a strange man with a strange name—he'd established that they didn't use harsh chemicals on their crops, and he'd taken off. Relieved to get away and, to be honest, relieved that they were so private. Both parties had made it clear during that single meeting that they weren't interested in each other's business. It had seemed perfect.

Which was another reason he was so irritated with that woman. How dare she ignore their unspoken agreement and invade his privacy like that?

Well, to hell with it. As he opened the truck door, the dog raised its head and made a noise not strong enough to be a whine. Luc hesitated, eye on the animal. Its paw shifted to nudge Luc's leg. Although there was no strength behind it, there was something else.

"You don't want to go there?" he asked.

The dog gave a low, rumbling response, which he could have sworn was assent—or a warning.

"I can't keep you if you belong to them," he argued, one leg out of the truck.

Slowly, painfully, the creature rose. Each step looked like torture as it made its way to his lap, where it collapsed heavily with a moan.

Luc opened his mouth to protest again, but the dog cut him off with a sigh, more eloquent than a howl.

It didn't want to go back, and Luc wouldn't force it. Christ, what was wrong with those people that they wouldn't even take proper care of an animal? He pushed away the mental image of that woman again, settled both legs back in the vehicle, and reached out to slam the truck door shut.

Okay. So they'd take a trip to the SPCA tomorrow. Or the vet. But first, he needed to give it something to eat. The dog, which weighed nothing, was more skeleton than muscle, its spine a series of fragile, pointed knobs under his hand.

Sliding one hand into the animal's matted fur, he put the truck into gear and reversed quickly, not letting himself think of the woman he'd turned away just a few hours before.

3

ONE THOUSAND AND FIFTY DOLLARS. THAT WAS HOW much the dog had cost him. Which meant he'd have to repair the ancient tractor himself after all, since he wouldn't be able to afford the new one.

There'd been a moment as Luc had bathed the dog the night before—a connection from its brown eyes to his—when he'd felt the animal's thank-you like a caress, heard it like words. "Don't get attached," he'd said. "I'm taking you into town tomorrow." That had been when Luc realized he was talking out loud.

After the bath, it had eaten half of Luc's ham and, more notably, drunk about a liter of water. How could anyone withhold clean water from a dog? After vomiting up the ham, it had settled onto a bed of blankets Luc made in front of the fire and gone to sleep with a satisfied huff.

Hours later, after listening to its noises, he'd gone down to tend to it and… *My God.* Every time he saw it, he was shocked anew. Even after the bath, its fur was patchy and thin, its skin flaked and mangy. One of its paws was a mess, no doubt infected—thus the limp.

A torn-up paw, heartworm, fleas, malnutrition, dehydration. What *wasn't* wrong with the creature? And when Luc had suggested taking it—no, *him*, not it, because the dog was a boy—to the SPCA, the vet had given him that look, the one that said that would be imminent death for a creature with so many issues.

Vaccinations, parasite treatment, antibiotics… The words had swirled into a great big invoice and a couple of overnight stays for the animal, who needed IV fluids, among other things.

Now, Luc was headed home alone after making the biggest mistake of all—naming the damned thing.

The memory made him smile. *Dog*, he'd called it, which the vet tech hadn't found funny at all.

"Just Dog?" she'd asked.

"Yes."

"That's it?"

"I could call it *Le* Dog?"

"Alrighty. *Le* Dog Stanek," she'd said, shaking her head as she typed the name into the computer. She handed him the bill with one of those big, fake American smiles on her face.

Back home, he made his way up to the barn to top off his barrels, irritated at the late start.

That nurse could smile, though, couldn't she, considering *Le* Goddamned Dog had cost him more than a month's bills, groceries, and gas combined?

Things were simpler alone.

∽◦⌒◦∽

Abby woke up, fed Sammy the last of her toast with butter and honey, and sent him over to the Cruddups' place with the excuse that she needed to check the fence line.

She mustered what little courage she had, along with a fresh bout of resolve, and trudged for half an hour through the dead grass back to the fence. Back to the hole. Back to big, stupid Grape Man. As she climbed through, she ignored the frigid rock face above and the few snowflakes floating from the sky, which looked thick, soupy, and ready to open up.

She approached the man where he clipped away at a different section of vines. His face was tight in concentration, every move sharp and precise—until he looked up and saw her. When he did that, his features dropped into an irritated scowl.

Goodness, how on earth had she thought he might be handsome? Nobody that stern could possibly be appealing. Not with those harsh features, that too-big nose, and that unfriendly gaze. She lifted her head.

"Morning, sir."

His eyes narrowed, the only part of him to move as they followed her progress. Indifferent, she'd say, if it weren't for that grim look of annoyance.

"Sorry to bother you again."

One sharp, dark brow angled up before he turned back to his work, ignoring her. Or trying to.

She forced a smile through the bubble in her throat and grasped one of the thin branches he'd just cut before yanking it up and out. "It occurred to me that I didn't let you in on the full array of skills I have to offer. You are one lucky man, because I just happen to be a crack cleaner. I can cook and sew, darn socks or—"

"No, thank you." He froze her with those iceberg eyes.

Don't cry. Breathe. Smile.

Doing her best to ignore him, she took another branch and yanked, throwing it to the ground as she'd seen him do. "You haven't tasted my—"

"I don't wish to taste anything."

Bless me, what kind of man is this, who—

"How about…?" In an act of desperation, she searched for something he might want. "You wanna taste *me*?" The words popped out, incomprehensible to her ears and so far from anything she'd ever said—much less *thought*—that she almost looked behind her to see who had uttered them.

No one budged. Five full seconds of silence passed before he turned to give her his attention. She wanted to take it all back.

"Pardon?"

Abby opened her mouth, but apparently the devil who'd prompted those words had decided to leave her high and dry. Nothing emerged.

Above them, the sky darkened. Or maybe that was just her vision. Why on earth had she said that? To get him to notice her, she figured. She saw Church kids do it all the time—acting up for attention. Short-lived, since the surest response was a beating—no matter how young the child.

His eyes raked up and down her body, way hotter than ice should be.

"Is this a proposition?" he asked. His voice was cracked and rough, like leather that'd sat too long and needed dusting off. But the accent, layered over the top? That was smooth. *Mellifluous* sounded like the right word. She'd have to look it up in the dog-eared dictionary she kept hidden under the bed—the only thing she'd ever stolen in her life. She kept expecting to burn in hell for that, but it had yet to happen.

Maybe this was it.

The second brow rose to meet the first. "You need money," he said. It wasn't a question.

"I need a job," she corrected.

"Find one in town."

"It'd take me hours to walk there." Besides, Church members drove the road into town all the time. They'd see her and pick her up and there'd be hell to pay. She'd be more hidden here, right next door. Nobody came over to this side of the mountain.

With a sigh, he hung his shears on one of the wires that held the vine branches up and ran one gloved hand through his too-long hair. "I will take you."

"Where?" she bleated, panicked that he meant he'd drop her back at the Church.

"Into town."

Her next words sailed out on a sigh of relief. "Any chance you could just give me a job instead?"

"I don't need your—"

The sky chose that moment to open up, spitting shards of icy rain down on them and drowning out anything else he might have said. Abby raised her eyes to where she could have sworn the rocky mountain face had curled up into a triumphant smile.

"You'll have to hurry if you wanna get this finished before we get iced in," she yelled through the loud, stinging patter. "If this goes on too long, you'll slip and slide right off the hill." She could see the words sinking in, could feel his change of heart…or maybe that was her Lord and Savior taking pity on her. Whatever it was, her words or divine providence, the man appeared to come to a decision.

"You will need gloves if you are going to do this. And a jacket." Abby thought of her coat, in a ball beside her hole in the fence. The thin wool would soak up this rain as fast as could be. The man walked a few steps in the direction of his cabin before turning back. "You are coming?" he said before continuing on toward the log cabin.

"Sir?" she called out.

He stopped again, huffing with annoyance. "Yes?"

"I'd like to…" She marched to him and reached out a hand, waiting through his perusal before lifting it higher, insistent. "I want to shake your hand, sir. To thank you for giving me a chance."

"Don't thank me. You'll just—"

"Please."

His lips tightened into a flat line, and Abby could see him wanting to back out, eyeing her hand like it was poison. But handshakes sealed deals. *Shake on it*, people said, and she liked the official quality of it. Liked that it put her on a level with the men out here. Men and women, doing the same thing. Equals.

No way would she admit how much she'd thought about the feel of those hands on hers the day before.

You're doing it again, warned the gleeful voice in her head. *Pushing too far.*

But the voice was wrong, which just went to show… something. Grape Man grabbed her hand, pumped it twice. He still looked mean and harsh—only this time, something had changed. The touch itself was just as shocking as the day before. On a purely visceral level, being touched by a man who wasn't her husband? It was… She didn't have the words for how wrong it felt. And how could the man's skin be so hot out here in the frigid January air? She stumbled at the warm connection.

Good Lord, she couldn't remember touching anyone besides Sammy or Hamish or Mama since…since she'd been branded a Chosen One and received her first mark. Isaiah had done that. And Hamish's touches, well, they'd been purely utilitarian.

The shiver slid through her again, from her toes out to the fingertips he'd just clasped. *Definitely the wind.*

He must have felt it, too. She saw it in the softening of his mouth, the way his eyes met hers. There was humanity there. And Lord, she'd been lying when she'd told herself he wasn't nice to look at.

That strong nose, freckled by too many hours in the sun. Wide, sharp cheekbones, kissed crimson by the wind. That dimple—or was it a scar?—on his cheek that looked more like punctuation than anything else. Most of all, the eyes: slate blue, clearer than a cloudless winter sky, and fringed with heavy lashes. When he met her gaze, it was almost painfully direct under thick brows and tempestuous, dark hair—which was too long by Church standards, but a perfectly poetic counterpoint to the blunt features beneath.

"I'm really—" *Grateful*, she was going to say, but he didn't let her.

Instead he interrupted, that gruff, accented voice sending shivers up her spine. "Enough. You'll be of no use to me if you freeze to death." He loosened his fingers and waited for her to do the same before turning away.

Her hand, pressed into a fist at her side as she walked, still held the hot imprint of his—a callused palm, fingers both coarse and gentle, and the space where that missing finger should have been.

After a brief hesitation, Abby followed the man, eyes glued to the tall, straight form that she'd watched as a small figure in the distance. She'd been so sure she knew who he was.

An image came to her—one laced with shame. She'd walked to the fence late last summer, when it had first become her official duty. The vines—these poor, wizened creatures—had burst out, big and green and so alive across the mountainside, their bunches of grapes dangling like jewelry much too heavy for their thin stalks. Amidst that fertile explosion, surrounded by a few men she couldn't picture if she tried, had stood this man. Smaller than the mountain, of course, tiny compared to the boulders and the vista beyond, but huge compared to the others. Alive. Elemental. More a part of this mountain than anything she could imagine.

There'd been other things that morning—her body, for one, had ached in a way she associated with physical need. She'd had it with Benji and experienced shadows of it at the *idea* of a man, but never, ever at the real thing. That nameless need she'd felt had been echoed by the creatures around her—the fecundity of nature, ripe and lush and begging to be plucked. Like those grapes. Like her.

He'd been bare-chested. He was the only man she'd seen so naked in her life, and though it had been too far to catch details, the things she'd seen had made her body prick up uncomfortably. Closer, she'd known, there'd be skin and hair. Sweat beading in places she could only imagine.

Wide shoulders; long, thick arms; slender waist; everything sheathed in muscle. The muscles a man would need to work several acres of vineyards on his own.

Trudging ahead of her through the mud, he looked efficient. No wasted movement. Like his words—just enough to get by. His body would have been tall and lanky without the muscles—bare bones. His was a strength born of necessity.

And despite how unpleasant he'd been, something about that appealed to her.

You wanna taste me?

Her words came back to her on a wash of heat. Oh Lord, had she said that? Where on earth had those words come from? If she didn't know better, she'd think someone else had controlled her tongue.

It occurred to her in that moment that he might very well choose to take her up on the offer. And she could choose to let him.

Sinner, hissed a familiar voice, knowing what she didn't care to admit: the idea didn't bother her nearly as much as it should.

He opened the thick wood door of the cabin—elevated and much bigger than the ones next door—and removed mud-crusted boots just inside, leaving his feet clothed in socks that had seen better days. *I could darn those*, Abby thought.

It wasn't until she'd toed off her shoes that it occurred to her: *I'm alone here, with a stranger.*

He had felt familiar, after watching him from afar for

so long. But close up…she didn't know a thing about
him. And he hadn't been particularly kind.

Halfway across the cabin's main room, he turned to
look at her, heavy brows raised.

"I…" She hesitated, taking in the sparsely furnished
room in search of some way to make sure this wasn't
a mistake. "It just occurred to me that you could be a
bad person."

That seemed to shock him. His features flattened,
pulling those thick brows back down into their natural,
taciturn configuration.

"You mean… Oh." His face cleared with understanding. He nodded and headed to a nook under a steep stair-
case abutting the front door, close to where Abby still
stood rooted to the spot. He came out with a gun—long
and shiny and nasty-looking—and for just a second, her
breath caught in her throat, telling her she'd made the
stupidest of mistakes. She could picture the sneering *I
told you so*s from the people next door. She could hear
Sammy's cries. Isaiah's sad, knowing sermon: *Abigail
Merkley died for her sins*, he'd preach, and everyone
would nod.

"Take this," the man said and shoved the gun into her
arms. "If I do anything you don't like, shoot me."

The laugh that bubbled out of her throat was unexpected. It was fresh and new, rejuvenating. *My first
laugh outside. My first taste of freedom.* She bit her lip
automatically, holding it in. It never served to appear
too happy.

But the man didn't seem to mind. For the first time
since she'd arrived, something besides irritation washed
over his features. He eyed her strangely, head cocked,

his gaze on the place where her lip remained caught between her teeth.

"I am funny to you?" he asked, and for a second, she considered shaking her head, forcing a more placid expression and casting her eyes down and away. Always down and away.

But this wasn't a Church member. This was outside. If she couldn't be herself here, then what was the point?

"This." She motioned with the gun, which was heavier than it appeared. "This is funny."

One thick eyebrow rose, and a comma flashed next to his mouth, which threatened to smile, although it never quite committed.

"The gun is funny?"

"Oh, course not. I didn't mean—"

"Never mind. French humor."

"Is that what you are? French?"

He blinked. "How did you guess?"

"You talk with this accent. Kinda—*Oh*. You're joking. Again." Her cheeks ached from the smiling, and his expression had changed from the hard implacability he'd worn outside. Melted a bit, perhaps. At this moment, he looked…young, maybe? Flushed and almost sweet. Almost.

Abby watched as he strode to a woodstove, opened it, and stirred the embers. He added a few logs and motioned her to follow him through a doorway. In the kitchen, he filled an electric kettle at the sink and set it to boil.

"You got electricity here."

"Yes. You don't?"

Embarrassed, she shook her head. "Not in our homes. Just in the main building. The Center."

He lifted his brows in an expression that struck her as being supremely French. As if she knew what that would be.

"Here." He pulled out a straight-backed wooden chair before heading out again, leaving her alone to set the gun down and sit at the small table.

When he reappeared, he held a thick wool sweater and gloves. "Put these on."

"Why don't *you* wear gloves when you work?"

"I like to feel the plants. Know what I'm doing."

"I couldn't take these from you. I'm fi—"

"You want work, you dress appropriately." Prickly Grape Man was back.

"Yes, sir."

"And please don't call me that."

"Sir?" Abby swallowed. "What should I call you?"

"Luc."

"Look?" she asked, confused.

"No. No, Luc. Uh, *Skywalker*. You know?"

She didn't.

"Um, *Luuuuuc*," he exaggerated, moving the vowel up from where he'd hidden it under his tongue.

"Luke," she said. *Bringer of Light.*

"What about you? You told me, but…"

"Abigail."

"Abi—"

"No," she interrupted, remembering her resolve. *Her* name, *her* life, *her* fresh start. "Not Abigail. Abby. Just Abby."

"Okay, Just Abby," he said, his lips quirking up

enough to tweak the scar—the one that made him look like he was smiling, even though smiling clearly wasn't his thing. "I'm called Luc Stanek."

"I'm Abby Merkley. Although Merkley's my…" *Husband's name*, she almost said, but suddenly she didn't want him to know about Hamish—her old-man husband. Suddenly, being given away to a man three times her age seemed wrong. A point of shame rather than a fact of life. And, for some strange reason, she didn't want this man to see her shame.

～∾～

You wanna taste me?

No matter how hard he tried, Luc could not push those words from his brain.

Ignoring the hot flush of his skin, he reached for two canisters and asked, "Tea or coffee?"

"Oh, no, I don't need anything."

Annoyed, he looked right at her. "It will keep you warm."

"All right. Either."

He huffed out a sigh. "Do you like coffee?"

"Never had it."

He blinked but let it go, spooning granules into a thermos before filling it with water and a splash of milk.

"This stuff is disgusting, but it's all I have. The tea's no better."

Armed with the thermos, an extra cup, and warm clothes, they trudged back out into the cold.

She was slow. With the shit already starting to fall, there was no time to waste. Already he regretted giving in to her request.

You wanna taste me?

No, those words weren't what had made him agree. It was her calm insistence that had finally worn him down, along with the ice. He hadn't believed that offer for a moment—although the image it had conjured…

"Do you know anything about grapes?" he barked, stomping toward the farthest, steepest field. The one he had to finish before bad weather made it too slippery and dangerous.

"I've…I've watched you."

He stumbled. God, was she going to continue with the explicit remarks, because he didn't think he could—

"I mean, I've seen you working," she corrected, a flush climbing up her face. At least he wasn't the only one who needed help with communication skills. "I can learn."

"Today, we work fast. That field is too steep to prune with ice on the ground."

"Thank you, sir. Thank—"

"Stop," he interrupted. "No talking. Just work. This is a pruner, or secateurs," Luc said, holding them up. "I will use this. And you will pull away the vines, yes?"

"Okay."

"This way, we go faster. I cut, you unclip and pull."

"Where do I put them?"

"Throw them down," he said. "Today, we don't worry."

She nodded, watching him closely with intelligent eyes. Trying his best to forget about her presence, he set to work. This was always easiest alone.

They made their way down the row quickly, the woman so quiet he could almost forget she was there. Except for those brief glimpses, of course, and the occasional brush of his arm against hers. One row to the next, picking up speed. More brushing of bodies: the side of her breast, the faint but nonetheless spectacular perfume of a woman, which he fought hard to ignore.

While they worked, his brain filled the silence with questions. How long had she lived in that place? How old was she? Not a child, but not old, either. Those freckles made her look young. He shot her a quick glance, found her eyes on him, and turned back to squint hard at the vine in front of him.

"It's so exact," she said.

He paused, blinking. "*Hein?*"

"The way you cut the branches. One but not the other. Looks like you've got a real specific way of doing it. *Scientific*," she finished, overenunciating the word.

Was it? It seemed so *instinctive* most of the time, but perhaps she was right. Perhaps it was more of a science than an art. It was just that some people were born to it and others were not.

A purple thumb, *Grandpère* had called it. Not everyone in the family had it. Certainly not Olivier. No, his half brother had been gifted with his father's money-making prowess. Funny how it always seemed to be one or the other. Wine or money. Money or wine. You couldn't have both. How disappointed everyone had been when it turned out that Luc was the gifted grower in the family. *L'Américain. Le Paysan. The half-Polish American peasant.* What a perfect cosmic joke, giving the gift to the only person in the family without the DeLaurier name, the one who was only half-French and all mutt. Well, they'd kept him in his place, hadn't they? Always the grower, never the winemaker. Only grudgingly permitted in the cellars. *Blood, after all, is thicker than wine.*

He glanced subconsciously up the mountain toward the barn with its winery and shook his head, clearing away thoughts that served no purpose at all. He wasn't a winemaker. Just a farmer—that was it. And if he'd tried his hand at making wine last year, well, that was just for fun. An *experience*. No. No, in English, the word was *experiment*.

"Why'd you pick that one to cut?" the woman asked, giving him a break from his thoughts.

"This grew two years ago. Thick and gnarled, yes? I cut here and cut this one down to two buds."

"That's a bud?"

"Yes, and these other knobs coming up. Also buds. They will grow into these...shoots or canes, and the bunches of grapes grow from there."

"Oh, I see!" She smiled with understanding, and he looked back at the vine, ignoring the tightness in his belly, the nerves building there. Why? Human contact? Had it been so long that he didn't actually know anymore how to talk to a woman without getting wound up?

Not that he'd ever been able to talk to a woman.

In search of distraction, he held out the pruners and indicated the next spur. "Try it."

"Really?"

"Yes." He cleared his throat. "Careful not to cut off your finger. I don't have time to take you to the hospital."

She struggled for a bit. "On a diagonal," he prompted before she figured out the angle and cut.

For a strange moment, the snipping sound reminded him of being young, the whole family out pruning

together. Neatening acres and acres of vines, preparing
them for the upcoming year. He remembered the cold—
not so bitter as this—and the camaraderie. Burning canes
in the *brouette*, and flasks of hot wine that *Grandpère* let
them drink, against *Maman*'s wishes.

He missed that—throwing branches into the *brouette
de taille* with its trail of smoke, the warmth it offered.

"Good."

Abby stepped back and handed him the pruners,
her brow creased as he cut into a more crowded area.
"Why'd you cut that one and not the others?"

"If there is a doubt, I keep the healthiest spur."

"How can you tell which is healthier?"

"Bigger, stronger-looking. Larger diameter. And this
one, the puny one? I snip. The healthy one is also closest
to the trunk and the *cordon*, see?"

"What was that word?"

"*Cordon*?"

"Yes. I like that."

"In English, you call it an arm. This is the trunk, and
these are the two arms. Spurs." He pointed to the knobs
that grew along the cordons, to last year's growth, dead
and messy and held up with wires. "Canes."

"So, the weak and the old get cut out? That seems so…
unfeeling." The idea didn't appear to please her, and he
didn't bother responding. Of course the runts had to go.
When he'd arrived here, the vines had been a mess. Left
to grow wild for years, the weeds rampant. He'd almost
turned around without making an offer at all. Luc's gaze
lifted again to the barn, nestled just beneath the precari-
ously perched boulders at the top of the mountain.

You didn't buy a vineyard for a barn, much less a

rock. He knew that. Everyone knew it. You bought for the location: the soil, the health of the vines. But while the real estate agent had gone on and on about the barn and its potential as a tasting room, Luc's attention had slid right over it, over the top-of-the-line equipment. The temperatures were ideal inside the odd structure, which was built into the actual mountain, its backside carved straight from the granite boulders. It reminded him of the troglodyte caves in France. And *Grandpère* had always told him to look for rocks like these.

After months searching this country where his father grew up for just the right place to make his own, it was that barn and its boulders that had decided him. Stupid, likely. Just more of his grandfather's superstitions, but...

"What about that little stump here?" Abby broke into his thoughts.

He looked at the spur she indicated. Older growth, without any visible one-year wood. "That goes."

He caught a glimpse of her face—the concentration as she watched, doing her own work but more interested in his. Learning. She looked good in his oversize Aran sweater. Although he wouldn't have had time to notice that if he were working as hard as he should.

A glance at the sky told him it was nearing the end of the afternoon. They'd worked straight through, both of them soaking wet. His boots squelched in the mud that was no doubt sucking at her pathetic shoes, and just as he wondered what awaited her back home, her hands dropped to her knees. She inhaled deeply.

"What is it?"

"I...I guess I should have had breakfast."

"You've eaten nothing?"

She shrugged.

"That's…*stupid*." The words were too harsh, he realized as soon as they were out. More proof that he wasn't fit to spend time with people, especially in America, where everyone was so *nice*. He avoided her shocked expression and set his pruners down. "Come. I'll give you something to eat."

"No. Thank you, sir. I…I should leave." She threw a look over her shoulder, toward the top of the mountain where she'd first appeared.

"You have far to go?"

She shook her head again—more to clear it, he thought, than any sort of denial. "I'm fine. I'll be fine."

He made an effort to soften his voice. "Why didn't you eat?"

"I…I was in a rush." It sounded like the truth, but he didn't quite believe her. "Is it all right if I… I mean, I need to be getting back."

"Of course. Come in, and I'll pay you."

"Could you hold on to it for me?"

"Hold on to your mon—"

She reached for the bottom of the sweater she wore, and Luc, who'd opened his mouth to ask…something… lost his train of thought. It came off—up and over her head, leaving her underdressed and cold in that odd-looking gown. A bit frantic, he averted his gaze from the sight of her nipples, perfectly outlined by the clinging material of her dress.

He concentrated instead on her hands as she pulled the gloves off—worn and full of holes, probably gritty on the inside from this summer's work—and handed his things over. They were still warm from her body.

"Thank you, Mr. Stanek," she said with a smile, putting her small, frigid hand out for another awkward handshake before turning away. From behind, her thin form was made shapely by the cut of fabric, tight at her waist and flaring at the hips. It should have expanded from there, leaving her bottom half mysterious and sexless, as he assumed was the intended purpose of that type of garb. Instead, the wet dress hugged her in a way that was decidedly appealing.

Rather than continue to watch the sway of her backside, Luc's eyes snagged on the straight, proud angle of her shoulders—which, though painfully thin, appeared strong. And if he wasn't mistaken, stubborn.

A few steps away, she turned back to catch him staring. "Can I come back tomorrow?" she asked, her eyes full of hope.

"Not if everything is covered in ice."

"Oh." She lost her smile. "Right. So…"

"Come if it isn't," he said in an effort to put the light back in her face.

She nodded before heading off again, leaving him to finish his vines cold and alone and hoping, despite himself, that she'd return the next day.

4

THERE WAS A DIFFERENT KIND OF EXCITEMENT AS ABBY headed out into the frosty morning. The buzz of fear and anxiety hadn't subsided, despite the hours she'd spent praying for forgiveness the night before. But beneath that, a bubble floated in her chest, and it felt an awful lot like happiness.

It must have been the idea of leaving again—on her own terms. It could have also been the work, which, though difficult, had been satisfying, the view so lovely and *new*. It couldn't possibly be Grape Man himself—the way he didn't waste words or movement, the way his eyes, an icy gray-blue that was almost warm, met hers. How he'd insisted on giving her the sweater and the coffee.

Out of habit, she sped up as she passed Brigid and Benji's cabin. Things had gotten unbearable with Brigid recently and the last thing she needed was a confrontation.

She'd just let her shoulders sag with relief when the door opened behind her. Too late.

Abby's shoulders tightened as she veered slightly off her path. If it was Brigid, it was best not to lead her to the hole in the fence. But maybe, if she was lucky, it was just Benji heading off to work.

"Heading over to the fence?" came Brigid's voice. No such luck.

Abby slowed. "It's my job." She forced a placid smile to her face and slowed her steps. If she stayed calm, maybe the woman would leave.

"I'll bet you enjoy it, don't you? Walking around all day with your head in the clouds."

Abby stopped, breathing hard, and gave the expected response. Brigid would, after all, report any mistakes to Isaiah. "There's nothing to enjoy. It's my duty. I do it because Isaiah decrees it."

"You're just too good for the kitchens, aren't you, Abigail? And the nursery? You're above the rest of us, aren't you? Wed to Hamish, your mother joined with Isaiah? You must feel special." The words were spoken so kindly Abby could almost pretend she'd misheard.

"*Special?* No. No, I didn't ask to work alone like this."

"Of course not. You'd have preferred working with the men," Brigid said with false innocence. It felt like a punch to the gut every single time.

"I'm not…" She searched for the right words to say. "Why are you… I never hated you, Brigid, the way you seem to hate me. I only wish that you could see—"

"Hate? Oh, no. No, you've got it all wrong, Abigail. There is nothing but love. I *love* you…*Sister*."

They had seemed like sisters, once upon a time. Back when Abby'd first gotten here, they'd been kids, singing together, loving each other. So proud to be part of this important mission here on the mountain. Something so much bigger than themselves.

The knowledge of everything she'd lose when she left was suddenly crushing, heavy and sad.

Stepping forward, Abby put a hand on Brigid's arm, that place where this woman had also received the Mark. "We'll always be sisters, Brigid. No matter what happens. You know that, right?"

The woman's blue eyes focused on Abby's hand where it touched her sacred brand, before lifting to narrow on Abby's face. She pulled away with a jerk.

"*Are you pure of soul, Abigail Merkley?*" The censure behind her words made Abby blink and lurch away. How could Brigid possibly know what she'd done? Maybe she *had* seen Abby cut through the fence. Seen her speak to the neighbor. "Eve in her garden of evil, tempting my husband from his righteous path. And him just a *child*." Brigid advanced, hissing, her words ridiculous in the face of reality—that Abby and Benji were the same age, that they'd both been fifteen when they'd done…things together. And that he'd been just as present as she. He'd touched her body as surely as she'd touched his, no matter where the blame had been cast.

"You don't deserve the Mark," Brigid continued, her face livid with anger that Abby couldn't understand. Why hold on to it after all these years? Why seek her out, if it was to express this kind of hatred? "Now a childless widow, with no man to tame your tongue, to beat your baser urges from you. Even Hamish, God rest his blessed soul, succumbed to your power. How'd you do that to him—make him change his mind in the end? Was it even the Almighty who took him, or did you—"

"Don't you say another word," Abby broke in. She took another step back from the woman, whose hostility was like an infection, worse than the cancer that had sickened Hamish before the end. "I swear to everything that is holy, I'll…" Gracious, what would she do? She had no threats in her. There wasn't even hatred when she looked for it, just a deep sadness for everything they'd lost.

Brigid stood, mouth tight and white around the edges, while her cheeks shone like two angry red flags.

"I'm sorry you lost your first baby, Brigid. But it wasn't my fault. Now you and Benji have little Jeremiah, who's—"

"Hush your mouth," hissed Brigid. "Don't you mention my son's name."

"I have work to do," Abby said, doing her best to keep her voice even. "And so do you, I'd imagine." She started to walk away before turning back. "And I did my duty by Hamish, Brigid. Till the end, I did my duty. In ways you can't even begin to imagine." She stopped, something occurring to her. "Things not as good as they should be with your husband? That why you're harassing me instead of heading off to your job in the kitchen? You're the one who got Benji in the end, you know. And I'm the one they gave to a fifty-five-year-old man. A marriage is what you make of it, isn't it, Brigid?"

Another pause while Abby thought of where she was headed—escape, right over the top of the mountain, so close she could taste it. For the first time, it felt as though she wasn't just leaving for Sammy.

Voice softer, Abby said, "I hope things are good between you and Benji, Brigid. I do."

It was clearly the wrong thing to say. "*Succubus*,"

Brigid hissed before Abby turned around and gave the woman her back.

It took a while to simmer down—probably a good half hour, during which Abby walked along the fence line in case she'd been followed. By the time she arrived at the top of the rise, she'd calmed enough to feel pity for Brigid's plight. The woman's miscarriage had been terrible.

It was God's will, she knew, that she'd never had a baby with Hamish, but there were other factors she'd begun to suspect. Perhaps old men weren't meant to sire children.

From this side of the mountain, looking out over the neighbor's land with the potential of everything the world had to offer, Abby understood that it was a blessing not to have borne a child within the Church.

Closing her eyes, she remembered arriving here with Mama, a half-starved seven-year-old. After those months of sleeping together in the back of their car, Abby had felt so alone when Isaiah had taken Mama in marriage—another couple without offspring—and sent Abby to the dormitory with the other children. Goodness, how that had hurt. Much as she'd loved the Church—the singing and the togetherness, the specialness of being a Chosen One of the Lord—she'd cried herself to sleep every single night, missing the warm, soft feel of Mama like a front tooth.

Sucking in a breath to push away those memories, she looked out over the valley, toward Blackwood and Charlottesville and everything that awaited Sammy and her beyond. She thought of the infinite potential of a life lived on terms that weren't this God's. And despite the heaviness in her gut that told her this was wrong, she felt full of life and hope and the thrill of possibility.

When she caught sight of him—the man who'd given her this chance, she lifted her head, straightened her spine, and did her best to be strong.

~ಬ~

The man greeted her without enthusiasm. He did, however, have the gloves and sweater she'd worn the day before. After she put on the sweater, he thrust a thermos of warm liquid into her hands.

She took a sip and—ecstasy.

"Is this coffee again?"

He nodded.

"Tastes different."

His face, already pink from the cold, flushed, the color concentrating high along the ridge of those sharp, wide cheekbones. His answer came out on a mumble. "Better stuff."

"Oh" was all Abby could manage as she took a second swig of the creamy, nutty brew. "Delicious."

Another sip brought out something close to a moan, and she opened her eyes to find him staring. Abruptly, he bent to pick up his pruners and went back to work.

They'd been at it for over an hour when Abby finally dared open her mouth.

"Guess we didn't get the weather everyone's all worked up about," she said.

"Apparently not."

"They said we'd get ice, but there's also talk of a couple feet of snow."

His only response was a grunt.

Wordlessly, they worked their way through three more vines, Abby's mind full of thoughts it shouldn't have. Of the man and his coffee—both earthy and dark. She didn't think she'd tasted anything earthy and dark before. Or quite so rich. She had a yearning, suddenly, for rich things: foods, tastes, smells, experiences that no God-fearing woman should want.

Experience. Even that word had her thinking of the man beside her, his broken voice and sad eyes. She didn't need to look to feel him right there, the two of them working in quiet, easy tandem. She unclipped the branches from the wires and pulled, over and over, with nothing to stop her mind from crawling on.

Are you pure of soul? She thought of Brigid, snide and knowing. *Eve in the garden of evil.*

Maybe the woman was right.

She remembered when they'd been caught, her and Benji in the orchard, their drawers around their ankles and their hands hesitantly exploring.

Mama'd been angry, but Isaiah…he'd seemed forgiving. *Poor Abigail Merkley. Always battling against your true nature.* With such tenderness, Isaiah had told her he understood—and she thought maybe he had. *We cannot help our sins, can we? We are the victims of our own transgressions, child.* For years, she hadn't even understood that word. Transgressions.

What had come after that hadn't felt like a punishment, at Isaiah's hands. It had been justice. An honor, even, to take the Mark.

In this place that felt a hundred times more sacred than the Church, she felt very much like the sinner that Brigid accused her of being.

If nothing else, this man's coffee proved that Abby was a glutton.

Gluttony. Yes, she might have moments of that, especially if everything out here was as full of flavors as this man's coffee. She glanced his way, but he remained concentrated on his plants, his hands slowing every now and then to caress a branch in a way that mesmerized her.

Unclip, pull. Unclip, pull. The crunch of her cold feet on frozen ground, the echo of Luc's feet turning it into a kind of music, accompanied by the smell of dead vines and unfallen snow. The movements hypnotized, the quiet calmed, the rhythm lulled her farther and farther away from salvation. She tried to push thoughts of God and sinners and the Church from her mind.

But the questions kept coming.

Am I greedy? Do I want too much? If greed harkened back to the sin of gluttony, then she might qualify. But not for material things. No, her cravings were for knowledge and experience.

What about wrath? Yes, she'd felt wrath. When Hamish had fallen ill and they'd refused to give him medicine. Not even to ease his suffering. That was all he'd wanted. Oh, she felt wrath all right. A brittle branch cracked in her fist before she flung it to the ground, a bit too hard.

There was no reason to go through the other sins. Envy wasn't something she liked to think about, since she was just about done comparing her life to anyone else's. In the Church, it had always been *Us* and *Them*.

Someday soon, she'd become Them. And Us would no longer matter.

What about lust? The question rang loud; she glanced at Luc to see if he'd heard it too.

Of course, that brought her right back to that hot summer day and the droplets of sweat she'd conjured in her mind. The way she'd dwelled on this man's slick chest and taut belly in the bright, bright sun.

She swallowed as her eyes slid to where his sun-bronzed hands worked, thick knuckles and long, strong fingers. Even the missing one had an appeal. Imperfect and interesting. Was there sensation in that stunted digit? And how would those capable-looking hands feel on her skin? Would they work over a woman's body with that same level of brisk efficiency, or would they linger?

Her tongue slicked over her bottom lip of its own volition, exploring things that had been forbidden for a lifetime. Lust. Good gracious, what would it feel like to taste, to touch, to feel the full weight of that particular sin?

"You are all right?" Luc asked, startling her back to the present.

His gaze was on her, brows drawn down quizzically. Abby realized, mortified, that she'd been caught staring. He'd tried to move on while she'd stayed stock-still, transfixed by his hands and stubble-covered, scratchy-looking jaw.

"Yes. Yes, sorry," she stammered out. "I'm…" Goodness, what on earth was she supposed to say to this? Nothing. Best to say nothing.

He put a hand to her shoulder, and she stilled. The contact was so charged, she couldn't move.

So few men had ever done this—touched her body at all. Only Hamish, toward the end, had shared touches with her. And Benji in that long-ago memory. Isaiah, too, but she didn't like to think of that time.

"Lunch."

Abby blinked through the haze of… What? What did his touch make her feel?

Best not to consider the weight in her belly or her frantic breaths. It could just as easily be from fear. Or disgust. Yes, that would be acceptable, wouldn't it?

"You go ahead," she forced out. "I'll keep working."

"Take this." He thrust something into her hand: a messily wrapped package. "You're not a vegetarian, are you?"

"No." She blinked dumbly. Something hot washed through her as she stared at the package. "What is this?"

"It's *jambon beurre*. Ham and butter. Eat."

"I don't…" Frustrated, she held out the sandwich. She had to give it back. "You didn't have to buy this for me. What do I owe you?"

Head tilted to the side, he watched her closely, earnestly, she thought, with what might have been a hint of insecurity behind that grumpy facade. "I didn't buy it, Abby. I made it. Now eat it, or I will think you don't trust my cooking." He turned and led the way to a large, flat rock at the end of the row.

After the briefest hesitation, during which she forced down a whole slew of messy emotions, she went to sit beside him and very carefully unwrapped the sandwich. Closing her eyes, she took a small bite and chewed, slowly savoring the first meal made for her by a man.

5

IT WASN'T UNTIL ABBY CAME OVER THE TOP OF THE
rise the next day that Luc realized just how nervous he
was. She'd made it about halfway down by the time Le
Dog limped up to greet her. An old friend, judging by
their interaction.

She squatted to give the animal a hug, sweeter and
warmer and kinder than anything this mountainside had
seen since Luc had moved in. Le Dog, in return, bathed
her face with his tongue, and Luc had to look away.

"You know each other," he said. Not a question.

"Rodeo. He and I… We used to spend time together."

He asked, "What happened?" and watched her face
whiten, wishing he hadn't said anything.

"He was taken away."

"Why?"

She shrugged, the movement perfectly nonchalant,
but the words… They were incisive. Sharp, like small
darts. "I wasn't supposed to get attached." The smile she
gave was a brittle shadow of her usual expression. He
hated it. "I'm glad you got him."

Curious but unwilling to delve too far into the work-ings of the lunatics next door, Luc nodded. "He is good company." He didn't mention that the dog had cost him a fortune. No point rubbing that in when the woman didn't seem to have any say in the matter.

Abby eyed the big barrow he'd worked late into the night to build.

"It's a *brouette de taille*," he said, tamping down the ridiculous edge of pride that tinged his voice. "For burn-ing the branches."

"Oh…looks kinda like a wheelbarrow. Do we roll it with us?"

The air was frigid, and this close, he could see the pink in her nose and cheeks. He'd been right to stay up working on the *brouette*, no matter that his body dragged today.

He nodded, feeling silly and proud of his accomplish-ment. A little *bricolage* in the workshop—not as easy as he'd thought, getting the parts. The steel drum, oddly, had been the hardest to find; he'd had to drive thirty miles out for that. Odd because burning a fire in a steel drum was one of those iconic images of America he'd always seen on TV. The rest he'd taken from an actual *brouette*. A wheelbarrow.

"And it keeps us warm." He reached into the sack hung on the end, took out a rawhide that he threw to Le Dog and a pair of gloves that he handed to her. "Put these on."

She looked up and caught his eye. She started to smile but flattened her lips. "They fit."

Was she upset? Why would she be upset about new gloves? Luc swallowed back his disappointment and spoke, all business. "We continue as before. I cut, you pull the branches and throw them in here." He indicated the place where he'd cut doors into the steel drum. It lay with its doors wide open now, flat on what had once been a wheelbarrow. He'd close it up when the day was done to avoid any risk of sparking a fire on the mountain or—God forbid—his vines.

"Okay" was all she said before getting right to work.

They made good progress together. Their rhythm was quick and easy, and they worked until the sun was high in the sky. He'd found a couple of adequate sticks and carved them into skewers that morning, just sharp enough to spear some sausages he'd gotten in town. While she continued to pull last year's growth out from the trellis and shove it into his barrel to burn, he turned to prepare sausages and small onions, setting them off to the side of the *brouette* to cook while they finished the row. Why hadn't he thought to burn the branches like this before? It was, after all, the perfect tool for pruning in a place this cold. Lunch, heat, and transport all in one place. No more hauling everything up to the enormous brush pile at the top of the rise.

The sight of her flushed from the heat and the work set off an unexpected spark of interest that Luc quickly tamped down.

Abby caught his eye, and Luc wondered if he had perhaps muttered something aloud. If he had, it would have been in French, which at the very least meant she couldn't understand. But what on earth would she think of a man who muttered under his breath all the time?

It didn't matter, he decided, as they approached their stopping point, Le Dog a few steps behind. His stomach grumbled as the smell of charred onions and meat told him that it was time for lunch anyway.

"Sit here." He indicated a log a few meters from the vines. He'd taken a chainsaw to the rest of the fallen tree when he'd bought the place. One of the many things he'd had to do in order to get the vineyard back up and on its feet. All of it enjoyable work, satisfying in a way his family would never understand. No, they'd been royalty—at least on their own small plot of grape-growing paradise.

He didn't like to think of what they'd done to the vineyard. Olivier, Maman, and Céline, with their new business partners. It couldn't last. It wasn't possible. The spraying and the abuse of the land. He pushed it from his mind.

What would *Grandpère* think of this place, he wondered—not for the first time—with its bright-red underlayer of soil? Farther down the mountain, it was red clay, making it impossible to grow grapes. Here, though, the ground was sandy, with just the right hint of tiny Bordeaux gravel. And if that rich iron color had an influence on the grapes, well…who knew how that would pan out? He'd thought he'd gotten hints of iron in his early tastings, but…probably just his imagination. It didn't work like that. Well, it did, but not overtly. Not in ways you could identify immediately on the nose. *Terroir*—that indescribable element of place. More a translation of sunlight and rain and the shape of the mountain than a simple regurgitation. Like how what you ate affected the way your sweat smelled.

He sniffed, unconsciously hoping for a whiff of woman. How would she smell up close? There'd be no perfume, nothing like French women with their designer *eaux de toilette*.

And there, he'd brought himself full circle—right back to thinking of Abby in inappropriate terms.

He shoved bread into her hand abruptly, along with his pocket knife. "Open that, for sandwiches."

"Oh. Okay."

"This is the tradition, when it is cold. The *brouette* to cook lunch."

"It's wonderful to have the heat, Luc. Thank you for thinking of that."

He shrugged. Alone, he'd been fine with the cold and the extra work hauling branches.

While they ate, he studied her face, watching her consume the sandwich the way she'd consumed everything he'd prepared for her, with such relish that he wanted to—

"*Putain*," he muttered, startling her as he rose. "I'm sorry, I'm just…a bloody mess today."

"Oh. Oh, that's okay. Do you want me to go or—"

"No, it's fine." Luc took a big breath and wondered where these nerves were coming from. It couldn't all be for her, could it?

Yes. Yes, it probably could.

∽൦∾

For the better part of a week, Abby had gotten up every morning and shoved back the excitement of what lay ahead as she dressed in her warmest clothes and headed off to work. The threat of the ice storm had been delayed, and so she'd pruned that whole week. Abby's body changed with the work, adapting to the movements and to the man's presence. She noticed things about him, little things, like the way he eyed her when he didn't think she saw, the way the gloves he'd given her a few days ago fit her perfectly. The way he fed her when he probably wouldn't have bothered to feed himself had she not been there.

Though his exterior was rough, he was a kind man. A good man, contrary to Isaiah's assurances that nothing beyond the fence could possibly be good. If the Church was wrong about that, then what other untruths would she uncover?

Things like medicine? And learning? She'd gladly give up her own place in Heaven to keep Sammy from suffering, but with every new day, the doubts piled up and up, until she feared her lifelong beliefs might topple.

And then what would she be left with?

Luc's kindness was magnetic, and she supposed it was the reason for this anticipation she felt every morning as she slid through the fence. Strange how it obliterated the fear of discovery.

Today, she paused and took in the view. Rows and rows of vines stretched out, their branches coated in hoarfrost, sparkling white in the morning sun. The valley below was lost in fog, while the sun beat hard on her head, and cold rime lined the ground. And there, up ahead, stood that man, majestic as the mountains. He moved, swathed in smoke, bending, cutting, pulling the branches out, and throwing them into the barrow before standing.

He turned her way and stilled. Abby's breath stopped for a moment or two as she stood frozen atop the rise, caught in the act of staring at him. The hand that she

wanted to lift in a wave wouldn't move. Her eyes, stinging from the sun, wouldn't blink.

His face, she could see even from this far off, was
stuck in a look of surprise or relief or…

Breath in, puff of vapor out. A bird cawed overhead,
its long shadow slicing through the landscape, breaking
the spell. She couldn't help the smile that took over her
face. Ignoring the shimmering thrill that ran through her,
she slip-slid down the slope to find him waiting, his only
greeting the extended sweater and gloves. Wordlessly,
Abby put them on. Almost habit after nearly a week.

Pruning was different now, almost pleasurable.
Together, they'd developed a rhythm. He'd snip, snip,
snip, usually about five times, and then go on to the next
plant while she moved in to unclip and pull. No more of
those branches like whips to her face—or his. Her movements had become spare; the pain in her shoulders faded
to a pleasant memory that kept her company at night,
alone in her bed. Their pace felt good, efficient. There
was pride in a job well done—not something she'd felt
since Isaiah'd taken her off market duty, claiming she'd
been too friendly with the evil outsiders.

It made her wonder why Luc had left France. What
would make this man move to an entirely different country to do this alone?

"What's it like, where you're from?" she asked.

She didn't expect him to answer, of course. Unlike
her, the man was not a talker, and he'd made it abun-
dantly clear that idle chitchat wasn't his thing. Only this
wasn't idle, was it? Not if a person was hungry for the
answer, like she was.

She'd given up on a response by the time he spoke,

his voice so low she had to stop to hear him. "Pretty."
He paused. "And warm, compared to this."

"It never gets cold there?"

"Not in my region. Not like this, no." His face lifted
to take in the landscape before them. "Everything is less
dramatic. More…civilized."

"You saying we're uncivilized?"

His eyes snagged hers before he bent back to his
task. His response was nothing more than a grunt, but
just that connection left Abby's body humming, her
fingers tingling.

He shocked her a few minutes later by asking, "What
is it you people do over there?"

"Why, you interested in converting?"

She was proud of the surprised huff she got out of
him—a challenge she'd won. And she wanted more. She
wanted a big, round laugh, a smile that reached his eyes.
She wanted his face to lose its solemn cast for a while.
It almost didn't matter what replaced it, although she'd
like to be close enough to see it, touch it, maybe catch
it in her hands.

"Do I seem right for your…group?"

She looked him up and down in a way she'd never
dare to back home. "No, sir. You don't seem like you'd
be a believer."

"And you are?" He returned to work, but the question
stalled her, held her oscillating in its grip. A few months
ago, she'd have responded without hesitation. Just days
ago, even, she'd been sure that out here was bad and in
there was good and there was no in-between.

He must have sensed her uncertainty, because he
stopped and said, "You are a believer."

Yes, she tried to say. *Yes, of course I believe.*

She couldn't.

"I was young when I got here," she finally managed. It sounded like an excuse. "At first, I thought this place was the bees' knees. 'Course you'd have to see where I came from to understand why."

"Bees' knees?"

She swallowed past the lump lodged in her throat. "Never heard that one?"

"I haven't."

"Means it's the best. So good you can't believe it."

Snip, snip, snipping in something that wasn't quite silence, they continued down the line.

After a bit, he surprised her again. "You never said what your days are like."

"Yonder?"

That made him smile. "Yes."

"Pretty normal, I suppose. Everyone's up at daybreak. Guess you could say we're like any farm. Some folks work with the animals, milking and gathering eggs and so on. Most women work in the big kitchen, baking for the market."

"I've seen you there."

"Me?"

"Not you. But your people. At the market, selling things with your…" He motioned toward his head.

"Our what?"

"Those hats." He stopped pruning to look at her. "Why do you not wear one?"

One guilty hand flew to the top of her head, where her bonnet should be. Her gaze slid to the sliced-up fence, beside which it currently sat. "Oh. I…" She swallowed, hating the truth but unwilling to lie for something so silly. "I don't like how the covering looks. How I look with it on. I leave it up there." *So you won't see me in it.*

One side of his mouth curled up before he reached for his vine in that affectionate way of his, taking whatever secret satisfaction he'd gleaned with him. "So, you work at the market?"

"Not anymore."

"No?"

"Banned from market duty," she said dramatically to cover up how much that had hurt.

"Why?"

"Too friendly with the customers."

"That seems…counterproductive. One hopes for friendly salespeople." He paused. "Especially in America, where the smile is king."

"People don't smile in…"

"France," he said, with that low, rolling sound that made her feel…warm. Curious. Itchy in places. "No. People don't smile."

"Ever?"

His lips turned down, and she could see how the no-smiling rule was well followed.

"*You* don't smile," she said.

He stopped pruning so abruptly that Abby almost ran right into him. "No?"

Shaking her head, she looked at his face and mirrored his frown before saying a purse-lipped, "*Non,*" in imitation of his accent.

And there, miracle of miracles, the man did it. His lips curved up. Or almost. One side of his mouth lifted—the side with the scar—and, oh goodness, it *was* a dimple.

What kind of trick was it that this big, burly man had to suffer through the indignity of a dimple? And much, much worse was her having to suffer through that smile.

She wanted to touch it, the divot in his cheek. Or those lips, or that thick, rough-looking neck, which was more cleanly shaven than the first time she'd come here.

Did he do that for me? she wondered as she turned away, reaching for…anything to stop herself. Branches. Those would do. Pull, throw, wait—red face averted—and move on.

They'd finished the row without speaking and moved on to the next by the time Abby could breathe normally. Surprise, surprise, he was the one to finally break the silence.

"Besides no cap, what else do you wish for?"

She didn't hesitate before saying, "A place of my own."

"Yes?"

"Nothing big, just a…a room. Where I could listen to music, maybe?"

"You can't do that there?"

"Oh, we sing all right. Best part of the Church is the singing."

"What do you sing?"

"Hymns."

"I don't know any."

Without thinking it through, she sang a verse from one of her favorites. "All things bright and beautiful, all creatures great and small, all things wise and wonderful: the Lord God made them all."

When she met his eye, Luc was…not exactly smiling, but close. His eyes were warm, his expression…

admiring, maybe? Abby blushed with the realization of what she'd just done.

He said one word: "Pretty." But something about the way he said it, his eyes eating up her face, made her cheeks burn hotter and breath come faster. To hide it, she turned quickly back to work.

Changing the topic, she cleared her throat and asked, "So, how much is a place to rent?"

"What?"

"A room to live in. How much money do I need for that?"

He shrugged. "Depends. Big cities, it's a lot, I think. Around here? I don't know. Maybe a few hundred a month?"

"Good Lord, that's a lot."

"Life is expensive." He shrugged and cut, the movement lifting shoulders massive enough to carry the weight of the world.

"Right. So…you have to pay for food, right? And what else do you pay for?"

"Electricity. Um, water and gas, things like that."

"Gas for the car?"

"For your car and for your stove or heat."

"Oh. So…I'd need a lot. To start a life."

"A good amount, yes. You need to pay a guarantee as well, I think, if it's like France. And references for the landlord." He glanced at her. "This makes you unhappy?"

"Guess I thought…I thought I could work for you for a couple weeks and have enough to start a life."

"It's hard, Abby." His eyes on her were steady and full of a new softness that she wasn't entirely comfortable with, like he'd taken off a layer of her skin to speak to her insides.

"Blue jeans, too," she said, forcing a touch of flippancy to her tone.

"What?"

"Jeans. I'd like to wear jeans with snaps and a zipper, like a normal person."

"Like a *slim*?" The word came out with two *E*s in the middle: *sleem*. She shook her head, not understanding. "Um, skinny jeans?" he clarified.

"Goodness, no!" She laughed. "I'd need time to adjust to just trousers first, but…" Letting her gaze rest on the valley before them, she thought of the hundreds—no, thousands—of women who walked around every day wearing practical clothing instead of these stiff cotton skirts and modest drawers she had to fight her way out of. "I'd like to look normal when I go into town, to feel free. Just a T-shirt and jeans. Those sneaker shoes to walk in. Maybe some—"

She stopped, hating how her current thought embarrassed her. It wasn't the wish so much as the fantasy surrounding it.

"Some?"

"Boots. Cowboy boots, you know? The kind you stomp around in." Except stomping wasn't what she envisioned when she said it. In her mind's eye, she pictured herself in jeans by all rights tighter than she should want to wear them; a cute shirt—maybe something sparkly, but not too fancy, since part of her just wanted a plain T-shirt; and those boots with their small heels and slightly pointed toes. And all of this dancing on the arm of a man. *This man*, truth be told. It was this man in her fantasy, which sent a new wash of heat prickling against the cold air, from her chest to her forehead and well into her hairline.

"I can't imagine you stomping."

"No? I'd be good at it."

Their eyes met as he said, "I don't doubt it." The words, silly and inconsequential as they were, sent blood rushing right down her body to where it didn't belong. Somehow that blood weighed her down, made her lids heavy, and sent her mouth to drooping in a way she was sure he could see.

And then she *knew* he could, because his eyes strayed there, lingering before one thick, rough-hewn hand followed. A single knuckle swiped her bottom lip in a gesture not so much affectionate as…curious? Compulsive? Like a baby who couldn't help but touch a ball or stuff it in his mouth. To taste. To feel. To *know*.

It was over too soon, that swipe. And yet, somehow, it lasted forever. Suspended here on the mountain, in their thick cloud of burning vine and sparks, the cold melted away by more than just the fire.

After that long hitch in time, Abby inhaled and let the air out in hiccups—the shaky kind you couldn't help making after a good, hard sob. But rather than the release of a big cry, his knuckle to her lip screwed everything up tight, made her insides overflow with whatever this was. She was sure she'd pop. She *had* to.

Because Lord only knew what she'd do if this pressure didn't release sometime soon.

6

LUC WAS A COMPLETE AND TOTAL IDIOT. HE'D SEEN that lip, poking out all pink and lush and sweet. In a trance, he'd let himself touch it, had watched his hand as if it hadn't even been his decision.

As they approached the end of the last row of the day, things awkward now that he'd gone and touched her, he wanted her in a way he couldn't control.

It felt so terribly wrong.

"What is it you do up there? In the barn?" she asked, breaking into his tortured thoughts.

"Nothing."

"Oh. I thought…I thought maybe you made wine with your grapes."

"Not really."

She looked unhappy at that answer, blinking away what might have been hurt. He'd said something wrong, as usual.

With a sigh, he explained, "I'm not a winemaker."

"You're not?"

"No. I'm a grape farmer."

She squinted at him and said, "It all looks to be in real good shape."

He shrugged. "I like to work on things."

"Machines and stuff? Like that tractor I've seen you tinkering with?"

"I enjoy making things work. The tractor gives me problems."

"I know someone who could fix it." She nodded slowly. Her body worked efficiently, which he couldn't help but admire. "What are you growing all these grapes for, if not for making wine?"

"I sell them. To wineries."

"Is there a lot of money in that?"

"Enough," he lied.

"But there's more in winemaking?"

"Yes," he conceded. "Not just making the wine, but selling to...a group of people. Wine clubs, they call it."

"How's that work?"

"People sign up to receive a few bottles at a time, regular shipments throughout the year."

"So, what? You'd send it out to them? Or they'd come pick it up?"

"Either. It's a very American thing. We don't do this in France."

"Did you make wine in France?"

"No," he said with finality. "I'm a farmer."

But, of course, she pressed on. "What if you did make wine? What if you did one of those clubs? That would be a big deal, right?"

"My wine is no good."

"Wait. You *do* make wine?"

He shrugged casually, a sudden tightness in his belly. Why had he let that escape?

"Not really."

"But you know how." She paused, eyes too intense on him. "You *have* made wine."

"I've...experimented. Not to sell. Just for fun."

She didn't immediately answer, leaving him scraped raw in the silence. He hated the doubt she'd stirred up, resented her for stirring it. Everything had been fine until she'd shown up and picked at his scab. In fact, there'd been barely a scar before she'd come here. She'd gone and destroyed his calm.

"This thing used to happen at the market with our customers," she said. "Especially with the cinnamon buns, 'cause people were crazy for those things, but I've seen it happen with anything. You'd get down to two or three of something, and suddenly, customers would just about tear each other up to get it. Some days, I swear we could have charged five times the price for one of those last buns."

He didn't think he liked where she was going with this, but he kept silent.

"Seen tons of folks heading to the other wineries in the area. All kinds of people down from the city, limousines and big buses, too. You could do that, couldn't you? Make your wine and—"

"I'm not a winemaker, Abby." He stopped and turned, abruptly enough to startle her. "Come. We need to finish."

He hoped his irritation would fade away, but instead it built over the next few plants, leaving him fidgety and inefficient. They should have been done with this section by now. Instead, they'd only gotten through about two-thirds. *Dammit.*

It was almost a relief when a fat drop landed on his cheek.

"Rain," he grunted. He met her eye for the first time since they'd spoken and found her…sad. She looked sad. *Putain*, that was the last thing he needed.

"It's time to go."

"Now?"

"It's raining."

After a moment of hesitation, she pulled off one glove and the other, her eyes knowing and compassionate.

"Good-bye, Luc."

She started to turn away, and instead of relief, he felt something frantic climb up his throat, pushing him to reach out and grab her. His hand landed on her elbow, and she froze. They both did, eyes locked where his hand held her. Slowly, his gaze rose to meet hers, expecting fear, disgust.

What he saw instead were big, black pupils swallowing up her irises, that unbelievable mouth pursed and slightly open, her bottom lip lusher than the ripest cluster of grapes. Suddenly he had to taste it. *Had* to. Instead of loosening his grip and letting her go, he tightened it and pulled.

She didn't resist, even for a second. He wondered if that was good or bad before letting his other hand—the one with blank space where there'd once been a finger—grasp the side of her face and pull it toward his.

You cannot do this.

With a pained huff—hers or his, he wasn't sure—he removed his hands, although he couldn't make himself step away. *She'd* have to do that.

"Go," he whispered.

But she didn't. She shook her head, eyeing his mouth like… *Hell.* Probably exactly the way he'd looked at hers—like she wanted to eat it.

Quiet surrounded them, but here, in the space between their bodies, their breathing was a hailstorm, her exhalations loud enough to heat his face and tighten his groin.

She swallowed and leaned in to whisper, "What were you gonna do?" The voice sounded nothing like hers. It was tight and hoarse, older than her twenty-something years.

"No idea. Keep you here." Slowly, as gently as his body knew how, he leaned in and nudged her nose with his. Her gasp felt like an invitation, and he took it. Up and back down the other side, until their mouths lined up and sweat broke out across his back and he wondered what in the hell had come over him.

She was the one, though, who finally pressed her lips to his. They were as soft as he'd imagined, but also solid, as if she were more real than he'd realized. Stronger. Just lips, dry and cold, the feel of them sensuous after more than two years without. When she didn't move, he did it for her, pursing and waiting for her to do the same. She didn't, and he shifted away. Did she not want this? Had he misread it?

Oh, but no. Not with that *look* in her eyes, all vague and heavy-lidded. That flush across her cheeks hadn't been there before, had it? And that expression? What would you call that look?

Dazed. She appeared dazed. He was about to step away, about to give her space, when she whispered, "I… I don't know what to do."

God, he wanted to show her. Badly, desperately.

Somehow, that single touch of their lips had been the hottest kiss of his life. And it hadn't even been a kiss, had it? Not a real one. Nothing but that brief brush of skin to dry skin, so small in such a wide-open space.

Luc couldn't blink the haze away.

What the hell was it about this woman that made him like this?

Okay, stupid question, he thought as he took her in. Funny, though, that it wasn't the usual things that attracted him to her. It was something else entirely. Considering the way she watched him—tense or expectant—maybe he'd underestimated the lust hiding beneath that drab dress.

It was the thought of the dress that finally snapped him out of it.

This wasn't someone whose mouth you shoved your tongue into. This wasn't a woman you had passionate sex with.

He stepped back, pulling himself away, and turned his face to the side.

"You have to go."

"I don't—"

"Go, Abby." She looked so hurt. Had she been another kind of woman, she might have realized that it wasn't because he didn't want her—quite the opposite.

"I thought we could—"

"No. You need to go."

She nodded, head down, shoulders bowed. This wasn't the woman to play around with, and he certainly had no intention of being her gateway to temptation or earthly pleasure or whatever he was to her.

After she'd taken a few steps up the slope, she turned

and said, "I won't see you tomorrow. We're one short for the market, so, much to Isaiah's annoyance, I've got to fill in."

He nodded and waved good-bye, wondering if this was a lie—her way of saving face, maybe.

The funny part was that he bet he'd suffer the most from cutting it off. Because while she may be experimenting or sowing her wild oats or whatever, he was on his own, stewing in the mess she'd leave behind.

He didn't watch her stomp up the hill with Le Dog by her side. Instead, he turned to clip listlessly at his vines. But once he was sure she'd made it to the crest, he turned and caught sight of her getting down on hands and knees to crawl through the fence. The animal, who appeared to enjoy the game, followed her progress with high, curious ears, his tail a wagging blur.

She'd cut through, hadn't she? Why hadn't it occurred to him before? The cult people hadn't sent her. In fact, now, he'd bet they had no idea she was coming here. To him.

He gave her a few more minutes before heading up the hill to where Le Dog stood by that tear in the fence. It was tiny and jagged. How had she not cut herself on those edges?

And wouldn't they catch her sooner or later?

The air on this mountain was too thin for Abby. She trembled as she made her way home, rain and wind battering hard at a body that felt anchored to nothing, flyaway and unsure, as the clouds scuttled madly across the darkening sky.

Breathless, she arrived beside Isaiah's cabin, unaware of how she'd gotten there so fast.

The door opened, and Mama looked out, as if she'd been waiting.

Abby blinked at how crisp everything was, especially Mama, whose bright eyes were almost blinding.

"Heavens, what's got you so worked up?"

How on earth could her mother tell from a single look?

"Nothing," she said, although words burned the inside of her mouth, trying to get out. Questions begging for answers.

"Come on in and help me make dinner," Mama ordered with that look that said she wouldn't take no for an answer.

Abby followed her inside. And then, because she couldn't help it, she asked, "What was it like for you? When you first met my father? Or Isaiah? Was it special?"

Mama set down her knife and covered the onion bowl with a towel before focusing on Abby. She set her hands firmly on the table, head tilted at an odd angle.

"Why do you ask?"

Abby should have guessed, from the stillness in the air and the forced quality of Mama's voice, that things were not as simple as they seemed.

She forced a shrug. "I was… Now that Hamish is gone, I was thinking about who I'd be joined with next. I wondered if—"

"You wondered what, Abigail?"

Abby blinked, surprised by the edge to her mother's tone.

"I wondered how it would feel to *choose* a husband."

"Choose?" Mama's face puckered in confusion.

"Well, like you picked my father and—"

"Look no further than our Savior, Abigail, for the answer to your questions."

"But, Mama, you wanted to be with Isaiah, right? You chose to come here. I mean, you could have—"

"Where, may I ask, is this curiosity coming from?"

Mama's breathing was loud in the silence that followed. There was a moment—just a second or two—when she'd have told the truth, perhaps. Whatever that truth might have been. That she'd changed, or the world had, and she wasn't sure she knew how to change it back.

"Just wondering who God will pick for me, is all." Or if, perhaps, God had already chosen.

"It is *not* your job to wonder, child." Mama's jaw was hard, her words crisp. "It is your responsibility to submit."

"Yes, Mama," she mumbled.

It wasn't long before Isaiah arrived, opening the door to the cabin and letting in another draft of that icy wind.

"I've got to go," Abby muttered. She made to move past him, and he stopped her.

"What's this?" he asked, reaching to touch her.

"I don't—"

"Got something in your hair here, Abigail."

He touched her hair and came away with a dry leaf on a branch. He squinted at it, hard, before looking at her.

"Grape leaf?" he asked.

"Must have blown over from next door," said Abby, throat tight with fear.

He examined it, and her, before tossing it to the wind, muttering something about the weather. Abby didn't wait before following one step behind. She had to get away from his all-seeing gaze and Mama's all-knowing one.

At her own cabin, she closed the door behind her and leaned against it, shaking. Why, oh why, had she spoken of this to her mother? Why had she gone into their cabin tonight at all?

She shut her eyes hard against the memory of that leaf crunching in Isaiah's hand, his yellow eyes on hers.

In the dark, something moved.

"Who's there?" She scrambled to light the candle beside the door, hands trembling so hard she needed a second match to do the job.

A moan, followed by a thud, led her to the kitchen. Dread heavy in her stomach, she turned the corner to see Sammy, curled up on a floor stained with blood and vomit.

Oh Lord, oh Lord, oh Lord. No, no, no. Please don't do this. Not to Sammy. Please, not Sammy. She dropped to her knees, heedless of the filth seeping into her skirt, and pulled Sammy's soft, golden head into her lap. His hair was matted brown, and crusty. Was he breathing? Yes. Yes, he was breathing, but—

His eyes opened, sweet and lucid. *Oh, thank you.*

"Sammy."

"Abby." His voice was thin as a thread, but his smile was real. Good. *Thank you, Lord. Oh, thank you.* She loved that smile, loved his gentle face with its high forehead and button nose. He was different, she knew. She'd seen people like him outside. But it didn't matter to her. There was no one in the world she loved more than this boy who couldn't be mean if he tried.

"What happened, Sammy-Boy?"

"Don't know, Abby. Don't know."

"Did you fall?"

"Uh-huh. Fell, shaking like the last time. Hurt my head so bad. Hurts bad."

He tried to sit up, and she held him tighter, stilled his body. "Hold on, pumpkin. Just hold on for a sec. Let's make sure you're in one piece first, okay?" He was getting worse. Just a week ago, he'd had one of these episodes, and she'd had no idea what he needed. No idea how to help. An image of Hamish flashed into her mind, so real it blinded her: those last dark months when his begging had gotten to be too much to bear and she'd finally done something about it.

Help me, he'd tried to scream over and over again. Only he'd lost his lung power, so the sound had been a howl, quiet and breathy and insufferable.

The voices blended in her mind—Hamish's becoming Sammy's—and she came close to weeping. So close. But it wouldn't help him if she cried, would it? It would do nothing but worry him, and that was pointless.

"Hurts, Abby," he said, a scared little boy with a man's voice. "My head."

"It'll be okay, sweetheart," she said, scared, truly scared. "Everything'll be just fine. I promise." Abby rocked him in her arms and wondered how she was going to make it better when she didn't have the resources to get herself away, much less another person.

Fear filled her chest, nearly drowning her. The only thing strong enough to push it back was shame. At her own behavior—the way she'd fallen so quickly into her own sensuality, forgetting why she'd left this place to begin with.

What kind of person let herself get distracted from a mission that could mean life or death for Sammy?

She got him up and cleaned the wound on his head, fed him, and set him up in her bed for the night. All of it hiding behind a mask of serenity while her insides were a mass of turmoil. How would she get Sammy out? And once out, how would she take care of them?

Once he'd fallen asleep, she got down on her knees and prayed. For Sammy. For absolution and understanding. But mostly, she prayed for an answer. She refused to think of Luc and the things he stirred up in her—it was too complicated to untangle. And not important enough when faced with Sammy's worsening situation. God might not forgive her for leaving Him behind, but if she didn't succeed, she would never forgive herself.

7

LUC HAD NO MORE WORK FOR ABBY. THE DAY SHE'D spent away, working at the market, he'd gotten through the last vines, and there was nothing left for her to help with. Luc didn't look forward to seeing her face when he told her.

But, jerk that he was, he didn't want her to stop coming. He wanted her here, the antidote to his anxiety instead of the cause. What was it about the woman that made him miss her when he usually couldn't get away from other people fast enough?

She didn't arrive first thing that morning, so he took off up the mountain to work on the stupid tractor. Le Dog, trotting beside him, had changed—his gait light and springy, limp nearly gone. They had a checkup with the vet next week, but Luc hardly needed the doctor to tell him the mutt was worlds better. That was what happened when you fed and took care of a creature instead of treating it like dirt.

His thoughts skipped back to Abby. The new curve of her hips, the slight roundness at her cheek, where before it'd been hollow. Like the dog, she'd developed a glow. He couldn't help but feel responsible. Not exactly ownership, but…a sort of pride. As if he had a stake in her survival.

He passed through the barn to get to the back. In the room on the right, dozens of bottles lay on their sides, awaiting a verdict. Beside them sat big, round barrels, full to bursting with juice that should have gone elsewhere—missed income.

He ignored them, moving instead to the back of the barn and out through the rear door, to what he called the graveyard. *Le cimetière*. Where the previous owners had left their machinery to die. An old tractor sat in the grass, with a rusted-out array of parts he had yet to go through. He had to get this tractor up and running now, especially if his newest idea took root.

Which it would. Luc knew. He'd have to buy plants—another expense he couldn't afford. But…if, against every expectation, his wine was drinkable and he sold it, he'd earn more than what he'd get from just selling the grapes. Grapes were practically worthless compared to a decent vintage. He'd seen what they sold bottles for around here, and although he'd never open up his place to visitors, he could sell at the local grocery stores. Maybe work out a deal with restaurants.

Idiot, he thought, climbing up into the tractor. *Nobody's going to want this wine.*

He clambered into the front seat and found a key in the ignition. He couldn't believe it. For a moment, he stared, dumbfounded. There was a goddamned key. He turned it, but nothing happened.

No surprise there, which pleased him in an odd sort

of way. This was a challenge Luc enjoyed—taking a mess of metal and making it work again. He went back in for his tool belt and returned to the *cimetière* to revive some old souls.

Time passed as he worked. A lot or a little, he had no clue. But at some point, as the afternoon light began to fade, Le Dog barked—not something he did often.

"*Qu'est-ce que c'est? Hein?*" He asked what it was. The dog, as proficient in French as in English, barked a happy response.

After a bit, he heard it, too. A voice. *Abby.* Finally. With a nervous leap of his pulse, he set off to find her.

∽∾

"I didn't think I'd see you today." Luc's voice came from the shadowy barn interior.

"Sorry I'm late." She paused, nervous. "I brought you something."

Now that she was here, thrusting her quilt into his unsuspecting hands, it was awkward and strange. The look on his face, which had flushed red, brought home the fact that Abby had just about no idea what was acceptable behavior in society and what wasn't. Maybe, she thought, this had been the wrong thing to do. Maybe…

"You should not have done this, Abby."

"I shouldn't?" she whispered, avoiding his eye.

"Did you make it?"

That brought up a laugh, straight from her belly and up through her chest and throat. "Why? Is it that bad?"

He blinked. "No. Not at all. It's…it's lovely."

"Oh. Well, I'm not much good with my hands. My work is nowhere near as good as the others'."

"No?" He considered her for a moment longer than was comfortable. "Well, you've done good work for me." He paused. "With your hands."

He held the quilt, probably catching fibers on his rough skin and hating it. This had been the wrong thing to do. She wanted to continue working for him without more tension between them, but she'd gone and done this, which would only make things worse.

"Where would you recommend I put it?" he asked, looking…pleased, perhaps?

"I thought in your cabin. Wherever you spend the most time. You could use it if you ever got cold. Or not. If you don't like it, you can give—"

"I like it."

"You do?"

"Thank you, Abby. It's…" He swallowed and looked away, his scar tight. "I'll take it inside. In a bit."

After a pause, Abby said, "I saw the vines. You're done."

He nodded.

"Must feel good." The thought made her frantic, not just because she'd have no more work, but because this would be taken from her. This place, this man. What on earth would she do now?

She waited for a few seconds, breathing hard until he turned and flipped a switch, illuminating the large space they stood in. Tools hung on one wall—pruners like the ones he'd used for the past week, gloves, and other things that she couldn't even begin to understand.

Behind him, at the far end of the barn, was a door—open and showing what looked like a scrap heap outside. Here, they stood in a room with big, metal tanks. It was massive and dark, even lit as it was. The tanks lined up like sentinels along one wall.

"Come," he said, leading her through a door, which opened up to…

"Oh my…" She wished she had more words—better words—to describe this place.

The room was immense. One entire wall was made of glass—the long one, facing down the side of the mountain, almost overhanging the valley. She'd seen it from the outside and had wondered what this much glass would be like.

Inside, it was extraordinary. She'd never seen anything so expansive. Never. And the windows didn't end at the wall. They continued up and bent to become the ceiling. It was the biggest, most open place she'd ever seen indoors. At the opposite end—yards and yards away—was an enormous fireplace made of stone. You could fit a person in there. You could fit a bear. The other wall held a long, empty bar. Beyond it was a room filled with wooden barrels. Everything was warm with wood and stone and so bright you could almost taste the light.

Her breath was audible in her ears, like someone else's. Like putting her head underwater. Like looking so far out that you actually saw inside yourself. She didn't wait for him to lead the way but walked ahead. Everything was muffled by the drowning of her mind, tamped down by the light and the view and the thin, thin air.

"What…what is this?" she asked.

"It was supposed to be the tasting room."

"Was?"

"The previous owners. The couple who started the winery and planted the vineyard. They had plans."

She shook her head. "Why did they leave? How could they leave this?"

"I don't know. A death in the family is what the real estate agent said—an inheritance or someone to take care of? Although…" He trailed off, leaving a heavy weight hanging between them, drawing Abby's attention back to him. Oh, his eyes. So blue in the setting sun, so pretty in that finely etched face. Something about the glass made the light in here brighter than outside. Sharper.

"Although?"

"I think it was you."

"Me?" Abby said, instantly horrified.

His mouth didn't smile, but his eyes softened, filling her middle with something squishy and good. "I wonder if perhaps they weren't comfortable with their neighbors."

"Ah." She turned toward the view and took a dozen more steps into the room, her undivided attention on the glass that overlooked…everything. "This is the most beautiful place I've ever seen."

"Is it?" he asked, looking puzzled.

"It's not?"

"Honestly, I hardly notice. It's the…" He paused. "The other side that interests me."

Looking at him, Abby had the distinct feeling he wasn't telling the truth.

"The other side?"

"Outside. Where I grow my grapes."

"But in here… This room. This is where people would come to taste wine? Buy it, too?"

"Yes. And back there, for making wine."

Abby took a turn around the big, empty room. "Through there?" she asked.

"Yes. That's the barrel room. In those barrels, the wine ages before bottling. Beyond that, where we first came in, are the tanks where the wine becomes…well, wine. And through that door, outside—not toward the tractor, but straight through—is the porch. Under the overhang is where the grapes are crushed and destemmed. That is where the real work happens. In a winery anyway. Harvest and crush. No sleep."

"Luc, this is…" Abby shook her head. She felt the huge hole in her vocabulary.

"I didn't make this," he said with a shrug, although there was something like pride on his face. "Come," he said, opening the door into the barrel-filled room and letting out a waft of pungent, earthy air. It smelled like blood and dirt, like this man's soul: wood and minerals and the mountain and something too human to describe.

She followed Luc between the rows of barrels to the other end of the room, where he gathered two stemmed glasses and a long instrument also made of glass.

"I thought you weren't a winemaker. Just a farmer, you said. That's it."

"I'm not a winemaker."

"Then what's this?"

Shrugging, he said, "An experiment. Here, I show you."

He handed the glasses to Abby and led the way to the barrel closest to the door. It had what looked like a small, round, plastic cork in the center. Slowly, carefully, Luc worked it out of the hole, which was ringed in purple. Once it was open, he slid the long glass implement inside, finger raised. She watched as he expertly pressed his finger to the dropper, lifted the entire mechanism from the hole, and put it over a glass, emptying the contents by lifting his finger again. He stuck the top back in, screwed it down, pounded it a few times, and moved to a barrel on the other side of the room to do the whole thing over again, into the second glass.

"What is that?"

"It's called a wine thief."

"Because it steals from the barrels?"

"Precisely."

"This must all be so…scientific."

"Yes?" He smiled. "There is some chemistry. Making wine is temperature dependent. Fermentation and aging and so on. But there is some alchemy involved, too, I think."

"Alchemy?"

"That mysterious blend of things. You know, like"—he sniffed—"the air. Mountain air versus flatlands. Instinct, earth. Not particularly precise." He waved his hand in the air. "Maybe Mother Nature or Bacchus or—"

"Bacchus?"

"The Roman god of grapes. Wine and *eu*—how do you say—*débauche*?"

"What's… Oh. Debauchery?" Abby asked with a jolt of excitement. "There's a god of debauchery?"

"Of course. In Greece, he was Dionysus." He paused, eyes on Abby's. "There are gods for everything."

"Where I come from, there's only one."

His mouth turned down dubiously at the corners as he

looked around for a place to set his thief. "I need a table in here," he muttered.

"You could set an empty barrel on its end," she said, picturing a row of them down the middle of the room. "You could have people in here, tasting straight from the barrels and—"

"No people."

She stopped, crushed.

"No people? Oh. I thought with that room out there and the—"

"No people. Here." He handed her the thief, which she held along with the wineglasses, and disappeared through a door. He returned rolling one of the enormous barrels before tilting it up to stand. It was obviously empty, but goodness, it must have been heavy. He set it upright, and Abby put the thief atop it.

"Which glass did I fill first?"

"This one." She handed him the one in her right hand.

"This one is native yeast. From my grapes. The yeast helps with fermentation." Luc pointed to the other glass. "And this is inoculated yeast. Purchased. Proven." He smiled at the question in her eyes. "The wines should be different. More science. Chemistry."

She nodded and caught his gaze, feeling something charged between them. Was this what he meant by alchemy? This particular blend of sensation and anticipation?

After a long few seconds, he spoke. "Go on, Abby." He sounded breathless, his face expectant, almost eager. "Taste."

The smile that blossomed across her features made his breath come in hard, hot, heavy. He felt like he was auditioning for something. Interviewing. Passing a test.

She examined the contents of the first glass, eyes alight but unsure.

"This is my first wine." Her voice was breathy, appealing in its excitement.

He figured. Although in France, children drank wine in church; here, even God's blood was treated like a sin. Ridiculous people.

"It's not finished, this wine."

"Not finished?"

"No. After the barrels, it goes into bottles. And more time before you drink it. But try it," he urged, hoarse with nerves. Anticipation thrummed through his veins.

Her hands were lovely on the glass, delicate and graceful, her lips pursed in preparation. Luc couldn't look away, reading clues into every tiny movement: the quirk of a brow, the vibration of her throat as she swallowed. Blinking, she took a second sip, which lingered longer in her mouth. Her tongue moved, testing, and her lips curved into a smile. Did she like it?

"What do you think?" he asked.

"It's so…" Another dip of the lips, her features scrunching together as if in search of the right word. "Bright. But dark. Rich. Kind of warm." Why was she blushing at that? Or was it the wine coloring her skin?

"Try the other." He held the air in his lungs, waiting.

She tasted. Her expressions were so vivid. Curious, serious. She was trying with all her might, and he loved that.

"Here, let me show you." Luc's fingers grazed hers when he reached for the first glass. He lifted it by the stem, swirled its contents, and dipped his face to breathe in the wafting odors. "You sniff, like this. What you're looking for is the nose. The…perfume, you know?" He handed her the glass and watched closely as she did the same, awaiting her prognosis. "You smell things, yes? Fruit or something else?"

"Cherries maybe?" She bent back to the glass she held, tried again, the movements so unpracticed they were pure. "But there's also wood. Is that because of the barrels? I smell lots of things, but not really grapes."

Luc couldn't help the smile that took over his face. "They're made of… *C'est quoi chêne*? Um…oak!" He snapped his fingers as the word came back. "French oak."

"I can smell that! In the glass!" she announced gleefully, her smile beautiful.

"What else? Anything else?"

"Hold on, hold on. Yes, there's something mineral to it. Like eating dirt."

"You've eaten dirt?"

"Yes!" She laughed, her golden eyes ablaze with humor. "Haven't you?"

"No, I…" It came to him—a memory, lost in the gnarled vines of his past. "Maybe? Once? Or once that I recall. I was in the vineyard, with Olivier, my half brother. We were… Oh, I don't know. I must have been five or six, and he was older. I remember *Grandpère* always talking about the importance of *terroir*. The…" At her curious expression, he fumbled the words. "The place. Like here, this mountain and earth, the sun and weather. It's all the *terroir*. My family's is Bordeaux, one of the world's most important regions. Everything about it is unique: the earth, the plants, the seasons, even the landscape itself. Olivier decided if I truly wanted to understand it, I should eat it."

"How was it?"

"Honestly? I don't remember the actual moment I put it in my mouth, but I remember the sensation."

She cocked her head, listening closely.

Luc continued, enjoying her concentrated attention. "That mineral thing you speak of, it was that, only I remember that it fed a craving in me. In my body, my blood." Looking up, he realized he'd lost her. "It's… silly, I know."

"No. No, I think I get it, because I don't taste it as much here." She reached for the other glass, which he handed over with something like intimacy, and took another sip. Her lips were already stained from his wine, and he couldn't look away, couldn't stop wondering how his grapes would taste on her skin.

"Taste what?" he mumbled, brain hazy, before forcing himself to stop. He'd die before he took advantage of this woman. With a deep inhale, he stepped back, blinking hard and pretending he didn't see the way her eyes skipped all over him.

"I don't taste the dirt as much in this one."

Needing to clear his head, he turned back to the tasting room. "Come with me," he said, picking everything up and setting it on the bar before taking a few steps away from her. He needed space or he'd do something stupid.

"Why won't you open this up, Luc? To outside people?"

"It's not for me."

"What isn't?"

"You know. People." He almost smiled. "I don't like them and they…generally don't like me."

Instead of smiling, Abby looked sad.

"I like you. I think you're lovely."

His hands tingled. His face heated, and he looked away. "Yes?"

She nodded. "Yes. You're so…good. To me." Why did that disappoint him?

"I'm not good, Abby."

"You are," she said with a wobbly nod. "I'm the bad one."

"*You're* bad?" He could almost laugh. "How?"

"I shouldn't be here," she whispered, looking devastated.

He shook his head in disagreement, slowly like the air'd gone thick, like he'd bathed in syrup or in the *moût*—the must. That dense mix of juice and skins and seeds and stems that gives the wine its color, its body.

"I'm sorry that you're unhappy here."

"No. It's not that. I'm here to work." She looked distressed. "I didn't come here for me. I'm not supposed to be doing all these new things."

"What new things?" he asked, frantic at the notion that she'd never come back.

"Things like drinking coffee or eating ham and butter sandwiches. Like today. I came here to work, and instead, I'm tasting wine." With her accent, the word came out almost as a long and fluid *waaaa*, so much better than the tiny, pathetic, one-syllabled *vin* of his native tongue.

But her expression was angry or frustrated, and Luc wanted to make that go away. "This wasn't at all the plan. This and all the other things I shouldn't have done."

Her gaze dropped to his lips, and he heard the words she didn't say about a stolen kiss in the vineyard. It had been his fault, all of it. He'd been the one to press the food on her—and the kiss and everything else.

"I'm sorry, Abby," he said, wracked with shame.

"Why are *you* sorry?" she asked, looking truly puzzled.

"For making you do th—"

"*Making* me?" Abby put down the glass and moved toward him, her eyes not even close to accusatory. "Don't you understand what I'm saying? I want more, Luc, now that I've had a taste. I know that I shouldn't, but it's all I can think about, and I do. *I do*."

LUC SWALLOWED, HIS EYES GLAZING OVER.

"We shouldn't have kissed," he said, looking angry.

"No. We shouldn't have."

"You've never done it before?"

"Not really," she whispered, knowing full well it was time to walk away. *But I don't want to.* "I want another one, Luc."

"Another what?" he asked, looking truly puzzled for a few seconds.

"Another kiss."

He shook his head, only instead of the refusal she expected, he said, "I can't stop thinking of your mouth."

She pressed her lips together subconsciously. Her body was glued in place, but her mind raced ahead. How would it feel, in here, with no eyes to see them? No weather to disrupt them? Would the wrath of God reach in through that enormous window and strike her down?

What if it didn't? What if…

It didn't matter. Let Him punish her. It was too late

anyway. What was a little kiss after the thoughts she'd denied since the first time she'd seen this man?

Slowly, she stepped forward, eyes on Luc.

"Kiss me," she whispered, full of the knowledge that this could well be the end. *What if he doesn't want this?*

She watched as he reached out to graze her dress with his fingers. Just the fabric, not the body beneath, but even that was heady, different. *New.*

"You want this." It wasn't a question. If anything, the words came out disbelieving.

"I want *you.*"

That did it. Whatever it was. Like they'd busted through their shell, only it was more like a dam had blown, and the man she'd known until this moment—quiet, contained, restrained—transformed into something wild. Unleashed.

A couple feet away one moment, the next, they collided. It was like falling, inside and out, a fatalistic succumbing. She could barely contain a sob when his skin finally touched hers, his lips moved to her neck, his hands on her shoulders. One hand went to her nape, cupping, cradling, but firm as well. And his face, as it made its way from the hollow beneath her ear, up and over her jaw, her cheek, to her mouth... Gracious, the man was drinking her in, learning her, smelling her.

And she wanted to do the same to him.

By the time his lips made it to hers, she thought she'd be ready for it. She was wet between her legs like she'd never been in her life, and heavy, too heavy to move. Only somehow, her hips were doing a dance all on their own, tilting toward him.

He stopped right before her mouth. "You want this,

Abby?" His whispered words felt wrenched from his massive frame, each one a small, hot brand against her face.

"I'm afraid," she whispered in his ear.

He stilled. "Of me?"

"Goodness, no." She almost laughed. "I'm afraid of what God'll think."

"Of this?" He pulled back and frowned. "A *kiss*?"

It might sound absurd when he said it like that, but they couldn't all be wrong, could they? Mama and Isaiah, Hamish and the other folks?

And was this really just a *kiss*? That hardly seemed possible.

She couldn't think straight with the smell of him so close. Like nothing she'd experienced, it was heady and intriguing, and all she could think was *This is what a real man smells like*.

"What happens, over there, if you do something sinful?"

"You're punished."

"By who? God or the man who leads the Church?"

Weren't they one and the same? "Guess I'm not sure anymore."

"We shouldn't do this, then," he said, running the back of his hand over her cheek and behind her ear, where his fingers sifted through her hair. She couldn't help but lean into his touch. "I don't want to hurt you, Abby." He sounded tortured. Was this the punishment—this strange, frenzied fluttering, this agony of need? "I've never…I've never been with someone like you."

"Someone like me?"

"*Innocente*." The word, his accent, the strain of his voice—all of it built and built until she could barely breathe. Her lungs were so full, she'd die if something didn't ease the pressure.

Tell me it's wrong, she prayed. *Show me a sign.*

"Just 'cause I haven't done things doesn't mean I haven't thought of them," she admitted.

With a growl, he dipped his head and kissed her, and Abby didn't stand a chance against that kiss. No, it was so much more than a kiss, drawing at parts of her body that shouldn't be connected to her lips. And not just her lips, but her tongue and teeth, her nose, her face, all of it prey to that mouth and those calloused hands. It came together in a mixed-up cloud of confusing sensation she'd never even fathomed. She'd never been so aware of herself before, of her own skin and the sensations, explicit, right, and lush.

I'm going to die, Abby thought. *This is going to kill me.*

She'd had no idea before. None. She'd seen people kiss when she'd worked in the market—had watched surreptitiously, entranced, as a couple in the alley went way beyond just mouths into certain sin—and she'd wondered what pushed them to act like that. Lord, now she *knew*.

He muttered something against her cheek before biting her jaw gently—not enough to mark, although suddenly, she *wanted* him to with something close to compulsion.

Never had she pictured this…this overwhelming wave of need. Goodness, the things she needed right now.

To be touched. Her skin ached with it. This body that had never had eyes upon it. She wanted him to eat her up with his gaze.

He stepped away instead, backing into the bar, looking agonized.

"I can't," he gasped.

"Why not?"

"I'll hurt you. I'm no good at…" His eyes closed as he searched for the word, the color high on his cheeks, making those freckles disappear. Her hand suddenly tentative, she reached out and brushed back the lock of hair that had fallen over his forehead.

"Restraint?" she whispered.

He met her gaze. "Exactly. I want to—" Biting his lip, he turned away, but she cupped his jaw and turned him back to look at her.

"What?" she asked, desire like lightning in her veins.

"Abby…" His voice was a dire warning.

"Please tell me."

"I want to do things to you, Abby."

"Like what?" she asked urgently. "Tell me."

"I can't."

"Why not?"

"It's too vulgar."

Those words lit her fuse. Because hadn't her whole life been about keeping herself at bay? Protecting herself from the vulgarity of her own body and the pull of natural instinct? And where had that left her? Not innocent, but ignorant. Stupid rather than pure. It had robbed her of the very essence of her humanity—her freedom to choose.

"Tell me," she demanded in a voice forged of steel.

After a pause, where he looked lost and young and a bit guilty, his eyes shifted back to hers, and he said the words. Every one of them pierced her like a dart. But instead of poison, they injected her with lust, filling her until she couldn't help but squirm.

"I want to lift up your dress and look at you, smell you. I want to run my tongue over every centimeter of your body before…" He paused and cleared his throat. He couldn't stop now. Not with the way her breath had gone wild with the shock of those images, her body over-ripe and ready to explode. "I'm not a poet." How could he be so sure when everything he said lit her on fire?

"I don't care. Tell me more."

She leaned back, and his eyes tracked her, his breath ragged and desperate.

Slowly, as if waiting for her to stop him, he lifted his hand to stroke her lip, an echo of that moment in the vineyard, so gently she couldn't be sure he'd even touched her.

"I can't stop thinking of your lips, Abby, and your—" He opened his mouth as if to say something and seemed to reconsider. The slide of his eyes down her body was palpable, solid and so real she knew he was imagining his hands on her. "Down *there*," he whispered. And at that, his gaze raced up to clash with hers. She ate up his words, the images, their unholy union. Wallowing in the sins he blanketed her with. The wrongs he fed her. The many, many transgressions they shared. "I want to slide into you. To fill you and fuck you. I want to make you feel good."

He stroked her cheek now, and letting her body lead, she turned her head and took his finger in her mouth. With a groan, he leaned in to kiss her again, only it was different this time. Deeper and more explicit, but play-ful, too. His tongue teased hers, his caresses asking for as much as he gave.

This was what she wanted. A man who sought her

pleasure along with his own. No more fumbling in the dark, but rather a give-and-take between their bodies. He tasted good, smelled right, and felt like desire. Abby couldn't stop replaying the image his words had conjured—of her lifting her dress, baring herself to him, inviting him in. Her breath came out in shuddery gasps.

From somewhere close by, the dog barked, startling her and sending her out of his arms, where she teetered, blinking blindly in the light of the setting sun, one hand pressed to her mouth. Finally, once she'd caught her breath and stopped her head spinning, she turned to Luc. With his cheeks bright red and his eyes hungry and vague, he looked as flustered as she felt.

"I want that," she said, taking a step back, head shaking. "But I can't."

Because nobody had told her that a kiss could kill you. That words, as surely as a melding of the flesh, could turn you into a sinner. Oh, they'd warned her that she'd lose herself in just this type of carnal embrace, but she hadn't believed them. And now look at her. Forgetting everything that had brought her here.

"This isn't what I'm supposed to be doing," she said, racked with a new kind of remorse. "I should go."

❧

Luc blinked, coming to with difficulty. He was worked up, his body more taut and excited than it had been in ages.

Beyond the window, the sun's last, sharp rays lingered behind a scattering of clouds. Enough to illuminate the room, but not for long. Winter nights came fast and hard around here.

"Wait. Why did you come here?" Luc asked. He took a step away from her, putting more air between them. He couldn't remember disappearing into a haze of craving like that. Ever.

"I came to see you." She glanced at the door, then back at him. "Things aren't easy back home."

"What's wrong?"

She shook her head, convincing him she wouldn't answer, and then appeared to change her mind. "I have a friend. He's sick. Don't know what's wrong with him."

"What kind of sick?"

"He shakes. Shakes and disappears. His eyes roll back, and he falls down, hits his head, and—"

"Epilepsy?"

"That what it's called?" She watched him, hungry for answers.

"In English, I think you call them seizures."

"Seizures." She sounded it out, as if filing the information away. "What should I do?"

"You have taken him to a doctor?" he asked. She shook her head, eyes intent on his face. "To hospital? When this happens, you take him to hospital, right?"

"We don't," she said with what sounded like shame. "No medical interventions. It's part of what we—what *the Church* believes. God takes care of his own." That last bit came out echoing and grand. Like she was imitating a preacher. "But Sammy can't take care of himself, Luc. He can't. He's young. Like a little boy. I have to do something. Tell me what I can do."

"He needs medication. Against seizures. A doctor would prescribe it, I'm sure."

Her eyes lit up. "There's medication? It would save

him?" She looked so hopeful that he wanted to give her medicine for Sammy right there.

"I don't know, Abby. I'm not—"

"But there's a chance?"

"It might save him, but it could be other things. I don't know why people have seizures, but I do know they live and they survive, if they're helped."

Nodding, she spun toward to the door, a whirlwind of excitement, took a few steps, and then spun back more slowly. "Do you think it's part of His design, Luc?"

He blinked. "Design?"

"Yes. Is it God's will? Do you think He intends for us to suffer?"

He had no idea how to respond to that when God didn't even exist in his world. "I don't know."

"Could this really be what He wants for us? For someone like Sammy to be in pain when there's a cure just beyond the fence? Could it be God's will?"

"No, Abby. I don't think this at all. We have science and medicine, and I think you use the tools you have. It's—"

"Okay," she interrupted with a decisive nod. "Thank you, Luc. I'm sorry. I have to go." She started toward the door again, leaving him to follow, dumbfounded, in her wake.

"You're leaving?" He could hear the disappointment in his voice.

"Yes!" she said with laugh. "There's a way to save Sammy! I have to do something! At least tell someone. They've got to know there's a way to save him. We need to help him. They'll understand. They *have* to."

"If there's truly no medical treatment at your…"

Merde, he didn't know what to call it. Could he say *cult*? Was that offensive to her?

"At the Church? There will be," she said, determined. "I'm going to make sure of it."

He trailed after her to the fence, where he and Le Dog waited while she prepared to crawl through.

"Uh…don't watch me do this. Okay?"

After a short hesitation, he nodded and turned, giving her privacy. Which was odd, after what they'd just done. Odd like this entire day. No—the whole week had been strange. Since the morning she'd stepped onto his land and into his life, nothing had been normal.

He had the feeling nothing would ever be normal again.

Abby ran back, elated.

There was a cure! No more pain for Sammy.

And oh, by the way, I had my first real *kiss!* And it was better than anything she'd ever imagined.

Oh Lord, she wanted to skip her way home, get into bed, and…and…and think about it, with her hand pressed to that place between her legs. But there wasn't time for that. She had to go to Mama or Isaiah. She'd tell them and make them understand that Sammy hadn't chosen to suffer, like Hamish had until the end. God would understand. Surely he would.

And if she could convince them to let Sammy take the medicine, then she wouldn't need to take him away.

She went straight to Isaiah and Mama's cabin. Mama'd be sure to see reason.

When she got there, it was dark and cold. Nobody

home. Rather than head to her own place, she tromped down the path to the Center, where the smell of cooking made her mouth water. Perfect. She'd talk to Mama and get a full meal. Even better, so would Sammy.

She headed through the big double doors and into the lobby area, where Sarah led the children in song. The sound made her smile, bringing back memories. If she had one wish, it would be to get that feeling back—the beauty and joy of singing, of knowing she was here for a reason and that everything they did here meant something. She'd been special. Important.

She walked across the thin, tan carpet—whose rough nap she remembered perfectly beneath her knees—to the rear of the room, where two doors led to the dining hall and kitchen.

In one of the doorways stood Brigid, focused on the kids, the half smile on her face probably a replica of Abby's.

She didn't notice Abby right away, but when she did, it took a while for her expression to change. For those few seconds of limbo, they shared something. A memory of a childhood spent as friends? A moment of regret for the past they'd had here? Singing and believing and just *being*, away from the reality of life outside this fence.

Just being.

Brigid's eyes cleared and her features dropped. The smile disappeared, and she squinted before disappearing into the kitchen. Well, Abby supposed, crossing the room to follow her, even bonds forged in childhood could be broken.

Gracious, wasn't it sad? She and Brigid had been

close once. Almost the same age. But as Abby pushed through the swinging door, she remembered things changing. They'd been about twelve, maybe, when they'd started to grow apart. No, not grown—more like broken, with Brigid splintering off from her life one summer. If not physically, at least in spirit.

There was a racket in here. The productive clatter and sizzle of cooking. Potatoes and beans, chicken and stuffing. A feast, it looked like. Abby's mouth watered as she sought out her mother, but she wasn't here. Abby made her way through the busy space, to the greetings of several women—not including Brigid, she noticed, who'd slid away to peel carrots, shoulders hunched, stiff back to the room.

What happened to you? Abby wondered before walking through the door. *What happened that summer?*

Ah, here was Mama. In the dining hall, preparing for dinner. Abby raced to her.

"Hi, Mama."

"Here you are. Wondered where you'd got to after the market."

"Checked my fences."

Her mother chuckled. "Looks like we finally got you the right job."

"I liked the market."

"Yes, well. You liked that a little too much, Abigail. Customers were asking after you. Fraternizing with outsiders is—"

"*Frowned upon.* I know, Mama. I know, but—"

"It's not just fraternizing, dear. It's sinking to their level. There's a reason we live here, you know. On this mountain." Above the fray. Yes, she knew that, too. She knew it all, and yet she couldn't seem to get it right—couldn't seem to want to.

"I need to talk to you, Mama."

"What about, child?"

"Sammy."

"Oh, honey, not that again. The boy was born with his cross to—"

"No, Mama. We can change it."

Hands busy polishing and separating flatware, her mother didn't say a word.

"Sammy's sick, Mama," Abby said.

"It's the Lord's will" was the response, although it sounded more like a single word: *Sthlorswill*. It came out smooth and easy, dismissive of the reality of it. That was what happened when you repeated something often enough. It turned into a meaningless sound.

"He's in pain, Mama. He's hurting. And we can fix that."

"If the Almighty's decided to—"

"We can save him."

"Who is *we*?"

"I've…" Abby glanced around and lowered her voice. "You could come with us, Mama. You and Sammy and me. I don't want to leave you here."

"Excuse me?" Her mother stilled, hands suspended above the flatware. "Lower your voice," Mama whispered, the sound harsh enough to burst the ridiculous bubble of hope Abby'd managed to ride in on.

"We could—"

"You shut your mouth right this instant."

"You don't understand. Sammy's going to—"

"Oh, I do understand. *I do*." Mama set a fork onto

the pile with a clatter and grasped Abby's arm tightly, leading her to the back door, face stiff and red. A few women watched their progress with curious gazes. Outside, Mama turned on her. "You think you know better than Isaiah? You think you know God's will?"

"No, Mama. I don't. But listen to me. *Please.* If God didn't want us to practice medicine, He wouldn't have let people create it, would He? Doesn't make any sense, does it?" Mama opened her mouth to reply, but Abby kept right on talking. No way she'd stop when there was so much to say. Mama was sure to understand once she'd explained. Mama would just come with her, and then there'd be nothing holding Abby here. Mama, Sammy, and Abby could start a new life. A family, on the outside. "Listen," she said, forcing an eager smile. "There're doctors and…and…surgeons and whatever helping people, right? God let that happen. And what about Hamish? You think it was God who took him? No, it was our own stupid refusal to use the tools we've been offered—"

"*Abigail Merkley. You shut your mouth,*" her mother said, the words harsher than any Abby'd heard in years— since the time she'd been caught doing dirty things with Benji. Mama's lips were compressed, her face rigid with anger, and Abby had her first real moment of doubt. Mama reinforced the feeling when she said, "Do not spew words of the Devil in my presence. *Do not* speak such untruths."

"Mama," Abby whispered, getting in close. "Come with us. Me, you, Sammy. We could be together. Out there. I don't want to leave without you, but—"

"*Not another word.*" With a step forward, she

tightened her hold on Abby's arm, and for just a second, it seemed to be in kindness—the start of a hug or some other symbol of warmth or affection. Instead, the older woman's hand grasped her forearm—nails sinking in— and twisted. The fragile skin beneath no longer hurt— the scars were too thick for Abby to feel pain—but even the numbness sent a message.

"Don't think *this*"—she squeezed hard—"makes you immune to God's will, child. Because it doesn't."

Abby stared at her mother, mouth open in shock. Before she could respond, Mama dropped her arm, threw open the door, and disappeared inside. Abby found herself alone behind the Center, blinking back tears of injustice.

Strange how she'd blocked out memories, like the one that suddenly came at her as fast as a freight train— her and Benji at the emergency Church meeting after they'd been caught in the orchard on that long-ago day.

Abby'd been the one on trial, though. Never Benji.

A defiler of men, they'd called her, Benji the inno- cent victim.

Stood up in front of everyone she'd thought of as family, summer light blazing in through the Church window, dust motes floating around her, Abby had watched the eyes change, turn accusing. Benji had cast his gaze to the floor when he'd admitted what they'd done, his voice almost too soft to hear. In his version, she was the one doing, taking, making him do things in return.

Mama'd been there, dry-eyed, her expression full of humiliation for what Abby'd done. Hamish and Isaiah had presided over it all, hard and judgmental. But in

Isaiah's eyes, there'd been something hungry that she hadn't understood. She'd cowered under that look, and when he'd offered her up to the man strong enough to tame her, she'd seen something off there. Like he wouldn't have minded doing it himself if he hadn't already been her stepfather. He'd used sibilant words like *siren* and *succubus*, and by the end, even Abby was pretty sure she deserved to go straight to Hell, sinful serpent that she was.

When they'd given her the chance at absolution, she'd taken it. Never mind that it had felt more like punishment.

What a relief when Hamish had claimed her—not because he saved her from punishment, but because someone still wanted her. Someone was willing to step in and save her from herself. She'd be forgiven in the eyes of the Lord and, almost more importantly, in her Mama's eyes, still filled with shame.

Here they were again, right back where they'd been all those years ago: Abby in the wrong for asking questions. For being different. For trying things and thinking for herself and wanting to experience things and live. Good gracious, if they knew about this knot of doubt inside her, they'd flay her alive, wouldn't they? The scars covering her arms itched with certainty.

Well, she'd just have to make sure they never found out.

It wasn't until she moved out of the light pouring from the back door that she saw the person lingering in the obscurity beside the building. Brigid again—her ever-present nemesis, always there in the shadows.

"Guess Isaiah's gonna find out about this, too, huh?"

Abby said in a low voice, unable to hold in her hurt for another second. "Got everything you need?"

Without another word, she turned and made her way back home, her heart as empty as her stomach as she dredged up another forgotten memory: it was Brigid who'd found her in the orchard with Benji that day and gone straight to Isaiah with the news. She could only imagine the damage the woman would do now.

9

Abby made her way back to Hamish's cabin to gather a few things, keeping an eye out for Sammy along the way. They'd leave tonight. She'd go to Luc, who'd take them in and—

She stopped short.

On the bench by her front door sat Isaiah.

How can he possibly know already?

He stood, somehow appearing both stern and tranquil. It was part of his gift—communicating a multitude of ideas without words.

Had Brigid already gotten to him? No. Abby'd come straight from the dining hall. It wasn't possible, was it?

She slowed her approach, tamping down the flood of anxiety sliding up her back. He couldn't know.

The smile she pasted on her face couldn't possibly look real.

"Evening, Brother Isaiah." With the glow of Luc and the hope of her mother's help long burned away, the cold penetrated the cotton of her dress and the thick, homespun wool of her coat. This man waiting here could not be a good thing.

"Abigail," he said, pushing his voice into that low register that said hours of preaching could ensue. *Hours.*

She bit back the words she wanted to let pour out—about Sammy and hope and God being everywhere—and waited, schooling her face into a close approximation of the interested believer she was meant to be.

"How are the fences?" he asked.

"Wonderful," she said. *Tell him about the medicine,* something inside her urged. *Maybe he'll understand. Maybe he'll agree.* "Perfect, but I've—"

"Good. Good." He cut through her words and paused, indicating that she should precede him inside. As she passed, entering the only home she'd ever had to herself, a slew of images hit her—Hamish coughing up blood, Sammy's face stained brown with the stuff. Resentment rose up on a tide of fear and frustration. It burned a hot trail through her belly and chest and throat to press like tears against her sinuses. Isaiah, their fearless leader, this man who ignored his own people's suffering.

"You worked the market today."

Slowly, she nodded. Should she tell him about how sick Sammy was? And about the medicine that could cure it?

"And where were you just now?"

"With Mama at the Center."

"Before then?"

Her throat seized up. Someone must have seen her with Luc.

"Checked the fences."

"Very impressive. *Ambitious.*" His smile was a

benediction. "I looked for you. Along the southern fence line. Up to the rocks. Didn't see you."

"Oh." She forced the word out as calmly as she could, swallowing back the lump of fear. He'd come across the hole in the fence with her coat and bonnet beside it, and now he was playing cat and mouse with her. He had to be. "Must have just missed each other." The words sounded artificial. She made her way past him in the disappearing light and slipped into the kitchen, where she filled the kettle. An image of Luc arose, unbidden, of his hot coffee and his hotter tongue. She almost cried, thankful that she'd gotten that moment with him.

"What's that, dear?" Isaiah asked, polite as ever, hat in hand, brim curled into his palm.

"May I serve you some tea?"

"Certainly. Thank you kindly, Mistress Merkley."

She could feel Isaiah watching her as she put the kettle on the stove and moved to fetch her single loaf of bread, hiding her shaking hands in the folds of her dress.

The silence was finally broken by the flare of a match when he lit the hurricane lamp on the kitchen table before going to work on the woodstove in the center of the one-room cabin. Once he'd gotten it crackling, she heard the creak of him settling into one of the wooden chairs that her late husband had built with his own hands. On the cushion she'd stuffed and sewn herself. The cushion Hamish had sat on every day, until he'd moved to the bed, never to sit again.

"The outdoors suits you," he said.

She nodded in return, since anything more would suggest that this was a compliment. Which it assuredly wasn't. Isaiah did not compliment. He spoke in simple truths. Proclamations.

"Sit with me," he said while they waited for the water to boil.

"Thank you. Sir, I have—"

"Sit, child. Listen. I think you'll be glad of what I have to share."

He sounded so reasonable, so like the man she remembered from her childhood, that hope flared. This was it—her opportunity to tell him. He would agree that medication was the solution. And with Isaiah on his side, Sammy would be fine. She had to try. She *had* to.

"If I may, Isaiah. It's about Sammy. There's a chance we could fix what ails him."

Watching her, he waited.

"What *ails* him, exactly?"

Ignoring the niggling voice that told her stop, she forged ahead. "He has…seizures."

Thin, reddish brows rose over bony features. "Seizures?"

"Yes, they're when a person—"

"I know what they are, Abigail. What I don't understand is why you see fit to question our good Lord and Savior. His judgment is true and supreme."

"I…I'm not questioning, sir, but…there's *medicine*. For seizures. We can help Sammy get better. It's not against the Lord if it's—"

"Sit." Face tight, Isaiah tilted his head and focused his eyes on hers.

Abby settled stiffly onto her chair and waited, urgency tamped down, frustration making her antsy.

"A decision has been made," he said with a smile.

He seemed to wait for some response before going on. "You've had a hard time of it, I know, since your husband died, Abigail. Hamish Merkley was a good man with a tight hold on you. With him gone, I know how easy it would be for you to lose your path. And the fault is mine if you have lost it. All mine."

Eyes downcast, face hot and prickly, Abby waited.

"I haven't lost my—"

Again, he didn't let her speak. "Had a few fine men request your hand, but I'm not sure they're strong enough for the way you need to be…*handled*."

Silence as Abby breathed, everything clenched, everything so tight she should, by all rights, have splintered into a million jagged shards.

"My concern, dear Abigail, beyond your usual challenges—oh, curiosity, pride, a dash of immodesty, and so on—is your *lack* of children, your inability to fulfill your duties as wife and mother. Are you barren? Would the Almighty so forsake one of His chosen few?" With a sad shake of his head, Isaiah lifted one hand, as if to touch her, but pulled it back. "I received word last night, Abigail, from our Righteous Lord and Savior. *Hallelujah!* I prayed, and He responded." Isaiah's voice rose, taking on the kind of fervor that usually preceded an important proclamation. Perfect, really, that tweak of surprise at the end, bewilderment that he'd been chosen, yet again, to deliver this sacred message. How modest.

The air grew stiller in the tight space. Even without an audience, Isaiah stole a room's oxygen. With people bearing witness, singing his praises, and giving him their air, he was legendary.

Why hadn't he saved this for a more public occasion?

"Would you believe our Lord has time to spend on such inconsequential beings as the two of us?" He chuckled self-deprecatingly, foxy teeth prodding his bottom lip. Righteous certainty lit him up from inside. Handsome and saintly. A deadly combination. "I could not believe it either, my dear. But He knows the importance of our work here, and He has, again, chosen you, Sister. *You.*" He nodded, narrowed eyes bright on her. Somehow, despite that light, he managed to look saddened, contrite—a martyr heading to his death. "I did not desire this, *Abigail.* I told Him so myself, but He did chasten me and remind me of my duties unto Him." He leaned forward and placed a hand on her forearm. Abby watched that spot—those fingers, that touch, both too familiar. The light sprinkling of gold hair along the back of his hand, the few freckles beneath, were too human for someone so close to the divine. "I will do the Lord's bidding," he whispered, and the hand grew heavier—whether in her mind or reality, she wasn't sure. "I will take *you*, Abigail." The hand lifted and alit on her face, caressed her jaw in a move she'd seen him perform over and over and over again. Just a fatherly motion, he'd say, but in reality, Isaiah never touched men like this, nor boys. It was more than fatherly, she was sure. It left her feeling filthy, wanting to shrug him off and scrub at her skin.

"*You?* You'll take me as a wife?" Her heart beat audibly in her ears. A fast, loud *thwump* that she could barely hear through. "What about Mama? Does she know?"

The corners of his mouth twitched as though at a memory, and something sick twisted in her chest. *I've got to get out of here.*

"I will do my duty unto her. And unto you. With no children between us, I see the error of our ways. And the Savior has decreed it." His voice was low, almost a whisper. "*I will plant a child inside of you.* Unlike your late husband, who was unable to do so," he added, a sad smile pasted over his features. And he believed it—that his was a nobler body, far more able than Hamish's.

No. Oh, no, no, no. She couldn't do this. She wouldn't. At least with Hamish, there'd been a marriage license. She may not have wanted it, but they'd been wed before God and government. What Isaiah proposed was preposterous on countless levels. No. Never.

A wave of nausea rose up, images of herself and Mama and… Oh Lord, the worst of it was the babies. The babies, if she had them, would be taken from her and put into the nursery.

"Four days hence, we will be joined in the eyes of the Lord. You will bear me children, *many* children, and we will prepare our people for the Day." He smiled. "Together."

In four days? It took longer than it should have for the words to truly sink in, because this wasn't supposed to happen. Isaiah didn't take women like this. There'd been whispers of God pushing him to do things with young girls, but not women who'd been wed before.

He'd want her to smile, to be pleased. She forced her cold lips to tighten at the corners, opened her mouth, and forced out a lie: "It would be an honor."

It wasn't until Isaiah took his leave that Abby let herself collapse. He'd just disappeared from sight when she rushed around back and threw up—halfway to the latrine. After that, she went inside and gathered the few

things that mattered to her: her birth certificate, stained
and worn, its corners dog-eared but still legible; the little
plastic farmer figure she'd kept from her life before
arriving at the Church—it had been her only toy when
she and Mama had driven away from West Virginia—
and her dictionary. She couldn't bring herself to look
at the Blackwood Library label on the spine, but she'd
taken the oldest, most tattered one they had. And she'd
always figured she'd somehow repay them. At least now
she might have the opportunity to do so.

Sammy was finishing up dinner in the dining hall when
she found him, which was just about the worst possible
place for him to be. She spotted him through the window
and waited, hidden in the trees, until folks emerged,
heading back to their cabins for sleep.

Finally, Sammy came out, and Abby took a chance
by going right to him, grabbing his arm, and pulling
him along.

"Oh, hi, Abby! Missed you at dinner. Brigid sat
with me and the kids. I got to hold Jeremiah! He's so
little. She said I can't give him regular food yet. Only
drinks milk."

She glanced over her shoulder and picked up her pace.

"Wow! That's great, Sammy. But listen, we need
to go."

"Where? Where we going?"

"We're leaving. There's someone who can help us.
His name's Luc, and he lives right over the rise, past the
fence. We'll—"

"You mean Grape Man?" She'd forgotten she'd

shared that name with Sammy. Well, good—that would make it easier to convince him to come along.

"Yes. Yes, we're going to Grape Man, and he'll know where we can go to get you help. Okay? Come on, let's—"

"Don't wanna go, Abby. Got too many friends here."

"We're coming back," she lied. "But right now, we've got to get to Grape Man. You have to listen, okay? You know where he lives, right? If anything goes wrong?"

"Yeah, but what about your mama? Don't you wanna tell her where we're going? I didn't see her at dinner, but she'll be sure to—"

"No, Sammy. No, we have to leave now. There's a hole in the fence that we need to get through. We'll worry about—"

"Oh, no, Abby. Almighty'll be angry if we do something 'Saiah don't like. 'Saiah always said not to tread on the other side of the fence. It's all monsters out there."

Abby stopped and turned to Sammy, hands tight on his shoulders, hating how firm she had to be. "Sammy. This is our only chance. Do you understand? Remember how you hit your head and it hurt? This isn't about Isaiah or God or my mama. This is about getting you all better." She paused, eyeing him closely. "How're you feeling?"

"Head hurts."

"Yeah? Like when you get one of your…fits?"

"Yeah. Before getting one."

"What if I told you we could stop the fits?"

"Oh, I'd be happy. I sure would."

Softening her hands into something close to a hug, she leaned in and grasped him gently by the forearm, urging him along. "Then let me make that happen, okay, pumpkin? Will you do that? Will you let me take you to Grape Man?" Another tug at his arm had him walking, if not quite agreeing to leave yet. But it was a start. Slowly, they made their way past the cabins, toward the uphill path. After a few minutes, Sammy stumbled to a halt.

"Don't want to leave, Abby."

Abby paused, one comforting hand moving to clasp his.

"Remember that ice cream they sell at the market?"

"Bubble gum!"

"Yes, that's right. Bubble gum. Well, you can—"

"Pink bubble gum."

She smiled, wanting to hug him but pressed by the need to move. "I'll get you some. I'll get you lots."

There wasn't time for the shame that washed over her at his acquiescence.

"'Kay, Abby."

"You know that section of fence, up there, by the rocks? The place above Grape Man's fields?"

"Yeah. Where we watched him in the summer." She flushed hot at the memory of dragging Sammy with her to watch Luc. "We're going there. To a hole I made."

"We crawl through the hole?"

"Yes, Sammy. And then—"

"He'll be our dad?"

Abby's chest caved a bit at those words. *Oh, Sammy.* She screwed her eyes shut and pulled him along. Even as a kid, she'd taken care of him. Like a little brother. Like her own child.

"Not exactly. But he'll help us." She closed her eyes, hoping she was right. "He's a good man."

From somewhere behind them—Abby couldn't tell

how far—came the sound of shouting. It took a few seconds before it sank in. When it did, she tightened her hold on Sammy and dragged him up and toward the fence. She worried as he struggled to keep up behind her. Would running like this set off one of his fits?

Another shout, so much closer now, had them doubling their efforts. Sammy, sensing her fear, didn't need to be told to hurry. Bless him.

It hurt her lungs to run so hard. It had to be worse for Sammy. It was when he started coughing that she began to lose hope. The men would hear them now, surely.

She pictured the path ahead. One last curve, the short, rocky climb, and then the home stretch. Picking up speed, she knew they could do this. *I have enough strength for both of us.* All they needed to do was make it to the hole and—

With a thump, she fell hard and rolled a few feet downhill. The air was knocked out of her, and her lungs hurt.

Pushing hard at the pain, she got up onto all fours, eyes focusing on Sammy's scuffed black shoes—no more adapted to this escape than hers—then up to his face.

"Go!" she hissed and pointed to the hole, invisible in the dark but only about fifty yards ahead now. "There. See where I'm pointing?" At Sammy's nod, she went on. "You go straight that way, to the fence. The hole is at the bottom. Get down and crawl through. Then you go to where there's light. Understand?"

"Not goin' without you, Abby. I can't do—"

"Don't you dare wait for me, or I'll be angry, Sammy," she said through gritted teeth, the lie bitter on its way out. She could never be angry with him, but now wasn't the time to show softness. Softness, right now, could very well mean death. "You go through the hole and down the hill till you get to the cabin. And then you tell Luc you need his help. Got it?"

He didn't answer right away, and she stood, cringing at the pain of her ankle. "Go on, Sammy. That way."

Behind them, footsteps could be heard, and the voices, louder, closer, more pressing. Dogs barked.

She'd dropped her things when she fell, but it didn't matter. None of this would matter if Sammy didn't make it. They were close now, too close. If she continued, they were sure to catch them, especially since she'd surely sprained her ankle and—

Oh Lord. Somewhere, not too far ahead, was the hole in the fence that meant escape. She took another step and bit back a howl of pain as she sank to her knees.

"See the fence?" Sammy nodded, and she shoved him, hard. "Go. The hole's right there. Don't look for me. Don't wait. And don't make a sound."

"Not without you, Abby," he said, that stubborn weight to his voice.

"Look. I'm slower than you right now, but I'm coming, okay?"

When he hesitated, she went on. "It's like hide-and-seek, Sammy. It's a game, okay? But you've got to win for me. Can you do that?"

She waited, breath held, for him to think it through.

"Find Grape Man—"

"Luc."

"Find Luc and wait for you."

She opened her mouth to protest and then closed it. No time. "Yes. Now go! *Go!*"

Once he'd taken off, turning back was the hardest thing she'd ever done, but Sammy would never get through if she didn't head the others off. Standing up, she gathered up her things, ignoring the swath of light that said someone was just on the other side of the rocks, until the footsteps were impossible to ignore.

Slowly, she raised her face to the spotlight, which picked her out of the dark night.

"Who's there?" she asked, covering her fear with bravado. Something she'd seen once, in town, flashed through her mind. A sports poster, she thought. It had read *Go big or go home*, and she decided to take that to heart.

"What do you want?" she yelled, loud enough to draw them all right to her—she hoped.

It was Benji, she saw when he approached, shotgun hanging at his side. Funny how, even as a silhouette, Benji's form was more solid than the other Church members'. She'd recognize him anywhere.

"Abigail," he said, voice low, friendly, in perfect imitation of their fearless leader. "Where you headed?"

"Oh, I'm just going to…" She swallowed. Why hadn't she come up with a story? No point, was there? "I'm leaving, Benji. Let me go," she demanded. There'd be no begging here tonight.

She could feel the intensity of his focus, despite the obscurity of his form.

"Over here!" he yelled, and everything ratcheted up. Answering voices and barking, followed by the dull scuff of footsteps. They'd hunted her down. Like prey.

One of the dogs approached, gave her a quick sniff, and then took off toward where Sammy had disappeared, and it was all she could do not to scream, *No!*

"I've got her!" Benji said, his voice rife with masculine pride, and Lord, she wanted to kick him in the face. She held back because that wouldn't do, would it? And then she decided she didn't care anymore. If they hadn't caught Sammy by now, he was free. *I've got nothing to lose.*

Her movements were decisive as she rose to full standing and stepped into Benji's space. Oh, she loved the uncertainty there once she'd gotten close enough to see. Needing to wipe every ounce of self-assurance right off his face, she lifted her right hand and swung as hard and fast as she could against his cheek.

His stunned grunt and surprised look—eyes big like a raccoon—would have been comical if everything wasn't so dire. *I'd better appreciate this moment*, she told herself as Isaiah led the others right up to them. *This might be it for me.*

She was right, she knew, as Benji's face tightened in a show of rage right before he shoved her to the ground and kicked her hard in the belly, all under the watchful, benevolent eye of Isaiah. One kick was enough to rid her of all air, then another for good measure. She curled in on herself, a body made of nothing but pain.

Nobody touched her for a minute. She'd just made it to all fours when Isaiah squatted beside her and spoke, voice inflexible and utterly deadly: "Where is Samuel, Abigail?"

When she didn't answer, he grabbed her by the chin and forced her to look at him. "If he's gone, we'll get him back. You know that, right? Just like we caught you, Abigail." To the group, he said, "Do whatever it takes to find Samuel and bring him home. Whatever transpires tonight is God's will." Leaning in, he put his lips to her ear, not quite touching, but close enough for his breath to send goose bumps crawling over her skin. "You had me fooled, all right, little Abigail Merkley. So good at playacting, aren't you? Honored, you said. It has since been brought to my attention that you want to play God, with medicine and other evils." He yanked her chin harder, brushing his lips against her as he spoke. "I suggest you make your peace with the Creator tonight, Mistress Merkley," he whispered. "You'll have your reckoning in the morning."

After a long evening spent working on machinery, Luc would normally have dinner and a drink and go right to sleep. This evening was different, though. Try as he might, he hadn't been able to fix the goddamn tractor. He had every part he could want, had tried every single thing, and yet nothing seemed to work.

At home, bone weary and exhausted, he couldn't sleep.

Because of Abby.

He couldn't lie down without thinking of her. And it made him crazy. He shouldn't have done what he did with her today. Shouldn't be thinking of her, much less touching her and…letting her experiment on him.

Because that was what she was doing, wasn't it? Testing out her newfound freedom on the first man she came across?

Seated in the kitchen, he refocused on the chunk of wood in his hands. Thank God he'd found it. The first good piece since *Grandpère* had died. No, it was longer than that. The last time he'd carved anything had been before losing his finger. It was odd working with one less digit.

It was a pointless exercise, carving wood. He wasn't even sure why he was doing it.

While he carved, his mind wandered—something he hadn't welcomed much over the past few years, but tonight he'd spent a good chunk of time planning the new field before letting himself think of Abby.

What was it about her that got to him? He didn't get off on innocence or freshness or whatever it was. No, it wasn't her innocence, but rather her thirst for experience that he liked. Her desire to *obliterate* that innocence.

God, whatever it was, it was dangerous. And while he'd planned to give her more work, he knew that wasn't a good idea. In fact, he should never have let her in at all.

Too late for that, he thought, more agitated than before. He shifted back into his chair and let his hands continue their work. Wood chips fell from the tiny block, revealing—or rather releasing—the object inside. Whatever that would be. He worked quickly, shaving here and there, until he gouged too deeply and had to consciously slow down.

His self-flagellation was halfhearted in comparison to the memory of today's exchange. That alone had him hardening. He couldn't stop thinking about her response to his words and the way she'd thrown herself at him, the way her nipples had pressed against the fabric of that damned dress, ten times more appealing than some lacy lingerie. Shave, turn, shave, turn. His hands continued, despite his mind stuttering to a halt on the thought of lingerie. What did her underwear look like under that thing? Did she even wear any?

Stop it.

Concentrating hard, he focused on the rough texture under his fingers, ignoring the sense memory of her skin beneath his, her mouth plush and hot and open and—

Concentrate, you asshole.

Funny how he'd found this piece of wood. Abby had just disappeared down the slope on her side of the fence when he'd spotted it, right beside his foot. More like stumbled on it. Long and oddly curved—and definitely not from his vines—the chunk appeared to have shown up out of nowhere. He'd ignored it initially, but something about it had called out to him, and he'd grudgingly gone back up the mountain to find it.

What are you? He squinted, trying to figure out with his brain what his hands already knew. Long and twisted, like a woman's—

A thump behind him had Luc turning and rising from his seat in one tense motion. Le Dog growled by his side, and Luc's hand was already tight around the dull carving knife. The piece of wood dropped to the floor with a thud. There, at his curtainless kitchen door, was a face, bright and demonic.

Without hesitation, Luc yanked open the door and prepared to yell at the idiot who'd broken his peace.

"Grape Man!" the kid said too loudly.

Luc blinked.

"I'm Sammy!" Not a kid. A man.

"*You're* Sammy?" A harsh sound escaped Luc's throat, and he realized with a shock that he was laughing. Jesus. This wasn't at all the person he'd pictured.

Everything fell into place for Luc. *Trisomie…* What was that in English? Down syndrome. That was it. Abby hadn't mentioned that, had she?

During his moment of hesitation, Sammy enveloped Luc in an uncomfortably personal hug.

Luc pushed away. *Space, I need space.* "What are y—"

"It's Abby. She said come here." He was out of breath and hard to understand. "There's a hole in the fence, and then I ran. It's hide-and-seek, 'cept I fell on the hill, it's so big. Got right back up and kept runnin'. It's the biggest game. Bigger than the fence this time. I ran."

"Abby told you to come *here*?" The boy nodded. "Where is *she*?"

"She's comin'." Sammy, who still stood in the wide-open door, turned to peer out into the night. Meanwhile, cold air poured inside.

For a few long seconds, Luc stood there, stunned. "Where is she, Sammy?" He looked over Sammy's shoulder, hoping that she would materialize and save him from this intrusion.

"Might be a while. Dogs and flashlights comin' over the hill and— Oh, hello, Rodeo!" Sammy walked farther into the kitchen and got onto his knees in front of Le Dog. "You're here, too! We're all here, in the same place!"

"Except for Abby. You said she's coming, but—"

"Yessiree! She'll be here. She'll come." Sammy bent and picked up the wood Luc had dropped. "It's a hand!" Luc blinked again, surprised. Yes, that was a hand emerging, attached to what would be a fragile-looking wrist, twisting off to disappear right before the crook of an elbow, delicate but capable. Luc had barely carved at it, so how could the kid possibly see all of that? Or did it just mean that Luc was blind to what he created?

Blind. That seemed about right. Like his hands could feel it before his brain knew what they were doing. Like Braille, he needed his body to interpret before his mind kicked in. Exactly like pruning vines. Thinking too hard destroyed the process.

He blinked at the tight feeling in the front of his head.

The man or kid or…Sammy had a way of moving into a space, sliding in so you barely noticed until suddenly you were in your living room and you'd never agreed to that at all. This was not all right. "She'll be here soon." Sammy looked around, eyes innocent in their curiosity. "Where's all your stuff?"

"Stuff?"

"You know, like home stuff."

Taken aback, Luc squinted at the space with a fresh perspective. It was sparse, he supposed. But what did he need things for? They just got in the way.

"Got nothing on the walls. No cushions or—oh, hey! You got electricity. In your house!"

In my house. My house. He's in my house. Overcome by panic, Luc tried to corral him. Maybe he could convince him to go back outside. On the porch, perhaps, where this boy's presence wouldn't feel so enormous.

"What am I supposed to do with you?" Luc asked helplessly.

"Abby'll tell us."

Wonderful. "But she isn't here. You need to leave. Go back, please."

Sammy looked crestfallen. "But you're my friend."

He ignored the weight those words placed on his shoulders and asked, "How old are you?"

"Nineteen."

Still a kid. But not quite.

"I'm not… I can't take care of you. You need to go. I'm not able to—"

Someone knocked at the front door. He hadn't heard a car pull up. Sure it was Abby, here to explain everything, Luc yanked open the door.

Not Abby.

Luc squinted into the dark, wishing he'd replaced the porch light bulb.

His visitors were a group of heavily armed men. About five, he guessed, although there could have been more farther out.

The hair on the back of his neck rose and the panic at Sammy's intrusion was replaced by a new sort of adrenaline. "Can I help you?" he asked, standing taller.

"Hello there, sir. Isaiah Bowden, from next door. Over yonder." The man in front wasn't the tallest or the most imposing, but he had the most presence. He was on the small side, especially compared to Luc, with orangish hair under a sturdy black hat. Beneath that, small, close-together eyes were shadowed in a pointy face. He was the only man not holding a gun, which, in a perverse sort of reversal of everything, made him more intimidating than the others.

"I recognize you," Luc said, forcing his jaw to loosen.

Drawing closer, the man—Isaiah—put one hand out for Luc to shake.

The second Luc's hand touched the other man's, something happened: the night darkened and clouds skittered across the sky, giving the moon her only appearance of the night. It wasn't a comforting cameo, and Luc wanted to take it back—remove his hand, step back into his house, lock the door, and never open it again.

After a half-dozen exaggerated pumps, Isaiah finally released his hand, and Luc fought the urge to wipe it on his jeans, scrub it with disinfectant.

He needed them gone. *Now.*

"That you, Samuel?" the man asked, yellow eyes lifting out of their shadows to focus over Luc's shoulder. "What are you doing all the way over here?"

Luc glanced back at Sammy, who didn't respond. For the first time since he'd arrived, the kid looked closed up, uncommunicative. In that instant, Luc decided that Sammy wasn't going anywhere.

"Looks like you found our stray, Mr…"

"Stanek," Luc supplied. "Sammy tells me he needs—"

"Oh, we'll take care of Sammy's needs. Won't we, boy?" The smile on the man's face didn't reach his eyes. Luc was tempted to close the door and lock it, but they'd get through eventually. He glanced at their rifles, picturing the walls of his cabin riddled with bullets in some kind of Wild West standoff.

"Poor Sammy simply doesn't know what he's about. We've always had a hard time with this one," said Isaiah. At a slight dip of his head, two of the men came forward to flank their leader, their old-fashioned clothes reminding him of a movie he'd seen, full of black magic and witchcraft. Complacent judgment. Unkind ignorance.

"What can I help you with?"

"We're just here to get our boy."

"I don't think he wants to go with you." Breathing hard

at the wrongness of the situation, Luc turned back to look at Sammy and said, "Do you want to go with them?"

"'Course I do," Sammy said with a smile. Luc immediately regretted the question. The kid didn't get it at all, did he?

"Do they care for you, Sammy? Are you safe there?"

The kid's bright eyes skipped to Luc, and his face twisted up in surprise. "'Course they do. It's my home."

"We take care of our own, Mr. Stanek," said the ginger-haired messiah on his doorstep. "We protect them with our lives." Luc narrowed his eyes at the man, pulse ratcheting up. Was that a threat? It sounded like a threat, especially with the way those men held their guns—stiff and at the ready. "We're also very attentive to our closest neighbors. We've been here a long time, sir. Hamish Merkley, the founder of our Church—God rest his soul—bought this land more than forty years ago. You understand how important it is that we all get along. We wouldn't want to get mixed up in your business, now, but we've always got an eye out, should you require attention from us."

The threat wasn't even subtle, was it? If he didn't do what they wanted, they'd get him.

"What of Abby?" Luc asked before quickly correcting himself. "I mean, um, the person Sammy spoke to me of."

Isaiah blinked and paused, jaw set and eyes narrowed on Luc. "Don't you worry about Mistress Merkley, sir."

Merkley. Was Abby related to the man who had started the cult? The one who'd bought the land they'd settled on?

"Like I said, we take care of our own, and she is currently *being taken care of.* I'd hate for anything to happen to her. Wouldn't you?" Something pounded hard behind Luc's eyes as the man took a slow step into his space. "Anything you need, sir. You let us know." Isaiah focused on Sammy, who lingered just beyond Luc. "Ready now, son?"

No! Luc wanted to yell, to throw himself in front of the boy. He had the sense that if he didn't stop them now, he'd never see Sammy again.

He'd started to move when the boy said, "Sure." He sounded perfectly happy as he slid by Luc's tense body and headed outside. Why was he pleased? None of this made sense. "Night, Luc."

"Where are you taking him?"

Isaiah wrapped an arm around Sammy's neck in a gross parody of a hug—the threat so clearly implicit that Luc didn't dare move. "Home, Mr. Stanek."

Luc's eyes met and held the other man's through three long breaths.

He finally gave in. "Good night, Sammy." His voice broke on the words.

The boy was swallowed up by the group of somberly clad men before disappearing into the night. Luc took another breath full of courage and spoke, tilting his head at the departing group. "I understand he needs medical care."

"Oh, sure enough" came the easy answer, with a smile that didn't look as carefree as it was probably intended. "Must have had a goodly amount of time to get acquainted if he told you all that. But like I said: we take care of our own. And I'd hate for anyone to get hurt." He tilted his hat down at the brim and lost the smile entirely. "Thank you again, neighbor. And God bless."

What was the right answer to that? *You, too?* Luc opted for a quiet nod.

Finally, the men disappeared down the drive with Sammy in their midst and Luc closed the door, heart beating fast. What just happened? And where the hell was Abby? Had they done something to her?

Turning, it took a few moments for him to spot Le Dog crouched under the coffee table, hackles raised high and ears flattened. As he turned the lock—something he never did—Luc wished he could get rid of the feeling that he'd just handed the boy over to the devil.

10

ABBY LIMPED INTO THE MAIN CHAPEL AND NEARLY collapsed, her knees turned to jelly by the sight of all these people, waiting.

For me. They're waiting for me.

The only thing that kept her standing was the knowledge that Sammy had made it out.

Isaiah started off the day with "Morning has broken," as if this were a regular service. As if she wasn't sitting in the front row like a witch on trial.

To add to the charade, she sang with everyone else, accompanied by the amplified strum of Isaiah's guitar.

When Hamish had been alive, they'd played together, Isaiah and him up there. They'd divided the sermon in half—Hamish's older, doom-filled words the perfect contrast to Isaiah's uplifting words of hope.

By the time the song wrapped up and everyone sat down, Abby's pounding heart had calmed. Maybe it was just a normal Sunday. Maybe she would be forgiven.

Isaiah's voice oozed through the speakers they'd spent hard-earned money to purchase a few years ago.

Funny how Isaiah's God was fine with this modern convenience but not the ones that saved lives. The sound came through strong and melodic, though a tiny bit of static came out with every brush of his beard.

"There is an enemy on the mountain today. A serpent among us." Isaiah's gaze ranged across the gathered crowd before landing, firmly, on Abby. "And that enemy is *doubt*." With a gentle smile, he paused before continuing. "Sliding into our hearts, it need take root in but one of our number. *One*."

She'd admired the sound of his voice, once upon a time. As a child, she'd looked forward to the sermons, their Sunday morning lessons, their daily Bible stories. Today, every syllable vibrated up her spine like the chords of a harp being tweaked. Exhausted, her mind wandered, taking in Isaiah's words like a rhythm without meaning.

She forced herself to focus back in.

"'For I am the Lord, who heals you.'" Isaiah stopped, eyes bright, breath puffing audibly against the mic. "'I will take away sickness from among you,' the Almighty did say. 'Heal me, Lord, and I will be healed; save me, and I will be saved, for you are the one I praise.'"

There was a long pause while the room sat quiet and the listeners rapt. With a startled jolt, Abby recognized what he was saying.

"*Some* among us—and you know yourselves—have deigned to question our Savior's capacity to heal. You have dared to doubt His very *choices*. And through that doubt, you show your lack of faith." He raised his brows at the agitation running through the crowd. It wasn't a sound, but a low rumble of excitement that showed he'd gotten through to them. They knew something was coming, just like the sheep at shearing time, although some of them still hadn't figured out who would succumb. It was excitement, Abby recognized, at the prospect of someone's condemnation.

Someone's punishment.

When Isaiah focused again on her, the sheep knew, with absolute certainty, that she was the object of this lesson. Eyes turned to her, wide and hungry.

"It is not our duty to question our Lord and Savior, nor His very word. It is our duty to *obey*." After a pause, during which his long, pale fingers reached out to the congregation, Isaiah smiled. "Let us pray, my children. For the prophecy is nigh."

Head down beside her neighbor's, Abby sat, heart pounding so loud and hard she was sure everyone else must have heard it. When she finally looked up, it was to meet Isaiah's fox eyes.

His inhalation rasped through the speakers. "Abigail Merkley, come forth."

Everything in her body tightened. Around her, the air crackled with expectation. Accusation burned. *Oh, look at the glee on those faces!*

Pulling in a long, shaky breath, she stood, head bowed, and made her way to the front of the room, feet whispering on the carpet. Silently, she chanted, *Sammy's safe, Sammy's safe.*

"Come here, child," Isaiah said in that friendly voice.

After only the slightest hesitation, she stepped onto the wooden platform before turning to face the audience. Her Church. Her peers. Her *people*.

Only none of it felt like hers anymore. These people

were strangers, with ideals and beliefs she could no longer understand.

Except Mama. Mama would be on her side. She'd forgive Abby's sins like last time. She searched the crowd frantically for that pale face and the love she knew she'd see there.

Brigid sat, pious and prim, with Benji beside her. Abby's ribs still ached with the echo of his zeal. Farther along sat the Cruddups and—

There. Mama sat a couple rows back, eyes wide and watchful, glazed with a visible sheen of unshed tears. Abby tried to catch her eye but couldn't.

Please look at me, Mama, she begged. *Please.*

Nothing. Not a moment of shared eye contact, not the tiniest acknowledgment.

Chest tight and heart tripping fast, Abby fought the fear and the drowning sensation. She lifted her chin, squared her shoulders, and awaited judgment, while her mother never once looked her way.

The day wore on—a marathon celebration, punctuated by singing and the sound of children crying, quickly hushed. Throughout it all, Abby stood before her only family, accused of more than just the crime of questioning God. It turned out she was responsible for Sammy's illness to begin with—along with afflictions endured by every Church member since the dawn of time.

It must have been around lunch when Abby sagged halfway to the floor, eliciting jeers from the crowd. When Benji and Denny Cruddup were called forward to prop her up, Abby tried to catch their eyes. *Nothing. I am forsaken. A sacrifice. To God, to the Church. To the mountain, maybe.*

Just before letting her go, Denny's hand tightened briefly, and though she looked to him for confirmation that this was, indeed, a communication, there was nothing. She'd no doubt imagined it.

By midafternoon, the Main Chapel windows were fogged over with the congregation's collective breaths, the air ripe with body odor, the room rank with Abby's shame and their blame. There was a ritual to confession at the Church of the Apocalyptic Faith. It was a balancing act, and from where she stood today, on the outside in a way she'd never been before, Abby could see it clear as day. Although she wouldn't call it confession today. She'd call it indictment.

In the Church, there was no right without a wrong, no wrong without a right to counter it. Punishment for Abby was someone else's reward, and they mostly enjoyed it. Oh, she could see it on their faces—that gloating pride. *Look how bad she is. The devil inside her.*

A cry rang out late in the day, interrupting the almost meaningless stream of preaching and startling the crowd. Isaiah, jolted from his tirade, turned to the sound, looking wrathful and out for blood.

"Give me the child," he said in that quiet voice Abby knew better than to trust.

Nobody moved, though someone whimpered. Brigid, Abby thought. Had it been her baby?

"Who was that? Bring it to me." The words rang out sharp as thorns. Nobody moved, and Brigid's face, always pale, was white as a sheet. Seconds ticked by as everyone waited with bated breath, the silence shocking after so much noise. And then it started up again—a snuffling, followed by the squall of an unhappy baby, kept too long inside. Brigid hushed her child, frantic now, only they all knew it was too late. God's wrath cut deep when His words were interrupted.

As Isaiah moved to step down from the altar, Abby opened her mouth to scream. She didn't think it through, she just let out an explosive wail, dragging the attention back to her. A long, high shriek emerged, piercing and raw, and it stopped Isaiah in his tracks.

Shaking, she went on screaming until she'd emptied herself of breath and inhaled in preparation for another. The next one was cut short by a slap from Isaiah, strong enough to knock her head to the side and rock her on her feet.

A stunned silence hung over the room.

"Get it out of here," Isaiah spat, his smooth voice torn raw with anger. "Get them all out. The women and the children. *Now!*" He lifted those yellow eyes from Abby's and directed them straight at Brigid, who wrapped her arms around Jeremiah and scuttled out fast.

Isaiah shook himself visibly and straightened before heading to the door. "Take her to the Small Chapel, gentlemen. Mr. Kittredge, stoke the fire."

There'd be no pain worse than this. She couldn't remember anything as bad as the branding of her arms: the hot press of metal to skin, the sizzle that took her out of her body and into the thin air, weightless and numb. There'd been a smell, at first, of her own flesh, but even that had disappeared after her mind had floated out of herself, up into the air.

"Abigail Merkley." The men muscled her down the hall, everything reminiscent of the last time, except for the place in her brain that used to believe. "This is your day of reckoning."

I can take it. Hands tightened into fists, she took in the men gathered there. Benji, Denny Cruddup, James Kittredge, and even his son, Carter. He was only fourteen and looked slightly green. A dozen more stood around them, all men she'd known most of her life. Men she'd trusted and cared about.

"I don't want this," she pled, looking from one man to the next, the agitation making her desperate. "Denny. *Denny*, you used to hold me in your arms, remember? You taught me how to play with a yo-yo?" Before Hamish had taken it away. She'd been eight, maybe.

And Benji, weak and repentant. *Holier than thou.* He grabbed her arm, avoided her gaze, and dragged her down the hall.

Eyes glued to her feet, Abby went along. Because Sammy was safe. He had to be; otherwise, he'd have been here today.

Isaiah was speaking, but she barely heard. The irons were in the fire. Three of them. The air stank of smoke and cinders, the ghost of burning skin. A sob tried to work its way up her throat, too big for the tight space. She forced it down.

Isaiah's words finally reached her. "Do you accept the teachings of Isaiah of the Mount? Are you a Disciple of the Apocalypse?"

Her attention rolled around the room, her eyes hopping from one person to another to the beat of that same comforting litany: *Sammy's safe. Sammy's safe.*

On the edge of hysteria, she squeezed her eyes shut and shook her head. "No."

Utter stillness. No one, as far as she knew, had rejected the Mark before. Even she had agreed to it that first time, convinced of her own wrongdoings. She'd wanted it. *Begged* for it.

"I need to hear your acceptance of the Lord, Abigail. Say it."

"No," she whispered. Then stronger. "No, I do *not* accept your Lord unto my heart."

She opened her eyes and focused them hard on the first man she saw—how fitting that it should be Benji. "I took responsibility for the sins of others. Not today. I do not take responsibility for your sins," she said, shocking them all. Except for Carter, who'd collapsed against the door, eyes wide.

"How dare you—" Isaiah started.

"*I don't!*" she shouted as loud as she could, lungs full, chest tight as if she'd just run back from the fence. Hands restrained her, angry fingers digging into muscle and bone. The air was full of something new—a violence she hadn't felt that last time. There was another element, too, as Isaiah drew close and the men held her for his perusal.

"Let her go," he said before drawing closer. "You think he got away safe, your little gimp?" he whispered in her ear. Abby stiffened and opened her mouth to protest. "Samuel is back. Did you know that? We found him, and he was so happy to come home, because this is where he wants to be. It's where he *belongs*, Abigail. Who are you to take him away from God?"

"No," she whispered, louder, harder, harsher. Pained breaths escaped her throat as the scissors came out, tips pointy enough to gouge her eyes. Instead, they cut open her dress and bared her back to these men. Oh, how they stared, soaking it all in, starving for this: her shame, her near nudity, her pain. Daniel, who'd watched her with lust for years, finally feasted his eyes on her. Even Benji, as he watched, lost that tiny bit of guilt she'd seen on his face.

Dry, racking sobs consumed her body as she tried to shake the men off.

Tried and failed. Again and again.

From somewhere by the door, someone retched. Carter, of course.

"Best cut the rest along the seams," came Isaiah's voice, calm and instructional as he ambled over to check the irons in the fire.

Waste not, want not. Always thinking of the good of the Church, isn't he?

Abby almost laughed.

Until the brand hit her back. Then she screamed.

11

Just a few hours had passed since Luc let the kid take off with the neighbors. Less than a day since he and Abby had kissed in the barn.

As the hours slid by, sleep eluded Luc, and his worry increased.

He shouldn't have let those men take Sammy back. He should have slammed the door, barricading the two of them inside, and called the authorities. He could just picture the standoff now. And where the hell was Abby? Were they holding her against her will? No. Of course not. He'd probably misunderstood the situation.

Or had he?

As morning dawned, he rolled out of bed, exhausted, and went right to work clearing the new field, halfway expecting her to appear over the crest of the mountain at any minute. By midmorning, it had started to snow, and he'd developed a crick in his neck from turning back to look at the fence line.

Maybe he'd head over there. Although that sounded like the worst idea. He'd never watched much TV, even in France, but he'd heard enough about cults to know things couldn't end well. Like that Waco place in Texas where everything had been blown sky-high, or the Solar Temple people in Switzerland, all dead in a fiery inferno.

Jesus. What if she was already dead?

He couldn't take it.

Back in the cabin, he picked up his phone and stared at it. Should he call 911? Was this an emergency? He put the phone down and rubbed a hand across his face. *Shit.* He had no idea. And would they even believe him if he called it in?

A glance out the front window showed the snow falling thick and fast. With a sigh, he grabbed his coat and went back out. After a few tries, the truck started, and he set off for town, nerves humming like they did every time he left the safety of his mountain—only worse. He hated himself for getting involved. Hated himself even more for waiting this long and knowing that if he didn't do it, the weather would make travel impossible.

He should have looked up the sheriff's number, he supposed, but he needed something to *do*. With his body, his hands.

The Blackwood sheriff's department appeared deserted when Luc pushed through its double doors, a blast of wind and snow sneaking in behind him.

"Help you?" asked a voice from somewhere in the back of the small reception area. Moments later, a man stepped into the room—not at all what Luc had pictured when he'd thought of an American police officer. He'd imagined someone gray and mustachioed, tall and wiry and weathered, with a paunch and a permanent scowl. A cowboy.

This man was dark and scarred. More hoodlum than lawman. As Luc took him in, he could feel the man doing the same, eyes narrowed, giving nothing away as far as conclusions went.

"I would like to…" He hesitated, at a loss for words. "A woman who worked for me is missing."

"She got a name?"

"Abby Merkley. Abigail Merkley."

"She have any family?"

"She… I'm not sure."

"How do you know she's missing?"

"She's…she's part of the cult on the mountain. The Church of the…something Apocalypse." Luc shook his head. How could he not even remember that about her? In some ways, he knew her so well. He knew all about that bright dash of humor, that thirst for life. He knew exactly how she tasted after sampling his wines. For over a week, he'd plied her with foods, taken pleasure in watching her taste them, savor them, but never once had he delved too insistently into her life. Because he hadn't wanted to know.

He should have asked. Should have found out if she was safe where she lived. Should have held on to Sammy last night with as much care as he'd kept the dog who awaited him in his truck, despite the threat.

"Come on back into my office," the man said before turning and leading Luc into a room, where he invited him to sit in front of his desk. "I'm Sheriff Clay Navarro. Your name, sir?"

"Luc Stanek. I have a vineyard up on the mountain."

The man didn't react, which was a surprise. Basically everyone he'd met since moving to Blackwood had something to say about the vineyard, its previous owners, or its nearest neighbors.

"Tell me what happened."

"She was working for me. For more than a week. I—" He stopped himself from saying more about her. Like, that he liked her, or that they'd… "She hasn't come back."

"You've only known her for a week or so?"

"Yes."

"Any chance she just got sick of the job?"

Frustrated, Luc shook his head. "She had to cut through the fence to get to me." The sheriff straightened up, his brows lifting. "I looked today, and they've patched it back up."

"Is she being held prisoner? Did she tell you that?"

"She said they…they don't practice medicine. I know she was unhappy with that."

"Did you see signs that she'd been hurt?"

After a brief hesitation, Luc shook his head. "No. She's too skinny, but that… No."

The other man sighed, rubbing a frustrated hand over his face. There was ink on his knuckles—faded-looking tattoos at odds with his neat, black uniform and close-cropped hair.

"Could you just go there?" Luc pressed. "Ask about her?"

The sheriff shook his head. "I've had dealings with those Apocalyptic Faith folks before. They're extremely averse to any outside presence, particularly law enforcement, and I'm concerned about stirring things up on that mountain. You know this storm's gonna be a big one, right, Mr. Stanek? I'm in no position to start something I can't finish. I'm ex-ATF." Luc must have looked as clue-less as he felt about that, because the sheriff expanded. "Alcohol, Tobacco, Firearms and Explosives—an agency linked to the Department of Justice. I wasn't around for Waco—a cult situation in Texas—but I know how easily something like this can go wrong. If you can give me some evidence of wrongdoing…something to substantiate what you're saying—"

"There's a boy. He might need medical care."

The man's brows lifted expectantly. "A child?"

"No. He's older. Nineteen, I think. But disabled."

"I understand there were complaints at one point. I know CPS got involved. Maybe a decade ago?" The sher-iff squinted hard at Luc. "How long you been up there?"

"A little over two years."

"Hm. Not you. Didn't realize anyone else lived on that mountain."

"There isn't. It might have been the previous owners. I believe they left in a hurry."

"If I head up there right now, by myself…" The man shook his head. "I could try to get some folks from CPS to head up there, maybe go with them." At Luc's questioning expression, the sheriff explained. "Child Protective Services. They won't like it, but we could couch it as a routine thing, since they're not sending any of those kids to school, far as I know. I understand you don't want to rock the boat if your girl's in trouble, but this storm is gonna shake things up around here, and I got two guys out with the flu. This isn't gonna happen today. And it's gonna be a few days before the weather clears."

Your girl. Luc itched at that.

"But you'll do something?"

"Yes, Mr. Stanek. I'll look into it." After a pause, he went on. "You're not thinking of going there on your own, are you? Because I can't do a thing to help you if you head up there right now, understood?" Luc nodded, pressing back the desire to ignore this man's advice and bust through their fence. "You got a phone number you can leave with me?"

On his way back out to the car, Luc glanced up and almost stopped walking. The stillness was unsettling. No cars driving by, not a sound besides the brittle crunch of his soles over asphalt.

It was bright, the night sky swollen pink, broken only by the dots of falling snow and the jagged line of the looming mountains. His mountain, whose sharp, eroded angles had drawn him to this place; the property he'd bought for a song: vines, broken machinery, and messed-up neighbors included.

He started up the truck and stared at that peak. He'd never seen it look so ominous or unwelcoming. And no matter how hard he tried, he couldn't conjure an image of Abby there, living her life with those people. What was she doing right now? Was it business as usual, or was she in trouble?

Compressing his lips, he threw the truck into gear, pulled out into the snow-covered street, and slid his right hand into Le Dog's fur. "What should we do?" he asked, his voice hollow in the cold cab. When the dog didn't answer, he gave him a quick squeeze and nodded. "I don't know either, boy. I just don't know."

How could she do this in the snow?

She couldn't. Not with the way she hurt. The ankle was bad enough, but it was her back that worried her now. Why did it hurt so much? It hadn't been like this before.

Just to the next tree. To the dogwood. The one that bloomed pink in the spring. She lurched, hurting, weak and cold—much too cold. No time to think about the cold.

With her body bent forward, the pain was the only thing that propelled Abby to the farthest pasture, almost to the hole in the fence. Sammy was someplace behind her, back with the Church. Isaiah had made sure she knew that. *He never made it out*, Isaiah had said. Which made no sense. No sense at all, since she'd sent him right to the hole.

Pain lanced through her ankle as she stumbled, and Abby reached for something good to help push her forward.

A memory: Luc with his knuckle to her lip. Just that one hot touch spurred her on as snow soaked through her shoes and left the bottom half of her nightgown plastered to her body. She shook as she tried to see through the driving snowflakes. This familiar journey was nearly unrecognizable. The night didn't help either. Abby slipped, stumbling on a rock. She tumbled hard to the ground, the air forced out of her lungs with an audible *oof*. While she lay there, letting the rest of her soak and waiting for the energy to get back up, the dogs started barking, flashing her back to that moment two nights ago when they'd caught up with her. Were they looking for her already? If so, there was no hope.

No hope.

Get up! a voice said, right there in her head, loud and clear enough to be straight from God himself. But Abby didn't believe in direct communications from Heaven. She'd seen enough firsthand evidence that those led to unhappiness and despair. She did, however, believe in Sammy, who deserved a better a life. A chance, at least. And she believed in Luc, whose steady hands were strong enough to put her back together again.

Feet caught up in her gown, she stumbled a few times as she tried to push herself to standing. Finally— *finally*—she rolled and got her feet under her. She pulled herself onto her knees, head pounding, eyes…wrong. Squeezed too hard by her skull. Time to go. No more resting. Go, go, go.

Up, moving, although she couldn't be sure it was her legs taking her. Hard, fast, frantic, lungs full to bursting, face burning from the cold, back weak, but now blissfully numb.

Faster, faster, faster, legs swishing, fabric grasped like wet hands, like ropes, until she yanked it up and gathered it around her waist.

There it was: the fence, the last barrier, and the hole she'd cut into it. Only… No. *Nononono.*

It was gone. Of course it was. Of course they'd closed it up. She scrambled to the spot—she knew this was it—and saw where it had been wired shut. They'd found it, after all. Of course they wouldn't just leave it open. Instead, Isaiah had had it reinforced with so many layers of wire, it felt like a message. It told her turning back was the only option.

Where were the cutters? Not here where she'd left them. Gone. Two steps back showed what she knew she'd see: eight feet of fencing topped with razor wire. The view from inside.

With a final glance behind her, she took in the cold, cold mountain, the miles of nothing. In front, frigid metal. Behind, Isaiah's rule.

Please help me get Sammy out, she prayed. She'd looked for him tonight on her way out. He hadn't been in the shed he sometimes used, nor had she been able to spot his sleeping form through the window at the Cruddups' or at Benji's cabin. She'd have risked going in if he'd been there.

Without hesitation, her fingers slipped over metal and pulled up, feet following suit, to no avail. The shoes had to go. She threw them over the top and started over.

She sucked back a sob, ignoring the strain and bite of chain link. Her body weight dragged her down, but she was driven by nothing but the need to survive. At the top, the galvanized coils, too high to be straddled, would slice her to bits if she didn't cover them.

Without hesitation, she struggled to pull off the cotton nightgown—immodest!—spread it over the wire, tried to press it down a bit, and followed with her leg. But thin cotton was no match for apocalyptic paranoia.

Don't think about it. Breathe through the pain. Breathe. The words pushed her to straddle the barrier that had held her prisoner for close to a lifetime. Up here, this high—closer than she'd ever been to the night sky, cradled by these mountains—Abby threw a long, aching look toward the compound. She said a silent good-bye to Mama, who didn't know better than this place. To Sammy, whom she'd get out if it killed her.

It wasn't until she'd made it all the way down that

she remembered her near nudity—and the clear signs of escape she'd left in her wake. Barking sounded again, muffled by the snow. It was impossible to tell if it came from in front of her or behind. She ascended to retrieve the nightgown, torn to bits and stained in places. It was necessary but tedious and it took too long, too long with her dry mouth and tight chest.

Not one for details, our Abigail, echoed the voices in her head. *Always in the clouds.*

Always! she'd wanted to scream. *It's better than here! Anything is better than here!*

Finally, she stumbled toward Luc's cabin, leaving the fence behind for what she prayed was the last time.

∼✺∽

Luc didn't think about going to the neighbors' place. He just went there, his truck barely making it up their drive, tires slipping all over the place. By the time he opened their gate, went up the drive, and pulled up to their main building—dark at this time of night—they'd been alerted to his presence.

But for now, he needed to know that Abby was okay.

"Help you?" came a voice from off to the right. A man. Possibly one of the guys who'd crowded onto his front porch last night. And like last night, the man held a rifle. Only now, it was pointed right at Luc. *Should have listened to the sheriff.*

"Yes." Luc girded himself. "I want to see Abby."

"Abby?" The man squished up his face. "Don't have an Abby living here."

"Abigail, her name is. I want to see her."

"I'm sorry, sir, but this isn't—"

"Neighbor!" came Isaiah's voice. The leader. He stepped out from the shadows beside the building and ambled toward Luc's truck. "What brings you here?"

"I want to see Abby. Where is she?"

Isaiah's smile was visible in the night. The rest of his face was shadowed by the wide brim of his hat. "How is it you know Mistress Merkley?"

"She…" Luc paused, suddenly recognizing the mess he'd gotten himself—and possibly her—into. "From the market."

"She hasn't worked the market in ages," said the first man.

"She was there last weekend." Luc looked from one face to the other. "May I see her?"

"No, sir." Isaiah's voice was hard.

Silence. Luc's hands ached from holding them too tight, his knuckles dying to connect with the bastard's jaw.

"Why not?" he asked, trying his best to keep his voice steady.

"I don't believe she is receiving right now, Mr. Stanek." Isaiah moved closer, not quite in Luc's face, but close enough for Luc to see the pores on the man's nose, smell the rank acid of his breath. "But we will let her know you paid her a call."

Isaiah lifted his hat and turned to walk away, dismissing Luc. After a few crunching steps, he turned back, eyes harder than they'd been a moment ago.

"I don't recommend trespassing on our land after dark, sir." He smiled, a quick, dangerous flash. Then lifted his chin toward the man who still held his weapon trained on Luc. "We've been known to shoot first and ask questions later."

12

A LOUD BARK FROM SOMEWHERE CLOSE BY STARTLED
Luc from his slumber in front of the fire. Bleary-eyed
but alert, heart beating fast, he took in his surroundings.

Living room. Right. America, not France. At the door
stood Le Dog, whose presence was more necessary
than ever.

"What is it?" Luc asked, standing up from his comfy
armchair. He waited a few moments. No more sounds
from outside.

Back to staring at the fire, trying to drown himself
in bourbon or… He grasped the bottle by the neck and
squinted at the label. *Virginia Straight Bourbon Whiskey.*
Made locally. If the locals drank it… He shrugged, took
a sip from his glass, and set the bottle back down. No
point going against the grain.

He settled back into the worn leather.

Another noise outside, a metallic thud, had him up
and out of the chair in a second, bottle and glass forgotten. His head cocked like the dog's, who let out an
alert *woof.*

"*Bon garçon.*"

Whatever it was, it was close.

Another noise, a softer scuffling this time, sent Luc to the window. Tonight, for the first time, he had closed the curtain. He tweaked it back and stared outside. Nothing moved, but Le Dog remained at attention. He jammed his feet into his boots, grabbed his coat, and yanked open the door. He shooed Le Dog back inside. "Stay here. I'll be back."

Outside, the air hit him hard, shocking his lungs into momentary paralysis. He inhaled sharply and zipped up in a hurry.

He took a few steps, walking straight through the fog of his own breath to the edge of the porch, and waited for another sound, a clue as to its direction. Nothing.

Well, merde.

That first sound had been metallic, like…

The old shed, which sat a couple dozen meters farther uphill. He hadn't bothered securing that door, since he had no current use for the building, but that must have been it. Or an animal. It could be an animal. *Possibly.*

This late at night? Too loud to be one of the chickens, who were all snug in their coop.

Perhaps it had been the wind. Unless…a fox? He grasped at that notion.

You could never be too careful with the fauna around here. He'd heard of bobcats and the like coming down from higher elevations in search of food. Although this blizzard should have been a deterrent, it could have pressed some poor creature to take extreme measures. Big cats, hungry and cold, might be attracted to a place like his.

Either way, Luc eyed the snow covering the ground, turned, and backtracked to the cabin, where he grabbed his rifle.

The snow was blowing, big gusts of it, with a cold that felt bone deep. Sharp.

A shiver of foreboding slid down his spine.

He tried not to think about the neighbors. Tromping over there might well have set off a shitstorm on the mountain. In his own damned backyard. Not his best move.

Another few steps, stomping through inches of snow—blinded by it—before he was stopped by that furtive noise. It told him whatever else this was, it was alive, awake, and up to something. A wave of adrenaline-fueled anger flooded him. He lifted his rifle, realizing a second too late that he'd have been better off armed with a piece of wood in the close quarters of the shed than something that needed to be aimed from a few feet away.

Too late to turn back, he yanked open the door, weapon raised…and stopped.

Nothing.

Dammit. He'd been sure it was in here. Slowly, with the tingle of another presence as solid as the shoes on his feet, Luc backtracked. Two steps out, and instead of left toward home, he turned right and almost walked right over her.

In the split second before he moved, Luc took in the scene. Against the outside corner of the shed, pale and ghostly and barely visible against the falling snow, lay a human being. A woman.

Abby. Her body a Rorschach pattern of light and dark, like something out of a Japanese horror film.

"*Putain de merde*," he breathed, not understanding what he saw. His stomach twisted into a knot of confusion.

"Luc?" She said his name, the voice soft and barely recognizable. Fear slammed into his body, hitting him hard in the chest. It drove him to the ground beside her, on his knees in the cold, cold snow.

Damn it. She was naked. Or close to it. She was wearing something wet and torn and spotted with…

He dropped his rifle to the ground and slid out of his coat, wrapped her shaking body in it before lifting her into his arms.

Abby was nothing but a crumpled heap when he picked her up, so tiny and light he wondered if she'd somehow disappeared, leaving nothing behind but her torn nightgown, a puddle of fabric like something out of *The Wizard of Oz*.

After his moment of idiocy—*I must be drunk*—his reactions finally kicked in.

Too light for a grown woman. Sparing a glance for his gun on the ground, he carried her back to the house, slipping on what felt like ice. She had to be frozen, half-naked like this.

He carried her up the three uneven steps to the porch and—after a brief struggle—through the front door, into the heat of his cabin. Le Dog woofed, jumping at him, showing energy for the first time all evening. Luc pushed the animal away and blinked down at Abby, hoping the light inside would turn the bloodstains back into shadows.

He moved quickly to set her down on the sofa and ran upstairs for blankets, feeling like his chest would explode with the panic.

Even in the yellow wash of firelight, she looked

glacial, her skin cold as marble, the filthy cotton of her nightgown an unearthly shroud. It was so different from how she'd been in the bright sunlight. He lifted a hand to touch her and hesitated.

What should one do to keep a person from freezing to death? *Hypothermia, hypothermia.* This wasn't something that happened much where he was from. Should he take off her dress? It was soaking.

"Abby?" he whispered, feeling like an idiot. "Your nightgown. I have to take it off."

Nothing. His hand hovered over her body before he let it settle on her cheek. Frozen. Her hands were cold, too.

"Talk to me, Abby. *Please.*"

He dropped to his knees beside the sofa, moving his fingers across her face to tap them lightly against her cheek. "Wake up, Abby. Please."

Luc's internal debate lasted only a second. A woman like Abby, so modest and sweet, would hate him for doing this. Or she would die. Right here, on his sofa.

She was waxy and pale, looking barely alive aside from the shivering that racked her body. Her torn nightgown was soaking wet and stained here and there with what might have been mud. And blood. That thick hair of hers was still trapped in its long braid, incongruously sleek and pristine.

"*Merde, merde et bordel de merde.*" He muttered obscenities while rushing to the kitchen for the scissors, wondering what would push a woman like her to run outside in weather like this, half-naked.

Back to the sofa, on his knees, the blades sliced through the soaked fabric with difficulty. The cloth was frozen stiff in places.

Frantic, he ignored the inappropriate thread of interest at what the gown revealed—a modest undergarment that he carefully cut off, then slid out from under her—and piled the blankets back atop her. Okay. More wood in the stove. He stoked the fire high, higher than he normally would, until it spat and popped angrily.

Behind him, she made a noise. He turned, hoping for her to be lucid, but all he found was more shivering, so hard that her teeth audibly clacked. The dog had settled right up against the couch, guarding her or watching over her or—

Skin to skin. The phrase floated to the front of his mind. A first aid video, that's where he'd seen it. Head, chest, neck, and groin. Those were the places to warm first. There'd been an electric blanket or hot water bottles involved, but if unavailable…skin to skin was recommended. Dammit.

No more hesitation. No letting whatever it was he felt for her decide. This was about her safety. Her *life*. He stripped to his underwear, the dog watching closely. Pulling back the blankets, he slid his arms around Abby and turned her onto her side before scooting in to press against her.

Take my heat, he thought. He envisioned it sliding into her, the cold from her body leaching into his. An exchange. He moved to run a hand along her back and encountered… What was that? A bandage? Gingerly, he felt up and up, only to find that her entire back was covered in them.

What the hell?

Avoiding her back, he put his hand on her arm. Rubbed up and down, and there, too, something was off. Strange ridges lined her forearm.

What the hell had they done to her?

Shifting back, he lifted the blanket to eye the pale, discolored shapes along her arm.

A moan drew his attention back to her immediate needs, and he let his questions go—for the moment.

He pulled her closer, molding himself to her, ignoring the tightness down below. Trying to ignore the fear that she'd die on him, right here…

After a few minutes of rubbing her arm and hands, then moving to rub her feet, all the while listening to her teeth make that horrible noise, he thought he detected a slight thawing. More time passed. Half an hour maybe, during which he held a naked woman who, in many ways, was a virtual stranger. Although she didn't feel like a stranger. She felt familiar and real.

The person he was closest to.

"Don't die," he said against the side of her face, the discomfort of their physical intimacy almost forgotten as he whispered into her ear. "*Ne meurs pas.*" He considered loading her into his truck and heading into town, taking her to a hospital. But there was nothing in Blackwood. He'd have to go all the way into Charlottesville, which would take an hour, longer in this storm. Not a good idea, especially considering he'd been drinking. Maybe he should call 911. This *was* an actual emergency. He couldn't imagine an ambulance getting up here, though.

After a while, something shifted. Abby's trembling subsided, and she let out a long, unhappy-sounding, "*Mmmmmmm.*"

"Oh, thank God," Luc whispered with relief.

Another pained groan from her pushed him slightly away.

"Are you okay? What do you need? You're hurt. Where are you hurt?"

"Burns," she slurred.

"It burns?"

Her only response was a moan. But that was good, right? Sensation returning?

"Okay. I'll call an ambulance or the authorities or—"

"No!" she groaned against his neck. "Please don't."

"Why not, Abby?" he asked.

"It's bad. So bad," she said, slurring.

"Okay. Okay, I won't call anyone."

Luc held her in near silence, the only sounds the gentle crackling of the fire, a sleepy sigh from the dog, and the dry rasp of his hand rubbing her arm.

He moved to her hand, relieved to find the fingers warm. He *had* to take her to the hospital, didn't he? Wasn't there something about the heart being affected if the body got too cold? He rubbed and rubbed her fingers, ignoring the feel of her against him, until finally he couldn't ignore it anymore and backed up to give her space. To give *himself* room to breathe.

"Please," she whispered. Luc lay stock-still, breathing hard. "It's better when you hold me."

He pulled her in again. "I've got you, Abby. I've got you."

❧

Hurt. Everywhere. Hot, hot burning, worse than anything Isaiah could do. Worse than God's wrath.

There were flames. They crackled close, popping like hellfire, growing, consuming. Tears rose up, and with them came regret. At all the things she'd never

see, never do. It used to be wearing jeans and boots. Or
flip-flops, with the sand in her toes. A milk shake for
Sammy. It was different, this new regret. Darker. Hotter,
rooted in her belly. Caresses. Aches to be tamped down,
desires to be satisfied.

Her lips moved, saying something. They hurt. Dry
and parched. Almost stuck together. More words came
out, and a hand touched her cheek, blessedly cool. Hard
against her lips, words floated through the air and cold,
cold water in her mouth. Sputtering, choking. Hauled
up, sitting.

I can't open my eyes, she thought, although suddenly,
the thought was floating in front of her, stolen from her
brain. Her lungs. Real words.

Other words in response. "Drink, *chérie*. Drink. Can
you please?"

Drink. Luc wanted her to drink.

She wanted that, too.

She drank. Each sip an effort, each movement controlled from somewhere outside her body, above or
below or perhaps a tiny spot in the farthest reaches of
her brain, telling her to pull in, slowly swallow, open
for the next sip.

He was there. She could see those harsh features,
lips set in a grim line, eyes too shadowed to make out.
Realer tonight than he'd been before. So real, she had
to reach out and touch his face, run a finger down that
chipped-looking nose, its texture exactly like the rock
on the mountain.

"Go back to sleep." His words gave permission, and
so she did.

13

Luc shot up, woozy and caught in a wave of déjà vu stronger than any he'd felt in his life. What was that? An engine? Something shifted against him, and he glanced down to see Abby asleep, mouth slightly open, face looking bruised in the moonlight. Bleary-brained, he startled again when the sound solidified into a car door slamming, followed by voices.

What the hell?

On the floor, Le Dog growled, golden eyes narrowed, muzzle curled aggressively. Another glance showed fur puffed up along his spine, ears flattened back. That sight brought every hair on Luc's body to standing.

He pulled back the curtain, like he'd done earlier this evening, only now there was something to see. Several men got out of a pickup with a snow plow attached to the front and disappeared around his property, leaving the truck running.

Once again, they were heavily armed.

He reached for his rifle, and his hand found nothing

but wall. *Bordel de merde*. Where…? The shed. He'd left it there when he'd carried Abby inside.

Moving fast, muscles tense with adrenaline, and anger making him fearless, he pulled his clothes on, raced to the kitchen, and made sure the back door was bolted. In the living room, he picked up the poker from beside the fireplace and went to the sofa, where Abby remained oblivious.

They were here for her. Of that, he had no doubt. Would they force their way in this time? Take her?

He'd kill them first. The poker in his fist proved that. A goddamned poker. It should be funny, this pathetic weapon against theirs, but it wasn't. There was violence in his muscles and bones. It made him stronger. He'd tear them apart with his bare hands if he had to.

Yelling reached him from outside.

"Abby!" he whispered, hunkered down beside her, face against hers. "Wake up."

Her breathing changed, eyes opened, almost focused on him. He put his mouth close to her ear and whispered, "Stay here and don't make a noise. No sound. Understand?"

She nodded, and without thinking it through, Luc pressed his lips to her hair in a hard, silent kiss.

He moved to the door, which he hadn't thought to lock. He hadn't planned for this, an all-out attack on his property. He slid into his boots, yanked on his coat, and stepped outside, poker clenched in his fist. He wanted to slam that asshole in the face with it, drive the end in through his neck.

But that wouldn't do, would it? With a glance, he took in the single set of footsteps leading up to his porch.

He'd carried her up here. *They don't know she's here*, he realized, awash with relief.

How would I act if she hadn't shown up here tonight? No frontal assault, although there would be enmity between them, certainly. He'd already confronted them once today. Scanning the night, he thought of the more than two years he'd spent without seeing these people at all. And here they were, at their third encounter in the space of just a couple of days. It was time for this to end. *Now.*

"Who's there?" he yelled. His voice carried a few meters and disappeared, soaked up by the heavily falling snow. He took a big, angry breath and stepped to the edge of his porch, the rage burning too hot for him to notice the cold.

From somewhere past the chicken coop, he heard voices. Goddamn it, he wished he had his gun. He'd fire a warning shot. Without waiting, he pounded down the steps, through the fresh snow, and straight to their truck. Its lights burrowed soft, yellow tunnels into his yard, speckled with falling snow. Holding up the poker, he approached—caution forgotten—and yanked open the door.

Nobody inside, despite the wipers and the engine and lights. Diesel exhaust wrapped him up in its cloud of stink. He leaned in and honked the horn twice, long and loud, before grabbing the keys, twisting them out, and sliding them into his pocket. *Fuck it*, he thought, laying his hand on the horn again and keeping it there. Nobody around to hear except these bastards, and he wanted them scared.

Here we go. One man, followed by a few more, came

into Luc's line of vision, all of them focused on him. He watched them, waited, breath painful from adrenaline or the cold. He took a step back, two, and one man approached Luc, separating himself from the pack, rifle in hand this time. Isaiah.

Damned bastard.

That feeling of excitable fear hit him—it made his muscles heavy and his brain buzz. Made him feel invisible and dead already—kicked into double time.

"What's going on here?" Luc asked, keeping his voice as low and calm as possible despite the man now standing just a few feet from him.

"Isaiah Bowden here, sir." The man moved into the glow of the headlights. He—unlike Luc, who was freezing his ass off out here—appeared to be dressed for this encounter.

"We've got to stop meeting like this," Luc gritted out, reaching for a grim glimmer of humor in this messed-up situation.

"Apologies for the late hour, but we have something of an emergency. Would you have a minute please, sir?"

So polite with his sirs and pleases, despite the veiled threats every time they met. All of this was so unbelievable, and just for one second, Luc let himself wish Abby wasn't here. That he'd never met her, that she hadn't come and turned his perfectly empty, uneventful life upside down.

Imagine that, he decided again. He needed to channel that cluelessness if he was going to convince this man that she'd never come here tonight.

He ran one soaked sleeve over his eyes, clearing them of snow, and shook his head. Play up the bewilderment and tamp down the fear—that was the key. "Bit late for a visit, isn't it, neighbor?" Luc said, moving out from the truck's door, edging two steps closer to the cabin.

"We've had an incident. Wanted to warn you."

So, that's how they're playing it.

"What kind of incident?"

"One of our residents is missing."

He fought the desire to glance back at his house and said the first thing that came to him. "Missing?"

"The woman you asked about earlier. Mistress Merkley. She took off on foot."

"Bad night for it," he forced out. His eye caught on the gun in Isaiah's hand. It looked like Luc's.

"It is indeed," Isaiah said, "and I'm sorry to say it's my own fault." The man didn't yell, but his voice carried. It was full and theatrical. A belly voice. A preacher man. "Abigail—poor soul—is *delusional*, sir." Sad pause. "I blame myself. When her late husband told me of her wayward ways, I didn't listen. I've allowed her to live on her own these past months." Isaiah compressed his mouth and lowered his brows in a parody of rueful regret. Oh, but he would be perfect in a pulpit. "She's taken off into the night, sir. All alone, barely clothed. And—I must tell you, neighbor—poor Abigail has done herself harm in the past. You've met her, you said. You must have noticed how…*capricious* she is." He looked away, removed his hat, and ran that same gloved hand through short hair, shaking his head with something like regret, before dropping the hat down again.

For the briefest moment, he wondered if it could be true. Could Abby be mentally ill?

No. Of course not. Curious, maybe, but capricious? Never. Imaginative and interested, yes, but never delusional.

He shoved back a wave of resentment that simmered up and tried to choke him.

"How is she delusional?" he forced out.

"She hears voices. Sees things. Thinks she's the conduit of our Savior." A sad chuckle from the man's mouth.

"Have you called the police?"

With a friendly smile, the man moved forward another pace or two. "Oh, no. We take care of our own, sir." Something slippery and cold worked its way down Luc's spine. Before he could come up with an appropriate response, Isaiah carried on. "You haven't seen her come through here this evening, have you, neighbor?"

Luc shook his head, eyes flicking from the poker in his own hand to the gun in the other man's. If they decided he was lying, he was screwed. But even worse, so was Abby. Tightening his hold, he shifted forward, gaze driving hard into Isaiah's. "I'm afraid you've wasted your time here tonight, Mr. Bowden." Letting his eyes travel over the rest of the group, he went on. "Now, I think it's time you moved on."

❧

Abby's internal debate raged for about five seconds. Her first instinct was to huddle up, hunker down, and let the exhaustion help her disappear into the sofa cushions. Her second instinct was to run up the stairs as fast as she could and hide in whatever nook she found there. But, as usual, her brash side won out. The side that told her to get up and find a weapon. To prepare for a fight.

She stood, blanket around her shoulders, and took a big, rasping breath, evacuating the dizziness and the pain. She took a slow look around. Luc had held a poker when he'd gone out, and she didn't need to be a genius to know what awaited him out there: Isaiah and the others. They'd hurt him for sure.

Hurry.

No more pokers beside the woodstove, so…

Hurry.

Kitchen. Knife. Rodeo walked close beside her, and she considered dipping to pat his head, but just the idea made her feel off-kilter. Like if she bent, she'd fall all the way.

Drawers opened and closed, cupboards inspected… Nothing. *Gosh…darn it!* She wanted to scream, wanted to curse and—

There, by the stove. A big jar of utensils and, in it, a boning knife. It brought to mind thoughts she could live without: Isaiah holding this kind of blade to her ear, threatening, slicing.

A head shake to clear it. Where on earth had that come from? He'd never threatened her like that with a knife. It was pure fiction…

She swallowed hard and grabbed the knife by the handle.

Her limbs were heavy. She fought the weight that made her want to sink onto the floor and returned to the living room, ready to help. She stumbled to the curtains, reached out one hand and stopped. What if they saw the fabric twitch? They'd know someone was here.

But she needed to see, had to know what was going on. She lifted a hand and gently nudged the material to the side.

14

Isaiah's posture stiffened, tensile but curved, reminding Luc of a copperhead he'd almost stepped on last summer. Not a snake he'd met before coming to Virginia, but immediately, he'd known it was deadly. Right there, among his vines, the creature had challenged him, stood up and made Luc back down. He'd gone to fetch a shovel, but by the time he'd returned, it was gone.

Even in the dark, Luc could see something unpleasant in Isaiah's face, despite his mask of sincerity. An eagerness or excitement that wouldn't be there if this was all aboveboard, and the threat of it thrummed through Luc's veins. It electrified and terrified him like the face-off with the snake had, zapping nerve endings in a way that was wrong, unnatural.

Actually, Luc realized as he fought the urge to shift back or show some other sign of weakness, the sensation was in fact *perfectly* natural. It went back to animal instinct, rather than relying on learning or intelligence. As the snake had lifted its diamond-shaped head, preparing to strike, Luc's body had acted faster than his brain, moving him out of harm's way. Instinct told him that the safest course of action was to run inside and bolt the door.

But it wouldn't be the action of a clueless bystander. He needed to be that clueless—if annoyed—bystander. For himself, for the woman on his sofa. For the dog, too.

"Well, if you see anything off, I would certainly appreciate it if you'd let me know." The snake moved in, flat, yellow eyes glancing over Luc's shoulder at the cabin, testing Luc's resolve. "If she does pay you a call, please remember she's unwell. We've been…we've been concerned about her for months." He shook his head. "Should have listened to the other women, rather than letting her go on as she was. Ever since her husband died. I'll never forgive myself if she comes to harm."

"I will certainly keep an eye out," Luc said non-committally. "She can't be safe wandering around in the snow."

Isaiah raised his gaze and smiled. "Indeed, sir. Not safe indeed." He turned and stalked to the passenger door of the truck. The others remained where they stood in the shadows, snow coating the tops of their wide-brimmed hats. Isaiah Bowden opened the door and got in. After a beat, he turned the rifle around and held it out. He did it with a nod, quiet and friendly. "Looks like someone left this rifle against a shed on your property. Might want to lock up your weapons, Mr. Stanek. Wouldn't want them falling into the wrong hands."

Luc was forced to walk around the truck to grab the gun, and for about five seconds, the other man held on. Three heartbeats, two big breaths, while some sort of message passed between them, the two men too close for comfort. Finally, Isaiah let go with a friendly, "God bless," and Luc stepped back—stumbled, really, chest rising and falling hard, jaw tight and knuckles white over wood and metal.

Luc turned away, ready to leave, and remembered the truck keys in his pocket.

Taking them out, he held them up, let them jingle in the quiet night. "Apologies for taking these, neighbor," he said, satisfied by the look of surprise on Isaiah's face. "I wasn't sure who would visit me at such an ungodly hour."

He tossed them lightly into the cab, where they fell with a clang. Why did this feel like a gauntlet thrown down? He hadn't done it on purpose. Isaiah's gaze rose to meet his, an odd smile on his face. He leaned out the door.

"You smell that?"

Testing the air, Luc said, "No."

"Hm. Thought I smelled smoke."

"Wood fire in my cabin."

"Yes, well." The man sized him up with a long, slow nod, his eyes hard as pebbles. "Be a shame for anything else to catch fire."

"Such as?"

A lazy shrug lifted Isaiah's shoulders. "Grape vines, for example. Seen a bad fire decimate a crop before." He wrinkled his brow, as if trying to call up a memory. "Maybe 'round here, in fact. Long time ago. Sure would hate to see that happen to your vines."

"Are you *threatening* me?" Luc asked as a long, slow shiver slid its way up his spine. He held still, because

nothing would be worse for Abby right now than shooting Isaiah or jamming the poker through his eye.

"Course not, sir. Course not. But I've seen stranger
things happen in these parts." With that, Isaiah settled
back on the bench seat and slammed the door shut.

Luc stood his ground and waited. No way he'd turn
his back on these assholes. Already he felt the crosshairs
on his chest as surely as if they were burned there. The
rest of the men climbed slowly into the truck, three in the
cab, two in back. Which must have been uncomfortable
as hell in this weather, but…it certainly showed what
they were willing to do. The lengths to which they'd go
for their leader. Or was it for their God?

The weapons in Luc's hands felt ineffectual, the rifle
tainted, as he watched the men take off, spitting snow.
Their arms bristled with guns, looking like some kind
of Picasso vision of aggression. It was only after they'd
disappeared down the drive that Luc felt his body again.
Wet and freezing on the surface, but hot at its core.
Burning up with rage.

Along with the return of sensation came the thought
that, for these people, Isaiah and God might well be one
and the same. The thought made him shudder, because
he knew what men could do in the name of God, and
he had a feeling this holy war was far from being over.

Abby sank to the floor. The knife clattered beside her,
forgotten. Her skin was tight, her brain swollen. She
watched Luc enter from her spot under the window and
waited for him to see her there. "I'll go," she said.

"You can't."

Luc approached her slowly, that poker in one hand, his rifle in the other.

"Why did he give you that?"

Luc's head dipped as he looked at his hands, and his "Hey, what are these doing here?" expression would have been comical if the situation weren't such a mess.

He hurried to kneel in front of her, and Abby couldn't help but pull back. It was just a little, but he noticed. He set the weapons down quickly, like hot potatoes.

"I left it against the shed where I found you. Earlier." He watched her closely for a moment. "You remember that?"

"No," whispered Abby.

"Abby," he said, quiet too. Like they had a secret between them.

In that voice of his, with that accent, she could almost—almost—shut down and pretend this wasn't happening. That he was feeding her something new, and she was tasting it, listening to him and thinking about all the things he could show her. All the new things she could experience.

"What's going on, Abby?"

Oh good Lord, where to start? And how...how could she... She shifted and the blanket dipped and Abby realized, for the first time since coming to, that she was naked underneath. "I'm naked," she said like an idiot, on a choppy exhale.

"Your clothes were soaked." He paused. "And your...undergarment."

That old thing?

She was delirious. Had to be.

She'd been naked with a man for the first time and

hadn't even been conscious for it. She could almost laugh. More than that, though she could cry, because this wasn't how she'd envisioned it—any of it. The final escape, coming to Luc. Asking him for help. Being naked in front of him—or any man, for that matter.

And how sad that she wanted to ask, *Did you like it? Am I ugly? Did you see how they hurt me?*

"What's going on, Abby?" Luc asked again, his words slow, his voice strange. "Why did you come here in the snow?"

Because I don't want to die, she thought on a wave of something too big, too heavy for her alone. It crashed right into her, like that fireplace poker to the chest. It caved her chest in, infiltrating the empty spaces her departing adrenaline left behind, and bent her over, deflated.

Without a word, Luc had her against his chest, in those arms—and they were as strong as they looked. Effortlessly, he lifted her and brought her back to the sofa, murmuring something. Comforting sounds, maybe. No—they were words she couldn't understand.

The blankets around her were warm. A nest. She watched vacantly as he got the fire roaring. After a while, he left and returned with his hands full. Some pills, a glass of water, and a pile of clothes.

"We need to get you to a doctor. A hospital, maybe. And I can call the sheriff—"

"No!" The word exploded from her, too loud for the room. "No police." Never the police. Police and hospitals wouldn't be good. They'd push Isaiah to do more violence. And everyone would suffer.

"You're hur—"

"No hospital."

"Okay, Abby. Okay," he said, placating her. Like an animal or a child. "We get you cleaned up." Oh, his English suffered when he was worried. How lovely. Abby smiled to herself as he disappeared up the stairs. A minute later, he returned. "Can you…" Luc started. He swallowed, his Adam's apple bobbing. "I brought you some of my clothing. It's too big." He held up a T-shirt with long sleeves. It looked soft and worn. "Can you do this on your own?"

"Oh. I think so."

"Good." He sounded relieved. "And this is ibuprofen. I'll leave it for—"

"How do I take it?"

He blinked. "What?"

"Just swallow it with water?"

"Yes. Exact." More English mistakes that sounded subconscious, exhausted. And that was because of her. Because she'd dragged him up and out of bed, and Isaiah'd been here, and now Luc would have problems with the Church. *It's all my fault.*

"I'll take them. What do they do?"

"You haven't—" He cut himself off with a quick shake of his head. "It's a painkiller. And reduces fever. Also inflammation."

Abby wished their hands would touch as he dropped the pills into hers. She wished he would look at her and smile and make it all okay. But he didn't. He stood, face turned away. "I'll let you…" He indicated a door leading off the living room. "You sure you don't need help?"

She shook her head and said, "Thank you, Luc."

"I've got to…check on something. You'll be fine going to the bathroom on your own?"

"Yes. Yes, fine." To prove her point, she grabbed the clothes and the pills and waddled to the bathroom on sharply hurting feet.

15

LUC WAITED FOR HER TO DISAPPEAR INTO THE BATH-room before going onto the front porch, pulling out the sheriff's card, and dialing. Straight to voice mail, which agitated the hell out of him. Instead of leaving a message—the hardest thing to do in English, as far as Luc was concerned—he called the other number on the card: dispatch.

"Blackwood Sheriff's Department, how may I direct your call?"

"I need to speak to the sheriff."

"Is this an emergency, sir?"

He hesitated, focused on where the cabin was and whether anyone could get to them through the pelting snow. Was it an emergency? He swallowed. "Yes. No. I don't know."

"If it's an emergency, we—"

"I just need to talk to him. Please. Tell him it's Luc Stanek calling."

"Just a moment."

He waited through half of an upbeat reggae song,

almost annoyed at himself for wanting to move to the music. My God, there was something diabolical about making people calling the authorities listen to those happy, happy words.

Finally, an answer: "What can I do for you, Mr. Stanek?"

"Sheriff." Luc breathed for a few seconds. *What am I doing? What do I say?* "They've hurt her."

"Excuse me?"

"The…cult people. She's here. At my house. Hurt and cold. I think she came close to hypothermia."

"Hang on. Did *they* hurt her? You know this?"

"No. No, she didn't tell me. She—" Luc cut himself off and swallowed hard, wondering, *Why didn't I get more information from her first? Why didn't I ask her? Because she didn't want me to call, that's why.* "I have no idea what they've done. What I do know is they came to my house looking for her in the middle of the night."

"Did they threaten you, sir?"

"Yes. Although, not in so many words."

"What does that mean?"

"The man—Isaiah Bowden, he's their leader— mentioned it would be a shame if my vines burned down, so…not overt, but definitely a threat. They said she was *mentally ill*." His voice went a bit rough at the end, and he paused. "*She's not.*"

On the other end was silence. He could picture the sheriff's face as he took it in, his eyes considering the situation, even over the phone, with as much focus as he'd given Luc before.

Finally, he asked, "Is she in need of medical attention?"

"Yes. I don't know the extent, but yes, she probably needs medical attention. She won't accept it, though."

A grunt. "Why not?"

"I don't know." Luc paused. "They don't believe in medicine over there. But I don't think that's it."

"Would she come with us if I found a way to get to her?"

Luc thought about the way she'd stiffened when he'd talk about calling the cops. "I don't think so."

The sheriff sighed, and Luc wanted to join him. Luc didn't understand what was happening either, didn't want to deal. And yet, when he was in the same room with Abby, beside her, talking with her... This distance was good. He wasn't himself when she was around. He liked her too much.

The phone crackled in his hand, the connection worse than usual.

"I'm sorry, Mr. Stanek. But we're in the middle of a major storm here." *No shit*, thought Luc, staring out at his yard, where the other truck's tire marks were already disappearing under a thin layer of snow. "I've got few resources, and unless this is a life-threatening emergency... If we get out there and she refuses care... Well, you can understand my hesitation. I'm not sure I can get anyone out there for...a day or two, at least."

Probably more, thought Luc, knowing what the roads would be like. He could attempt his driveway—the neighbors had done it after all—but the road to town would be risky, and getting stranded with Abby in the shape she was in was too risky.

"Even if this were a major medical emergency, we can't call in the chopper on a day like today. Nobody's

flying that thing till the snow stops," the sheriff said.
Another sigh, this one sounding exhausted. Luc pictured
the man, still in his office, not making it home with the
weather. "Honestly, sir, you'd have to have more of
an emergency at this point. We only get Pegasus over
from UVA for life-or-death situations. Like the multicar
pileup I'm headed to right now, up on the interstate."

Luc nodded, knowing the man was right.

They said their good-byes, leaving things up in the
air. He'd get in touch when the storm blew over. *If necessary* had been the subtext.

Now what?

Luc shut the phone off, shoving it into his pocket,
and stood on his porch. The wind was blowing hard,
visibility limited now to just a few meters. Usually, from
here, he could see his vines, standing sentinel above
the valley.

Tonight he stood, waiting for that sense of ownership and rightness, like the evil king in those *Lord of
the Rings* movies, searching, searching, and…nothing.

He turned back to face his front door, and there, his
internal radar found what he was looking for—*belonging*.

With a jolt of unease, Luc realized it wasn't the
vines calling to him. No, tonight, the ping came from
another place entirely. Like a beacon, he could feel her
in there.

Abby. Today, with his vines out of sight and everything else a tangled ball of confusion, when Luc sought
an anchor, he found Abby.

And that scared the hell out of him.

∽⦿∾

Abby examined the two pills before putting them into her mouth. They were orange, which struck her as odd. Not bright orange, but the color of plant pots. The color of the soil on the mountain, if you dug down a foot or two. Sweet on her tongue and down her throat, disappearing on a wash of water that felt good, so good. She drank the whole glass before standing up from the toilet and coming face-to-face with her reflection in the mirror.

Oh goodness, look at me.

Her face was a mass of bruises, her hair a bird's nest in the braid she hadn't redone in ages. Days, likely, although she'd lost track of time.

When she let the blanket drop and turned, the bandages on her back were stained with fluid, unhealthy. She'd need new ones.

Had he seen those? He must have. And what about her arms? Had he seen the older scars on her arms? The usual wave of pride rolled through her at the sight of those scars, only to bottom out, sharp and acidic in her belly.

Her vision shifted, and with a dizzy lurch, Abby clutched the sink.

A collage of images burst into her brain—*standing there, her back exposed, while the men she'd always known as family destroyed her. Sammy, Mama. Hamish in pain. Making the tea for Hamish and leaving it beside his bed. "You can drink it," she'd said.*

The room swirled, too fast to be real, and she sank to her bottom on the bathroom floor. Up was down; good, bad. Sacrifices made as a badge of honor suddenly burned with shame. She'd scratch them off if she had the strength.

Shaky, cold. Bleary-eyed. Not far behind her was the bath. *Just get to the bath and wash off the mess. Just do that, and I can sleep.*

The bath, once she ran the water and got into it, was torture.

Feet first. Hot, hot, burning against her thighs, not yet reaching her back, where the real torture would begin. But she needed to unstick the bandages. Ignoring the places where the razor wire had cut into her, she sank down, the water cloudy red and smelling of blood within seconds. It wasn't until she'd submerged fully that she noticed the soap on a ledge high above her head.

Sucking in a hard breath, she leaned on the rim, lifted herself up, grabbed the soap, and dipped back in. The burn of her thighs was sharp, the ache in her back already familiar.

It hurt to sit in this bath—real, physical pain. So much better than the pain of knowing what she'd left behind.

Where are you, Sammy?

The water was hotter than she was used to. Not that they took baths like this at the Church. Sponge baths were pretty much it. It made *her* feel like a sponge, soaking it up, her muscles adjusting and turning to mush. With a big sound—an *ah* that came from somewhere deep in her marrow—she sank in farther.

Movement behind the door, almost furtive. *Isaiah. He found me.*

She sat up fast and pushed to standing, arms up to keep her modest, trembling. She didn't even notice the honeycomb of gray spots as they crept over her vision, barely recognized the wooziness until the bathwater sloshed around her ankles and she slid down with a thud.

That woke her up.

Was this Hell, this heat? Had Isaiah finally—

A knock—knuckles on wood.

"All right in there?"

Confusion continued to crowd Abby's vision, held her tongue, belabored her breath. She'd banged her head on the side of the tub, maybe.

Yes. No. No, I am not.

The squeak of hinges. Cool air. A slow turn of her head. Wet, water, coughing.

It was all too fast. Luc's arms came around her, and she gave him her weight. *Luc, Bringer of Light.*

She nodded, let the nod become a face rub, noting the cold and the smell of the outside on his clothes before sinking into him with relief.

∽ಲ೭

As Luc cradled the towel-wrapped woman against him and scanned the bathroom, the word for abattoir came back with crystal clarity—the one he could never seem to remember: *slaughterhouse.*

Every time he came or went from his property, he was forced to drive right by the neighbors' *goddamned slaughterhouse.* The place where they killed and skinned and bled their animals. Pig carcasses, sheep, and chickens. For food, he assumed, although images of sacrifice floated through his head. With Abby in his arms, he could think of nothing but sacrifice.

A dog barked in the distance. One of theirs, no doubt. *Hunting her still.*

"I'm sorry." Abby's voice reverberated against his chest.

Luc sighed. *Et merde.* "It's okay." He sat on the toilet, soaking wet from her bathwater, wondering what the next move was.

Luc couldn't guess where to begin. For the second time tonight he held a shivering, near-naked Abby in his arms, her eyes squeezed shut with pain. *Call the fucking helicopter. We need the helicopter.*

He sucked in a breath. Blood. So much of it. He swallowed, ignoring the earthy smells billowing up from the bath, and eyed her legs. A long gash ran from a gently curving shinbone, up to where it disappeared above her knee, seeping more blood.

"Why didn't you tell me you were so badly hurt?"

"I didn't…I didn't realize," she gasped. "I was running. Couldn't feel it till I got up. And the bath…"

"Did they do this to you?"

"No, I did."

He shook his head to clear it. "What?"

"Running. Climbing the fence. I cut myself."

"You didn't crawl through?"

"They closed the hole."

Anger rose up, hard and hot.

"How are your feet?"

"I don't know."

"Let me see them," he pushed out through tight lips.

She hesitated.

"We've got to take care of this, or it could get worse."

"I've never done this before."

"Done what?"

"Been…" She gave her head a quick shake, sucked in a shaky breath.

"Here." He set her down on the edge of the bathtub and

lifted her foot into his lap, slowly, gingerly. Even after her bath, traces of mud and dried blood coated her sole. Leaning back, he grabbed a washcloth and busied himself with soaking it at the sink. He did it all without rising from the toilet seat—the advantage of a small bathroom.

Sparing a glance at Abby's face, he said, "Tell me if this hurts too much." At her stoic nod, he set to work, gently rubbing at the layers of grime. "Let's see the other one." Carefully, he cleaned that foot, too, revealing cuts and areas that looked rubbed raw. Such a tiny foot, naked-looking without the toenail polish that so many women wore like armor.

"Let's bandage those," he said, not wanting to set her feet down, to let her go.

"I'll do it," she said, trying to pull away. "I'm fine."

He doubted that. "You need medical care."

"I need privacy." Her voice came out stronger, her gaze boring into his.

"You practically fainted in the tub."

"The water was scalding. I didn't realize." A pause. "Please, Luc. I can do the rest myself."

He eyed her doubtfully.

"I can do it." This time, her voice was firm, certain, and Luc chose to believe her.

"You can stay sitting up on your own?" he asked, getting a bleary nod in response. For such a small person, she was made of tough stuff, this one. "I'll be back." He headed to his kitchen, where he kept his first aid kit—the one he'd bought when he'd hired help at last year's harvest. He grabbed the big bottle of hydrogen peroxide and a pair of scissors and returned to where she sat, barely propped up on the side of the tub.

"Do you know how to use this? It's—"

"We may not practice medicine, Luc, but we're well versed in the art of hygiene." The look she gave him, full of humor, softened her words. "And cotton," she said with a half smile. "We know our cotton."

He smiled in return, because even torn apart and bleeding, this woman had liquid steel running through her veins. He'd seen it outside, in the way she worked, uncomplaining in the cold. He'd seen it in her ability to adapt, learning new things with openness and curiosity. And he saw it in her humor. In the way she smiled and never appeared to feel sorry for herself. He'd never known another woman with such fortitude. Or man, for that matter. How could he not admire that?

The humor meant she'd be okay. Didn't it? You didn't laugh at death's door, right? "What about the bandages on your back?"

"Please, Luc. Please let me do this on my own."

"Okay," he answered, breathy with irritation, relief, and some admiration as well. "I'll be right outside if you need anything."

"Luc."

Her voice stopped him at the door, and he turned back. She was beautiful, even wounded and hunched in on herself in his bathroom. Maybe even lovelier, with the bright-pink patches on her cheekbones and the damp curls sticking to the skin along her hairline. Her eyes on his were a fathomless, liquid gold, and all of it, every little thing that should have made her into a victim translated instead to strength. *Mistress of her destiny.*

"Thank you."

He left with a muttered, "It's nothing."

In the living room, he wandered. The fire, just low-burning embers, needed to be fed. After that…after that, he'd clean up this mess. Only he wasn't sure which mess he meant—the wad of blankets on the sofa, the bathroom…or Abby's situation. His situation.

And whatever the hell this night would bring next.

16

WRAPPED IN MORTIFICATION, ABBY LET HER SHOULDERS curve and her breath come. She'd been unclothed in front of him—again—and still not on her terms.

This wasn't how she wanted her body to appear to him—bloody and battered.

The sting of hydrogen peroxide on her wounds was good. It made things sharper, made her feel more focused, more in control.

In control of my own pain.

A knock on the door jarred her out of that odd train of thought.

"Yes?"

"I've got ointment. You can spread it over some of the cuts before bandaging them."

"Thank you," she said.

"Can I…can I open the door?"

She pulled the towel up tighter around herself, taking special care with her shoulders and back before responding. "Yes."

"Here, I'll hand it through."

"Thank you," Abby said, expecting him to leave.

Instead, he spoke from behind the open door. "It looked like... You can't do your back on your own, Abby. I could do those for you, if you—"

"No!" Abby's voice was close to a shout. *I don't want you to see me like this.*

Silence.

"You want me to go?"

"Yes." A pause. "Thank you."

She waited for him to leave before doing her best to clean and clothe her body. Her back would just... *Have to wait*, she'd been about to tell herself. But why? Why would it wait when there was a person here who could take care of it for her? He could help her. Why refuse the help?

Modesty? Ha! A lot of good that's done me.

She knew from experience that the bandages wouldn't unstick themselves, and if she didn't do something about it, healing would turn into a painful, never-ending cycle of sticking and removing, sticking and removing, until it scabbed up. And the scars.

The scars were the whole point, of course. Keeping God's Mark on her body, wearing it as penance.

She shouldn't care about the brands. A modest woman wouldn't worry about her looks. She wouldn't concern herself with the eyes of men like Luc on her body. She shouldn't care that he'd find her ugly.

How skewed her priorities were—choosing an antiquated, man-made notion of impropriety over her own well-being. Choosing beauty over health.

And that thought decided her. *Bare your ugliness. Stay alive. Forget modesty; forget everything but survival.*

"Luc!" she called before she could change her mind.
"I would like your help."

She waited as he came in, dropping the towel in back
and letting him see the bandages.

His breath came out harsh and surprised.

"Did they cut you?" he asked. She heard the moment
he saw her arms, the gasp he couldn't help but release.

"No," she said, shutting her eyes tight. She wished
she wasn't here for this, wanted to disappear up, up, up
above the world, on a tiny planet of her own. The way
she'd disappeared when they'd done this to her back.

~∞~

"What did they do to you, Abby?" He stared. Bandages.
Big, yellowing bandages. They looked like they'd been
on her skin for ages. And those scars on her arms.

She didn't answer, only hunched her shoulders, silent.
Nothing disturbed the steamy, warm air of his bathroom,
except for the shuddery sound of her breathing.

"Burns," she finally whispered.

Luc's teeth clenched so hard his jaw cracked audibly. His hands felt like battering rams without a target,
knuckles white.

"Can you…" He held back, breathing hard. "We need
to get those bandages off."

She nodded in agreement, and like a fool, Luc wasn't
at all sure he wanted to see.

In the end, it wasn't a simple matter of taking off
the bandages, since they were stuck to her skin. But the
more he saw, the angrier he got. *Putain d'enculés.*

Brands. Those pigs had fucking *branded* her.

Regret, that's what he felt, at having let her go back

to them. And fear, too. Not the fear of facing off against that smooth and slimy snake bastard, but the fear of Abby dying here. Fear of being responsible for her. For getting it wrong and losing her when she'd only just appeared in his life.

"You should have come to me sooner, Abby."

"Couldn't get away," she grunted. "Nothing I haven't dealt with before. Just takes a little while to heal. Needs air."

"Right," he said. He pushed out the fear and anger as best he could. Not anger—something stronger.

Rage. Pure, unadulterated rage. "Who put on the bandages?" he asked.

"I did. The arms healed best when I let 'em air, but that wasn't easy, since modesty dictates that I—" She dropped her chin to her chest with a huff and spent a few seconds apparently gathering herself before craning her neck to meet his gaze. "It has done me no good at all. And I don't know how my back could heal while maintaining my modesty. Modesty wasn't an issue when they…"

She didn't finish, and in all honesty, Luc didn't really want her to. If he heard any more about the brands, he wasn't sure what he'd do. He pictured himself going back to their side of the mountain, his truck plowing straight through the glass double doors fronting that ugly building.

Gathering himself, he soaked a washcloth in the water, wrung it out, and set it on the bandage, covering as much as he could.

Her body tensed. Nothing else.

Luc didn't know what he'd expected. Histrionics, perhaps? Freaking out from the pain? Instead, she turned her head, and those glowing eyes sought out his face, landing on his lips and lingering a little too long. Somehow, the insane attraction replaced the worry. It was more than just physical, he realized. Here she was practically naked in front of him, and what got to him wasn't her nudity. It was those eyes.

She nodded. He had no clue why.

"Try now," she finally whispered, breaking the spell.

"You'll tell me? If it hurts, I mean?"

Again, she nodded.

He reached for one corner—already unstuck—and pulled.

One of Abby's hands left the towel in front of her, lifted, sought him out. He grasped it tightly, which made his work more difficult. He sank to his knees on the floor beside her, their faces close enough to share air, their fists shaking with her pain as he teased the once-white cotton from her skin.

About halfway through, the bandage stopped coming off.

He reapplied water, pulled at the other corners, concentrated on the second bandage, and got that almost all the way off. The yellow stains worried him the most. That couldn't be good, could it? A sure sign of infection.

When had they done this to her? Could he have stopped them?

Yes. Yes, he could have. He could have told her to stay here, with him. He could have offered her a safe place. *Made* her stay.

Should have kept Sammy, too.

No, he wouldn't even think about that. How could he have done it without risking all of their lives?

A glance showed her eyes screwed shut, lovely face tied up in a knot of pain. Her hand convulsed in his, and he squeezed hers back.

He had to unstick the rest of this *foutu* bandage, fast.

After what felt like forever, he got them off with a little more tugging and exposed her back.

Nom de Dieu, her poor, poor skin, defiled.

"Thank you," Abby whispered.

Mouth open, all he could do was take it in. The brands covered every inch of skin up her arms and across her back. Fresh burns and old ones, scars that had whitened with age, shiny on the raised parts. In places, the brands overlapped.

Luc took in the damage, and his only lucid thought was *I'm going to beat that bastard to a pulp.*

∽ↄ℘ↄ

It was getting light by the time they made it out of the bathroom. Abby let Luc take her upstairs, half-naked, with her back in full view. He'd run up to get her a button-down shirt, helped her slip it on backward, and left it undone in the back while he smeared some ointment over the new brands. He made her drink water before having her lie facedown on his bed, where he reapplied clean bandages and presented her with a small, white stick.

"Here," he said, handing it to her, clearly expecting something.

"I don't…" As she examined the object, memories came back—sweet ones she'd lost beneath layers of fire and brimstone: sick in bed, Mama's cool lips on her forehead, one of these sticking out of her mouth. Another flash: a white room at school, back when she still attended school— posters on the walls and a nurse shaking her head, tutting at whatever she read on the…the…

"*Thermometer*," Abby said, the word suddenly clear, along with the feeling of safety it engendered. Once this was inserted into her mouth, things would be taken care of.

"You know how it works?"

"I remember."

"Under your tongue," said Luc. When she hesitated, he moved to sit beside her on the bed. "Open your mouth. Like this."

He stuck it in and waited until it beeped, then removed it and looked at the small, red, flashing screen.

"*Merde*," he exhaled. "Here, take two more of these, and we'll check again in a bit."

"Okay," Abby said, watching as he shook two more pills out of their bottle and put them on the table beside her glass of water.

"Get some sleep, *chérie*. I'll be back."

"Wait!" she called as he moved to go. "I have to get Sammy out."

"Not tonight, Abby. You can't tonight."

"But he'll die, Luc. He'll die."

"He could die trying to escape, Abby. Just like you came close to dying out in this weather."

Blinking, she nodded.

"Where is he, do you think, tonight?"

"Possibly with the Cruddups? Or with Benji and Brigid."

"You think Isaiah doesn't have him under lock and key?"

Luc's words chilled her for their truth. Slowly, it dawned on her. Things were different now. Totally, inexorably changed. Forever.

"You're right," she whispered.

"We'll get Sammy out." She opened her mouth to protest that *we*, but he kept right on going. "But not tonight. Not until you're well enough and the weather is clear enough. Otherwise, it's suicide."

And she was tired. So tired. "Okay, Luc," she whispered. With one last caress of his hand to her forehead, he went back downstairs.

After sitting up to swallow the pills, Abby collapsed onto her belly, wondering how she'd ever thought she'd survive in this unfamiliar world. Even thermometers had changed since she was a child. They had a little window that flashed red, and it beeped and… What had her temperature been anyway? He hadn't even told her. And if he had, she wouldn't have understood what it meant. Wouldn't have known what flashing number she was looking for.

Even here, in this man's rustic cabin in the mountains, Abby felt unprepared, uneducated, and inadequate.

After a short while, the pain lessened, and she found herself disappearing into fitful sleep.

More bleak dreams, peppered with oddly happy ones. Unexpected moments she grasped, only to lose them again.

Hours passed. Or more. Days, maybe?

A cold weight on her forehead, an angry voice. "*Shit.*" Something in her mouth, a high-pitched sound, and more curses. It took a while for Abby to recognize these modern conveniences, the sound of Luc as he reapplied ointment to her back. His hands were gentle and cool.

When he'd finished, he shifted as if to leave, and Abby reached for him. She turned her head, unable to open her eyes. "Wait," she croaked. "Please don't go yet."

"You need something? I'll get you fresh water."

"Yes, but…"

"Hold on," he said and disappeared down the stairs.

Decades later, he was back, with fresh, ice-cold water, just enough to soothe her aching throat.

"Luc," Abby rasped out, "don't go."

He sighed. Even in her current state, she knew that meant he wanted to leave, but she found his hand again and squeezed it as hard as she could.

"It's cold in the snow," she said.

"You're burning up, Abby. I don't have anything stronger than ibuprofen. I've got to get you to a hospital."

"No. No, no, Luc. Don't you get it?"

He stilled, stopped trying to pull away from her.

"Get what?"

"We're burning. It's all gone. Everyone on this mountain. Them. Us. The world."

"Gone?" His voice was hesitant. Slow and quiet, like he didn't believe her, which made Abby need to say it louder, stronger, to *make* him understand.

"He's killed the babies. The sky's orange with it. The Cataclysm."

"You're dreaming, Abby. You're delirious." He peeled her hand off of his and placed it beside her. "You need more sleep. Go back to sleep."

"I have to go back. For Sammy."

"Not tonight. Not until the storm clears, Abby. You'd die out there."

"When the storm clears. I'll go when the storm clears."

With a moan, she shifted until her face found a cool spot on the pillow and sighed before sinking again into the fiery inferno.

ABBY WOKE UP DRAINED BUT HUNGRY. SHE LAY ON her side in Luc's bed and watched the light fade as the snow continued to fall, enclosing her more fully inside. What time was it? Had she slept through an entire day?

Somewhere outside, beyond the cabin's thick log walls, a rhythmic thud told her that Luc was chopping wood. Pressed by the demands of her body, she got up, hobbled to the top of the steps, and slid downstairs on her bottom. Slow, so slow, with her stinging feet and sore ankle, every part of her body aching.

She watched him through the kitchen window as he hauled big logs and took an ax to them. His movements were practiced and skilled—the swing constant, like music—and he piled pieces neatly before repeating the entire process. Every movement was big, because the man was, but concise as well. Lord, it wasn't right, was it, for her body to feel this…sluggishness when she looked at him? Bright and alive, but slow and heavy, all at once. It seemed wrong, given her condition.

After a bit, he tromped through the snow to his vines. Lord only knew what he did there before heading up to the barn.

Once he disappeared from view, Abby shook herself, as if coming out of a spell, and realized just how ravenous she was.

Turning from the window, she took in the kitchen. What could she eat? Bread. Bread was good. She took a slice from the loaf, munched it dry, and decided to make herself useful. She couldn't just sit in someone's house all day and get nothing done. But after a few minutes of puttering—sweeping and cleaning his already-spotless kitchen, ignoring the pain in her extremities—exhaustion took over. She slid another log into the fire and collapsed onto the sofa, pulling a blanket over her shoulders.

A grunt woke her up—was that her own voice?—tearing her from dreams of arms tight around her, too tight but warm, and fire on the mountain. Fire all around them.

Mindlessly, she pushed to standing and looked out the window, scanning the landscape for Luc's form. It was almost night, although everything still had that vague, light snow glow, and the stuff was still coming down from the sky.

Oh! There he was, a silhouette against the pale earth, too far to see in detail. As she watched, the figure—just a spot, really—drew closer. With every step, something bubbled higher in her chest. Anticipation or excitement. She searched the landscape for Le Dog, who never ventured far from Luc. When she couldn't find him, her eyes flew back to the figure, suddenly racing through possible scenarios—Luc in the barn, overtaken by Isaiah. Luc working in the fields and not hearing the attack. And now, Isaiah was here, marching toward her.

She leaned against the window, breath fast, stomach tied up in knots. Oh no. Isaiah'd hurt Luc, which meant she'd brought this to him, and now he'd come to find her. To take her back. To punish her as she'd never been punished before. Could he see her?

She shoved the curtain closed and lurched back into the room, heart racing, air wheezing through her lungs.

Beside the door stood Luc's rifle, and although she'd never fired one, she took hold of it, let her fingers get to know its cold, steel edges. Not in the awkward, hesitant way she'd held it that first day, but decisively. She'd shoot Isaiah if she had to. Shoot any of them. No way would Isaiah or any members of the Church scare her. Not out here in the world. She wouldn't let them.

Hefting the weapon, she hobbled to the armchair and sat, ears pricked and eyes darting, shivering with the cold.

The fire threw shadows across the room, and Abby forced her breath to even out, sinking her body deeper into the chair, ignoring the press of leather to her back. After a while, the heat calmed her—although it never warmed her bones—and her mind traveled past the possibility of immediate threat.

What was happening back home? Was Sammy having supper with the Cruddups? Were households full of the gossip of her departure? Were they looking for her? Condemning her? Escape couldn't possibly be this easy, could it?

Was she *actually* free? She was. Still close, granted,

but that couldn't be helped. And she wouldn't leave without Sammy. Tomorrow, maybe, she'd feel well enough to head back over the fence and—

A bell rang from somewhere in the house, a bright, electronic sound that had Abby jumping out of her skin before she understood what it was. It took a moment to locate its source—a small telephone, sitting on a table by the front door.

For a few seconds, she considered picking it up. Should she? No. No, it wasn't hers to pick up. But... what if it was Luc calling the house?

It gave out another high-pitched *dring*, with an insect-like vibration. *Don't touch it.*

A step back, then another. The phone eventually stopped, only to start up again. It did that five times, until finally, she reached out and picked it up, touching the green circle that said On.

"Allô?" said the voice on the other end. A woman. More words followed—not in English.

Abby couldn't respond. Frantically, she looked for a button to stop this call she shouldn't have taken. She finally found a red End circle and put the thing down, returning to the chair to wait.

❧

Luc felt the strangest, most unexpected warmth at the sight of his cabin with smoke billowing from the chimney and light glowing from the windows. It was pleasant, although he wasn't keen on the reasons for it. Nobody would wish this situation on a woman.

Nobody would wish it on him, either.

Her presence in his life—and everything it seemed to

bring with it—had been clawing at his throat all afternoon, burning at his gut as he worked.

Anger at what they'd done to her, anger that there was nothing he could do about it, and anger that he'd let that kid go back. But how the hell was he supposed to have stopped them?

It speared him in the chest, that thought, so mixed up with everything Abby made him feel. He'd gone up to the cabin before noon to find her snoring quietly on the sofa, and if he hadn't forced himself back out, he could have spent the rest of the day there, warming her in his arms. Or just sitting with her. But neither of those things would have satisfied this jumbled, roiling, ball of emotions inside of him: the anger and frustration, yes, but also something so protective it burned his sinuses and hurt his chest. And all of it laced with a sexual need that felt entirely inappropriate with her injured and snoring on his sofa.

So he'd gone back out into the never-ending snowstorm to work, with only the occasional break to check on her. The last time he'd gone in, her forehead had felt cool and her sleep hadn't seemed so fitful, which was an enormous relief.

He spent a good chunk of time making sure everything was prepped for the power outage they were sure to get. Last year's storms had been nothing compared to this one, and the power had eventually gone. He'd learned that it was just the way things happened here on the mountain, which was the last place the power company checked on their route. The generator was gassed up and would at least ensure the winery stayed warm enough. The cabin would be fine with the woodstove.

He was hungry by the time he got home and shoved

open the kitchen door, a pile of firewood balanced in his arms. The smell of cooking hit him in a moist burst of steamy air, and there she was, at the stove, stirring the pot, as if she belonged.

"You heated up the sauce," he said in lieu of greeting.

"Oh."

He squatted, dropped the wood beside the kitchen stove, and looked up at her from his spot on the floor. "Oh?"

"Sauce."

"Yes. For spaghetti."

She looked at him blankly, brows raised.

"You don't know spaghetti?" he asked. She shook her head. "Pasta. Noodles?"

"Oh. I used to eat that when I was little. I remember sucking down these long noodles." She paused, red as the sauce in the pot. "But I thought it was a stew or something. I didn't know." She lost her smile and indicated his sparsely stocked cupboard, chewing her bottom lip with what looked like consternation. "So many things. So much choice."

"In *there*?"

"There's rice. I recognize rice. But the package said it was dirty. Beans are obvious, but that one said risotto and there it's orzo and... What on earth is orzo?" Her eyes met his, and for the first time, he understood the enormity of this for her.

But she was smiling, which alleviated some of the tension inside him. Not just fear and anger from what those men had done to her, but the pressure of being host and guide to this stranger in a strange land. Of all the people in the world, he was probably the least qualified.

"Let's get some water on to boil," he said finally.

He filled a pot at the sink, relieved that the power hadn't gone out yet, and thought about how it would feel to have no experience of modern life. Because even Luc, country boy though he was, had flown on an airplane to get here. Backward though he was, he still used a mobile phone. He glanced at her, beautiful despite being covered from neck to toe in his ugly clothes. Except for her back, which he wouldn't let himself look at—partly because those scars would only rile him up again and she didn't need his rage, but also because he *wanted* to so badly.

Ripping his thoughts away from what he now knew about her body, he sought for something mundane.

"Orzo is another kind of pasta," he explained. "Also Italian, like spaghetti."

"It's shaped like rice."

He smiled a response, put the water on to boil, and strode into the other room to check the fire. Everything seemed to be doing just fine without him, which he appreciated. She'd taken care of things in his absence.

"Where do you usually eat?" she asked when he returned to the kitchen.

"At the kitchen table."

She nodded, got the second wooden chair from the living room, and set it at the table before pulling two forks from the kitchen's lone drawer and two plates from the cabinet above.

They were quiet, and with six minutes on the timer when they finished setting up, there was nothing left to do but stand there and not look at each other.

It made him nervous—her proximity, her presence in his kitchen.

Without thinking, he reached into a lower cabinet for a bottle of wine, which he opened and served. He lifted his head to find her…staring.

"Are you okay?" he asked, because really, she looked at him as though he were an alien. Which wasn't all that odd, considering how bad he was with these situations. He'd clearly done something wrong, not asked her something he should have or—

"Thank you, Luc."

"Oh," he stammered. "You're welcome."

With a breath in, she looked at the table. "So. Spaghetti is Italian."

"Yes," he said. "And with spaghetti, you drink wine." He handed Abby the cork from the bottle he'd opened. "Smell that."

After examining it for a moment, she put it to her nose, breathed in, turned it, and did the same on the other side. The wine-stained side.

"Smells old."

"Yes? Anything else?"

"It reminds me of that room up in the barn, with all the barrels." She looked at him. "Is that strange?"

Heart quickening, he shook his head and looked away. No. No, it wasn't strange at all. It was beautiful, like this woman. Though she was injured and just recently feverish and dangerous to begin with, he couldn't help wanting her as he'd wanted nothing before. He reached for his glass and took a long swig of wine.

And all of this, he knew, was a bad idea.

Abby watched Luc use tongs to take two knots of spaghetti from the pot and put it onto their plates with a deft twist of the wrist and top each with a ladle full of thick, red sauce. All of it—her intense hunger, the smell, that practiced move, the way his handsome face creased in concentration—settled in her chest.

His back, thick and vital, stretched the shirt he wore, his strength painfully evident. And despite that obvious strength, she felt no fear when she watched him. Only affection.

That was a lie. There was more than affection simmering inside. There was that tension he always seemed to bring out in her. Like excitement, except darker. Deeper, maybe.

A clatter from the sink brought Abby's mind back to the mind-boggling fact that he'd helped her prepare dinner. And *served* it to her, while she sat at the table. The sight of him rinsing off the serving spoon should have made everything seem practical or utilitarian, but even that didn't rid her of that *feeling*.

"I can do that," she said, rising to stand beside him.

"I'm sure you could" was his only response. She waited impatiently for him to stop, turn around, leave the job to her. *Women's work.* He put the spoon in the drying rack. "Sit and eat your food," he said, holding out her chair with a smile.

Oh, that smile.

After a brief hesitation, during which everything— every life experience Abby had ever had—did a final, definitive flip-flop in her brain, winding up somewhere below her belly button, she finally sat down. *I belong here.* The words shimmered in her brain, although she wasn't sure if they meant "out here in the world" or "here, with him."

She smiled at him shyly and turned her eyes to the food on her plate—much easier than looking at the man, because goodness, he was blinding.

As they ate, she found herself sinking again into a desire to touch him, to test his skin and run her fingers through his hair. She couldn't guess if it would be soft or coarse, and in a moment of utter certainty, she knew she didn't want to *guess*. She wanted to *know*. All of it—how the longish hair would feel against the skin of her face. And those hands, deft and efficient—how would they touch her body? With power and competence, she suspected, which had quite the appeal.

She felt his eyes on her and wondered how long she'd spent in her dreamland.

"There's a specific way to eat spaghetti, if you're interested."

"Like pruning?"

He smiled. "Yes. We Europeans enjoy our traditions."

Using his fork, he gathered the long strands and wound them into the bowl of his spoon. For a brief, nearly hysterical moment, Abby thought she might swoon from the beauty of him. In any other household, anywhere in the world, this would be mundane—but here, with her a freakish outsider, this was incredibly sensual.

Only the man doesn't know it. Time to calm down.

She tried imitating his moves, with half of his ability and some success. Still, the spaghetti was...

Around a mouthful of the stuff, she said, "This is *divine*." Her eyes closed of their own accord, giving her tongue a chance to take it all in without him distracting her. Another bite—*not too fast, not too fast*—was slightly different. The flavors came together with notes she recognized: herbs, tomatoes, onions. She'd thought the pasta would taste like bread, but it didn't. It was soft and chewy. And—

Luc cleared his throat across from her, and Abby looked up to find him focused on her, his blue eyes glittering, mouth not quite closed. Goodness, she'd disappeared again, hadn't she? Embarrassed, she swallowed too much too soon, sputtered a bit, and said, "I've been told I have my head in the clouds."

After a beat, he answered, "If I had to guess, I wouldn't say in the clouds."

She swallowed. "Where, then?"

"Right here," he said with a smile that Abby couldn't help but return.

"They just meant that I'm always dreaming. I go into my head or—"

"I see what they meant. They're wrong."

Abby stopped, fork and spoon suspended in the air. It felt like it might matter, this response. What did he see that nobody else had?

As he opened his mouth and closed it, color rose to his face to settle high and pink on his cheekbones. It was charming how often he blushed.

"Here, drink."

He shoved one of the glasses of wine toward her, hard enough that it sloshed over the edges, and she watched as his cheeks darkened even further.

Lord, would he look like that if they… If he…

She took a sip and sighed again at the richness in her mouth, heat blooming from her throat to her middle.

He interrupted her thoughts. "I…I'm not good at this."

"At what?"

"Small talk."

"I'm not even sure what that is," said Abby, feeling the holes in her education more keenly than ever. But his response helped. It helped a lot when he laughed first, because he was wonderful to look at. And the laugh, though rare, settled on his features comfortably, arching his brows, turning up the corners of his mouth, and creasing his cheeks, breathing new life into those high swathes of pink.

"We should continue to get along, then."

The laugh disappeared, the sound of his voice faded, and their eyes met awkwardly in a dance Abby had neither learned nor perfected but was suddenly keen to understand.

She exhaled quick and hard while her body grew heavy and warm. From the wine or the man, she wasn't entirely sure.

"I think you're fine at talking," she said.

"Yes?"

"Good at other stuff, too."

His brows rose and his lips parted, making her want to taste them. His attention slid to the side, away from her, as if he was searching for something to say. Finally, he said, "You've never told me, and I can't help but wonder: What is it like to live there?"

"With the Church?" She set down her flatware and thought. "I couldn't describe it. It's been my only life."

"Forever?"

"Yes. Well, no. Mama brought us when I was little, but I hardly remember before."

"Why?"

"Why?"

"Why did she bring you? What was in it for her?"

Abby took a moment to answer. She lined her thoughts up one by one, pushing away memories that hurt too much to examine, lingering on good ones from when she was younger. This place had been much better than where they'd come from: safe and so much cleaner. Such a dream for a little girl who'd spent most of her life living out of the back of a car with her mom.

"She believes in the teachings. She's been devout forever, went to prayer every week, no matter where we were, then she met *him* and…" Everything changed.

"Isaiah Bowden?"

Abby nodded. "Hamish started the church here, but Isaiah's the prophet. He went out finding believers, while Hamish stayed here, welcoming and building. The mountain was supposed to be sacred land. Only, things have changed."

"How so?"

"Isaiah's not just a prophet anymore. He's the Second Coming. Hamish was still alive when Isaiah started saying he was the Messiah."

Abby took a sip and stared at nothing. A light film of tears covered her eyes as she let herself feel alone and maybe a bit sorry for herself.

Beside her, Luc puffed out a breath. "I can't believe this is happening right next door to me. At least now I know why this place was so inexpensive."

"I suppose nobody wanted us for neighbors." After a pause, she turned to him. "I'm glad you're here," she said, her voice small. "You gave me the courage to leave."

"*I* did?"

She nodded, flushing hard at what she was divulging. "I watched you over here, doing everything on your own. You had workers when you pruned and picked the grapes, but...you were mostly alone, and you were strong and bent on getting things done. I admired that."

Another sip, a smile, as she thought about the truth. He'd been driven and strong and able. For over two years, she'd watched him and wanted to see him close up, fantasized about the possibilities.

Reality, of course, had taught her not to dwell, but... Well, those dreams had gotten her through the hardest of times. And it had gotten her here, which wasn't all that bad, actually. Not bad at all.

He seemed shy as they got up, and he sent her to sit in front of the fire while he did the dishes. The lights flickered, and Abby shivered.

After a bit, he joined her, wine bottle and two glasses in hand. "Want to help me kill this?"

"I'm sorry?"

He looked away, boyish and cute again. "It doesn't work, does it? When I try the very American expressions? It means would you like to help me finish the wine?"

"Oh."

She mulled over the question. The wine felt good—it had loosened her joints, softened her muscles, dulled the pain to a throb. But it also made her say things she normally wouldn't say, and that might not be wise, given...everything.

But I want to say those things. I want to drink and kiss, ask questions and live.

"Yes. I'd like that," she finally said, knowing she was agreeing to more than the drink.

18

ABBY TOOK HER GLASS, HER HAND BRUSHING LUC'S IN
the process. It sent a zing of awareness down her arm,
reminding her of how little she knew about life out here,
about men and women and reality.

About seduction.

Was this man a seducer? No. No, he was too gruff,
too straightforward, all matter-of-fact with no frills. She
quelled a tremor with a warming sip from her glass, but
deep inside, something raw and uncontrollable reared its
head, trying hard to burst free.

Another sip, and Abby rolled her head on her neck.
She sucked in a long, shaky breath to relieve the nerves
that bubbled up, reveling in the feel of this shirt she had
on—big and soft, like the pants, and brazenly open at
the back. She'd wear men's clothes all the time, she
decided. No starch, lace, or modest undergarments. No
struggling with too many buttons and ties.

"How do you feel?" Luc asked, shifting the sofa
cushions as he sat down beside her, close enough to feel
his warmth. It took Abby a moment to understand he

meant her burns and not the cotton rubbing her breasts into achy points.

She blushed and coughed, but her nipples didn't go down.

"Much better, thank you." She lifted the glass and sipped again, glancing sideways at his profile. "This seems to be helping."

He smiled—oh, goodness, he was lovely—and she squeezed her legs together, hard.

"It's been known to do the trick." He turned the glass to the single lamp in the room and eyed its burgundy glow.

"Would this be different if I were a normal woman?"

He stilled, looking slightly suspicious, before lifting the glass higher and asking, "This?"

She pointed toward him with her wine. "Sitting with me. Having a drink."

After another brief silence, he set down his glass and shifted beside her, suddenly seeming too big for the sofa. "I'm not exactly a *normal* sort of man."

"I figured as much," she said with a smile of her own. "But what if…what if we'd met in town? At the market, maybe. What would it be like?" She took another swallow of wine, and it lit her right up. Or maybe that was his interested gaze.

"Strange."

She sputtered, nearly losing half her sip in the process. "Well, thank you very much."

"No, not you. I mean me. I'm not good at being natural."

"Okay. When you meet someone usually, what's it like? You go out to dinner? To see a movie?"

"Oh. Yes, I suppose so."

"You suppose?"

He opened his big hands, looking almost as clueless as she felt. "Well, not *me*. I don't go out to dinner."

"What do you do?"

He looked to the side, and she couldn't tell if he was searching for the right answer or sifting through memories. "My encounters with women tend to be more...casual."

"Oh." She pictured him in loose, low-slung jeans, slouching and shrugging in that way teenagers did. *Casual.* "What's that like?"

His expelled breath sounded frustrated, and she came dangerously close to letting him off the hook, until he answered. "It's just sex, I mean. No real relationships. Well, I had one, but..." He trailed off, leaving her with nothing. She wanted much more.

Sex? She wanted to know.

Instead, she asked, "How did that start? Your one *relationship*." Even that word felt funny. Grown-up and modern.

He frowned. "She told me she wanted me. We fuc—" He cleared his throat, which had turned a mottled red, the color disappearing into his neckline. Abby had to see how far down it went. The need was ravenous, pulsing, painful, and hot. "We did the...sex."

"Where?" she whispered, picturing a barn or a vineyard—she had a hard time imagining this man anywhere but in the great outdoors.

"Why do you want to know?"

"I..." She couldn't tell him the truth, could she? That she liked him. That she was curious. That she had absolutely no idea how to be normal, but there was this demon inside, stretching her skin painfully taut in its bid to get out. "I want to do it right."

The look he gave her said she was crazy, and yet there was something else in that expression.

"What, with me?"

"Yes. How…how would you touch me? If I were normal?"

"How would I—"

"Start? How would you start?" She barely forced the words through a throat that was hoarse with embarrassment, not to mention that yearning inside her—coarser and baser than anything she'd felt. This wasn't an emotion, exactly—more of a compulsion. "Where would you put your hands?" the demon goaded.

He looked at them—his hands—where they sat on his knees. Such vital parts of this man's body, cut and scarred and torn apart and missing a piece. They were lived-in and beautiful. Hands that had seen a thing or two, like these softly folded mountains with their low profile and vast knowledge of time. Would they feel that way on her? Experienced? Wise?

Sounding as frayed as she felt, he said, "I told you, I'm not good at *speaking*." It wasn't until the words sank in that she understood the underlying meaning.

"You're good at"—she swallowed, more brazen than she'd been in all her twenty-two years, because, despite the accusation that put those old scars on her arms, she'd never actually seduced a man before—"*doing*, though. Is that what you're good at?"

They were so close, sitting on the sofa in the warm living room, by the light of a single lamp and the glow of the fire. It was surreal, all of it. Dreamy.

In the time it would have taken to find something else to say, something proper to take them back to familiar territory, Luc's hand rose to her face. His knuckles skimmed her mouth in that signature move, shutting her up definitively. It didn't even surprise her that he'd use the back of his hands instead of the pads of his fingers. With those calluses, he probably couldn't feel anything at all.

They were warm and dry against her lips. She opened her mouth enough to let her tongue out to taste him. His indrawn breath made her think she might need to do it again—just to see how he'd react this time. She licked the crook between his fingers and got a long, slow exhale in response.

So she moved, just a little. Just enough to grasp the edge of his finger in her mouth, to bite it and let it catch on her bottom lip. She watched him closely—him watching his own hand, the place where their bodies touched, the flush of blood under his skin, the way the islands of his pupils, already big, ate up their surrounding sea of blue entirely.

"You are sure you want this, Abby? With me?" he asked, searching her face but not moving that hand away.

Abby's only answer was to grasp his other hand in hers and press it hard against her neck, against skin that felt hot. So hot.

~∞~

At the sound of Abby's words, then at the touch of her skin, Luc's cock went from thick and heavy to unbearably hard and ready to explode.

He wanted her. There was no doubt about that. There

hadn't been, if he was honest, from the first time he'd laid eyes on her. But he wasn't supposed to do things with her, and she wasn't supposed to do this seduction thing. Luc had come to America to work and to make something of himself. Not to seduce an innocent, religious girl—the equivalent of a nun, in his mind.

Or so he kept telling himself, because, sitting there in his oversize shirt and pants, Abby was the sexiest thing he'd seen in his life.

"What are you doing, Abby?" he managed to ask. He hated the way her features fell in response. But they shouldn't be doing this. She didn't need to get embroiled with him; she needed to leave, to get far away. And Luc was not skilled enough in the ways of seduction to do this right—whatever this was. He'd only mess it up, the way he'd messed up every other time he'd been with a woman.

"I was…" She inhaled, maybe taking in a dose of courage, before she lifted her chin and went on. "I wanted to… I want to…"

"We shouldn't." He stood and took a couple steps back. She needed someone smooth and knowledgeable. Someone who'd take her out and show her the world. Not a man who'd rather do anything to avoid crowds.

Her shoulders squared up. "Why not?"

"I can't kiss you again," he said. He knew this, but he wasn't happy about it.

"Because it's a sin?"

He blinked, confused, and shook his head. "No, Abby—"

"I *want* to do it again. It's wrong, I know that, but—"

"Of course it's not wrong." He paused, searching

for words. "It's just…you should do this with someone more…like you."

"Like me? You mean sheltered and inexperienced? Or another sinner? Because people out here do things. I've seen 'em, even in public. It's so…shameless. Maybe… Is kissing bad where you're from?" Her words came out breathless, the consonants almost inaudible.

"Bad? You mean wrong?"

"Yes. Is it bad that I want to kiss you just because it feels good?"

He huffed disbelievingly. "No. No, that's not bad."

Luc strode to the steps, thinking he'd go up there and… What? Get himself off while she sat down here, expectant and waiting?

No, to the bathroom. A cold shower would clear his head. Or outside—yeah, he could go out into the snow and—

"I want to try more," she interrupted. Jesus, why couldn't he catch his breath?

"Not with me, Abby."

"Oh. You don't want me like that."

"That is not what I mean. I mean you are…" He lifted his hands, trying to describe the perfection of someone so bright and crushingly lovely. "I mean I'll ruin this. I'll ruin *you*."

How was he supposed to explain the things that got him off, the images that crowded his brain? How could he tell a woman like her that he always liked the bounce of tits and the sight of his cock sinking in? That foreplay was a hand wrapped in hair, conversation, a nod, and a few grunts? He pictured trying to explain how far he was from a romantic. His fantasies… God, if she only knew.

He had no idea how to keep his desire civilized enough for someone so innocent.

"I still don't understand. If you want this, then why are you stopping?" she asked.

"Because I don't want to hurt you, all right? Your back, but also your"—he made a pointless motion in her general direction—"your person. I'm not gentle, like you need. I'm not...slow and romantic. I don't spout poetry or...or *dance*. Or do *foreplay*." And then, because he needed to shock some sense into her, he said, "I *fuck*, Abby. I fuck hard and fast. I do it for *me*. I'm a selfish lover because I'm no good at communicating, and I've never understood *how*. So, no. *No*, I'm not the man to introduce you to the pleasures of the flesh."

He stood there breathing hard, wishing he could escape the soft accusation in her eyes.

"I'm sorry, Abby." He looked away. "I need to sleep now. You should sleep upstairs in my...in the bed. Could you... Could we..."

Eyes downcast, she stood, her freckles lost in the blotchy wash of red that took over her pale, pale skin. His hand itched to touch it, but damn it, he wouldn't be the one to break whatever seal of abstinence this woman had been brought up with. He'd let some other man do it—a man whose flowery tongue could ease his way.

The thought of tongues made him angry, while his prick ached in his pants. There was nothing to do but storm into the kitchen, petulant but righteous in his restraint. Another man would give in.

But not me.

"All right then. May I..." She motioned toward the bathroom, not meeting his eye.

"Yes, of course," he said, feeling only slightly contrite as he went about the business of closing the house down for the night. He let the dog out, stuffed a couple more logs into the stove, all of it with the hot, guilty strain of his erection between his legs.

When she reemerged from the bathroom, he'd turned on the stair lights, turned off the others, and sat on the sofa, waiting.

"I like you, Abby."

She stopped.

"I am trying to say that I like you too much."

She nodded but nothing else. He wasn't sure what he'd expected.

"You have everything you need?"

"Yes. Thank you." She watched him for a long moment, those eyes seeing right through him, filled with something close to pity. Or maybe it was regret. "Good night, Luc."

"Good night, Abby."

"Thank you for helping me. For saving me, I mean."

He started to shake his head to deny and then stopped. "I would do it again." *And again. And again.*

With a last nod, she turned and disappeared up the stairs, leaving him alone with Le Dog's quiet snoring and the suffocatingly cozy crackle of the fire.

He couldn't sleep, of course. Not twisted up and turned on like this, hot and aching like a teenager, consumed with a teenager's guilt. Knowing she was ready and willing, right up those steps.

But her *back*.

Right. He concentrated on the memory of her back, the shocking, red lines printed deep, the fresh ones still too puffy to make out the patterns. The way the burns went to the edges of those perfectly curved shoulders, the way her breasts, braless, hung heavy against the fabric of his shirt. He'd seen her nipples stiffen. Her mouth slightly open, her eyes pinned on him... He could smell her, still, could almost taste her and— *Merde*, he couldn't stop thoughts of her body from haunting his brain. Didn't want to stop.

He reached down and clasped himself. He pressed hard at first, in hopes of abating the pressure, but it only served to chafe and stir things up. What would she feel like down there, between her legs? She'd be tight, wouldn't she? Tighter than anything he'd felt around him, he'd bet. And pink, like those lips. The same color and probably plush in the same way, ripe and wet and...

He was breathing hard now, with his hand on his cock, shamelessly working up and down over his pants, until the fabric was too much in the way. He worked it down to midthigh, exhaling hard at the feel of cool air on his hot, hot skin.

And then, taking a tight hold of himself with his left hand, he worked it up and down, added a twist at the top, imagining that twist like the hot glove of her sex, only she'd be tighter. Suppressing a moan, he turned slightly to the side, wanting to see his hand in the firelight and hoping it would look like hers. He was closer to coming than he'd have thought possible after just a few strokes. So close that, when his eyes landed on her silhouette on the steps, he almost kept going. Almost.

But the figure let out a shocked, ladylike gasp, and instead of finishing, he pulled the blanket back over himself, stilled, breathing hard, and waited.

"ABBY?" LUC SOUNDED STRANGLED.

Abby swallowed, tried to reply, and then shook her head.

"What are…" He sounded tortured and a bit shocked. "What do you need?"

He shifted, the movement nothing like that frantic self-flagellation she'd been mesmerized by for those few seconds before he'd seen her.

Need? Goodness, what didn't she need right now? She needed lessons, firstly, on how to navigate all the newness and these frighteningly raw sensations. How could she have known that the sight of a man doing things to himself would shake her so thoroughly?

She opened her mouth again and tried to speak, only her voice was gone. Broken apart, dried up, and splintered into hot shards embedded in her throat. In fact, there was nothing left in the bright, hollow upper half of her body, only a shell of craving. *Thirst* beyond anything she'd ever known.

Her bottom half, though, was different. Everything

below her stomach was warm and full, weighted down by that same hunger—only there, it was swollen and plush, hefty with her desire. And she was wet. Absolutely soaking through the trousers she wore, making them uncomfortably damp against her skin.

"You. I need you, Luc."

He sucked in a harsh breath but didn't say anything.

She moved slowly, almost despite herself, toward the sofa, her eyes glued to that man. She sank to the sofa beside him, close enough to smell him.

"You were supposed to stay upstairs." The words were like bright slaps, lighting her up in places she'd never fully explored.

"I don't want to stay upstairs. I came down to tell you that I understood if you didn't want me, but..." She took him in, from the wild halo of hair around his head to the broad, tense shoulders, over his flushed face with that scar she wanted to lick. "But you do want me, right?" When he looked to the side without answering, she went on. "I don't want you to protect me from yourself, Luc. I've been protected enough, okay? Over and over and over again, I've been told what I should and should not do—for my own good, you see. Always for my own good. And I'm done with that. You think being with you would be bad for me? I can take that. In fact, I want it." He was watching her now, eyes glittering on hers. Feeling brazen and raw, she lifted her hand and set it on his knee, saying, "Show me what you were doing under there, Luc. I want to see. *Please.*"

On a muttered curse, he reached a hard hand out, hooked her behind the neck, and pulled her closer, bringing her face near to his. His breath was harsh against her cheek, but even those agonized puffs meant something. They confirmed that he *did* want her.

"I want to help," she finally managed to eke out, breathless and hoarse. "I've never… I didn't know men did that. Will you show me?"

His hand started rubbing audibly up and down his… his… She didn't have a word for this. No words for the motion she could hear, could imagine but couldn't see. She was dying to see. "What do I do?"

Touch me, she wanted him to tell her.

His face, when he finally spoke, was a picture of reluctant submission, as if she'd forced his hand somehow. "Take off that shirt." The words zapped her, lit her up, made all the soft parts of her body feel stiff and painfully alive.

Wordlessly, hands shaking, she reached for the back of the shirt, shook it forward, and let the sleeves slide down her arms. Oh, how odd that showing her body would make her want *him* more.

This is it. My succumbing.

No. Not succumbing. Overcoming.

The thought was unclouded, her decision self-aware, this descent into depravity utterly *hers*.

And oh, that got her wetter, screwed her up tighter, and made her ache for more.

Eager now, she flung the fabric away. He stopped moving and exhaled audibly, his jittery eyes flicking over her.

"I want…" he started, one hand frozen in midair. A glance down showed her braid, a thick rope draped over one breast. "Take it down for me? Please?"

She pulled the strands apart, letting her hair cascade over her shoulders, and he started moving again, slowly, the sound of his palm rough and explicit in the fire's warm glow.

Just as she opened her mouth to ask what was next, he grated out words, raw and vulgar and almost incomprehensible to her ears.

"Pinch your…"

She frowned in those few moments before she understood. The sizzle of shock worked its way from those two sharp points, all the way to that unbearably empty place between her legs. She lifted her hands, almost afraid to touch herself. She was so sensitive, so needy. But his rasped "Do it," in that voice, with that accent, and that look on his face, compelled her.

She tweaked her own nipples as Luc looked on, his eyes somehow watchful and lazy all at once. As she moved, she couldn't even begin to picture the other times she'd been touched. What she'd done before— even with Benji—had absolutely nothing in common with this ocean of sensuality. It felt deep and limitless in a way she couldn't begin to describe. This felt inevitable, natural.

Right.

She moaned, the sound as tortured as the man before her, and he stopped. But Lord, why did he look so angry, still, as if she'd cornered him and made him do horrible things?

And I haven't even touched him.

"What do you want me to—"

"Would you…take the pants off?"

Oh. Oh no, she couldn't do that, be completely

unclothed, and wet to boot. Goodness, what would he think of all that wetness between her legs? He'd think she was—

"You don't have to, Abby." Funny how those words made her want to.

"You're right. I don't." But she did want to. Lord, wasn't having a choice the most addictive thing in the world? Their eyes caught and held, shared something profound.

It lit her up as surely as her fingers on her breasts.

Shoving away the doubt—not easy when there was a lifetime of shame to get through—she stood before him and pulled off the pants he'd loaned her.

He let out a breathy groan that sounded like it hurt. When her eyes went to his, she saw exactly what had brought it on. That place between her legs was glistening with need, her hairs curled and visibly damp. She hurried to cover herself, but Luc, fast as lightning, moved to still her wrist, just grazing her in the process. That wisp of contact—barely a breeze over the light hairs there—was enough to still her. It also broke through the wall he'd built between them. The wall that had allowed them to talk and move and touch themselves but hadn't even hinted at this connection.

Oh, but they'd known about the connection. They'd felt it before, every time they'd touched. Only now it went from thrilling to something bigger, more electric, harsh and almost unbearable in its intensity.

He didn't make a move. Abby, mesmerized by her outrageous desires, slid her wrist into that sandpaper hand.

It took him a while to grasp her. Long, slow seconds,

thicker than heartbeats. One…two… With a twitch, his hand tightened.

He'll do it now. The thought came out of nowhere. *He'll put it in me. All business, like Hamish.*

But no—with Hamish there'd been no zinging and need and emptiness. There hadn't even been a discussion when he'd done it.

This time, she wanted it. This time, it was her doing it. The two of them.

She let him coax her up and over his reclining body, too far, until that wet place hovered directly over his face. He eyed her hungrily before grasping her bottom and urging her back down, right onto his face.

She screamed when his mouth hit her there. Not a breathy sound, like the others, but a tormented *ah* that had Le Dog lifting his head by the fire.

He pulled back. "You want me to stop?"

"Stop?" she gasped. "No! Goodness no! Show me what's next."

Like a starving man, he dove back into her body. If she'd thought the sensations were too much before, now they were… Oh Lord, it was sheer decadence, what he did, his face in her…in her… Oh, goodness, what was it called? It was too much, too much.

His tongue slid along her center, then up, up, so soft and—she let out another sound, this time darker, the sensation so sharp where he was that she knew she'd go there. To that place she'd been once or twice with her hand between her legs. This would be with Luc, though, humming into her flesh, consuming her in a way that was earthy and demanding and inexorable. She'd die, she knew, if he pushed her too far. So, hands scrabbling at his head, she yanked at his hair. "Stop, stop, no, stop," she begged.

He pulled back with a groan and shifted her down a few inches, his face lost and hungry and shining with wetness. Her wetness, she knew, the thought as thrilling as it was mortifying. He let her wipe him off with a swipe of her hand, and then he trapped her hand and held it while he ran his tongue from her palm to fingertip.

He's licking my juices. The realization hit her hard in the gut, and her womb clenched down.

"You ruin me, Abby." The words sounded puzzled and a bit lost.

Abby opened her mouth to apologize and froze. She could never go back to the lies and denial—to that life she'd been bred to believe in.

Her answer, when it came, was from deep down inside—that bright, little heart of a sinner.

"What do we do next?"

This was Luc's problem. This uncontrollable yearning to feel things—things he'd gotten away with avoiding these past couple of years. He didn't just want to touch and feel this woman's body—he wanted to throw her over his shoulder and ransack her. Not just experience her, but consume. He'd held on until tonight, but then he'd gotten his mouth on her, and he was gone.

There were women who wanted this sexual voraciousness, he knew, but not Abby. He would never do that to Abby. He'd rather shut himself down, tie himself up...disappear.

But then she sat back, eyes glittering, and asked for more. *What do we do next?* A siren's song of pleasure.

"What do you want to do?" he asked. "What do you feel like?"

"How do I... I don't know."

He swallowed, taking her in where she sat astride him—those breasts that were soft and warm and heavy, her skin lighter than he'd imagined, her nipples sharpened by desire. Her smell was different from any other woman he'd been intimate with—pure in its humanity. She was sweet musk, unadorned—unadulterated by the chemical stink of perfume or fancy shampoo.

Face crinkling, she asked, "If we were normal—and I know we're not," she added with a smile, "what would you do?"

He half shrugged and swallowed. "I'd touch you, probably. Find out what you like."

"Do that, then."

"I like this." He worked his hand out from under her and ran it over the underside of one breast. It was plump and pale and so soft. From there, he let his hand slide away and ran his knuckles down to the slight swell of her belly, around to one lush, freckled hip, and then did a slow, rasping drag up her arm, over her shoulder, to her neck.

Christ, this neck had haunted him—so slender and sweet, untouched by the sun. He shifted her down so their crotches lined up, with just the blanket separating them. From there, he sat up a bit, bringing their torsos close and letting him breathe her in.

The sounds that she made spoke of undeniable pleasure, arousal, and surprise. When he caught her eye, she shook her head and looked away.

He wished, in that moment, that he was a different sort of man. One who knew the right words, could spout a line or two of poetry.

"*Qu'est-ce qu'il y a, chérie*? What is it?"

His hand cradled her throat as she swallowed. "I didn't know."

"Know what?"

"What I was missing."

"This is good? When I touch you?"

"Better than good."

His smile was satisfied as he ran his hand from her nape, along that braid, and down her back, where it brushed a bandage.

Everything stopped.

Everything except for the pop of the fire and the crazed whimpers she made while she rocked against him.

He blinked, reality setting back in. Her scent and her taste and the sight of her eager and open had made him forget those marks on her back.

He sat still, upended and suspended—on the cusp of so many things.

Breathing hard, he waited, cock pulsing, painfully close to that tight, hot promise.

He wasn't sure he actually wanted to know when he asked, "Will you tell me what they did to you?"

"Right now? That would kind of ruin the moment, wouldn't it?" She gave him a forced-looking smile.

"I don't want to hurt you, Abby."

She shook her head. "You won't."

"How can you be su—"

Her weight shifted, and she leaned into him, hands tight on his shoulders, face inches away. "I know what it's like, Luc, to be taken without an ounce of excitement or desire. I know how it feels to be a duty and nothing else. To be used for my body in the worst possible way." Those strange animal eyes caressed his face. "Could we stop talking about this? I want to do something for the sheer pleasure of it. At least once in my life." God, how could she be so innocent and yet not? He couldn't get his mind around that.

"But what of"—he grazed her shoulder with his thumb—"what of your back?"

"Can we do…" She paused and looked to the side, awkward for the first time since they'd started. "When you…licked me. It didn't hurt."

On a hot exhalation, Luc reached up and tweaked her nipple—just a little. "Does that hurt?"

She shivered and shook her head, her gaze glued to his hand as it slid down to cup her sex, where his fingers found her clit and circled it. He watched the goose bumps perk up across her skin.

"What about this?" he whispered, entranced by her reactions. She was so pure in her pleasure.

A low *oh* emerged from her half-open mouth.

"*Hein*? What, Abby?" he teased, taking hold of her hips to line her up with the outline of his cock and slide against her, up and back. The movement was so wonderfully sexual that it made him want more—he wanted to see.

"It's good. So good." As if reading his mind, she reached for the blanket separating them and tugged it down, lifting herself up to shove it out of the way. When she sank back down, her bare, slick heat slid against his cock with explicit perfection, and he thought he'd die.

The woman needed no direction. She put her hands on his chest and slid up and back, up and back, each slide bringing him closer to coming.

He eventually tore his attention away from the silky glide of their sexes long enough to take in her face.

"You're beautiful, Abby. So beautiful."

"I want…" She was out of breath, her eyes vague.

He let his hands guide her hips for a few beats, marveling at how she soaked him down there. "What, *cherie*? What do you want?"

"Oh Lord, I can't say it."

"Then how will I know?"

He continued to move, even when she slanted forward and hid her face in his shoulder. "I'm not…I'm not even sure how to…" They both made a low sound when the head of his cock notched right at her entrance, stopping everything but the beating of their hearts. She turned her head into the crook of his neck and whispered, "I'm so bad. I shouldn't want this, but I do."

"Yes?" He was practically gasping when he spoke now, his control a pathetic, frayed thing. No surprise after years of abstinence. Looking at her, he amended that thought. It wasn't the years without sex that made him lose it. It was this woman. Unfettered desire, utterly unashamed. She was perfection, sexier than anything he'd seen in his life. "Tell me what it is that you want, *ma belle*." For a man who had no time for words, he suddenly wanted them badly. What would she call this? Would the descriptions sound dirty tumbling from her perfectly curved lips?

"I want you to"—she swallowed, the sound dry in the quiet room, and the rest of her words were a barely audible whisper, just a hot puff of air against his earlobe—"put it in me. *Please.*"

His balls, hot and tight, came close to exploding at those words. It was the most delightfully filthy thing he'd heard in his entire life.

He'd just reached down to take himself in hand when a thought cut in. *Condom.* How had that escaped him? What was he thinking? That would be ruination of an entirely different sort.

This woman stole his breath away and shut his brain off.

"We need a condom," he said, squeezing her hip. "I have some in the bathroom."

"I don't…I don't know what that is."

"No?" For some reason, that made him laugh—just a soft chuckle of affection that turned into a kiss, languorous and warm as the fire.

How the hell am I going to survive once she leaves?

He pushed back the thought as fast as it had come.

Finally, he extricated himself from her embrace, ignoring the chill as he shifted out from under her, and said, "I'll show you."

He stood and pulled his pants back up before walking to the bathroom.

It was too bright while he rooted around in the medicine cabinet for the box he hoped hadn't expired. He'd bought them shortly after arriving here, although even then, he'd figured it would take a miracle to actually find someone with whom he'd use them. He almost laughed at that. It *had* taken a miracle, hadn't it? A woman literally falling—if not in his lap, at least on his land.

After what felt like an eternity, he found them, closed

the medicine cabinet door…and there he was, his face in the mirror an ugly thing.

Strange how many thoughts could race through a person's mind at the same time. A picture of her on his sofa, wanton and wanting, immediately transposed by that feeling he got when he had to deal with too many people at once—a flash of something close to panic. But he wasn't sure if it was because of those lunatics over the hill, just waiting to destroy her—and him—or if it was the idea of her leaving after this.

Staring hard at himself—through the sun damage and the scar from that last fight with Olivier—he wondered what the hell she saw in him. A savior, probably. A doorway out of here.

In his hand, the condom crinkled, and he blinked hard at it for a second or two.

Leaving the bathroom door open for the swath of light it offered, he returned to stand in front of where she still sat on the sofa, condom package in hand and heart in his throat. Something about the way she watched him from under the blanket, eyes fogged up with incomprehension and lust, made him stop.

"Is it me you want?" he asked.

"Excuse me?"

"Or is it just sex on your terms that you need?"

Something in her shifted, and she ran narrowed eyes over him from top to bottom and back up to his face again.

"Would it make a difference?" she asked, her expression hard.

"Yes. Yes, I think it would."

Gathering the blanket to her chest, she leaned

forward, crooking her finger for him to get down to her level. He squatted.

"I could ask the same of you, couldn't I, Luc?" He blinked. "Am I just a convenient happenstance? Naked and ready and in your house?"

"God no. You're…" He sucked in a breath and admitted what he'd been trying to deny since the moment he'd laid eyes on her. "You're everything." What he'd meant was "you're innocent perfection," but that wasn't right either, because he didn't care about virginity in a woman. He wanted a different sort of purity. He wanted her because she'd never play games, and he'd had enough of those for a lifetime. He wanted her unadulterated beauty, her guileless desire, her truthfulness.

She huffed out a disbelieving laugh and slid a hand down his scarred cheek, while something inside of Luc loosened, maybe even disappeared entirely.

"All right, then." Her eyes went to the condom crushed in his hand. "Why don't you show me what that's all about?"

He turned to kiss her palm and imagined—for just one second—how this could be if she stayed. If, one day, they stopped using condoms. He'd build onto the cabin and… No point, though, was there? For her safety. For his.

Throwing off the fantasy, he asked, "You've never seen one?"

She shook her head.

"This is to keep you…us…from having a"—he swallowed back another totally misplaced wave of regret—"a baby."

She blinked. "Oh."

"Men put it on for birth control. But also against disease." Was that hesitation on her face? "We don't have to do this if you don't want."

"I've never…" Oh hell. What was she going to say? "I've only ever done this with the…man on top."

"But you've done it?"

"Yes." She paused, pursed her lips, and lifted that strong chin. "Or it's been done *to me*, I guess."

He shoved away the anger that brought up in him and focused on the other thing. She wasn't a virgin. That was a relief. She was a virgin, though, when it came to pleasure. That notion got him riled up again. He could be the one to give her pleasure for the first time. And with that excitement came a sense of responsibility.

"Okay." He swallowed and rose from the floor to settle onto the sofa beside her. Eyes on her disheveled body. "*You* do it. You're in charge."

"Me? I couldn't. I'd—" She stopped, her expression a caricature of denial and then…excitement? She smiled. "*Really?*" Her whisper covered him like a caress, and all he could do was nod and smile back. Had anyone ever looked at him like that? Like he was something to be enjoyed, not just the other way around?

"Yes. You can do it. It does not have to be me."

Her gaze turned greedy, her eyes more potent than the touch of her hand.

"I don't…I don't know how to start."

"We don't have to do the condom right away," he offered, wanting to kick himself. "We can…do whatever you want. What do you want, Abby?"

∼∾∽

Abby was finally doing what she'd once been accused of: defiling a man. And it was glorious. This time, she couldn't seem to dredge up any guilt over it. All she could find was excitement, warm and electrifying.

Never mind that she was sitting naked with a man. Being unclothed was a novel feeling as it was, but to be close enough to feel his body warmth was… Drawing in a shuddering breath, she shifted closer. It was exhilarating and frightening and liberating all at once.

"What do I do first?"

He sounded breathy when he asked, "What do you want to do?"

"I want *you* to take off your shirt. I want to see the rest of you."

"Help me do it," he said, the words sharp spikes of need between her legs. "Undo my shirt. *Please.*"

With trembling hands, she leaned over, reveling in the brush of her breast against his arm, and undid one pale button at a time, until he sat there in a tighter, long-sleeved top.

"Will you help me with this one?" She pulled at the fabric.

Almost impatiently, he yanked the cotton over his head and—

"Oh, goodness." Abby was without words. She let her eyes take him in. The warm humanity of him was so different close up—breathtaking and a bit intimidating, but above all, real. She'd underestimated his size, somehow assuming that layers of clothing added to him. Instead, he was bigger, more physical than she'd imagined. His wide chest was packed tight with muscle, so vital that she ached to taste it.

"Good or bad?" Was that insecurity in his eyes?

"Oh, heavens, you're lovely." That made him laugh. A rough bark of a sound, loud in this enclosed place.

"Can I..." She lifted a hand.

"Go on."

Heat simmered off him, palpable before their skin even met.

First, she touched the hair she'd seen from afar, sprinkled across his skin in a pattern whose perfection was no doubt dictated by God. She brushed over it lightly, expecting it to be coarse.

"Soft," she murmured before bending forward and setting the side of her forehead against the center of his chest. His heartbeat thumped against her temple, connecting them somehow even deeper.

He let out a strangled noise but made no move to touch her, which was both a frustration and a relief.

Slow as syrup, she nudged him with her nose, drew him in—here, where his smell was potent and addictive—and let her lips rest on skin that was burning up. His heartbeat turned frantic, the rise and fall of his lungs fast, his breath shaky.

"Is this good?"

"Yes," he breathed.

Abby pulled away, eyeing his tiny, brown nipples.

"What do I do next?"

"You tell me."

"I want to do the bottom, too."

Standing, he helped her pull down his trousers, baring long, muscular legs, with a sprinkling of black hair that she wanted to feel...against her face, if he'd let her. Lord, Isaiah was right. She was utterly licentious.

That made her smile, the guilt softened by the firelight and the affection in this man's eyes.

Shifting back gave her the chance to take him all in,
everything from the broad expanse of his shoulders, down
over arms sculpted out of something harder than flesh and
blood, to those hands, every inch of him taut and full of
energy. But oh, those hands. What could they make her
feel? She imagined how it would have been if she'd been
given to this man in marriage instead of Hamish. Would
she have felt differently, then? Would climbing into bed
at night have been a pleasure rather than a chore?

"It's too dark in here," she said.

"For what?"

"I can't…see you properly."

With a half-strangled chuckle, he went over to turn
on the lamp, casting more light on his body, along with
a good dose of hesitation.

"What am I supposed to do next?"

"You're asking me, Abby?"

"I don't understand how this works," she said,
frustrated.

"What?"

"There's this impulse in me, like an itch I need to
scratch. What do I do with it?"

Now she was the one pleading.

Dropping his chin, he seemed to gather himself, the
muscles along his shoulders such a solid frame for his
indecision. But when he looked back at her, something
in him had changed. His eyes were bright, his jaw tight,
his next words a bright, red flag in the air.

He sat back down beside her. "Use me." His voice
was low and eager. "Use me to figure it out."

She didn't need a second invitation. Life was moving too fast as it was. She needed to get Sammy out and disappear, so this could be her only chance, over in the blink of an eye. She swallowed back the lump of regret that formed in her throat.

Funny, though, because the progression to this moment had actually been long and slow. She'd watched him for years, memorized his shape—from far away, at least. Above the neck, she knew every line, scar, and freckle. Every frown, every questioning curve of the brow. But she knew only one facet—like smelling a meal and never getting to taste. She wanted more. And Lord, wasn't that just her in a nutshell? *More, more, always more*, Mama would say.

Now, she was assailed by the prospect of tastes and smells and the feel of him under her skin. All of the experimentation and discovery she could do with that body at her disposal.

She voiced her last remaining fear. "What if I do it wrong?"

"There is no wrong."

"And if you don't like it?"

He smirked. "I'll like it. What does your body tell you to do, Abby?"

Everything! her skin screamed, nerve endings so alive that even the burns truly hurt for the first time after being numb for hours. But it didn't matter. The pain was sensation, and that was key.

She didn't answer. Instead, she scooted closer to him, subconsciously licking her lips, as if admiring a feast spread out. From the top of his windblown hair to the bottom of his toes, she wanted this man.

He patted his knee. "Come here." She hesitated, and he went on. "Put your leg up and over."

With alacrity, she hooked one leg over him, straddling him so that their sexes fit snuggly together, with just the fabric of his underwear between them. The need to rock her hips and rub against him was too strong to resist, and she shuddered as pleasure ran up her spine, something like an ache settling in her belly.

Her body took over, leaving her mind behind to watch in shock from her perch above him. The noise she made was primal and ugly as her hands tore at Luc's hair. Luc, instead of being offended or hurt or angry, as she'd imagine any other man would be, seemed just as hungry. His eyes ate her up, and his hands guided her, urging her this way and that, all the while fulfilling his promise to let her do the doing.

He shifted below her, his movements almost frenzied as he rubbed and rubbed. She answered in kind, her body making the decisions her mind hadn't yet considered.

But my body is *me*, she recognized. She took the idea and owned it, letting it light her up from the tips of her fingers to the depths of her soul.

It shimmered inside, that sensation, high and floating and spinning in the air. It settled into her limbs until they grew limper with every new shift of her hips, every lifting of his. All the while, he watched her with those deep-sea eyes. Playing her, accompanying her, coaxing her body for more, until there was nothing left to give, and she slumped forward against him. The pleasure was almost too much to bear, but something was still missing.

"Luc, I want…"

"What, *mon coeur*? What?" He was breathing hard,

his face tense and concentrated, the look of him...
Goodness, was there anything more lovely than the
expression on this man's face? So serious as his gaze
flicked to hers, then down to his hands on her body, then
farther to where they connected—or nearly, if it wasn't
for that cloth barrier. Sucking in a breath full of their
combined, earthy scent, she glanced down.

In shock, she took in how lewd it all was—that
navy-blue cotton stained by her. She couldn't tear her
eyes away.

"Fuck me, Abby," Luc begged, sounding nothing like
himself. The same voice, familiar but lost. Abby blinked
in shock at that word.

"I don't..." She swallowed. "I don't know how."

"Up," he ordered, swatting at her bottom. It was too
gentle to hurt, but the sting echoed with pleasure.

Using his shoulders as a support, she pushed up
to kneeling and watched as he shifted, pulled down
his shorts, and used his hand to lift his...his what?
Frustration swept up inside of her. She didn't even know
the words for these things. *Manhood*, she'd heard, but
that sounded stilted and wrong.

"What do I call your...your..." She reached out, gingerly, and ran a finger up it.

"*Ma bite*? In English, people say 'cock.'"

"Your cock," she said, eyeing it on a satisfied exhale,
hovering somewhere between hunger and uncertainty.
That was what Hamish had put inside of her? No. No, it
couldn't be. This was so much bigger...more imposing,
and appealing. She yearned to taste it.

Could she? He'd put his mouth on her, hadn't he?
Could she maybe just...

"It's big, Luc." It hadn't looked nearly that big against his hand earlier.

He stilled, his expression somewhere between pride and uncertainty.

"Oh yes?"

"Can Ic"

It was strange, the things that occurred to her as she took him in hand. It was surprisingly heavy, the skin softer than her own. Every part of him was hard and scarred and callused, but not here. Not this sweet, intimate place. There was no give, which was fascinating. And there, at the tip, was a clear bead of fluid. She ran a thumb over it, then, eyes on his, lifted it to her mouth for a taste. Salty.

Her only warning before Luc took over was a groan, so desperate it clawed at her insides and made her nipples ache. Apparently, the time for exploration was past. In a frenzy, he grasped her hips and pulled her back above him, took hold of himself, and ran it up against that aching, soaked place in her body. He moved himself—his *cock*—back down, up and down a few times, lighting her up with every glancing touch against that magical spot. He stroked himself to a glistening shine before notching tightly to her, his one hand squeezing, tight, tight, tight, his eyes flying to arrest against hers, waiting. On the edge.

"Wait," he breathed, more to himself than to her. "Wait. Hold on. Condom." His hand searched the sofa, sliding between the cushions and coming out with the foil square. He ripped it open, gripped himself, and pumped hard a couple of times before rolling the ring all the way on. "Okay. Now, you do it. Lift up, and I'll…" He swallowed audibly. "You can take me inside."

She glanced up at those words to catch him biting his lip, his eyes concentrated hard on that place where their bodies met, and steadied herself with a hand on his shoulder. Slowly, full of defiance and excitement but not an iota of fear, she lowered her body onto Luc's.

An animal sound came straight from her chest as he pressed in, in. It felt dirty, but in the best possible way as his body worked its way into hers. There was no pain, though, no cringing hesitation, nothing even remotely resembling duty in this taking. *And who's taking whom anyway?* she asked herself as she took him in, swallowed him up. There was a moment when the big, blunt crown of him caught at her opening, that she felt a hitch of something familiar—more of a stretching than pain. But one look at his eyes, so intent and so warm, brought her back to the here and the now, where desire reigned supreme. So she gave in to the pressure of his hand on her thigh and let her baser instincts guide her down, his body easing into hers, filling her and bringing her pleasure like nothing she'd ever felt.

His expression, though—good God, the man looked shocked and pained and suspended, mouth hanging open. His lips were ripe and as needy as her whole body, just begging for a kiss that she couldn't give him, because she couldn't move. She was stuck, impaled, waiting for the next tiny advance, the thick, thick reality of her body accepting another.

"Oh, Luc." She shuddered as her bottom finally settled on the top of his thighs and their chests came together with a different sort of friction, the tingling of her tight nipples like sparks in her veins. Somehow, her insides tightened even further around him. He groaned, bent forward enough to put his teeth on the cord that connected the top of her shoulder to her neck and bit.

He moved, fingers tight on her bottom, lifting and drawing back down, every slide hitting something inside and forcing her tighter, tighter.

"I want," she gasped, with no idea what the next words would be. None.

Only he seemed to get it, because he muttered, "*Oui, c'est ça*. Keep moving," while one of his hands shifted forward, to the place where their bodies came together, and pressed that tiny, wonderful, sharp place.

She screamed, *screamed*, because the shock of it was electrifying.

Luc met her eyes, looking almost surprised, before concentrating on that place even more, his fingers agile.

"Fuck, Abby, I've got to come."

She looked at his face, all flushed and drawn. "Come?" she asked, bleary-eyed.

"Climax. Orgasm." The words emerged as quick, staccato shots. They felt perfect and dirty.

"When the…" She swallowed, not understanding any of it, just rolling her hips against his. The sofa beneath them squeaked with every bounce of their bodies, and even that sound made her hotter, weaker, closer to that… thing. "That thing when the *procreation* happens?"

Apparently that wasn't right, because he huffed out a laugh, but the sound was more self-deprecating than insulting. She felt the vibration inside her.

"Oh, yes. *Procreation*. How to… I… My *cock*… It spurts out fluid. In French, it's called *jouir*. *Jouissance* means…'enjoyment' or 'pleasure.'"

"For me?" She didn't even understand what she meant by that.

"Yes. Yes, you can do it, too." He breathed through a particularly tight twist of her hips and worked his hand harder between their bodies. "*Jouissance*. Joy."

"Oh," she said as he hit her in that spot again. Pulling back, she watched him work at her, shocked by the visuals that she'd been missing for years. She was close enough to that climax to feel it approach, rumbling toward her fast and furious and inevitable.

"It's coming," she whispered, and he nodded.

"You feel so fucking good." He looked down, concentrated on what his hand was doing. "You hear that?" he growled, and she did. The sloppy, wet smack of their joining was slightly mortifying and exceptionally arousing.

His fingers tweaked her again and again as they slipped and slid through her. She moved on him, less of an up and down and more an internal clenching as their bodies lost control and the want took over. As her climax arrived, bigger and stronger than anything she'd had to endure, she leaned in and put her lips to his, eating his moans and breaths and uncontrollable joy.

She reached it—that crest—pressing down onto him, his hips straining up to meet hers and tightening against her as she clamped him inside, mouth to mouth, forehead to forehead. Just as she blinked the first wave of pleasure away, the lights went out with a bang, leaving them in total silence and utter darkness. Abby tingled from her fingers to her toes as she sat out of breath, the two of them all alone in the world.

20

"Did we do that?" Abby asked. She was collapsed over him, warm and perfect.

"Make the power go out?" Luc smiled, his cock just starting to soften inside her. He didn't want to pull out, didn't want to leave her, but he'd have to. *Just a little while longer.* "Possibly. Probably," he managed to say and tightened his arms around her.

She snuggled into him and sighed. At his spot beside the woodstove, Le Dog woofed lightly.

"Was that—"

"Are you—"

They both spoke at once and fell into a lazy, giddy sort of laugh, although hers was more of a giggle. Luc couldn't remember being this happy in…forever.

He angled his face toward hers and asked, "What were you going to say, *mon coeur*?"

"It's silly. I…"

"No, go on."

"I…I don't… What happens next?" she asked, and

he had the distinct impression that wasn't what she'd planned to say.

"I go turn on the barn generator so the wine won't freeze."

"No generator here?"

"I have never had anything I cared about keeping warm before." He gave her thigh a squeeze, feeling strange about this conversation that ignored everything they'd just done.

"And us?" He heard her swallow and waited a few seconds before realizing she'd meant them the first time. Their bodies. *What next* because she had no experience with a condom or any of those messy practicalities that modern women faced with so much aplomb.

"First," he said, pressing his softening cock deeper into her for one final, languorous taste, "you give me another kiss."

"Oh." She sounded slightly flustered until he bent his head, finding her mouth easily in the dark, and touched his lips to hers. Light kisses, a swipe of his lips, stroking tongues, and quick, noisy inhales. He was getting hard again inside her, which wouldn't be a good thing with the condom, so finally, he pulled away. "*Oh.*" Her voice this time was lazy and full of understanding, laced with humor.

"Next, I have to hold on to the condom, or we could have an accident."

"Okay."

He reached between them, eliciting a gasp when he ran his hand over her pussy to the place where their bodies came together. He pinched the latex against himself and nudged her until she shifted back.

"Where do you…put that?"

"In the trash. It clogs up the septic system, and these things never disintegrate." He paused. "We won't be able to bathe, with the pump not working. If you want a bath, you might be able to get what's left of the hot water, but you have to go now."

"Oh, that would be nice." She got up and stretched, her silhouette visible in the faint light of the fire.

"Does it hurt?"

"My back?" She tilted her head, seeming to consider. "Not really."

"Will you tell me what happened?"

Another hesitation. "It was the only way."

"What?" When she didn't answer, he advanced on her. "The only way what?"

"The only way I could think of to make sure I could leave."

"But they did this to you, yes?"

"I let them."

"Let them?"

"I accepted it."

"I don't understand."

"I accepted the Mark. If I hadn't… Not sure what he would've done."

Frustrated, Luc looked around for his flashlight or a candle or anything. What the hell could be worse than brand marks on her back?

"You mean you let them burn you? They hurt you in exchange for…not hurting you?"

"I pretended to repent. For my sins."

"And what were those?" He spread the blanket over her, pulled his underwear up his hips, and reached for his pants.

"Wanting to save Sammy. Wanting to leave."

He blinked, the anger swelling on a wave of understanding of what he'd done—he could feel its flush across his chest and face, prickly and uncomfortable. Somehow, he'd managed to forget the boy's visit. He'd pushed it out of his mind, which had made it easy not to mention it to Abby. He should tell her.

He threw on his clothes and loaded the fire up with logs. He dug his Maglite out from its drawer in the kitchen and handed it to Abby, who'd put on some clothes of her own.

"I don't want to leave, Abby, but I have to." She took the flashlight and fiddled with it for a moment before he showed her where to press.

"Lord, you must think I'm ridiculous."

"I think you're charming," he said, and watched the smile disappear from those lush lips. Something passed between them. It might have been awkwardness or embarrassment. Maybe for her it was an *oh shit, what have I done?* moment, but it felt different, more intimate than any post-sex experience he'd had before.

"I might be gone a while," he whispered, then leaned in to put his lips to hers in a quick kiss. It was meant to be chaste, with the secretive taste of the Sammy betrayal still in his mouth. But how could he keep it that way when she was so soft and smelled of sex? How could he resist the sounds she made?

And when had kisses been this sexy?

Never before Abby. Not once. Not Sandra Couron in the barn, not even when her cousin from Paris had joined them. He'd been, what, thirteen? And the girls more like seventeen. He'd always wondered why they'd chosen him and not the older, more handsome Olivier, who'd actually known what he was doing. It wasn't something he'd ever gone back to ask. Certainly not as an adult when he'd run into the exhausted-looking Sandra working the checkout line at the local Leclerc supermarket.

They kissed for a while, until finally he drew back to look at her, a knot of guilt sitting too large in his chest.

"I have to tell you something, Abby." He waited for her soft, blurred eyes to focus on him and then spoke. "Sammy did come here."

"What do you mean?"

"He made it here and then…then Isaiah came, with his men. They were armed to the gills and I…" He bent his head and rubbed his eyes at the memory. "He said he wanted to go with them, and they…they threatened you, Abby. And Sammy."

She swallowed, her eyes flicking back and forth at his. "He just went with them?"

A chill went through Luc as he remembered that moment—Isaiah's arm slithering around Sammy's neck. There'd been a threat there, but something else, too. Something almost gleeful. "Sammy was happy to go. He had no idea that his life was in danger."

"He's too good to understand people hurting one another."

"Does he know what they did to you?"

She shook her head and sounded fierce when she spoke—a mother hen protecting her chick. "I'd *never* let him see that."

"Of course you wouldn't." He smiled, wishing she'd touch him again, let him know he'd done the right thing. "I wanted to go out and find you, Abby."

"They had me locked up."

"I would have kept him if I could, but they would have killed him and—"

"I know," she whispered before reaching up to touch the side of his face, the rasp of her fingers against his stubble audible. "But he'll die anyway, if he stays there."

Luc shook his head. When had he felt this *responsible* for another person? It was a terrible feeling, really. Wonderful and terrible.

"I'll help you get him out." When she started to protest, he talked over her. "It's my fault he's back there. I'll go on my own if you won't let me help. You understand?" After a pause, he went on. "But you have to promise me one thing, Abby. You have to promise that you won't go until you're better and the weather clears. If I leave you here tonight and find that you've gone back over the mountain, I'll rush in after you and—"

"I won't go without you."

Luc stared at her hard. Was she lying?

"Promise me, Abby."

"I promise not to go without you."

"And not until you're well enough and we can leave this mountain, if necessary. If we get stuck up here with them after us…"

She nodded, shuddering. "I promise, Luc."

With a small huff, she put out a hand for him to shake. He shook it a few times, remembering that first handshake out in the middle of his vines. The feel of her hand in his that day had been like a door opening, letting sunshine into his life for the first time in years. He just hadn't known it then.

He didn't want to go up to the barn. He wanted to

take this woman—the best thing in his life—upstairs to
his bed. He wanted to lay her on her side and slide into
her from behind, face in that thick, red hair. Instead, he
leaned in for one last kiss, inhaling her scent so he'd have
something to take with him into the cold, snowy night.

God, he couldn't remember a woman tasting better
than this, couldn't bring up an occasion when he'd
wanted someone more. But he had to get the generator
up and running at the barn, so he pulled back and sent
her to the bathroom. He gave her another kiss, because
he couldn't help himself, and then left her alone.

Abby'd wanted to stay on that sofa forever, lolling around
in the vestiges of her excess, but Luc urged her to the
bathroom and into a shallow, steamy bath before leaving
her alone with a burning candle and that little flashlight.

Alone with this body, this hedonistic shell she'd been
blessed with.

She was languorous still, and slick down there, the
pleasure taking ages to seep out of her. It wasn't until she
started to slide down into the water that reality returned:
her back, a mess; Sammy, out there still. The power was
out, which made no difference in her world, but now she
was alone here and that did. It wasn't until Luc was gone
that she realized just how safe he made her feel.

Which was ridiculous, wasn't it, so close to the
Church? And Sammy hadn't been safe here, had he?

Chilled now, she washed quickly, got out of the bath,
and turned to her dim reflection in the mirror. Mirrors
were not something they had at the Church of the
Apocalyptic Faith. Mirrors were for sinners.

She twisted, trying to catch a glimpse of her back and worrying about that unpleasant numbness.

It didn't hurt. She hadn't lied to Luc about that, but that was because it was numb—not necessarily a good sign, although it could have something to do with the wine she'd drunk. The memory of that wine gave her a tight thrill in her abdomen. Would he give her more tomorrow? Would he do that…touching himself again? Would he kiss her in that deep, lewd manner she'd never guessed would feel so good?

Or maybe I'll do things to him, she thought, looking directly into those eyes in the glass and seeing nothing familiar there. He'd put his face down there. A long, slow shiver worked its way through her, leaving her skin pebbled with goose bumps.

Could I do that to him?

With another shiver, she pushed that thought aside and forced herself to concentrate on her back.

It was numb and stiff, despite the days that had passed since they'd marked her. The best sign that things were improving, she'd found, was when it started to itch. Right now, she felt nothing.

Squinting in the low light, she eyed one of the topmost burns. That yellow tinge couldn't be good.

Was it getting worse?

No. Her arms had healed just fine. She'd be fine now.

No matter what, there'd be no police. No hospitals. No authorities.

One time, years before, someone had called Child Protective Services on the Church. Goodness, she'd been just a kid back then. Ten or so. Those people had shown up with their badges, police with their lights and guns. She and the other kids had been told to sit in the Hall, to smile and sing. So they had. They'd sung every hymn they knew, while the police took them out, one at a time, leading them to one of the cabins, where they asked all sorts of questions. Stuff about touching and beatings and food and school.

The police had come up empty-handed and eventually left. But beneath the fear of separation from Mama and the Church and everything she knew and trusted was the knowledge—even at that young age—that if anything was to happen, if there was to be any sort of confrontation at all, they would all be forced to endure God's Wrath.

It wasn't until recently that she'd fully understood what that meant. The adults wouldn't go down without a fight. And the ones who tried to get away... Well, Abby remembered Becca Bernstrom—barely. She'd had the cutest twins—two itty-bitty girls, born early, their heads like warm apples. The birth hadn't gone well, and her husband, Richard, had wanted to take Becca and the babies to a hospital. There'd been a fuss in the Center— Becca's blood and her husband's shouts. She remembered watching the family leave in the Church station wagon, disappearing down the drive toward town.

There'd been gunshots.

After that, the twins came back to be raised in the nursery, but their parents never resurfaced. Gone to a better place, everyone said, and she'd thought for the longest time that they meant some other town.

That didn't seem likely anymore.

Abby did her best to resalve her back before dressing, feeding the woodstove, and heading back upstairs to crawl into Luc's bed, chilled by more than the air. Again, her thoughts returned to the other side of the mountain.

What were they doing? Was Sammy okay?

Goodness, how could she be here, partaking in earthly delights, while he could have had one of his seizures again? When he could be hungry and ignored?

Luc's bed smelled like him, which warmed her almost as much as the blankets she crawled under, but even that wasn't enough to keep her mind from wandering back there, over and over.

And what about you, Mama? Are you worried? Did you search for me? Do you wish you'd done something to stop the branding this time?

Abby shivered, wishing for more blankets. Where was the one she'd given him?

And then back to Mama: Did she wish, like Abby, that they'd never come here to begin with?

Although Abby couldn't regret it, could she? Not with the things she'd experienced.

Not with tonight. Hesitant, she reached a hand down to that place between her legs. His had a name, but what, she wondered, did they call it for a woman? A hen, perhaps? That made her smile. Sliding a hand inside the big pants he'd loaned her, she marveled at how much pleasure it could give her.

Slowly, she let her fingers explore in a way she'd never done before, all the Church's complicated garments making skin-to-skin touching nearly impossible. Oh, she'd pressed there, through cotton, and felt things, but not like this. Not explicitly, with the memory of a man holding himself in his hand for pleasure. *Thinking of me.*

Did all women know about that little spot? She pressed it with a shuddery breath.

In Luc's warm bed, surrounded by his scent, she explored herself: her breasts, heavier than God would have wanted. They'd bounced as she'd moved atop Luc earlier, and she'd caught the way his eyes watched—so intently. He'd looked at her hungrily, and she understood that hunger, could feel it surging through her body, from that warm, heavy, pulsing core to her tingling fingertips.

Sinner. The voice whispered in her head, the notion of sensuality so linked to being bad that she wasn't sure she'd ever be able to separate them entirely.

But what she'd done hadn't felt sinful tonight, had it? It had been as joyous as the hymns they sang at Church.

A thought burst through her mind, a flash in a sea of uncertainty: What if sinning was just another part of life? What if it was okay to sin?

That would be... Lord, it would be beautiful, wouldn't it? If you took the person, the whole person, as they were—if you strove for goodness, kindness, empathy, but the things you did with your body were your own? Eating and drinking and...fucking. He'd said it earlier and she'd heard it before. Oh, that word alone felt sinfully perfect, sliding along her nerve endings and reminding her of the man who'd blown all this wide open for her. Luc. Bringer of Light.

With a deep sigh, she flipped from her side onto her belly and sank her face into the pillow, to suck in his smell the way she'd soaked up his caresses. The way she'd taken in his body.

And on a lazy haze that felt almost happy, she recognized how much she'd like to do it again.

⚬∾

The stupid generator wouldn't start. Which meant Luc had to light the fire in the barn fireplace and keep it stoked, which just barely kept the place from freezing. If the sun came out in the morning, he'd be fine. Everything would be fine. He'd just have to spend the night here.

He got the fire up and running and returned to the cabin to tell Abby before heading back to settle in front of the barn fire on Abby's quilt.

The sun emerged at daybreak, thank God, bright and brassy and piercing.

Exhausted and grumpy, Luc tried to start up the generator again—without any luck—before making his way back down to the cabin, Le Dog at his heels. He'd have to set up a proper bed in the barn for tonight if this continued.

As he got closer to the cabin, he was surprised to see no smoke coming from the chimney. Well, it wasn't that surprising, actually. Abby was probably snuggled in his blankets. God, he wanted to join her. Maybe he would. The thought brought a smile and a burst of excitement to his chest.

On the porch, he knocked the snow off his boots as quietly as possible—he'd let her sleep, get the fire started, maybe brew some coffee, and slide into bed beside her for an hour.

That sounded perfect. Surely the barn would be fine with this sun.

Though warmer than the outdoors, the cabin was still cold as hell, and he quickly relit the fire. In the kitchen, he fed the dog, made coffee, and started breakfast for his guest. *Pain perdu*, he decided, since French toast was the perfect way to use up stale bread.

He would bring it to her in bed.

Halfway up the stairs, something frantic skittered down his spine, but it disappeared when he found her snoring lightly on her side.

He should let her sleep. She was clearly exhausted. But maybe he'd just check her forehead.

"Abby?" he whispered as he drew nearer. She looked normal, as far as he could tell.

"Abby?" He set down her plate and put a hand on her arm.

She moaned slightly, a breathy, sleepy noise that made him remember what she'd sounded like while fucking.

Her expression was stern, brows drawn, two harsh, red lines bisecting her pale face, and Luc began to worry in earnest. Did she look worse today? She'd come to him thin and naturally pale, but today her skin had a gray tinge that wasn't right. His worry drove him to sit on the bed beside her and put his hand to her forehead.

Merde, she was hot. Hot and dry and—

She opened her eyes. They were like cognac, not whiskey as he'd originally thought. Liquid, shiny, and warm. His hand lingered, and he forgot, for a moment, his purpose in being here, especially when she smiled at him like that, those ridiculous, pink lips curving up and losing almost none of their plumpness. Luc, caught in the burnt honey of her eyes, sat like an idiot on his bed and grinned, her smile and smell bringing it all back.

"Hi," she whispered in a voice he'd like to sublimate and add to this year's vintage.

"Good morning."

Instead of answering, she turned her head, just enough to make it an actual caress. Luc didn't pull back. He couldn't. She was magnetic, those glowing eyes focused solely on him.

"Feels good," she said.

"What?"

"Your hand. So cool."

Shit. That wasn't normal. "You're burning up, Abby. I think you—"

With a groan, she turned, curling in on herself and baring her back to his gaze. The shirt, stuck in places, was stained darkish and—

Oh fuck. The marks that had been red the day before were white- and yellow-tinged with infection. He needed to do something. Now.

21

HOURS PASSED. OR MINUTES. OR DAYS, DAYS SPENT GOING in and out of fires, tight, hot arms, bullets tearing into the compound, bullets tearing into crying children. Sammy strung up on the cross and burned.

A voice, warm and rasping, but the words so smooth. "Abby. Abby." Her name so soft on those lips. Soft-looking lips. Lips she needed to touch again. "You're burning up."

"It's just a dream."

He stilled when she touched him. So still, caught in the moment. Unmoving, hanging there above her. Her fingers, of their own accord, slid from his mouth to the side, across that scar and to the edge of his jaw, where the stubble thickened. They moved down over the angle there, to his chin. Through it all, he held himself still.

"This dream's better." She smiled. "Better."

His breath was hot against her fingers, and she turned them, letting him heat the back as she bit her lip. Wanting to bite his.

"I have to call someone, Abby. The sheriff. I can't let you—"

"No. No police, or they'll die. The Center's rigged. The kids will burn. We'll all die."

He put his hand over hers to still it, pressed it briefly before pulling it away. Pulling her away. She blinked and moaned and let him pick her up and carry her down the stairs.

∽◦∾

Luc was frantic, and he wasn't the only one. Le Dog, sensing that things were off, paced in front of the door, whining.

Luc picked up his phone, prepared to call the sheriff or an ambulance or the helicopter or whoever would come save her. It wouldn't turn on. No batteries, of course, and no way to charge it.

That was when he remembered the snowplow. When he'd bought his truck, the thing had been mounted to the front. He'd taken it off himself, so he knew what a pain in the ass it would be to mount. For the past two years, the thing had sat filthy and rusting behind the barn, because…well, because he almost never felt the need to leave his place, with or without snow. Or he hadn't before.

He hated leaving her here alone, but with no choice, he trudged outside.

Sliding the stupid thing down the hill and then getting it on took forever. By the time he finished and managed to plow a path close to the cabin, the sun had slid even farther to the west, its reflection blinding on the snow-covered mountain.

He lifted her, wrapped in the blanket from his bed. She wasn't heavy, he knew from carrying her before. That was the heartbreaking part—she was light, way too light. So dry and hot, she felt like a husk of a woman. The thought sent a new wash of panic through him, and he squeezed her too tightly as he took her out to the truck.

The dog insisted on coming, so Luc let him climb into the back of the cab, comforted by the companionship.

Once in the truck, Luc had a moment of hesitation. He couldn't exactly buckle her in, could he, half-conscious, with her back a mess? But shit, plowing the drive with this amount of snow—he had no idea how dangerous it would be. The last thing he needed was Abby flying through the windshield.

He buckled her, pulled out the ancient cigarette lighter, and plugged his phone in.

Slowly, steadily, he rolled down the drive, Abby sagging in the front seat beside him. It wasn't until he approached the neighboring property that he realized he'd be in full view of them—the cult. What would they do if they saw her?

Merde! Luc's pulse went nuts. The nerves made his skin cold, his hands so tight on the wheel he couldn't imagine prying them off. In front of them lay all that pristine white to plow through—nothing but obstacles, and as their fence grew closer, he pictured them plowing through that, too.

From the back, the dog whined.

It took a while, plowing through the drive alongside their property—that place where they hung the animal carcasses to bleed them, where he'd picked up Le Dog. Every second, he was sure he could feel them watching, could sense their ire, the crosshairs on his back. A group of men emerged from the big building in the distance, the one they seemed to use as their headquarters. Did they know he had her? Could they guess?

Goddamn it. He had to hurry. He couldn't hide her well enough from someone looking in the window. Behind him, Le Dog let out a quiet and menacing noise, different from anything Luc had heard from him thus far. A low, visceral growl that made the hairs stand up along Luc's arms.

That was when he spotted Isaiah, the snake, as he stepped out of the building.

Luc tapped the accelerator, praying he wouldn't speed up too fast and get them jammed in a snowbank.

I never signed up for this, he thought for one brief, selfish moment, before shifting back into first and forcing the truck's engine forward through the snow.

They were halfway there. Halfway, and the copper-haired man walked steadily to where their drives ran parallel to each other, only a low fence in this section, before separating again closer to the road. *Don't let him get here in time.* If he got in front of the truck, Luc would be obliged to stop. The truck moved another few feet, gravity doing all the hard work, and Luc pasted on a sick, weird smile, lifted his hand in what he hoped looked like a neighborly greeting, and rocketed past.

Safe, safe. Go, go, go.

Relief flooded Luc—until he saw the hairpin turn another thirty meters down, and he knew they were screwed.

Unable to slow down enough, he took the turn too fast and wound up on the uphill side of the mountain, almost windshield-deep in a snow drift. He tried to reverse. Nothing. The tires turned in the snow like hamster wheels, going nowhere.

"Abby?"

No answer.

"Wake up, Abby," he whispered. Fuck, was she alive? "Come on, Abby, you've got to get in the back."

She moaned. *Good, good.*

"Come on, Abby, *ma chérie*, get in back. Go. I can't lift you back there—you have to do it on your own."

The men approached in the rearview mirror. Even through the sound of the truck's engine, he could hear the crunch of their feet in the snow.

These figures, so familiar now in their wool coats and gloves, a few of them holding rifles, looked like an old-fashioned army closing in on his truck. It reminded him of something from *Gangs of New York*. Weird. Weird to think of that at this moment, the pulse behind his eyes making his head ache. *Hurry. Hurry.*

Okay. Okay, he could do this. He could pull this off.

He got out of the truck, forcing himself to move slowly. He meandered to the back for the shovel, all the while shaking his head, exaggerating the movement so they'd see it, pasting on a rueful smile. With the strangest sense of certainty, he knew that they'd kill her if they found her.

They'd kill him, too.

He didn't think about how they might have killed her already. If he didn't get her to a doctor, and soon, she could be dead.

That thought dug the smile deeper into his features, hardened his muscles, made him wish he'd remembered to grab his rifle. It was back there, in his cabin, standing useless against the wall.

He forced himself to dig, tires first. The group drew closer, unnervingly silent aside from the inexorable crunch of feet in crisp snow. The back windows of his truck, fogged up now, reflected nothing but bright, white light. No movement. Maybe they wouldn't see her if they didn't approach the front.

"Morning, neighbor," the man's voice rang out. Isaiah, the sick mastermind behind this strange cluster-fuck of humanity.

"Good morning," Luc said through lips that were suddenly loose with nerves. Another shake of the head as they reached the truck, maintaining his self-deprecating smile. He could pull this off. He could. "I was sure that if I drove fast enough, the plow would get me out, but…" *Flatten smile, shrug, indicate truck, pretend a half-dead woman isn't inside.* A woman they'd done this to. A sweet, passionate, intelligent woman they'd damaged.

No anger. It wouldn't help. He pushed every single splinter of rage into a smile, made his shoulders relax, took some easy swings at the snow. *I'm just a dumb city boy. Foreigner*, pronounced *furner*, like they said it around here.

"Took it *real* fast," Isaiah said as two of his guys peeled off, not even pretending.

"Never really driven in the snow before," he lied, shoveling faster. *Elmer fucking Fudd.*

"Well, first thing you wanna do is let the truck roll, just roll it." Oh, this guy was all helpful advice, all warm fuzzies, wasn't he?

Luc managed to dig one wheel out, and half the

plow, too, with enough room to roll forward. As long as nobody blocked his progress. The uphill side of the truck was flattened against the bank, which was to his advantage, Luc realized, as the two guys who'd separated from the group leaned nonchalantly on the driver's side and peered in.

What could they see?

"Yes, I figured that. Too fast to stop. I hit the brakes and…" Luc indicated the truck again, that silly smile frozen in place and his arms working so hard he couldn't feel them. If he sped up, he'd be nothing but a cartoon blur.

"Where you headed in such a hurry on a day like this, son?"

Son? Son? The man couldn't possibly be more than a decade older than Luc. *Putain*, his shtick was over the top.

"Ran out of…" *Milk*, he almost said before replacing it with "Beer." They'd have milk, wouldn't they? They'd offer him milk, and he wouldn't have a choice but to accept it.

And why the hell hadn't the two men looking in the window sounded the alarm?

"You got a dog in there?" one of them asked.

Forced chuckle. "Yes. Stray. Some hunter must have lost him in the woods. He just showed up at my door, right before the snow, in bad shape. Took him to the vet in town. Nobody claimed him, and I'm out a thousand bucks."

Beside him, their leader lifted something he'd been holding loose at his side. *A gun!* screamed Luc's brain, and he barely kept himself from flinching. Slowly, the man sank the blade of a shovel into the snow, threw it off to the side, sank it in again. Like a cat playing with its prey, he helped Luc dig out the tires. One of those orange cats with yellow eyes. Taunting. Helping before hurting. Sounded like a good motto for these guys. He wondered, in a brief moment of hilarity, if that was the message behind Abby's brands. *Help first, hurt later.*

"You're a real Dr. Dolittle, huh? Have to remember that if we have any creatures show up, needing looking after. If they're lame or require too much care, we usually just shoot 'em, put 'em out of their misery. We'll bring 'em to you now." Oh, God, they *were* toying with him, weren't they?

Why hadn't they said something about the woman in his truck yet? What were they waiting for?

With a small shake of the head, one of the men stepped away from the window. Isaiah's strange eyes followed his progress before flicking back to Luc.

"Looks like you got yourself dug out, neighbor," Isaiah said with a hard *thwack* of one gloved hand to the truck's hood.

"Thank you," Luc breathed, wondering when they planned to strike. Wondering, waiting, his back a target as he climbed into the cab and watched the men move reluctantly away. A final lift of the hand and slowly, as calmly as he could manage, Luc disengaged the emergency brake, shifted into first, and let the truck rock a couple times before it crawled out from the drift. He let it roll with his foot on the clutch, no accelerator, and kept on going down the hill.

It wasn't until he'd made it to the road that he let himself turn and take in the front seat. Empty.

"Please tell me you're back there," he said, because she had to be. She couldn't have gotten out with the passenger door wedged into the snow.

"Yes." Looked like she'd flattened out on the seat under that blanket with the dog flopped on top of her.

Luc let out such an overwhelming breath of relief, he thought his body would deflate to nothing.

"I'm sorry, Abby," he said, turning onto the main road. "But I'm taking you to a doctor."

～⌒～

After giving Le Dog a big scratch and a kiss, Abby climbed slowly out of the backseat, into the front. She ached. Every bit of her ached, even the rush of relief running through her felt like an ache.

"Where are you taking me?"

"Hospital."

"I won't do it, Luc. Hospitals are official. Official means police. Police means…"

"What does it mean, Abby?" he asked, his voice gentle.

"You don't want to know."

"Oh, I think I do." He sounded angry, but could she blame him? Lord, none of this had turned out the way she'd have wished. This wasn't how her new life was supposed to go.

Abby bent forward to stop the pressure against her back and let her face fall into her hands. She wanted to weep, wanted to scream and curse.

"Tell me a curse word," she said. "The worst one you can think of."

"*Enculé*," he said, his voice vicious but the sound so lovely on his lips.

"What's that mean?"

"I can't tell you."

"Why not?"

"It's very dirty."

"Good. Tell me."

"Fucked in the ass," he said, shocking her. She blinked at the *ass* part, not ready to even think of the possibility, and concentrated instead on *that* word again—the *F* one. That was the one she wanted.

"*Fuck*," Abby spat. Then again, "*Fuck*," and again. *Fuck, fuck, fuck, fuck*, until it didn't sound like a word anymore. It lost its meaning, turned into nothing but curt, harsh sounds in her mouth, on her tongue.

Beside her, Luc said nothing.

"It also means...what we did last night, right?" Some things you picked up, no matter how protected you were.

"Yes. Not in a nice way, though."

"Is it mean?"

"It can be. Insulting or...dirty."

"Dirty?" she slurred. Why was it so hard to talk?

"Like..." He breathed out hard, looking reticent, like this was the last discussion he wanted to have with her. "Like if you're talking dirty to someone. Not dirty, but...sexy. If you're talking to someone about what you would like to do to them." Was he blushing? He *was*. He was getting red. "If you were trying to seduce someone, you might say fuck."

"Oh. You said it." She blushed at the memories. "Last night."

Through narrowed, bleary eyes, Abby watched his lips puff out into that pout he had when he said French words, almost smiling as he expelled a breath. He looked at her, pupils pinpricks, irises bluer than blue, reflecting the bright wonderland of snow.

"Do you regret it, Luc?"

"Regret what?"

"What we did last night. Me."

He slowed the truck to barely a crawl and took his eyes off the road again to meet hers. "Never." There wasn't a hint of doubt in those two syllables. "Never," he said again, almost a whisper, and a wave of happiness swelled up inside of Abby, as bright as the snowy landscape around them. His hand left the steering wheel in search of hers. For several long minutes, he held her tight like that, until they got to the main road into Blackwood, and he had to pull away to downshift.

And now, as they entered civilization, everything was different. The distance between them seemed to stretch, their intimacy left behind as surely as the threat of the Church.

"No hospitals, right? You promised."

"No hospitals, Abby."

After another few seconds, she went on. "I need to get Sammy out. Soon. I can't leave him there."

"I know."

"And Isaiah won't go down without a fight."

"What do you mean?"

She'd skipped too far ahead, she could tell, straight from *fuck* to furor. "If the police come, he'll be...dangerous. He believes it's his divine right to live on that mountain, to be there and protect what's his."

"I don't—"

"They're all waiting for the Apocalypse, Luc. They're

expecting the End of Days. And Isaiah would not be against bringing it about himself, if need be."

"Why?"

"He's the Messiah. At least, he thinks he is. And everyone there believes it. The ones who don't…" She spread her hands, sank forward more.

"The ones who don't?" he asked, his voice harsh.

"Well, you've seen what they…" She blew out a hard breath. "My back was the best-case scenario."

"*Fuck*," he whispered, which made her release a small, strange laugh, even though laughing hurt.

"Yes indeed. Fuck."

They were on Main Street, which was fully plowed, the few unfortunate cars parked on the sides covered in snow. A couple businesses appeared to be open, and the town's holiday lights were still up, each old-fashioned lamppost trimmed with greenery and a bright-red bow, even though it was too late in the season.

Out of the blue, she said, "We don't celebrate Christmas like the rest of you."

"*Hein?*"

"In our Church, Christmas is for praying, on your knees. There's no celebration, no gifts. Just singing. And listening to scripture. And Isaiah's word."

"What does he say?"

"The Cataclysm is nigh. We must prepare for the Day. We are all upon this earth to suffer."

"He makes certain of that, doesn't he? Does every-body… Does he brand all of his people?"

She shook her head, let it wobble on her neck. "No. No, no. Only women get branded. And…and girls."

"All of them?" He looked at her and back to the road.

A harsh laugh erupted from her lips, and Abby fought it back, because it hurt. Everything hurt. "No. You ask for the brand. I've gotten so many now, I'm *special*." In the silence, Abby turned to look out the window, admiring the town under its blanket of snow. She'd like to live on a road like this; she'd like a house with black shutters like the ones on the antique place, which doubled as a bed-and-breakfast. Smoke puffed out of its chimney. They were racing by, racing by so fast, all of it smears of color against the window.

"Abby?" Luc's voice was far away, and when she turned, she couldn't seem to catch him with her eyes. If only things would stop spinning so she could catch him with her eyes.

❧

Frantic, Luc pulled over into the first plowed parking area he found, in front of the coffee shop. He checked the phone, which had charged too slowly and was only at eleven percent. Without considering his actions, he dialed the sheriff's number. After a couple of rings, the familiar voice answered.

"Navarro."

"Sheriff, it's Luc Stanek. I…I have an emergency. I need help."

"What's the emergency, sir?"

"Abby. The woman I told you about? She's here, I have her. She's…she's hurt and…" He swallowed, feeling his betrayal of her, as solid as the dog in the back seat.

"Where are you?"

"Main Street. In my truck. She won't go to the hospital, but they've… Her skin. She's feverish and…"

"Her skin? What's wrong with it?"

"She's been burned. Branded."

"Hold on." There was a pause while Luc heard voices on the line. A woman, followed by the sheriff murmuring. Finally, he came back on. "You know where the Nook is, Mr. Stanek?"

"Yes."

"There's a dermatologist there, a skin clinic. You see where I mean?"

"Ummm." Luc squinted ahead. There. A small, official-looking sign just two doors up. CLEAR SKIN BLACKWOOD. He'd never paid attention to that sign before. Why would he? "Yes. Yes, near to the martial arts place and the café. I'm almost in front of it already."

"Perfect. Wait for me. We'll meet you in front."

"Wait." Luc stopped the sheriff before they hung up. "This isn't an official call, okay? She doesn't want the police involved."

The man exhaled audibly before replying. "Fine. See you in a few."

It felt like forever, but only ten minutes passed before he caught sight of the black SUV in the rearview—the third vehicle to come through what was generally a busy road. No lights, no sirens. Good. They parked, and a small woman got out, bundled up in cold-weather gear, while Abby had only a blanket. He should have wrapped her up better.

Luc got out to meet the sheriff and the woman next to the passenger side of his truck, blocking the door for a moment. Stupid, he knew, but he needed something first.

"I promised her no authorities."

The woman nodded and turned to the sheriff. "I'm fine, Clay. You go."

"Hang on." Navarro nodded toward Abby beyond the fogged-up window. "She unconscious?"

"Yes."

"Well, let me help you get her in."

"I've got her," Luc insisted, feeling...not ownership. No, no, that was the last thing Abby needed. But responsibility, certainly. She was *his* to carry. He'd carried her this far, and he wasn't about to allow someone else to do it. He opened the door and slid his arms beneath her body. Her eyes fluttered open, and she smiled at him blearily, which was good. Conscious was good.

She murmured, "You're my bringer of light," and Luc fretted even more.

"Would you mind watching the dog in the backseat?" he threw over his shoulder to the sheriff before turning to walk behind the woman.

Nobody spoke, and when the man followed them in, dog clicking at his side, Luc couldn't muster the energy to protest.

22

CLEARLY NOT AN EMERGENCY CLINIC, Luc THOUGHT AS HE helped Abby through the door, into a small waiting room. He caught flashes of things: dried flowers, decorating magazines. Klimt posters on the walls.

The person leading the way was still too bundled up to identify. *What if I don't trust her? What if Abby doesn't?*

At this point, it probably didn't matter. It was this or the hospital.

They were led through a door, where the woman switched on some lights. Her boots squeaked down the hall, leading him the few meters to a door. An exam room, where Luc felt out of place, too big and in the way.

I should go.

The person unwrapped herself from all the winter gear—red scarf, tan coat, hat, and sunglasses. What emerged was a smallish, blond woman. When she slid into her white lab coat, she looked like someone playing doctor.

"I'm Georgette Hadley." Calm, even tone. Luc's breathing was choppy in comparison. "I'm a doctor.

You're Luc." She turned to Abby with a smile. "What's your name?"

Abby smiled back, and he almost screamed. What was this? A fucking tea party?

"Abby. Abby Merkley."

"Oh, I know you!" the doctor said. "You used to sell me bread and those cinnamon things. I remember you, Abigail!"

"She prefers Abby."

The woman's eyes met his and lingered, searching or measuring, before patting the exam table.

"Let's get you up here…Abby," the doctor invited before washing her hands at the sink.

Luc helped Abby onto the examination table, his hands cradling her body as she curled up on her side.

"Abby, can you tell me how you're feeling?"

Nothing.

Luc glanced down to find Abby watching him. "Can you tell the doctor?"

Abby whispered, "Hold my hand," with a sweet, sweet smile, and Luc's fear ramped up two hundred percent.

"Help her," he rasped, not wanting to look away from her. "I thought she was better, but I couldn't get her up. She was outside the other night, in the cold. I should have brought her to you then. And the…the *fièvre*. The fever continues." Shit, he was rambling, frantic.

Nodding, the woman grabbed a thermometer, put it into Abby's ear, and noted the temperature without reaction. She slid a cuff over Abby's arm and took her blood pressure. All the while, she kept one hand on Abby.

"Clay said you'd been burned."

"You won't let the police go there, will you?"

"No. No, Abby, you're my patient, and I won't do anything you don't want me to do."

Abby sighed. "My back was branded."

"How does it feel? Does it hurt?"

"No. No, it doesn't hurt."

When the doctor lowered her brow, Luc elaborated. "She says it's numb."

Dr. Hadley leaned in, her face close to Abby's.

"Abby?" she whispered. "Abby. Do you remember me? From the market. I've missed seeing you there."

Abby smiled. Good. That was good.

"Can I look at your back, Abby?"

"I was too friendly."

The woman blinked. "I'm sorry?"

"At the market."

"Too friendly?"

"My favorite job." Abby's lips curved up even further. "You were so nice. I wanted to *be* you."

"Yeah?" The doctor stayed there, bent forward, face in front of Abby's, as if she had all the time in the world for chitchat. She reached out to brush a few stray hairs off Abby's forehead and let her hand linger. It was an affectionate move, one that made Luc's heartbeat slow, calmed his breath, something like relief flowing in.

"I need to look at your back, Abby. I need to make you feel better."

Luc stepped back, cut out from this exchange.

"That man outside," Abby said. "Who is he?"

"He's my boyf—my fiancé."

"You were in a police car."

"He's the sheriff."

"What's he going to do? When you tell him what you saw?"

"I won't tell him. There's this thing called doctor-patient privilege. I can't talk about your condition to anyone. Not my fiancé, not Luc here, unless I have your permission."

"You can talk to Luc."

"Okay, Abby. Can I look?"

Abby nodded. With one last stroke, the doctor stood straight, legs or back cracking in the quiet room. She walked around Abby and carefully peeled back the layers.

Luc watched the woman's face, waiting for some reaction, some crack in her professional veneer. And there it was. O-shaped mouth, hand raised to cover it. No sound—nothing so obvious as that—but the expression... Good thing Abby couldn't see her.

"You were branded multiple times." The woman's voice came out flat. There was anger there, but it was well hidden. "Overlapping burns."

Over and over again, Luc thought. He'd seen the marks, and he wished he could forget.

No response from Abby, other than a look that begged him to answer in her place. How did he know that? How could he read her so well?

"Yes," he said, eyes on Abby's.

"These older ones are—"

"They've done it before," Luc said, saving Abby the trouble.

"Are you allergic to any medications?"

That pushed a dry chuckle from his lungs and dragged his attention away from Abby. "They don't do medication. I've given her ibuprofen for the fever."

The way the doctor looked at him, full of empathy, made Luc's knees nearly give out with relief.

"Would you mind taking a seat out there?" She nodded toward the door, and though he ached to stay, he gave them privacy.

~◦~

The calendar on the waiting room wall was stuck on December. He wanted to flip it to January. But there wouldn't be a January, would there? They'd need a new calendar for that. Next year. *This* year.

Luc hated December. He hated the inactivity in the vineyard, how the vines appeared dead. It was a time of death all around.

The doctor walked in. She had one of those faces that looked eternally concerned. Caring. Was that something they taught you in med school?

"Luc?"

"Yes. How is she?"

"We'll take care of the infection, and I'll do what I can for the scarring. You did well bringing her in. Thank you."

He nodded.

"She wants to talk to you."

"Yes. Good."

The woman needed to stop giving him those looks. He didn't need her pity.

Inside the exam room, he stopped. Abby looked like she hurt. He walked to her, put his hand on her forehead—it was almost a habit now—and sighed hard when the skin against his felt almost normal.

"Thank you," she whispered, clutching at his wrist,

pressing it to the side of her face. He wanted her to kiss it.

He nodded and didn't pull away, although the gratitude made him nauseated.

Her eyes opened him up.

"So…I have a choice to make."

"About what?"

"What happens next."

"What do you mean?"

"The doctor says she can help attenuate the scarring on my back, so I don't have to live with the Mark forever."

"That's good news."

"I don't think I want it gone, Luc."

He blinked and pulled away. "No?"

"Is it wrong that I want to keep it? As a reminder of where I've been?"

He shook his head, ignoring the itch of his ring finger.

After a pause, Abby spoke again.

"Dr. Hadley—she has a guest room at her house. She can take me."

"Oh. Yes. Yes, of course." He nodded, jaw hard. "You must go with her."

Was that disappointment on her face? But they didn't have a choice, did they?

"You don't want me to go back with you." She watched him. "Right?"

"I—" Luc couldn't meet her eyes this time, turning instead to gaze at the calendar. This one was turned to the right month, and his eye went straight to the fourth. Two weeks before *Grandpère*'s death. Three days after his father's. "Going up the mountain's not the same as coming down, Abby. If I have to leave the truck and walk, you would have to do it with me. We can't have you tromping up the drive right in front of them."

Abby's nod was stoic, her eyes too wet. "Of course. It wouldn't be safe." She smiled at him. That fucking smile, bestowing absolution.

"Besides, you want to get away, right?" It hurt to say it. "You have to get away from them. Promise me you'll leave town."

"When I'm done, I'll leave town. I promise." She glanced at the closed door and whispered, "I didn't tell her about Sammy, what with the sheriff being her… person and all. But I have to get him out, Luc. *Now.*"

"I know, Abby. And I'll help you do that." *Or maybe even do it on my own*, said a reckless voice inside his head. She wouldn't meet his gaze for a moment, and he leaned in. "But you will wait until you're better, right?"

After a long few seconds, she nodded and looked him in the eye. That connection resonated down to his bones. Though she looked ready to pass out, she hardened her gaze, squinted at him, and said, "You don't go in either."

"How do you—"

"I know you, Luc Stanek." The whispered words were harsh, but so close to loving, it almost hurt. "And that's why you're going to promise me, right now, that you won't go in there and risk everything on your own." When he didn't answer, she went on. "If you don't give me your word, right this minute, I'll steal the sheriff's car the first chance I get and—"

"Yes. Yes, I'll wait. I will wait for you."

"You won't go in there and destroy your entire life for Sammy."

"I promise," he whispered, caught in her sharp gaze.

On the heels of those words came another thought, so unexpected it nearly bowled him over: *No. But I'd do it for you.*

❧

The door closed behind Luc without a sound, as if he'd never been there. There'd been no kiss good-bye, no hug, nothing but an uncomfortable look before he was gone, and Abby couldn't be sure any of it had happened. *Any* of it. Had they really touched each other? Kissed and done…those wonderfully sinful things just the night before?

Perhaps I imagined it. The soft tastes, that clenching need, those shimmering moments. Did I make it all up?

When the doctor came back in, her expression asked a question that she wasn't rude enough to voice. And Abby, who typically liked to share things, kept her mouth firmly shut. Not this. She didn't want to share this. Not the secret or the unexpected hurt of rejection, nor the memories that might not be real.

"How do you feel?"

"Strange," she said.

"Let's get you home and into bed."

For someone who hadn't taken medication since she was a young child, Abby had been dosed up to her gills today. She was tired. Sleepy, sleepy tired. She squinted down at her clothes. Luc's blanket kept her warm. Beneath that, his clothes had been replaced by scrubs adorned with pink elephants. With wings. Elephants with wings.

"They don't have wings, do they?" she asked as they emerged into the front room.

"Excuse me?"

"Elephants. I thought they just stomped."

"No wings." The doctor opened the front door, letting in a whoosh of fresh air. Abby lifted her eyes from the animals on her clothing and caught sight of the black SUV, lights on top. She stopped.

"What is it?"

"I forgot about the... He's police." Police were bad. Isaiah would—

"It's okay. It's okay, Abby. He's with me, remember? With us. He's my ride. He watched Luc's dog."

"Luc's dog."

"Right."

Abby calmed down a notch.

The doctor hung back for a moment, appearing to consider. "Like I told you, he's my fiancé. The sheriff of Blackwood County. We live together."

"I can't—"

"I won't tell him what happened to you, Abby."

"But he's your—"

"It doesn't matter who he is. He's not privy to your personal, private medical information. It would be illegal for me to tell him."

Abby relaxed. A bit.

"He's also... Did you get a look at him earlier? He's a little"—Dr. Hadley glanced at her, then back out at the snow-crusted road—"intimidating. His face is...marred, and he's been through a bit. He won't ask you questions, but he's the type of person who would get involved if he thought it was the right thing to do."

"So, should I—"

"You should not worry. But don't mention anything

in front of him, unless you want him to…do something about it."

"All right."

"And remember. Clay's not as mean as he looks." Dr. Hadley smiled. "He's a pussycat."

She looked at the doctor, considering. This woman had been one of Abby's favorite customers, a regular who'd taken the time to chat every Saturday, without fail. A relationship Abby had been made to understand she shouldn't be forming. No talking to the clients, even though that was ridiculous. They'd liked her. Part of the reason some of those people bought from them had been Abby's gregariousness. She'd been sure of it.

When they'd taken her off market duty, she'd wondered which of the women had told on her. Who out of the other three had decided she needed to be reported? Brigid, no doubt.

It didn't matter.

"I'm ready," she said with a cold breath in.

At the car, the doctor performed introductions. "Abby, this is Clay. Clay, meet Abby. She'll be staying with us for a while."

Abby opened her mouth to protest then shut it, eyes focused on the man who was indeed intimidating, but not nearly as frightening as Dr. Hadley had implied. He was handsome, the snow a perfect contrast to his dark good looks.

He nodded at her but didn't offer to shake, which made her think he was giving her space.

After a short drive, they pulled up in front of an old farmhouse, cozily blanketed in white. All that was missing was a curl of smoke from the chimney.

Inside, the doctor said, "Let's get you some clothes, okay?" She turned to Clay. "Would you mind putting together a snack before you go back out?"

"'Course." He glanced at Abby. "Anything you don't like?"

"Oh." She considered. She ate whatever was put in front of her. *Like* had never been an issue before. "I guess not. Thank you."

Taking her arm, Dr. Hadley led Abby to the stairs. "Come on, we'll get you set up in the guest room."

Everything about the house was beautiful. Old and glowy warm with lots of color and layers of fabric. A memory slid out from the depths of her mind: *Little Women*, a book. She remembered characters sitting around in their house, talking and loving one another. A house like this one. *Did I read that?* she wondered, with a vague recollection of another lifetime. A child named Abby. Maybe she'd seen a movie.

The bedrooms upstairs were inviting, her bed not only made, but also turned down. Waiting for a guest. The bathroom was clean and white. Everything smelled good. Like herbs and pie.

The woman brought her clothing.

"Dr. Hadley, I—"

"It's George. Please call me George."

Abby nodded.

"Here," George continued. "This should be comfortable, but I'm happy to get you a dress, if it's more to your—"

"No!" Abby cut in, breathless. "Trousers are perfect."

"Trousers it is," George said, a smile tugging at the corners of her mouth. "You're taller than me, so they'll be short, but maybe this weekend, we can get you some stuff."

"I'll repay you, Doctor. Thank you."

"George. Please. And you don't have to—"

"I want to, George. I want to get a job. I have to repay you." She fought to keep her attention away from the mountain looming behind the house. "I want to repay Luc, too."

"Oh, I'm sure he's not—" George interrupted herself, clamped her lips shut, and nodded. "I understand."

"Thank you," said Abby. "Thank you for everything."

"Oh, Luc gave me this for you." George reached into a pocket and held out a bundle of paper. An envelope with a curlicued *Abby* scrawled on the front, filled with cash.

Alone in the room, Abby set the envelope down and took off the blanket and the scrubs. She pulled on a pair of clean, white underwear—snug and soft and so different from what she usually wore—and the trousers. They were loose but short. An oval mirror stood on a stand in the corner of the room. She should go look at her reflection.

In just a second.

She ran a hand along her body, from waist to thigh. This was it. She'd joked with Luc about the jeans and the boots and the puffy coat, but really, they were all part of that shell that she'd craved for so long. A uniform of normality. No, of...what? What was it these clothes represented?

Not quite ready to face the future, she spun toward the bed and caught sight of Luc's crinkled envelope.

The money for her days of work. He'd thought to bring it, had left it for her.

With a sob she just barely managed to contain, Abby sank to the bed, the envelope clutched in one hand and Luc's blanket in the other. After a few deep inhales, she couldn't contain the tears any longer and pressed the fabric to her face, sucking in the smell of his home and wishing it were him.

~❦~

Someone is here.

Luc stepped into the living room, breathing hard, head shifting from one side to the other. Nothing had changed, really, nothing immediately discernible, but... He sniffed. There was something in the air that shouldn't be. A presence, now gone.

Although he hoped not. A confrontation was exactly what he needed.

Rifle in hand, he searched his house, one room at a time, Le Dog at attention beside him.

In the bathroom, right there in the rubbish bin, was a wad of bloody cotton and gauze pads from Abby's back. If Isaiah and his men had been here, there was no way they'd missed that.

But what about the brown-stained floral of Abby's torn nightgown? Though he looked everywhere, he couldn't find it. Had Abby somehow gotten rid of it without him knowing? Burned it, maybe? Or had *they* taken it? The ghosts of intruders he felt sure had been here.

Upstairs, he almost expected some hellish gift. A horse head in his bed or whatever it was cultists left as calling cards, but there was nothing out of place. Nothing at all.

Maybe he was imagining it, their presence in his home.

But he didn't think so. And neither did Le Dog, who seemed as agitated as Luc felt.

A wave of anger rose up—against those people for trying to intimidate him, against himself for getting caught up in someone else's business, against Abby for dragging him into it.

But that last part was a lie. He wasn't mad at Abby for coming to him or for bringing these assholes into his life. He just couldn't handle the hollow feeling she'd left behind.

Which made no sense at all, since he'd wanted her to leave and never come back. To be *safe*.

Get Sammy to her and she can go.

He was overcome by a strange mix of fear and anticipation as he considered just how he'd do that. Why hadn't he asked Abby about the layout over there and where Sammy might be?

The day was getting dark and cold, the shapes taking on an eerie blue hue that reminded him of a dream. Surreal and unpleasant, especially with the sensation of eyes everywhere. Were they watching him? He felt alone and surrounded at the same time. Angry and afraid.

Settling in was impossible. Nothing beckoned. Not the kitchen for dinner, though he'd need to eat before heading back up to light the fire in the barn. God, what was this ache?

After packing up some food, he grabbed what he'd need to bed down in the barn, whistled for the dog, and headed out into the night, rifle over his arm, hating this feeling even more now that he'd figured out what it was.

"I need a drink," he mumbled, going back in for the hard stuff and wishing, for once, that he could have stayed in town, gone to the bar, maybe met someone and let them take him home. Someone he could fuck who would obliterate the tenderness he'd built up with Abby over these past few days, the want and need. Someone to help bandage his raw parts, which, though invisible, chafed immensely.

Not that he did that, of course.

Not that he'd want to, even if he could. Not with memories of Abby in his brain and his body.

It was a relief, he realized, that he wouldn't have to sleep in his own bed tonight, which was thoroughly steeped in her essence.

On his way up to the winery, he checked on the chickens. They were ruffled and angry at being cooped up, but nonetheless happy to see him, Lady Godiva doing that stomping dance that told him just how irritated she was. He went to the barn next, where he looked in on his barrels. The barn, at least, had remained locked and felt untouched, the temperature only slightly lower than usual. Nobody could get through those doors without a key. They'd have to burn it down to get inside.

After building a big fire, he headed straight for the interior room, where he checked the temperature and topped up the barrels.

Odd how he couldn't muster up the usual feelings of ownership at the sight of all that oak.

Back in the tasting room, he waited. *For what?*

"What am I waiting for?" he asked Le Dog.

For her.

For the first time in his life, Luc Stanek felt lonely.

He paced the room, agitated. Paced and paced as Le Dog hunkered by the fire, brows twitching as his eyes followed Luc's movements. Finally, after a useless ten minutes of this, Luc grabbed the rifle and went outside. He'd just head over to the fence, check out the spot where Abby had come through, maybe cut through and investigate the other side under cover of darkness.

Adrenaline coursed through him, pushing him close to running as he went, his feet crunching loudly on the snow. It wasn't until he neared the fence that he heard it—another set of footsteps. He stopped cold, feet sinking in, and waited.

Probably close to a minute passed, his heart beating in his ears the only sound in the frozen night. And then it started again: the crunching. Steady, slow steps, from across the fence. He followed the steps with his eyes until he saw a shadow against the snow, and a glint of reflected moonlight. They'd put up a guard to keep him away.

Or to look out for Abby.

Either way, he knew better than to face off against them. Not like this, raw and spitting rage. The chilling reality was that they could do anything they wanted... unless he sought help.

No cops and no going in alone. Those were the promises he'd made. *Merde*.

Slowly, more carefully and quietly this time, he returned to the barn and locked himself in.

He grabbed the bottle and glass before forcing himself to settle down in front of the huge window, with Le Dog pressed to his side and Blackwood nothing but a sprinkling of fairy lights below. The first pour was big, enough to burn on its way down, enough to shove back this chaos burning inside him. Another pour to follow the first—only as he lifted the glass to his lips, it caught the light from the flames. He froze in place, gaze riveted to the liquid within.

Firelight through Virginia bourbon. The exact color of Abby Merkley's eyes. He slugged it back and doled out another.

Hours later, something woke him up. The cold, he thought at first, seeing that the fire had burned down to a handful of embers. But when Le Dog leaned into his body and growled, Luc knew that wasn't it.

Just as he rose from his makeshift bed, a noise came to him, piercing through the usual middle-of-the-night silence. An animal sound, spectral and strange, brought another growl from the dog, whose fur was standing on end.

"What is it, boy?"

With the next noise, he knew exactly what was happening. Something—or someone—had gotten into the henhouse.

With a curse, he struggled to get his boots on, took way too long to throw on his coat and grab his rifle and stride out into the night. There was nothing to see below. When he stopped to listen, breathing hard in the cold night, adrenaline pumping through tight muscles, he thought he might have imagined everything. Until from the direction of the henhouse, he heard it again—that unearthly sound.

He didn't consider what he might be getting himself into by running right into it. He thought only of the animals, but by the time he got there—not even a flashlight in his hand—it was too late.

Whatever it was had gotten in and done its dirty work. Was it a fox? How could a fox have—

He ran his fingers over the latch. Bent backward, which meant this was no animal attack.

Although it wasn't something he could prove, was it? That those fuckers had come here and killed his chickens. Gagging from the smell of blood, he stumbled back a step, then a second.

The air stank of death and rage.

"Fuck!" he said under his breath, then louder, "*Fuck!*" Lifting the rifle, he fired a shot into the air before bellowing again. "Don't you fuck with me, you hear?" The gunshot's echo muffled his words. It didn't matter anyway, because he couldn't see a goddamned thing, but they were out there. He could feel them watching.

And he understood the message loud and clear: His closest neighbors had just declared war.

23

"ANYTHING TO PROVE IT WAS THEM?" ASKED CLAY Navarro when Luc called him the next morning.

After a sigh, Luc asked, "The armed guard along the perimeter? The threat?"

"Thought they didn't threaten you."

"Right. Of course not." He let out a dry, unhappy half laugh. "They want her back."

"Yeah, well, she's not talking about it. And George will do me bodily harm if I mention anything to Abby, which—"

"She has to get better," Luc cut in.

"Everybody agrees on that point. Problem is, while she's healing here, you've got Armageddon on that mountain."

"I'll take care of it."

"Don't do anything stupid, Stanek. There are dozens of 'em, for Christ's sake."

Breathing out a hard huff of frustration, Luc looked out over his vineyard, wondering what the hell to do next.

After a pause, Navarro asked, "You considered

coming back into town? Camping out here till things blow over? It'll give me time to put together a team that can actually handle the kind of clusterfuck you've got brewing up there."

"And return to a devastated vineyard? No. No, I'll stay here and make sure they don't do any more damage."

"How you planning on handling that?"

"I'll stand guard every fucking night if I have to. I'll sleep out here and—"

"Look, I'll pay 'em a visit, all right?" Navarro cursed under his breath and went on. "Nothing confrontational, 'cause I can't prove a thing, but it'll at least tell them you've been in touch. Got the law on your side."

Luc barely held back a cynical laugh.

"But you stay put," Navarro continued. "Don't go over there. Don't talk to 'em. Do *not* engage. You got that?"

After a pause, Luc answered. "Yes. Fine. No engaging."

"Anything happens, you give me a call. I'll be right up. Top of my list. Got it?"

"Yeah. Thanks, Sheriff."

"Call me Clay."

"All right. Thank you, Clay."

"Not everyone would have done what you did for her."

This time, a small, choked laugh came out. Nothing he'd done had felt like it was for her, he thought before ending the call. Everything had felt selfish.

All day, Luc thought of those people, his anger not dissipating, although after hours of watching over his vineyard, weapon close by at all times, he wondered if perhaps they'd done their worst.

And he thought of Abby. In his house, in the barn, while clearing the newest patch of land. He thought of her in the evening while he carved his hunk of wood into what turned out to be her arm and neck and her back, the skin perfectly clear of brands.

During that second long, lonely night, he thought of her in his arms. He could feel her there, even with the power back on and the sheets washed and the smell of her gone.

She was safe at least, if not gone for good.

And whose fault was that? She'd be long gone if he hadn't handed Sammy back to the cult.

Over and over again, he beat himself up about returning that kid to that hell. Sammy. Poor Sammy.

After another uneventful day, he even started to wonder if he'd dreamed it all—the night watch and the threats, and maybe the chickens had fallen victim to a fox after all. Or coyotes. Were there wolves around here?

After everything that had happened, how could he possibly go back to his wine and vines and dog-eared issues of *Vigneron* magazine by the fire? With the tension tight in his neck, he spent every waking hour working hard, wishing thoughts of her and the fucking neighbors out of his brain and out of his life.

The craziest thing of all was how bored he was. *Bored*, for Christ's sake. Today, after working himself raw clearing the new vineyard, he set off for his cabin, where the choices of activities were limited—something that had never bothered him before. Because boredom just wasn't part of his makeup. Before Abby, he'd been content to sink his hands into soil and just exist. He'd been happy when his back ached and his body was sore, happy to think about nothing but the weather conditions, always alone.

I miss her.

The phone in his pocket rang. He grabbed it, checked the number, and as usual, let out a disappointed sigh. French mobile number, not Blackwood or some other place farther afield. Not Abby calling to... What? To check on him or chat or tell him she was coming back? That it was time for them to go in and get Sammy?

Which would be horrible news anyway, because he didn't want her going in there. He should tell Clay Navarro of her plans.

Although, *putain*, he wouldn't mind seeing her face, touching her, feeling that soft skin, so pliable under his hands.

When the phone rang again, he came close to hurling it against his door. Instead, he shut it off and spent the evening cooking another pointless, tasteless dinner.

∾⦵∾

For three days, Abby slept off and on, waking only to eat the food George pushed on her. Her slumber was fitful and anxious, filled with flames and the certitude that it was too late. By the fourth day, she left the bed awake, if not refreshed. It appeared to be midmorning, and the house was quiet.

She went to the stack of clothes that George had left her, selected the warmest items, and took a much-needed shower before heading downstairs.

George's note awaited her in the kitchen, beside a plate of biscuits. The first couple of days, her hostess had fed her in bed, but Abby had put a stop to that yesterday.

After eating a hasty meal, Abby squeezed into an old pair of rubber gardening boots and a coat and tromped out into the backyard. Slowly, she spun around, in search of those telltale boulders at the top of Luc's mountain. Nothing.

She'd been an idiot to hope that she could just walk out back and up until she ran into his land and then the Church's. It was probably miles away.

Well, without a vehicle, she'd walk if she had to. Not in these boots, though. She shivered. Nor in this too-light jacket.

Letting herself mutter a frustrated "Fuck," she turned around and jumped when she caught sight of Clay, standing on the back porch steps, looking rumpled and tired in his sheriff's uniform.

"Whoa. You scared me."

"Sorry about that," he said with a self-deprecating smile. "Figured you'd heard the door open."

Abby shook her head and waited.

"You plotting your escape?"

His question, though posed lightly, made her jolt. His eyes widened before narrowing.

For a few taut seconds, she stood trapped like an insect under his gaze. Finally, he released her with a smile and said, "Come on in. I'll put on a pot of coffee, and you can tell me what it is that's got you looking for a way back to the people who hurt you." He turned to go in and swung back to add, "If you want to share, of course."

The door slammed shut behind him, leaving her alone again, toes trapped in the too-tight boots and her heart trapped in a too-tight chest.

The quiet garden was such a stark contrast to the thunderous mess she was inside. Something moved behind her, and she turned to see a bright-red cardinal alight on a quaint, wooden bird feeder staked into the ground. It leaned in to pull out a sunflower seed, cocked its head to stare at her, and then took off in a blur of scarlet, leaving her blinking in its wake.

As she searched the nearby branches for the bird, another one appeared, the same shape but darker, its feathers a dull brown, but its beak that same bright orange. A female. When Abby shifted again, this bird didn't take off. It glanced her way before continuing to feed. Fearless.

But cautious, she imagined. If Abby made for the birdhouse, the animal would leave. It just wouldn't let itself be scared off from such a treasure trove.

She glanced at George's house—her safe nest these past few days could also be her prison. Unless she was smart about it.

Pulling her resolve around her like a cloak, she tromped back through the snow and up the steps into the house, where Clay stood with his back to her, watching coffee drip into the pot.

The problem with coffee was the smell. Goodness, every time they made it was like walking into Luc's cabin all over again—that nutty aroma brought her back to her first sip, softened with cream and sweet with sugar. The warmth of his fingers against hers as the mug had changed hands. It made her want to cry.

Without turning, Clay said, "Wondered what you'd decide."

The urge to tell him about Sammy was strong, but she fought it. Sammy was her responsibility. "You can't go in there with guns blazing."

He turned to look at her, face tight. "All right. What does that mean?"

"It means the Church members await the Apocalypse. Going up in a blaze of glory is the goal."

"What can I do, then?"

"I...I don't know." She shook her head. "You need to get the kids out of the Center. The main building. The nursery's in there, and if you can get them out, the adults..." She paused, ignoring the stab of pain in her abdomen. "The adults chose this."

He poured two coffees, stirred in sugar and a splash of cream, and handed one to her. "All right. So we can't go in with guns blazing. Not as if I have the resources anyway." He took a sip, eyes on her. "I'll talk to the Staties and the FBI. Put together a team." Her face must have reflected how little she liked that idea, because he lifted a hand and went on. "I'll get those kids out, Abby. You believe that?"

She eyed this harsh-looking man who'd shown nothing but kindness toward her. "I do," she whispered, ignoring the tears that swamped her, unbidden.

"I'll need intel from you on how things are laid out. What's your plan for now?"

"I need a job and a place to live."

"I'll ask around," he offered, to which she nodded. After a bit, he excused himself and headed upstairs for a shower.

He left a bit later, leaving Abby alone with George's three-legged cat, Leonard.

She must have dozed, despite the mounting anxiety and the knowledge that she'd done the wrong thing.

Lord, she needed to get out of here. She needed a

vehicle at the very least. With a vehicle, she could get close enough to the Church to get in and pull Sammy out before everything blew sky-high. Never mind that she didn't have a proper coat or even the footwear she'd need to get in and out without losing a limb to frostbite. She eyed the telephone, wishing she had Luc's number. Although the last thing she wanted to do was get him involved.

It was night by the time George got home, and Abby was jumping out of her skin.

"I want to go out," Abby blurted, nearly attacking the doctor at the door.

George blinked and smiled, slowly. "Okay." Abby almost sank to the floor in relief. "Let's go to the Nook."

"What's that? I feel like I've seen it."

"It's Blackwood's one and only watering hole." When Abby didn't respond, George went on. "It's a bar and restaurant."

Oh, that would be perfect. A bar. People. Distraction, but also the first step out of here. The thought was unforgivably ungrateful. "Yes, please. I'm… I can't stay here anymore." At the look on George's face, Abby corrected herself. "I mean, stuck and feeling like there's nothing I can do. I want to pay you back for all you've done."

"Come on. I'll take you out to dinner." George eyed her. "Let's find you something more appropriate to wear."

"I'll pay you—"

"You'll pay me back. I know, I know. But for tonight, let's just get you out of the house for a few hours, shall we?" She eyed Abby. "We need Jessie, though, because none of my stuff is going to fit you."

"Jessie?"

"Neighbor. And friend." George grabbed Abby by the hand and led her to the front door. "Come on. I saw her car. Let's go."

⁓∾

An hour later, George and Abby took off for the Nook with Jessie, the beautiful amazon of a neighbor, driving. Abby wore jeans that looked too tight but were stretchy and as smooth as butter, with a too-low top and a soft sweater. She'd stared at herself so long in the bathroom mirror that George had come to check in on her. *I can't fall to pieces every time I wear something new*, Abby'd decided, shoving back the tears and greeting George with a smile.

On the way over, the women buzzed with excitement at the prospect of introducing her to this new experience.

"It's just dinner," George insisted for the third time. "I mean, Abby shouldn't be staying out too late. It might—"

"*Hamper your recovery*," Jessie and Abby declaimed in unison before breaking into a fit of giggles. Gracious, it felt good.

She tamped down the nervous excitement as she followed the other two women into the Nook. The big room was dim, which gave her an impression of intimacy and dark corners, with the light focused primarily on a bar.

Jessie hung back, and George took the lead, finding them a booth and grabbing a couple of menus before settling down.

"What would you like?"

Abby picked up the menu, glanced over it, and set it carefully back down, overwhelmed.

"Know already?"

She could only shake her head. George caught her eye. "You okay?"

"No," whispered Abby.

The man who'd been behind the bar—tall and slender, dark-reddish hair shining a bit under the dim lights—approached the table and spoke. "All right, ladies? Renee left me in the lurch, so I'm on me own tonight. What may I get you to dri—" The man stopped talking, his eyes on Jessie.

Jessie, however, looked hard at the menu. George finally broke through the moment.

"I think we'll get a bottle, Rory. Red or white, ladies?"

When Jessie didn't respond, Abby said, "I've only tried red." *And*, she thought, *I'm not sure I can taste it again without thinking about Luc.*

"White it is," said the man. "Shall I bring you the house?"

"Please" came George's response.

"Back in two ticks."

As soon as the man had gone, George turned to Jessie. "You and *Rory*?" she asked, brows shooting sky-high.

Jessie, who'd flushed bright red now, just shrugged.

"How did I not realize this?"

"We always do our drinking at your place."

"Because you never want to come to the Nook. Because of—"

"I can't talk about it now. Or ever," Jessie interrupted, and George just looked at her through those pale-green eyes. Turning to Abby, Jessie asked, "Know what you'd like to eat yet?"

"You pick."

"Really? I'm not even sure what you li—"

"It's too many choices," said Abby, at a loss. "I have no idea where to start."

"All right." Jessie looked between George and Abby. "There's a story here, isn't there?"

George left it to Abby to nod.

"I'm…I'm not from around here."

"So, no clothes, no idea what to order, first time out. You're an alien?"

"Something like that." And then, because she felt bolder than usual, Abby lifted her chin and went on. "You tell me about *him*, and I'll tell you about my…origins."

Though she looked taken aback for a second, Jessie quickly recovered and held out her hand with a smile. "Deal," she said with a firm shake. "But not tonight. Tonight we drink wine and eat…cheeseburgers?"

"Cheeseburgers it is," said George, setting down her menu with a smile and a decisive slap.

The man—Rory—returned with the wine and took their order, leaving the three of them alone again, full of stories and a new sense of adventure. They held up their glasses of white wine, which Abby could already tell wasn't nearly as interesting as red. Or maybe it had just been Luc.

"As your doctor, I'm supposed to tell you that you shouldn't drink while taking antibiotics," said George. She held her glass up high, eyes soft on Abby's. "But as your friend, I'd like to make a toast. To a new life."

Jessie lifted her glass, adding, "To new adventures."

Trying not to cry, Abby did the same. "And to new friends," she whispered as the others touched their glasses to hers.

"To new friends," they echoed.

The place filled up while they ate and drank and talked. It was so easy with these women. People came in off the street, bringing the chill with them but laughter, too, and the space quickly crowded. After a bit, the lights dimmed, the music and voices got louder, and the energy shifted. When the man came to remove their plates, George asked, "What's happening tonight?"

"Dancing."

"That might be a bit more than we can handle for tonight." George's eyes slid to Abby. "You mentioned someone leaving you in the lurch. Are you looking for waitstaff?"

"Indeed I am."

Abby piped up before she'd fully considered what it would mean to work in a place like this. "I'm looking for a job."

"Yeah? Got any experience?"

"No, sir." She looked him straight in the eye, deciding not to be afraid. "But I'm good with people."

"Hm. You know anything about cocktails?"

"No."

"You drink wine."

"It's my third time."

Although his face was in partial shadow, his smile shone big and brassy.

With a chuckle, he reached down a hand. "You're hired."

"What? I…I'm not sure wh—"

"Just say thank you"—he wiggled his fingers—"and shake my hand."

She reached out and let him take her hand in his grip,

expecting to feel something from his touch—excitement like when her skin had touched Luc's, or tenderness or desire.

But no. Nothing. The second man to shake her hand in her entire life, and she felt nothing more than the pleasant warmth of human contact.

What had Luc done to her?

"My waitress quit on me, and I've been buggered ever since. Luckily, the punters don't come 'round as much after the holidays, which gave me a bit of a respite, but still. Look at this crowd. Just turned February—love is in the air. And it's almost the weekend, which means there'll be a good dose of lust, at the least." Jessie made a loud huffing sound, quickly smothered, and Rory's eyes narrowed on her before returning to Abby. "When can you start? Tomorrow?"

Tomorrow. Abby's body hummed with the possibility. She'd find a way to get back to the mountain. She'd walk if she had to. "I don't have a car or a place to stay that's—"

"Still got the apartment upstairs?" Jessie cut in, and everyone turned to look at her.

Rory's face broke into a long, slow, syrupy smile, and there was something different in his voice when he focused on Jessie. "Matter of fact, I do. Remember it, do you?"

When nobody responded, he looked at Abby. "It's nothing fancy, but I'd be happy to give it to you."

The Church would never find her here. A den of sin like this. She could hide in plain sight. Heavens, she could get Sammy out tomorrow. Not wanting to seem too eager or ungrateful, she glanced at George before focusing back on Rory. "How much is the rent?" She swallowed hard.

His expression was interested as he took her in—or curious, maybe. "For you, darling, nothing."

"Oh, I couldn't do that. I'm—"

"She'll take it," Jessie said, chin up, face obstinate as she looked Rory head-on for the first time. "He may seem like an ass, but you'll be safe with Rory. He's only an asshole to me. Besides, he owes me for all the grief he's given me over the years."

He narrowed his eyes and smiled hard before turning back to Abby. "You can bring your things tomorrow."

"Thank you, sir." It was a relief, suddenly, to feel like she wouldn't be a burden to George and Clay. Besides, Rory wouldn't care where she went when she wasn't working. Being here would make getting Sammy a cinch. She thought of the walk to the mountain and then the return trip, with Sammy in tow, and amended that. It would be a trial, but one she was up to.

She hoped.

"No, darling. Thank *you*. The pub'll be even more packed tomorrow, and I'd be stuck with me trousers down, if not for you."

Abby blinked, resolutely ignoring his lower half. "Your trousers."

He cocked his head and looked at her—really looked, in a still, direct kind of way. "You're not from 'round here, are you, love?"

"Uh…" She swallowed and tried for a partial truth, which she wasn't all that good at. "I'm originally from West Virginia."

He nodded slow, still squinting, reading something

into her words or body language or appearance that she couldn't begin to guess.

"What's your name?"

"Abby."

"All right, Abby." Rory was speaking louder now, over the music and the dancing. "Come in tomorrow, and I'll put you to work."

"Thank you," said Abby.

"We ready to go?" asked George.

Jessie yelled over the music, "I wouldn't mind a dance, actually." She looked worked up by the exchange with Rory. Abby could only guess at whatever history had made her edgy like that.

Abby turned, and her mouth fell open. "Good Lord," she said, her attention glued to where a jumble of bodies moved together, some frantic, some languorous, sinuous limbs wrapped around and around until she couldn't tell where a person began or ended.

How had she not noticed how hot it had gotten? It smelled different now, too—perfumed and musky and a little bit desperate. There was sweat and alcohol in the mix, but something else… Not the smell of sex as she knew it, as she'd shared it with Luc, but bodies in motion, working hard. Not toiling in the soil or a kitchen, but toiling to a different end. Procreation? No. No, nothing as biblical as that. Working hard for the sake of pleasure.

Oh, what a novel concept. Toiling for sensation.

She took the last sip of her wine and let it heat her in new places.

I want to dance. Ignoring the little voice that whispered, *With Luc,* she stood up and looked at Jessie, pretending not to see the slightly worried, surprised expression on George's face. She'd do this tonight. Just this once. And then tomorrow, she'd get Sammy. Lord only knew what came next.

"I'll dance."

"You coming, George?"

Jessie forged a path to the dance floor, tall and willowy and easy to follow. She immediately started moving with the music, her body sinuous and easy in its undulations. George, smaller and curvier, was different, her movements limited to shoulders and hips.

And Abby... After a few seconds of hesitation, she closed her eyes and sank into the sea of sensation. The music, the beat, came from inside her. Her heart, her blood sliding through veins, limbs heavy but full of a new sort of energy. Sin—a sea of it. A hand landed on her hip, and her eyes shot open. *Isaiah.*

Turning, panicked, she encountered someone she'd never seen before. A short, older man.

Not the Church. Not Isaiah.

With a quick smile and a shake of her head, she backed away from the man. She took in the other women with a smile and danced. The way she'd always wanted to dance.

My choice. Me. If I'm going to sin, I'm going to sink into it, do it for real. Live in my body this once instead of floating high above it.

On she danced, through to the end of the song. The music wrapped around her as surely as the safety net created by these two other women. Another song came on, and she opened her eyes to find them beside her. Another hand landed on her hip—one belonging to a younger, bigger man this time. It tightened, pulled her in too close, the smell of cologne cloying. She pushed away, turned to catch sight of the man. He was fine, nice-looking, smooth and shaved and perfect in a way she'd never experienced. But everything about him was wrong, and suddenly, she was too hot, too sweaty, the music too loud, the sensations overwhelming.

Jessie appeared in his face and said something Abby couldn't hear. Immediately, the man disappeared into the sea of revelers, but Abby'd had enough.

Pushing away from the throng, she wound her way back to their table, where she picked up her glass of water.

Jessie joined her. "I'm done," she said, out of breath.

"Shall we?" asked George, and when Abby nodded, they grabbed their coats and took off for the door.

"What'd you think?" George asked on the way to the car. "Of dancing like that?"

"I like it." On a sharp exhale, Abby added, "Not really what I'd pictured, though."

"No?"

Abby couldn't bring herself to extrapolate, but an image arose in her mind, unbidden: a man behind her, messed-up hands on her hips, tightening like that other man's had, but…but different. Funny how, in that hot, sweaty place, there'd been nothing of Luc, but out here, she could smell him perfectly, on the clean, cold, snow-drenched air. And she missed him so much it hurt.

24

AFTER A LONG DAY OF HARD, HARD LABOR, WITH HIS neighbors keeping a constant watch, Luc was twitchy and tired and ready to jump out of his skin. With those assholes following his every move, he hadn't been able to sleep in days. He missed Abby and couldn't count the number of times he'd caught himself wondering what she was doing and where she was, or why she hadn't called him. What if she wasn't recovering properly? Could that be the problem? He hadn't considered that possibility before, focusing instead on the worrying possibility that she'd attempt to get Sammy out on her own.

He ran back to the cabin, propelled by fear, and after a frantic search for Sheriff Navarro's card, realized he had the number on his phone. The man picked up after a couple rings.

"Navarro."

"It's Luc Stanek."

"Luc."

"I was…" Jesus, he was breathing hard. He swallowed, trying to calm down. "How is she?"

The sheriff didn't answer immediately. When he did, his voice sounded more hesitant than usual.

"She's left us."

Oh shit. Shit, shit, shit, what did that mean?

"Got a place to stay in town. And got herself a job."

Luc breathed a sigh of relief. Christ, was this what it felt like to have a heart attack? "My God, Clay, you nearly killed me there."

Clay huffed out a laugh. "Sorry about that. We've been... I was planning on calling you today. We're going to be heading your way."

"Who's we?"

"Look. I should warn you that you might be asked to evacuate your place in the next couple of days. We're putting together a joint—"

"No. I won't do that. The second I leave, they'll... Fuck, I don't know what they'll do."

"We can't just go in there without being fully prepared. Can you hold out a couple more days? I don't have the manpower yet, but I'll send a deputy out if I have to."

Luc glanced at his front window, constantly covered by the curtains now, when before, he'd never closed them. He'd even tacked a piece of fabric onto the kitchen door. "No. No, I'll be fine for now."

"You'll let me know, though, if anything changes?"

"Yes." He was about to hang up when he remembered why he'd called. "Wait! Where is she? Abby, I mean. Where's she working?"

"The Nook."

Surprised, Luc asked, "The bar in town?"

Clay chuckled. "Yeah. She'll be good at it. Even

sick, she was chatty, friendly." He paused. "She's a good kid."

Luc nodded. *Kid.* What an inadequate way to describe so incredible a woman.

After ending the call, Luc made his way to the front window and pulled back the curtain, with Le Dog's curious eyes on him. There, at the top of the hill, directly behind the fence, stood his twenty-four-hour-a-day armed guard, keeping watch over the house. Making sure he didn't cross the fence. But also, he suspected, waiting for him to leave his place. One wrong move, and they'd be on him.

In the past forty-eight hours or so, fear had given way to frustration, which he knew was just a thin veneer over the anger that threatened to swallow him up and push him to do stupid things. Like find a way through that fence in the dead of night, locate Sammy on his own, and bring him to Abby. The thought of presenting her with the boy, like some kind of knight giving her his obeisance, made him feel both pathetic and excited.

Stifling that energy, he went to make dinner for himself and Le Dog, noting that there wasn't much left. He'd have to go to town soon, or they'd starve. He'd finished up dinner and was thinking about heading to bed when the sound of an engine reached him, struggling up the drive.

It's her. Excitement bubbled up, and he leaped down the stairs, nearly stumbling at the bottom. Pulling up his pants, he opened the front door, started to run out on the porch, and stopped short.

The woman who stepped out of the car was not Abby Merkley. She wasn't pale and soft-looking, with long, burgundy hair. This woman was all sharp angles, plucked and perfumed, with razor-thin bones and an imperial nose. Starlet sunglasses perched atop her polished hair, and she wore a slick silver coat over skin-tight jeans. Who in their right mind wore stiletto boots in the country, on a vineyard?

A second, different wave of hope rose in his chest, though, as she made her way up to the cabin, heels crunching on the remnants of two-week-old snow. *They want me back*, yelled the voice in his head. Pathetic voice, quickly tamped down, especially as nobody else emerged from the car. Not Olivier or *Maman*, the ones who mattered most.

Luc swallowed his disappointment and ignored the tightening in his chest.

"I was just heading out, Céline," he lied, grabbing his keys from the hook by the door as if his ex traveled from France to see him every day. "What do you want?"

"*T'as vu comme tu me parles*, Luc?"

"Yes, well," he responded in French. "I'm sorry I'm curt. Your visit is a bit of a surprise."

"Can we talk?"

The last thing he wanted was this woman in his house—his space—but with that constant presence up the hill, he had no choice.

"Come in," he finally said.

"What the hell are you doing here, Luc?"

"What do you mean?"

"You go from one of the most prestigious *terroirs* in the world to"—she waved dismissively at the cabin's rustic interior, Le Dog, even him—"to *this*." Trust a Frenchwoman to express such scorn in a single, innocuous syllable. "There's nothing wrong with being the peasant in the family. The earth, the life's blood. Without you, the wine is nothing. Nothing. But this…"

"Yes, well, here everything is mine."

"So? You're selling the grapes."

He hesitated, oddly nervous at the idea of outing himself. "I'm making wine."

She stopped in the process of removing her coat, eyes wide. "Really? How is it?"

"Young," he said. "But good. Interesting."

"Are you selling it?"

"Not yet."

She laughed, taking off her coat and handing it to him. "No surprise there. Do you even own anything besides work clothes?"

"It's different here," he said, irritated at her immediate assumptions. "You sell to individuals. Tastings and wine clubs and—"

"And you plan to do that? Luc"—she leaned in and put a hand on his arm, sweet and condescending—"you don't like people, remember? You love your vines and animals. No time for anything as base as us humans."

Luc looked down at the coat in his hands. Her signature perfume wafted up. He hung it up and turned back to her. "What are you doing here, Céline?"

"Don't you listen to my messages?"

"No."

She made a long *pffft* sound through pouty, red lips, making Luc feel sick with the excess of it. Too much. Too much everything. "Things are not going well at home."

"Home?"

"Our home, Luc. Your family home."

"It's not my home."

"How can you say that? It will always be home, Luc."

He studied her earnest expression, tinged with a jot of desperation. And then he knew. "Is it the upper fields?"

"What?"

"It's the upper fields, right?" She didn't have to answer. He could see it on her face as she sank onto his sofa. All the pressure, all the stupidity of planting those fields when he'd warned them. *Grandpère* had told them not to. Nobody, in all the generations of growers and winemakers before, had planted that field. They'd given it instead to the villagers, those without gardens, to plant for food.

Not profitable enough, Olivier had said. And *Maman* had agreed. Céline had, of course, stayed silent. She'd had his back then, not Olivier's. At least he'd thought so.

"When did you and my brother start fucking?" he asked, fueled by curiosity but still unable to stop the anger that rose up at the memory.

"Oh, Luc, we're not going to—"

"We damn well are. You came all this way to discuss things. To drag me back there, right?"

"I didn't think—"

"No. You didn't, Céline. You never did. If you or any of the others had ever thought about a damned thing besides your own personal gain, you would have realized that the upper fields were meant to stay fallow. That the gardens *Grandpère* let the villagers plant were full of roses and marigolds and fruits. Those fruits attracted the stupid flies." He paused, standing above, waiting for her to catch on. "*Away* from the vines."

The look of surprise on his ex's face would have been comical if it hadn't meant he was right. And if he was right, he should—

No. He wouldn't go back to France. Not unless Olivier got down on his knees and begged. Let them save their own asses. Their own *heritage*.

"It's the fruit flies, right, Céline? *Hein*?"

Her voice came out close to a whisper. "Yes."

"You all thought it was hocus-pocus. You and *Maman* and Olivier. You thought *Grandpère* and I kept the vineyard small because we weren't ambitious enough. Or to control you. You thought our decisions were absurd, superstitious fantasy. Like biodynamics. Like planting near to rocks or burying the horns." He paused, pent-up anger dangerously close to the surface. "Where's Olivier?"

"At home."

"He sent you here? To get me?"

Her mouth tightened, those overly full lips compressing, her face losing some of its confidence, and suddenly he understood. He sank down to squat in front of her, but not too close. Christ, he didn't want to risk touching her.

"He has no idea you're here, does he?" Luc whispered, the certainty burning a hole in his stomach. His half brother didn't even want him back. His mother would rather deal with their problems on her own than ask her son for forgiveness. "Where does he think you are? Girls' trip to Saint Tropez? Spa weekend at Aix-les-Bains?"

She didn't answer, but her face, normally perfectly pale in the winter, had taken on a sickly greenish hue.

"Always going behind one of our backs, aren't you? Were you planning on telling him you came here? Or would this be another seduction?" He shifted away, righteous anger humming in his veins. "Well, good luck, *ma chère*. Good luck getting out of the pit you have dug. You can go." He stood up and backed up even farther.

"Where am I supposed to go?"

"I don't know. You must have had some kind of plan when you came here."

"But there's nothing here, Luc," she protested. Shit. She'd planned to stay here, hadn't she? To seduce him, no doubt. Christ, what a sick, sick woman.

"There's a B and B," he said, thinking of the frou-frou establishment in downtown Blackwood. "Or better yet, get on the motorway and head back toward Charlottesville. They have places almost fancy enough for you there. Not the *George V*, but you can make do for one night."

She stood, tall in those deadly looking boots, and assessed him openly, eyes sharp and admittedly beautiful. "Always the martyr, Luc, aren't you?"

"Excuse me?"

"Always the one being taken advantage of; always the one pushing everyone away, *so wounded*. Did you ever ask yourself why I slept with your brother to begin with?" When he didn't answer, she continued, relentless and in his face. "You weren't the only one who was hurt in our relationship, Luc. You gave me *nothing*. You're the victim because I was obvious about it, but if you take a step back, you'd realize you never cared to begin with. All you cared about then was your vines. And now..."

She ran her eyes over him, to his left hand with its

missing finger. "Your finger? Olivier's fault, right? Because of the secateurs he forced you to use? Your *Maman*'s fault they didn't get it sewn back on in time?" With a cynical smile, she went on. "If you'd stopped working that night, maybe you'd have a finger. You were out there late, in the cold. Olivier didn't force you." She looked him head-on. "You're not a recluse, you're a *misanthrope*. More interested in being alone than trying to make things work. You're so afraid of compromise, aren't you? Of anything that would take away from your stupid vines. Growing them your way. The *right* way." She leaned in and focused on him, that smile dropping from her perfect features. "You can't stand to be hurt, can you? I don't mean *this* kind of pain." She grasped his hand, lifted it, and then shoved it away. "*This* you enjoy. You enjoy being right, even if it means alienating your own family. You're not capable of love, Luc. You're too interested in being the wronged party. That's it, isn't it? You've never loved anyone in your entire life as much as you love those stupid plants."

He opened his mouth to respond and then shut it again. She might have been right before. But now, God, she was wrong. So totally wrong he wanted to laugh.

He loved Abby. The knowledge was so clear, so right, that he could almost have hugged this woman for showing him.

Almost. Instead, he smiled and put out his hand—to her obvious shock. Now, he wanted one thing and one thing only: to get rid of her so he could go to Abby. He'd have to brave the crowds at the Nook to get to her, but what did that matter?

"Thank you."

"What?"

"I appreciate you coming here and trying. I know how hard this must have been." She blinked. "But I've got to go."

"You're leaving?"

"Actually…will you take me into town?" he asked, to Céline's obvious surprise.

"What are you talking—"

"Don't ask, all right? Just…just go out to your car. Pretend to say good-bye to me on the porch, drive past that curve down there, and then wait. Will you do that?"

"You've gone mad," she whispered, eyes round with shock and pity and a hint of revulsion.

"Please. Just take me into town and drop me—"

"Luc, you're worrying me. Let me take you back to France. Back to your life, not to this…wild place."

"If you don't want to give me a ride, fine. I'll just—"

She huffed a sigh, looked around the cabin, and turned back to him. "Around the bend? That's where I wait?"

"Yes."

She shook her head but finally agreed. "You will explain this to me?"

"Yes, of course," he lied. But he didn't owe this woman a solitary thing. Nothing.

It was night outside when he made a big show of waving her off before heading inside again and locking the front door. He stuffed the fire full of wood, turned off the lights, grabbed his coat, and whistled for Le Dog. No way he'd leave him out here alone when God only knew what those crazies would do next. As quietly as he could, he made his way out the kitchen door—too bad he didn't have a key for this one—and down the hill, half expecting that Céline had left without him.

He ignored her protests when Le Dog hopped in first, then got in, pulled the door not quite closed, and said. "Let's go. *Go!*"

They rode in silence, Luc ducked low until they'd gotten to the main road. Céline's driving, too fast and choppy at the best of times, was much worse with an automatic. Her hand hovered over the gearshift, as if she itched to grab it.

"Pull in there," he said as they sped down Main Street, past the dermatology clinic where he'd last seen Abby, and on to the Nook, the only place open at this time of night. His breathing picked up speed at the possibility of seeing her.

She pulled over and looked at him, her expression almost comically shocked. "You're going in there? You? In a bar?" And then, totally unexpectedly, she burst into laughter. "Oh. My God. It's a woman! You're… Wait. Are you *stalking* her or something? Is that why you had me drive you? Because I will not—"

"Of course not." His face flushed red. "It's…it's more complicated than that."

"I see." Although he didn't think she did. She stilled, then, her eyes serious on him, and whispered, "You're in love."

His chest convulsed.

"Okay, okay." She smiled, almost affectionately, and nodded. "Okay." She patted his hand. "Go on. I'll… Good-bye, Luc." She gave his hand a squeeze and released him, looking sad now.

Luc got out of the car and stood on the sidewalk to watch her pull away. He looked down at Le Dog, noticing for the first time that, though he'd gotten him a collar, he'd never bothered with a leash. Not that they needed one. Le Dog was never far.

It suddenly occurred to him that he couldn't very well bring the animal inside the bar with him.

Luc lifted his gaze to the Nook's bright sign and fogged-up windows and the long line of cars parked out front. Christ, what had he gotten himself into?

Only, the question was about more than tonight, wasn't it? It was about Abby and the cult and…and everything. Although, for the first time, there wasn't an iota of doubt that he was on the right path, no matter that it had flipped his life upside down. At the end of Main Street, Céline's taillights disappeared, and right here, the bar's door opened, letting out light, music, and a few laughing people. They stumbled happily to a car as he stood out here in the cold, knowing that he wasn't good enough for the woman inside.

∽ഊ∾

"Order up!" André called from the kitchen window, but with no outstanding food orders, Abby couldn't figure out who it was for.

Rory clarified. "Abby, it's time to take a break."

"No, I'm fine."

After a full day here, she had already gotten used to her boss's sardonic brow and his amiable way of bully-ing her into things. "Had André make you pasta, love. Pick it up from the window and settle your arse on a barstool. Or, if you need some quiet, use my office."

The food did look good. Somehow, Abby hadn't noticed how hungry she was, but her stomach was gurgling embarrassingly. She wouldn't pay attention to the exhaustion weighing down her limbs.

"I don't—"

"Dinner's on us, love. Always during your shift, remember? Otherwise, you'd never get any food in you. Go eat."

She did as he asked. He was the boss, after all. And, Abby noticed, she was starving. It was… She glanced at the office clock as she collapsed onto the sofa. Ten thirty. Goodness, where had the time gone?

Remembering how Luc had forked and twisted his pasta, Abby did the same, careful not to make a mess of her apron.

That reminded her. Digging into the big front pocket as she chewed, she pulled out wads of cash. She was shocked by how much there was.

It turned out people paid for food and drinks, and on top of that, they gave her money. Rory had refused it earlier when she'd tried to hand some off on him.

"It's yours, darling," he'd said in his British accent. British, she thought, where they don't pronounce that *t* in the middle of words like butter or water. Amazing how she'd barely set foot off the mountain and already she'd met an English bar owner, a half-Peruvian sheriff, a Mexican cook, and…the obvious, of course: the Frenchman she did her best not to think too much about.

There was way more than a hundred dollars in here, which would pay for more clothes at the thrift shop for Sammy. Maybe she could start a car fund.

She looked at the clock again, anxiety tightening her

back and neck. There wasn't time to buy a car before getting Sammy out.

She'd leave at two, when the bar closed. Two in the morning sounded right. Nobody at the Church would be awake at two.

She looked down at the pasta and forced herself to take another bite when what she really wanted was to pack it up in one of those white cardboard boxes and sneak it into the refrigerator upstairs for Sammy to eat tomorrow. Common sense told her she should eat more. She took another bite of pasta, which was good. A little too sweet, maybe? Nothing like the rich red sauce that Luc had fed her. The herbs in his pasta had been greener and the tomatoes brighter. The brightest time of her life.

Goodness, would she ever stop thinking of him?

After another few bites, she packed the food up and made her way back to the dining room, where the crowd was changing. More men, fewer families, the bar thick with people and the tables nearly empty.

"Dancing again tonight, love," Rory said when she joined him behind the bar. "I'll take care of these punters, and we'll clear those tables off our dance floor, get things ready for the DJ. You're welcome to clock out now or…you can stay and tear up the dance floor again. Either way, I won't need you." After a lascivious wink, he turned to a group of men at the bar, charmed his way through their order, and joined her on the floor to help her move the tables and chairs, transforming this place into the closest thing Blackwood had to a nightclub.

I work in a nightclub, she thought with a private laugh. What would Isaiah say? What would *Mama* say?

She glanced at Rory—a man who pretended, with

every fiber of his being, to be lazy. Every movement appeared somehow slow and laconic, yet look at how much he accomplished. There was an art to it.

When they'd finished, she went to the back to take off her apron, again eyeing the clock. Eleven. Still too early, but her nerves jangled in anticipation of what she planned to do. She didn't figure she'd be able to sleep with the thumping of the music beneath her. Nor, for that matter, with the thumping of her heart. Lord, she could hardly breathe.

"Here, love." Rory's voice cut into her thoughts as he handed her a drink.

"What's this?"

"Vodka cranberry."

"Oh. Thank you."

"Not big drinkers where you're from, then?"

She shook her head and avoided his eye, because he'd been kind—beyond kind, considering he'd given her the room upstairs to live in for next to nothing—but there was a light in his eye that she didn't trust.

"Something on your mind?" he asked.

"Oh. No."

"Come on out and watch the crowd, then."

"Yes. Yes, I think I will."

She followed him out and settled at the bar, where she watched him work. A handsome man, she thought, but not…not Luc.

"Abby?"

The voice, so familiar she felt it in her belly, couldn't possibly be real.

"Abby? Could I speak with you?"

She spun around in her seat. And there he was,

looking flushed and disheveled and so much better than she remembered.

"Hi" was all she could manage, the vodka and marinara threatening to come back up. She was intensely aware of her clothes, stained despite her best efforts, the flat, white sneakers, scuffed by whoever had worn them before, the hand-me-down jeans, and…everything.

"You are well?"

Abby forced a smile, powered a big breath in, and nodded. "I'm great. Great, thanks. I'll just… What are you—"

"I just wanted to—"

"Oh," Abby said, turning to hide her embarrassed smile. "You go ahead."

"You *are* working here."

She nodded. "Yes."

"Ah." He glanced over her shoulder—avoiding her eye?—and back, straight at her in a way that proved how wrong that theory was. His voice lowered to a whisper. "How is your…?" He motioned over his shoulder.

"Better. I'm… It's… George was finally convinced that I'd healed well enough to leave. So…"

"Good." He looked down. Definitely avoiding. "Good."

"Yes. The beauty of modern medicine."

"I'm glad you're well."

"So." She let her eyes slide to look at the people behind him. "What brings you here?"

"Just came in for a drink."

"Shift's over, Abigail, my darling." Rory appeared by her side, his voice quiet but sharp as he eyed Luc in a decidedly unfriendly manner. "I see the Cape Cod's not to your taste. What's your poison?"

"My poison?"

"What do you like to drink, dearest?"

"She likes a good Bordeaux," Luc answered, his focus shifting to Rory in what looked like a challenge, before returning to her.

"How about a cheap Chilean red?" Rory asked.

"If that's what you"—*think I should drink*, she'd been about to say, which was ridiculous; instead, she finished with—"have, then that's what I'll take." And then, because she couldn't help it, she added, "But if you ever decide to upgrade, I know of a wonderful local vintage."

Luc's blush intensified at those words, and he looked away when Rory eyed him. "Shall I get this man a drink, as well?" he asked her, waiting for her nod before taking off to serve their drinks.

"I lied," Luc said, eyes finally settling on her face.

"Excuse me?" she asked.

"About coming here for a drink." He shook his head with that self-deprecating expression that made her want to wrap her arms around him. He had to speak loudly to be heard over the music, which, she could tell, only served to make him uncomfortable. "I came here to see you."

Oh, that did it. That woke her up. Swallowing back whatever she'd been about to say, she watched him and held back her smile.

"But Le Dog is outside, so I should—"

"Hold on." Abby turned to call to Rory. "Can we bring the wine upstairs?"

"Course, love." Rory threw a look at Luc, which she appreciated.

"Meet me at the back door. I'll open it up for you,

and you can come up to my…my place," she finished. The words felt strange in her mouth, like she was an imposter, or a child pretending.

"Yes. Yes, I'll do that," Luc said before walking off, his big body cutting a too-large swath through the crowd.

Rory set down two glasses and an open bottle of wine on the car beside her.

"So that's your poison, then." She frowned for a second, thinking he meant the wine, until she followed his gaze to Luc's departing back. "We've all got our Kryptonite, haven't we?"

"Our what?"

He blinked slowly, eyes focused sharply on her, and she had the distinct feeling she'd divulged too much information with that bit of ignorance.

"Man of Steel? Superman? The only thing that fells him?" he asked, and rather than continue to show her ignorance, Abby smiled and forced out a tight chuckle.

"Oh, right. Of course," she said and turned away.

"You're not in Kansas anymore, darling."

"Definitely," she said, with absolutely no idea what he was talking about. Picking up the bottle and glasses, she turned and headed to the back.

25

THE TINY APARTMENT UPSTAIRS FROM THE NOOK reminded Luc of something you'd find on the top floor of a Paris apartment building. A real estate agent would no doubt call this "character." Le Dog didn't seem to mind, though. With a satisfied huff, he settled next to what looked like a heating vent. Not even the thumping floor seemed to bother him.

"You're living here?"

"Yes." She indicated that he should sit, but he couldn't. Who could possibly sit with this much... energy running through him?

He shoved back the anger he felt at Abby living in a place like this. Cracks in the ceiling, a kitchen sink stained beyond repair, linoleum that should have been replaced decades ago. She didn't belong here.

Not like she belongs in your crappy cabin, came a voice from the back of his mind.

Swallowing back the hounding voices of doubt, he served the wine and waited for her to sit. When she didn't, he stayed standing, suddenly filled with doubt.

"I've...I've missed you." The words didn't sound like his. They sounded too weak. Too real.

"You have?" Her eyes were massive and liquid, and fuck, they made him feel so damned alive.

He huffed out a strangled laugh and slugged back a glass of wine rather than throwing himself at her feet.

"How are you feeling?" he asked in lieu of a response.

"Fine. Better."

"Your back?"

"Yes." After a pause during which they both drank, she elaborated. "It's better. Not perfect, but better."

"Good." Why was this so awkward? It shouldn't be awkward, it should be—

At the sink, she reached up for a glass—a jam jar—and filled it with water. She slugged it back and splashed her face.

Only then did he take in the details of her—not their disgusting surroundings or his disgusting thoughts, but her. She looked...good. Tall and full, her body different in clothing that was her size. Blue jeans that fit her. A shirt that flowed from her strong, slender shoulders, down over breasts that were lush and full and suspended. A bra, which both delighted and dismayed him. The thought of fancy, frilly lingerie on this woman was enough to heat his blood.

He pictured men seeing her in the lingerie. Other men, many men. Like that barman downstairs, whose throat he'd rip out, whose fucking heart he'd tear into pieces, whose stupid, lascivious grin he'd—

Her hands grasped his face, and she kissed him, hard.

"I missed you, too," she whispered in his mouth, and Christ, he couldn't stop himself from crushing her with his arms, pulling her in tight and seeking out the hollow of her neck, that place where the smell was purely her. Even with the scents of the bar layered over top and odors of cooking, he found her there and drew her in. Home. She felt like home.

Her lips went to his again and gave him the kiss he'd been missing for so long, sensation, yes, but so full of emotion, he thought he'd drown in it. Christ, what had he done before her?

Her mouth was hot and hungry, the sounds she made even better.

"Take this off," she whispered, plucking at the coat he still wore. Hurriedly, he removed it and then, at her urging, his shirt.

Everything stopped when she put her head to his chest—an echo of what she'd done the week before in his cabin—and breathed. Just breathed.

"What are you doing, *amour*?"

"Listening," she whispered. "Just listening."

"There's nothing there."

She exhaled loudly and shook her head from side to side.

"You have no idea, do you, Luc?" she asked, finally pulling back to look him in the eye, her face...tragic, maybe, which he hated. "No idea."

"About what?" he asked, truly puzzled.

"Your heart, Luc. You have no idea how beautiful it is."

All he could do was watch her, this woman who didn't realize she'd stolen it right out from inside him.

∼◦∽

Abby meant to tell him what she planned. But then she'd seen his face—that sweet, scarred face—and she couldn't help but kiss him. After that, his shock had been so palpable, and she'd known in this instinctive sort of way that he was shocked at her desire and her emotion. He was shocked by how much she wanted him.

It made her want him so hard she couldn't stop touching him, caressing him. Good Lord, if she could, she'd consume every inch of him.

Which gave her an idea.

The impact of her body against his was jarring. It rattled her foundations. It probably jolted the dancers downstairs in the bar. Her hand in his hair, yanking his head closer, his face near hers, their teeth clashing too hard. His lips were torture; he could kill her with that tongue, and oh no, his smell. His smell was torment. *Excruciatingly perfect.*

She'd sell her soul for that smell. To the devil. She'd let Isaiah and his minions burn every inch of her. Something purely animal escaped her mouth. No containing it, but that was fine. Fine when he took it, ate it up, gave her a noise of his own.

Goodness, where was this coming from? The need and the…greed? Where had she kept it all these years, up until she'd met this man? It was old and deep and strong, an overflowing well.

Luc's shoulders were hot under her hands. Her fingers scrabbled at his waist, tore at it until he helped her get whatever it was off, down, down, landing at their feet with the clunk of keys.

Bless me, this body.

She glanced down to see his underwear—navy-blue shorts—and the need to consume him swelled anew.

I can't breathe. I can't... I can't.

Slowly, she sank to her knees.

"Don't do that. Don't, Abby," he said, his accent thick, choppier than she'd ever heard it. She tucked her fingers into his waistband and dragged it down, slowly, slowly, while his voice faded away to a pained-sounding groan.

He seemed far away up there now, with her face next to his cock and his smell so warm and potent and perfect.

She bit her lip to hold back a sound of her own and slowly reached for him. He was big and thick, and the color of him here was darker than she remembered. Above her somewhere, he protested, but his hands hung limp at his sides, which made the protest feel halfhearted.

Full of curiosity and desire, she brought him—his cock—close to her face and ran it along her cheek. It was so soft she had to do it again, and Luc sounded like he was dying. With a half smile, she eyed him. "You okay?" she asked. Goodness, how had she not known the power of this? Of holding a man's desire in her hand? Of drawing it out until it stretched thin and tight between them like a guitar string, taut enough to break, but so perfectly pitched when she plucked it.

On that note, she ran her nose along him, breathed him in and then lowered her mouth to his crown, where she ventured a taste—just a lick, really, but enough to make Luc shudder above her, and she met his eyes and smiled.

Look at me now, she thought as she took him into her mouth, slow, slow, filling her, so ripe and lush and perfect until it was too much and she withdrew, a touch out of breath but ready for more.

More, oh God, more. She might have actually said it, because he released a noise that sounded like aching and pushed into her mouth a little deeper, another time, even deeper, until she took him in far, and then his hands pulled her up.

"Come on, Abby. Not like that. Not on the floor like that."

She stood, and her shirt was gone, rent open with nothing but the echoing ping of eight tiny buttons to remember it by. It took her a second to realize she'd been the one to rip it off. She'd paid ten dollars for this shirt today. Too much, but she'd liked the color. The stupid thing was the exact color of Luc Stanek's eyes. Beneath it, she wore her first modern bra—complete with underwire, which held her in a way she found erotic against her skin.

She didn't get rid of the bra like she had the shirt. Instead, he yanked the cups down, baring her, opening her up, thrusting her breasts even higher, served on a platter. He stroked a nipple, not nearly hard enough when she wanted him to bite. Abby stopped breathing, her underwear suddenly too tight. The blue jeans lost their appeal. Too complicated, too…constrictive.

"Would you…would you bite it? Please?"

And his face—Luc's furrowed face, too tender and full of surprise, focused on her breasts for one, two, three seconds before he leaned down and touched his lips to her. Not the bite she'd been craving, but she knew he wasn't the brute he pretended to be. And oh, the noise from her lungs deflated. Half scream, half pained moan, her head flopped back, and her hips… Why did they do that? Rocking, rocking, in search of something.

He took his mouth away, hot and wet where it had sucked at her nipple, and brought it to the other one, pinching the first and lifting them both, drawing them together, muttering. What was he saying? He sounded lost. Some of it was in French. She liked the way those words tore at her, a little at a time, but some of it came out in English, and it was crass.

"You missed me, Abby? Did you? Because I could not stop thinking of you. Every day. Every fucking minute." He didn't look happy about it.

"*Lord, yes,*" she bit out, taking hold of his hand and putting it between her legs. *When did I get this bossy?* she wondered as he rubbed her through her jeans.

And there it was again, that pressure in her abdomen, warm and electric. Hands at her waist, fumbling, the sound of a zipper, stiff material scraping down her legs, his rough hands following it down. At the bottom, the fabric got stuck in her boots, and with a frustrated sound, he squatted, yanked hard at one boot until it gave and the fabric slid off with it. Without doing the other side, he paused where he was.

Inhale. Exhale. She took in what felt like her first breath since this all began. No wonder things were out of focus.

"Come here," she said, her voice hoarser than she'd ever heard it.

"Wait." He was looking at her—not her face, but down there. His breath was warm on her, and she could smell it: her own female scent. The one she equated with pleasure—with him.

"Come *here*, Luc. Hurry. I want…" *Everything.* Her

hands—God, they had a mind of their own—tried to pull him up. "*Now.*"

Instead of obeying, he reached out and touched her, right where the hair sprang up in unruly curls between her legs. And while his hands had been a bit rough when they had rid her of the trousers, now they were gentle, even shaky.

The back of his knuckles brushed against the hair, before his hand twisted and cupped her, one finger straightening and reaching beneath, between her lips, where it slipped and slid. Back and forth once, twice, and back, circling her opening before sliding in.

Ah, sweet relief.

Her knees loosened and almost gave. Downstairs, the music was turned up a notch, and the floor shook rhythmically under her feet, but here the only noise was the messy, slick slide of his finger pressing in and out of her body. She looked down to find his brow furrowed, his features tight with concentration, gaze fixed on where his finger disappeared between her legs. She'd never seen that look on his face, none of the peace he showed when he worked or the light humor he'd shown other times. He looked intense, focused.

"From that first day, Abby, I've been yours. Yours," he said, the words sounding torn from his throat. And Lord, for a moment, she thought she might cry.

Instead, she pulled at his hair, reached for his face, because right now, she wanted him thick and deep. She wanted him so deep she'd never forget.

"I want you to fuck me, Luc," she said, her voice more decisive than she'd ever heard it, that word lighting her up.

It worked though—seemed to wake him from his daze, got him up and moving, tugging at his pocket, pulling open his wallet. What on earth was he doing with his wallet?

She tried to slap it away from him, but he kept on, pulled something out. A foil square like the one they'd used last time. A condom. How strange. And serendipitous.

She watched him rip it open with his teeth and pull it out before slipping the ring over the tip of his *cock*. She'd just had it in her mouth, but still it surprised her, made her want to taste it again, which felt like a tragedy, since she couldn't keep doing this to him. She had to get Sammy and go. That was it. Get Sammy and go.

Stop it. Enjoy this moment.

She held her breath and let her eyes meet his. They watched her. Waiting.

He'd stopped. "You want this, Abby?"

"Yes," she admitted.

"I'm not good at...talking about things. Making them pretty."

"I know," she said, but she also knew it wasn't true. He'd made her feel special with his words, but also his looks, his touch.

"I want to fuck you so hard."

Oh, that sent a new wave of heat into her face. It prickled her scalp.

"Do it." That felt like a challenge. She liked the way his fingers pinched her nipple in reply.

"I want to forget about everything."

What? What did he want to forget about? It didn't matter. Nothing mattered when he grabbed her hard at her hips and pushed her back, back, back to the chipped Formica edge of the kitchenette counter, lifted her up. It didn't matter that the surface beneath was wet with water or that she was just as wet between her legs.

And hungry. Terribly hungry.

"Don't forget," she muttered, pulling at him, trying to, but he wouldn't let her. He caught her hands in his, held them behind her back with one of his, and kissed her. Slow and deep and wet.

This. This was the kiss she'd remember for the rest of her life. This was the kiss that would warm her bed when she was far from here. This was the kiss that would make her forget what Isaiah might still be doing to the others on the mountain when she and Sammy were long gone.

This was the kiss.

～～～

Luc hadn't meant to go all sweet. He'd wanted to fuck her, hard. But then he'd caught sight of her face and those lips, and the kiss just happened.

One moment he felt nothing but animal desire and the next…

Soft lips, softer whimpers, soft breasts against his chest. Why did it make his lungs go tight? Instead of keeping her hands trapped behind her back, he let them go, begging, "Put your hands on me, please," in a hoarse voice. He waited as she slid one in his hair; the other stroked down to his waist and up to his chest, where her nails dug in.

He'd never experienced anything like Abby's touch. Nothing was better than the soft edge of her tongue against his or the way she nipped at his lip. Nothing more satisfying than the rasp of his chest against her pointy, pink nipples.

No. That wasn't entirely true, he knew, pulling away long enough to catch her eyes with his.

"You want this?" he asked, looking down at where his cock stood up, thick and demanding. Aching, aching to press into her.

"Yes."

"You want to put me in you?" he asked.

"Me?"

"Yes," he breathed, barely controlling his voice. "You do it."

What was that on her face? Surprise? Some anticipation? Her hand was hot on his cock. Just her fingertips, at first.

"Hold me harder."

"Like this?" Her palm tightened, but not enough. Not nearly enough.

"No." His voice was harsh as he clasped his fist over hers, tightening painfully. "Like this."

"Oh goodness."

"Squeeze and pull."

He took his hand away, because leaving it would mean taking control. Shoving in, thrusting, fucking.

"Put me in you, Abby."

"Wait, I want to see you first. I need to—"

"Please," he interrupted, his voice threaded with need. Her gaze rose to meet his.

One pass of her fist over him, as they held each other's eyes, and fuck, he was a goner. Worse than before, because he understood that she'd hurt him. How could she not when he was already so chafed and raw? She scooted to the edge of the counter, lowered the tip of his cock, and slid it against her.

Luc's breathing filled the air, along with her smell. He glanced up, catching her looking at him. Together, their attention flicked down, up and down. As her hand found her opening, he took that last half step into her body so they did this together—the giving and the taking. And together, their voices entwined in the air between them, wordless grunts on his end, a long, whimpering moan on hers.

His attention was fixed firmly below, his forehead pressed hard to hers, and fuck, it had been too long without her. His balls were high and tight, slapping gently against her at first, before her legs went around his hips and pulled him in harder.

She was as hot and snug as his own skin, and those curls between her legs made him want to tug. He'd do that next time, take his time. Now, though, he couldn't, because his hands were planted on her hips, where he could pull her in, tighter, tighter, harder, with every thrust of his body into hers.

He was going to orgasm too fast, he realized. Too fucking soon. But he couldn't slow down. Instead, he pulled one hand from her and slid it between them, to bury into that hair, find her clit and rub. No time for slow, no time for pretty. He used everything he had to make it quick, rough, the pad of his thumb and the side of one finger going fast and furious.

"Oh, oh, oh." Abby's noises were beautiful, musical, as he slowed his hips and quickened his fingers, almost stopping altogether when she clamped both hands to his wrist to slow him down.

"Let me. Let me make you come."

"I can't…"

"You need me to stop?"

Her eyes flew to his. "No. No, just…lighter." She bit her lip. "Make it last longer."

He almost chuckled at that, but it turned into a groan. "I'm not sure I can, *mon amour*."

"It's coming too fast," she said, sounding slightly frantic, and he slowed his pace, and oh fuck, this was almost harder. Watching each long, slow slide into her was excruciating. Torture.

"I'm going to come," he warned, and her eyes shot up to meet his.

"Okay." She nodded. "Do it. Make me come, too."

Christ, he loved how direct she was. How could she be like this after everything? *How?*

She convulsed around him tighter than he'd ever been clasped, and he couldn't have stopped his climax for anything in the world. He lost it, deep inside her, holding her hard against him and wondering how on earth he was ever going to let her leave.

26

THEY MOVED TO HER BED, WHICH WAS SMALL AND SAGGING but clean—none of which mattered with her in his arms.

They'd lain there for a while, her head on his chest, when she broke the silence.

"I'm getting him out tonight."

He stiffened.

"I'll drive." He paused. "Shit."

She leaned up on an elbow. "What is it?"

"I don't have my truck."

She looked at him, confused. "What do you mean? How'd you get here?"

"It's a long story."

She sat up and leaned forward until the numbers on the microwave came into view. "We've got time."

"You have this planned out then?"

She shrugged. "I leave here at two."

"How were you planning to get there?"

"Walking."

"Jesus, Abby. And then, what? You and Sammy would walk back here?"

"Yes."

"You weren't going to tell me, were you?"

Slowly, she shook her head, softening the blow with sweet, shiny eyes and a soft hand to his cheek. "This is your life, Luc. I can't ruin your life."

"No?" He mirrored her movement, touching the backs of his fingers against skin that was crushingly soft. "*Non, mon amour*?"

She put her ear back to his chest and her vigil over his heart, which was quickly breaking beyond repair.

When her breathing grew deep and regular and he was pretty sure she'd fallen asleep, he pulled away as carefully as he could, got out of bed, and dressed, shocked that she didn't wake. He wanted to kiss her again before leaving but couldn't risk it.

The hardest part, as he left her small nest above the Nook, was nudging Le Dog back inside and hoping he didn't start crying or doing something else that would wake her. But it was a risk he was willing to take. Bringing the dog—or the woman—with him was not an option.

He crept down the stairs and out the back door into the cold, clear night. Above the parking lot, a single bare bulb shone, a solitary glow against the night. Nothing like the fancy streetlamps on Main Street meant for the tourists; this mean bulb was purely utilitarian. No prettiness here, nothing to distract from the dumpsters and the stink and what was possibly a puddle of vomit a few feet along the gravel drive.

He sucked it all in on a whoosh: the stench, the remorse of leaving her. A look around showed a dead downtown, cars congregated around this building,

but nothing else moving. Luc didn't want to go back
into the bar. Nor did he want to call a cab or an Uber.
Nobody else should be involved in what he had to do
right now.

∽◌∼

Abby woke up alone and groggy, in the half-light of her
new apartment, sure that something was wrong. It took
a few beats for things to click into place, but once they
did, she was up and getting dressed. It was still before
two, the bar downstairs audibly winding down for the
night. Luc couldn't have left that long ago, could he?

How dare he? How dare he leave when this was *her*
mission to accomplish? Le Dog got up and stretched
as she pulled on her new clothing—suddenly too tight
rather than freeing. At the last minute, she remembered
to grab the keys she'd have to get used to carrying
around. Someday. Someday this would all be normal,
and then maybe she'd wish for her old life again.

Doubtful.

She patted Le Dog on the head and, after a few seconds' hesitation on the landing, went toward the bar
instead of out the back door.

Rory blinked when he saw her.

"You here to help close up, love?" he said above the
loud music.

"Oh, I hadn't—"

"That was a joke." He paused, eyeing her closely
before his eyes flicked over her shoulder. "Where's
your bloke?"

"He left."

Rory frowned. "You give me the word, and I'll—"

"No. I just… I need to go after him. What's the best way?"

"You can't call an Uber in Blackwood, love."

Abby blinked. She had no idea what that meant.

"Right." Rory went to grab something from behind the bar and threw it at her. A set of keys that dropped to the floor before she could catch them.

"The truck's old, but she runs fine. Just don't too push her too hard on the uphills. She's out back, parked beside the rubbish."

She blinked. "Oh, I couldn't—"

"Go catch him, love." He paused. "Go on."

She turned to go and then stopped to turn back. "I'm sorry, Rory. But I have another favor to ask."

His brows rose. "Go on then."

"There's a dog upstairs. Luc's dog. I hope that's okay."

"As long as it doesn't piss all over, I don't mind what you do up there."

"Thank you, Rory. I owe you—"

"Go. Go on. Catch your bloke and give him what for."

He shooed her out and went to calm a loud group of men insisting they hadn't missed last call as Abby went out back to find the truck.

∽◎∾

The walk to the mountain was long and cold, despite working up a sweat inside his parka. Somewhere around mile five, it started snowing, which would have added insult to injury. But by that time, Luc had developed such a steady rhythm that he hardly noticed it at all.

Jesus. He was really going to do this, wasn't he? Forget about everything he'd worked for, ignore the danger to his land, his livelihood, and himself, and attack the crazy cult next door.

Not attack. Stealthily infiltrate.

The strange thing, though, was that there was no regret when he considered everything he risked losing. Not an ounce of fear, either, which he couldn't possibly attribute to the glass of wine he'd consumed earlier.

His feet crunched up the road, gravel and snow and ice making the footing treacherous, keeping his mind on the here and now.

The smart thing would be to call Navarro, to get him involved now, because that made sense, instead of rushing in there on his own like some demented, French Rambo.

Rambeau, he thought with a snicker.

Going serious again, he reminded himself that Abby didn't want that. And Abby had good reasons for things, didn't she?

They're all waiting for the Apocalypse, she'd said. *They're expecting the End of Days. And I'm beginning to think Isaiah would not be against bringing it about himself, if need be.*

The whole thing rigged to blow.

Abby doesn't want me to do this either, he reminded himself with a stab to the gut.

By the time Luc reached the bottom of his drive, the sweat inside his coat didn't keep him from shivering. He'd left his place open to attack again, gone for hours—although they wouldn't know that, with his truck parked in front of the cabin. But there was that same fear at the back of his throat: the possibility that they'd attacked him while he was gone, and he was impotent against them.

Well, fuck that. He was done being scared, done worrying. Done letting them walk all over him. And more than anything, he was done letting them walk all over Abby.

∽ঞ৹

Abby hadn't driven in a while, although she'd done it a few times on market duty. In fact, she'd even had a driver's license made. Of course, Isaiah'd taken it away from her. For safekeeping.

The closer she got to the mountain, the tighter her stomach twisted, and still, there was no sign of Luc. This truck was older than anything she'd driven before, and she kept her pace slow, despite the nerves trying to shove her foot onto the accelerator. It was a good thing, too, because she might not have seen him if she hadn't been inching along in the newly falling snow.

She pulled up beside him, leaned over, and used the hand crank to roll down the window.

"Luc!"

He stopped and turned to squint at the truck, and even from here, the man looked cold.

"Get in! Come on!"

Shaking his head, he turned and waited for her to pull up the lock before opening the door and climbing in beside her.

"What are you doing?"

"I'm getting Sammy," he said, and for the first time in her life, Abby had the urge to hit someone. Not hard, just...

She grabbed him by the collar instead and shook him before plastering her mouth to his in a hard kiss.

He kissed her back with equal vigor, his lips as cold as ice.

"You are a...a nightmare." She bit out the words before letting him go and putting the truck back into drive. "You have a plan?"

"First, I was going to get my gun," he said with what sounded like humor, "and possibly defrost my feet. And then I was going to get Sammy out."

"Yes?" She nodded, as slow and calm as she could.

"Yes."

"You're a...a *stupid* man."

"I am." His hand covered hers on the steering wheel. "But you were going to do the same."

"I wasn't going to go in like some...*dumb, stupid man*."

He chuckled, and the feeling that sound brought up in her chest should have worried her. Instead, it warmed her up.

"We go in quietly and get him out. Together."

"All right," he said with a sigh. "Together. We go together." He moved his hand to her thigh and gave her a squeeze that lit her up inside, the sensation utterly inappropriate in this moment, but so good that she almost purred.

"We can't drive in now that they've put up the guard."

She swung her face around. "Guard?"

He sighed, hard, as if he hadn't meant to say that. "They've been watching me."

"That's why you don't have your truck tonight?"

"Yes."

"Through the fence, then."

"We'd need tools for that, and we can't drive up to my cabin without them seeing us."

"Right." They must have been keeping Sammy in the Center with the kids. "Your driveway. That place where it runs up on the fence."

"The snowbank we got stuck in on the way out."

"Exactly. By the slaughterhouse."

"Where will he be?"

She doused the lights and started up his drive, passed the slaughterhouse, and parked, hidden from view, keys dangling from the ignition. Ready to run.

She laid a gloved hand on Luc's, stalling him.

"Let me out, Luc. I'll do it. I'll go in."

He shook his head, pressed his forehead to hers, and whispered, "We do this together, Abby. Now, where is Sammy?"

She inhaled his warmth. "The Center."

"Okay."

He gave her a hard kiss and pulled away, then seeming to change his mind, he grabbed her hand, threw a sidelong glance her way, and whispered, "We're in this together. But once we get him out, you leave town. You take him and go."

"I know, Luc." Though she didn't want to. She wanted to stay with him. She wanted to be his family.

"Don't worry about me. Just leave town."

"I will." Lord, those words were the saddest thing she'd ever said, each syllable like ripping out a piece of her heart.

"That way?"

"Yes." Before they took off, he went to the back of the truck and came back with an ax.

Abby followed closely behind Luc, marveling at how much better these boots were than the shoes she'd had to walk in before. The sky over the mountain was changing as they climbed the low fence and trudged toward the Center as quietly as they could over the hard-crusted snow. Strange to see this place in the cold light of dawn.

Dawn. It shouldn't be dawn for a few hours yet.

About twenty feet from the main double doors, Abby stopped and threw her head back. The clouds shone bright orange.

"Luc," Abby gasped, but he'd already seen it. Probably smelled the smoke, too. "Go, Luc. Run. Go take care of your vines." Her whisper came out harsh and frantic and much too loud. She expected him to run, but he didn't. Of course he wouldn't.

Instead, he took hold of her hand and continued the trek forward, shaking his head and muttering what she thought might have been "Together."

27

INSIDE THE CULT'S MAIN BUILDING WAS A BIG ROOM, LOW-ceilinged. It was too dark to make out much detail, but it smelled musty, like old carpeting. Camp Jesus, frayed at the edges. Luc ignored the way his pulse pounded in his skull, doing his best to concentrate instead on getting them out of here alive. Squinting, he could make out crosses and prints on the walls. Rows of wooden chairs faced what must have been a sort of altar at the opposite end of the space.

This was it? The place where these people worshiped their angry god? Luc had never been much for religion, but he'd always felt a sort of awe in France's cathedrals and ancient stone churches. This windowless space inspired nothing.

There were doors off to each side and a double set straight ahead, but Abby was already headed to the left. When she paused, he got close enough to stir her hair with his breath and whispered, "Open it. I'll go in."

She turned the knob and pulled, and he entered a

room that felt immediately different. First of all, there was breathing.

A lot of breathing.

He could see enough to realize that there were people waiting here, together in one big space. It felt like a trap, like some demented surprise party.

Only…that was snoring, wasn't it?

Somebody snuffled, a quiet, high-pitched, plaintive sound, and everything crystallized. All the kids were here. Not with their parents in those cozy-looking cabins, but here, in this big, cavernous space.

It smelled like…like urine, he realized. Diapers, maybe. Other things, too, that he couldn't identify, but the entirety of it freaked him out like nothing had before.

They're expecting the End of Days. And I'm beginning to think Isaiah would not be against bringing it about himself, if need be.

Abby's words came back to hit him hard in the chest, and his instincts told him to back out.

That was when the voice whispered.

"Abby?"

His breath rushed out with equal parts fear and relief.

Abby responded from right beside him. "That you, Sammy?"

"You come to get me?"

"Yes. Come on. Let's go."

"Don't wanna leave without my friends."

Oh God, why did he have to say that? Why did he force this into a choice that they couldn't possibly make?

There must be adults in here, right? Watching over all these children? *Mon Dieu*, how many of them were there, right now, hearing this conversation?

As his eyes adjusted, he barely made out a row of cots or pallets or mattresses, one after another, after another. What looked like cribs lined the far wall. He squeezed his eyes shut, wishing he didn't know about this.

Babies.

He'd just opened his mouth to whisper that it was time to go when a voice cut in.

"Who's there?" A woman.

"It's Abby, Brigid," said Abby. "Just here to get Sammy, and then I'm leaving."

"*Abigail?* You ain't takin' nobody. I'm callin' Isaiah and—"

"He's sick, Brigid. You heard me tell Mama. You know he'll—"

The woman made a strange, frantic sound.

Someone snuffled on the other side of the room, and another kid coughed. Abby whispered again, "It's his only chance."

Luc came up against something and stiffened. A person, who let out a bleat of a sound, and after a beat or two, he recognized it as Sammy. "Sammy, it's Luc," he whispered as quietly as he could.

"Who else's here?" came the other woman's voice, louder now.

"I brought a friend. To help."

Harsh breathing told him where Brigid stood, and Luc wondered if he needed to subdue her. In the meantime, she spoke again, something different in her voice. "Take Jeremiah, too." The words were electric, stopping them all in their tracks.

"What?" breathed Abby.

"Take him," the woman said. "I won't tell."

Luc's skin pebbled over with goose bumps. This whole thing was so wrong.

"We can't take your baby, Brigid. He'd—"

"Just do it. Or I scream." A rustling sound and footsteps, then she went on. "Here. He needs to see a doctor. And vaccinations. I want him to have those. You can"— she cleared a clogged-sounding throat—"you can say he's yours."

"No, I—"

"I'm *beggin'* you. *Please*." The last word came out more like a wail, and Luc cut in.

"Take the child, Abby," he said, grabbing Sammy's hand and pulling him toward the door.

A noise came from outside. A man's voice, yelling, followed by another and the loud crunch of footsteps in the snow.

"Let's go," he said again, moving fast until he was stopped, midstep, by Brigid's voice.

"Too late," said Brigid. "Through that door. The Small Chapel."

"No," said Abby, her voice strange. "I won't go in there."

"Go." Brigid pushed the group toward a door. "Out the back."

"Come on, Abby," Luc urged. He grabbed her arm and pulled. Reaching past Sammy, he found the door, twisted the knob, and they stumbled through. The door slammed shut behind them, cutting out all light and air.

Blind in the pitch black, he felt around for Abby and found her, child in her arms. "Which way?"

"I can't, Luc. This is… Down this hall is the Small

Chapel. It's where they…" She shook as she spoke, and a shiver slid up his spine.

This place smelled of stale ashes. And fear.

He waited.

"I can't go through that room. They hurt me there, Luc."

"Okay, Abby. Okay. We stay here. Or we can turn back and bust our way out, if you want. I can do my Rambo impersonation."

She didn't speak for a second, and he stood, with Sammy breathing hard against him and the men's voices getting louder next door. "Rambo? Is that a superhero?" she asked finally, and oh fuck, he wanted to kiss her. No, he wanted to marry this woman.

They started moving again, Abby leading them through a door, and *putain*, he could smell the ashes stronger in here. He almost gagged, not from disgust, but from anger. And another emotion, stronger, more protective. Some kind of instinct he'd never known he possessed, inexorably linked to this country and this woman.

Suddenly, Luc didn't want to hide anymore. He wanted to tear through this place, swinging the ax he still held at his side, to knock them down like a goddamned Viking raider. And then he wanted to tear Isaiah apart. With his teeth.

Beside him, Abby whispered, breaking through the shimmering sheen of rage. "The exit's right over there."

Blinking, he moved, making sure the others were right where he could feel them. Their breathing was loud in his ears.

The fucking door wouldn't open, and Luc felt around until he encountered a massive padlock. Behind them, a door slammed, and somewhere outside—hopefully not too far away—Luc thought he heard a siren.

"Step back." He nudged the others to the side and hefted the ax, determined enough to chop through the lock on the first swing. A kick finished the job, and they were out in the fiery night.

~∞~

Abby's breath was loud in her ears when she spoke. "We can't leave the children."

Luc said, "I know." He sounded resigned but certain. "This stops now."

"I'll go—"

"You take these two to the fence, and I'll go back."

"Okay." She wanted to argue, but what was the point? Besides, if she could get Jeremiah and Sammy out, she could come back and—

Brigid appeared in the doorway along with several women, their arms full of groggy children, others dragged behind them. Her old adversary nodded at her once, and suddenly they were on the same team, aligned in their rejection of this life that had been forced on them. "This is all of them," said Brigid.

On a rush of adrenaline and something that felt like love or pride, Abby turned to run. Behind them, something popped, and one of the children started to scream.

Pulse beating hard and fast in her throat, Abby pushed herself harder. From behind her came the loud pop and crash of the Center roof caving in. It smelled bad, like gas and...

A gunshot sounded out from not too far away, and Abby couldn't even look. She refused to turn back, wouldn't look behind her, because this baby in her arms, and all the others, depended on her to get them out. Smoke billowed out from behind them now, thick enough to choke her as she nearly fell. Gagging, she pulled her coat over Jeremiah's face and ran faster.

Someone yelled—nothing but a disembodied voice in the blinding wreckage. *He would have killed the babies*, she thought over and over and over. Seconds more, and he'd have killed the babies. Who could possibly side with him after that? None of them would, right? Mama couldn't possibly want to stay with that man?

They were close to the property line, the part where the fence was low enough to climb, when a shadow broke out from the trees and turned into a man. Benji, rifle in hand, blocked their way, and the scene was like something she'd lived before. Just days ago, but it could have been a different life.

"You going to shoot me, Benji?" she asked, slowing. "You planning to shoot your own son?"

Benji's face turned strange enough to stop Abby in her tracks. He didn't know. He hadn't realized she held his baby under her coat. At first, she thought it was anger or disappointment, but when he dropped the rifle and moved toward her, his mouth open wide, expression a broken thing, she understood it for what it was: relief. He sobbed with it when he saw his boy, and had she been a different person today, she'd have let him take the baby.

Instead, she held on tighter, but when she moved to walk around him, he put out his hand to stop her.

"Stop your cryin'," Brigid's voice hissed from a few feet away. "You pick up that rifle, Benjamin Sipe, and make sure we get out of here alive. It's your job to keep your boy safe. All of the kids, after what you let Isaiah turn this place into."

Everyone stilled, except for Luc and Abby, who was pretty sure Benji had never had a woman speak to him like that before. But being less of an idiot than Abby had believed, he complied, picking up the rifle and looking to them for direction.

"Hold up the rear," said Luc, the ax in his hand ten times more threatening than the firearm in Benji's. But then again, he was ten times the man. Something like pride swelled in Abby's chest.

An explosion from the Center sent them all running again, toward the fence. Finally, they made it to the truck.

Luc turned to Abby. "To my house?"

"We don't know what it's like up there."

"I see lights. Probably fire engines. We'll call the sheriff."

They shoved the youngest children into the back and a couple of the bigger ones climbed in front with the babies. The others—adults and older kids—melted into the woods to continue on foot.

Up they went, staring out the windshield at where the reflection of emergency lights lit up the smoke and trees. One more bend and she'd see it: the destruction.

The sight knocked the breath out of her. It wasn't just the vines they'd burned. It was the cabin. *Luc's home.*

No. No, no, no. Over and over she thought it, but denial apparently didn't work. How could it be this cold with that inferno raging outside?

"*Fuck!*" Luc muttered, along with some French words that didn't sound nearly as pretty as usual. For a few dull-witted seconds, Abby watched him slam out of the truck and stalk to where Clay stood, a good distance from where the firefighters worked on the cabin.

It was no use. She knew it even as the people toiled, their blue and red lights ironically festive against the rock face above the barn, the only structure they'd left intact.

His home was a pile of destruction. Beyond it, a lighter cloud of smoke rose from the vines, the few surviving vines standing like eerie scarecrows in the dawn light.

She waited another beat or two in the shelter of the truck. *This is because of me.*

Even from this distance, Luc's silhouette looked exhausted as he indicated the truck. Clay turned, his expression hard, and moved toward them. Around her, the kids stirred, antsy and crying now when their lives were no longer in immediate danger.

"We need to get you all into the barn, and I'll call for backup." Clay looked at Abby. "You get all the kids out?"

"Yes. But we need to drive back down for the others—they're headed up on foot."

"We'll go." Clay's mouth tightened. He was no doubt beating himself up, although it wasn't his fault either. He yelled for a deputy, and they called for reinforcements, sent someone down to pick up the others, and moved the group of refugees into the barn, which, if nothing else, was warm.

"You okay?" the sheriff asked her once everyone had been located and brought to safety.

"I think so."

He looked at Luc, who nodded.

"We'll get these people out of your hair as soon as we can. Someplace where the kids are safe and..." His phone rang, and he stepped away to answer it, running his fingers through his short hair.

Abby lifted a hand to Luc's face—to wipe a smudge off, ostensibly, but really to touch him. To keep him to her, to apologize, to hold the pieces of him—of *them*—together. He looked wild and desperate. All she wanted was to make this right. How *could* she make this right? Down below, the men continued to fight the remaining flames.

"I'm sorry, Luc. I'll help you. We'll—"

"May I have a word, Luc?" It was Clay, sounding official, wanting to get to the bottom of everything. This was bad. It was all so bad. And what was happening next door?

On that thought, she was done. Done with it all. No more tolerance, acceptance be damned. What she felt was... Oh Lord, it was good. Pure. That amorphous guilt hardened like crystals, hot like the brightest spark, but calm and cool like the dingy snow lining the ground down below.

She stopped listening as the two men discussed the mess they'd find next door. Gesturing vaguely, she mumbled something about going to the bathroom and, instead, headed right for the door, then down the hill to the truck they'd driven up here. Rory's truck, with its farm vehicle license plate.

Weird how she noticed the tiniest details right now.

It was an amazing fuel, rage. Stronger than anything she'd felt in her entire life, it propelled her to the truck, where the keys hung in the ignition. It helped her get it started on the first try.

Without headlights, she rolled down the hill, finally accelerating through the curve and pushing it harder when she heard the first shout behind her. Of course they'd yell. They'd follow her, too, she assumed, which meant she had to hurry the hell up.

Motherfucker, cocksucker, and all those other choice expressions she'd stored up in her time outside rose up, but none of them seemed right. None of them felt like the insult she intended.

God hater. That would be a fitting insult to the man who'd set out to destroy her. *Infidel*, she thought, hatred and hysteria filling her head with idiocies. Every last bit of emotion she'd denied over the past months—*no, years*—coalesced into a solid wall of fury, righteous enough to run down anything in its path. She'd kill Isaiah. That was it. The only fitting punishment for what he'd done. All the lives he'd ruined. The one he'd destroyed by burning those vines. And for what? To hurt her? To get her back?

From somewhere close by came another explosion, and from the direction of town, more emergency lights added to the fray, blue ones, along with sirens. It rocked the truck and left her half-deaf. She shook her head to clear it of an image of Mama dead, planted her foot on the accelerator, and shot down the mountain.

~~∞~~

There was Denny, watching her as she drove up with eyes she couldn't understand. He looked as charred as the wreckage of the Center. As destroyed as she felt, as she gagged on the smell.

On a moan, she shoved out of the car, bent over, and vomited, narrowly missing his dusty, black shoes.

When she lifted her head again, there were more of them—the men. They'd lost their self-righteous sheen, which she didn't understand until it occurred to her: *They don't know the kids are out.* She looked around. *And their wives. They think they've killed their own wives.* Oh, no wonder they were such burnt-out husks.

"*You were willing to kill the babies but not yourselves?*" she tried to scream, but it came out raspy and weak.

Betrayal hung in the air around them, coiling in oily layers, thicker than smoke. The memory of Jeremiah's tiny, warm hands, the smell of his head as they bumped up the drive, made her push just a little more. They deserved the pain of not knowing.

And it might not be the Christian thing to do, but she wanted to punish these men. Every single one of them.

"I can't believe we were ever family. Or friends," she spat.

"Friends?" Isaiah's voice broke in as he appeared as if by magic in a cloud of smoke. How could he remain so unmoved by the poisoned atmosphere?

His voice cut through the air, slick as Sunday morning. "You were only friends with these men insofar as Adam was friends with Eve. Or the snake." He smirked, and Abby could see that snake clear as day, right here before her. "You think any of these men hold a torch for you? How many did you take liberties with? How many did you defile?"

The men shuffled awkwardly, but not one moved to defend her.

Slowly, Isaiah walked to the front of the group, his steps measured, theatrical. *Good*, she thought through

painfully rushing breaths, *come here so I can claw your
eyes out.* "God's will is done on the mountain tonight.
With the flame of His wrath, the balance is restored and
the sinners shall be punished."

"Are you *kidding* me? Sinners? *Murderer!*" she
screamed and lunged for him, but the men stopped her,
yanking at her arms. Trapped. Always trapped by this
man and his vile army. "Who's the sinner here, Isaiah?
Me? *I'm* the sinner? Is that what you're saying? What
about the babies? You did your best to kill the babies!"

"It was their time."

Through a half sob, half laugh, she spoke. "Oh?
Was it? Well, then your God's not as powerful as you
thought, is he?"

"What are you talking about?" Isaiah's step faltered.
Oh good, she'd taken him aback.

The hold on her loosened, and she stood her ground.
Ignoring his question, she let her voice grow stronger.
"No more hurting children. I was *fifteen years old* when
you gave me away. Who's the sinner there? Me? Or
you? Or the man old enough to be my grandfather? Oh,
but he sinned in the end. Did you know that?

"I tried to take him away. Bet you didn't know that
either, huh? Tried to get him to a hospital at the end. He
wouldn't let me. Because of your stupid version of God,
who would allow His most devout subject to suffer."

"If it's God's will, what may we do but obey and—"

"God's will!" she broke in with a choked laugh, not
moving a muscle as Isaiah drew closer. "Oh, you think it
was God's will that Hamish died when he did? Did your
God tell you that in one of your dreams? On one of your
treks to your magic rock? Is that it, O fearless leader?

You'll be disappointed to learn that *Hamish died by his own hand*. Not your angry God."

The men around her started to step back, her arguments widening the cracks in their conviction. She took in the horrified faces around her.

"You didn't think I'd sit back and let another person suffer, did you? Oh no, I helped him put an end to his misery. *Foxglove*, it's called. Such a pretty flower. And the best part? *You* chose it. Remember how you had us selling flowers at the market last summer? Remember those pretty purple flowers just so tall and graceful? Who'd ever think those sweet flowers could fell a grown man? 'Course, by the time he started begging for death, there wasn't much left of Hamish."

"You killed Hamish?"

"He killed himself."

She gagged on the memory but forced herself to remain strong, knowing just how much this hurt him—this hateful Messiah. More folks arrived during her confession, gathering silently together in the lightening night. Behind her, she heard the sounds of vehicles approaching, saw the red and blue lights reflected on smoke, but it didn't matter. Worse than killing Isaiah was embarrassing him in front of his men—his people. It would be all the vengeance she needed.

"What about the Mark, Isaiah? Is everybody here aware of what you and a few of the men did to me?" He took another step in her direction, this one furtive rather than self-assured, but she ignored him, turning in the glow of the headlights and unexpectedly catching her mama's eyes.

Her breath caught in her throat, and her thoughts

briefly scattered. "Oh, *Mama*, I was so afraid you were dead. I thought—"

"What are you doing?" her mother asked, looking horrified.

Abby forced herself to go still, not to rush to her mother. Instead, she studied her, trying to put the pieces of everything she knew and remembered together. The mother of her childhood, before this place; the woman standing in front of her now.

"Did you accept the Mark, Mama?" Abby impulsively asked.

No response.

"You did, right?"

Her mother nodded.

"Did you know they forced me? To take the Mark on my back? Over and over again?"

Abby wasn't sure what she expected. Maybe some sort of acknowledgment that her mother hadn't wanted this for her. What she got instead sent her back a step.

"You're a *wicked* child," her mama hissed. "Always been that way. Too curious by half."

"He tell you he was gonna take me as his wife, Mama? Two wives for this man?"

Her mother blinked and glanced at Isaiah—at her husband.

"Didn't know that, did you?"

The crowd parted as Abby made her way to her mother and grasped the older woman's hand. "Did he tell you how he cut open my best Sunday dress to get to me, Mama?"

Behind her, people whispered. From farther off came the sound of footsteps in gravel, but no one interrupted.

"My back…here." Turning, she urged Mama's hand up the back of her coat and shirt, to where the ridges of her shame resided like braille, the letters scabbed up beneath her fingertips. "You feel that? I didn't want it, so I got it tenfold. All over my back. You think God wanted that, too? Huh?"

"Oh, I knew all about it," spat Mama, pulling away and shocking the words right out of Abby's mouth. "You think Isaiah's the one who gave you to Hamish? You think he's the one who hears God?" Her gaze swung around to take in the crowd, her body vibrating. Everyone was still. "Isaiah may be God's tool on this mountain, his mouthpiece, but I am the eyes and ears. Only God told me the people wouldn't heed the word of a woman." As she leaned toward Abby, the words came low and vicious. "If he'd let me, I'd have marked you every day of your life, you vile, wicked child. Defiled and rotten to the core. With a father like yours, I'd have—"

"Were you the one who ordered the children killed, too, Mama?"

Silence.

"Lord, I knew you lot had this place rigged to blow, but I didn't think you'd do it." She threw an accusatory look at the crowd behind her. "You all let him do it?"

Someone in the crowd said an outraged *No!* and people moved, the tide changing. From out of the murmuring came a woman's voice.

It was Brigid. Lord only knew how she'd gotten back down here so fast. "The children are fine." To the side, behind the men, Brigid stood stiff, her skin black with soot, her chin held high. She met Abby's gaze with a burning one of her own, and a strange sort of sisterhood bloomed between them.

Isaiah jolted, a look of sheer surprise on his face. It would have been comical if this weren't such a tragedy.

"She helped us get them out in time." Brigid's attention moved from Abby to Isaiah. "You could hurt anyone else you wanted, Isaiah. I'd take it, for the sake of our Lord and Savior. But I couldn't let you hurt the babies." She looked around the crowd, her eyes soft and sad. "We've all been defiled here, ain't we? I never did like Abigail, but she's right. God surely don't want the babies to suffer. So we got 'em out. While you men were guardin' your perimeter, us women saved the babies."

Isaiah was livid. "You're just worried about your own child, aren't you, Brigid? Always—"

"*Yours*, you mean?" she responded, and everyone stopped.

Benji, mouth open, turned between his wife and his leader, looking lost.

Isaiah spoke. "Listen, Brigid, you're—"

She spun toward Abby. "You think you had it bad with Hamish? I was thirteen when Isaiah started making me do things. For God, he told me, over and over. Then he got me with child and used Benji to cover it up."

"Oh, Brigid," whispered Abby, but the woman wasn't done.

"I let you destroy my childhood," she continued, focused back on Isaiah. "But you won't destroy another child's. I'll kill you first. And, lucky for us all, Jeremiah's not yours."

"This is the Blackwood Sheriff's Department."

Clay's voice came over a loudspeaker, breaking the group apart. "I need you all to put your weapons down."

Slowly, the men complied, setting down their rifles. All but Isaiah.

The crowd shifted again, and from out of the fog came the crunch of footsteps. A glance to the side showed Clay and his deputies, Luc with them, weapons raised.

"I want to see hands," Clay yelled.

A sea of hands rose into the air, the men and women backing away from Isaiah.

Minutes passed, punctuated by the sound of walking on gravel, men and women switching sides, leaving just Abby, Brigid, Isaiah, and Mama.

"You, too, sir," said Clay.

Silence.

"I want him to suffer," said Abby.

"He'll suffer in prison."

"I want to press charges."

Clay was a few steps away now, where Luc also stood.

"You can do that. But you don't need to."

"Against her, too. My mother." She stared hard at the woman who was supposed to protect her and had instead thrown her to the wolves. "For whatever you'd call branding a woman against her will."

"I believe I'd like to do the same," Brigid said at Abby's side; her voice was strong. Her eyes held Abby's for a few moments as they waited for what came next.

"Yes, ma'am." The footsteps crunched closer, and with a new energy, Abby watched Clay move—flanked by deputies—to Isaiah, who surrendered his shotgun. He looked small and scared facing off against someone he couldn't bully. "Isaiah Bowden, you are under arrest for arson, assault, and battery…" Clay recited a litany as he led the man away.

With one last, long look at her mother, Abby turned her back on the only family she'd ever had and headed into a future that she couldn't possibly begin to imagine.

28

ABBY WAS DOWN BELOW WITH ONE OF THE DEPUTIES, giving her statement, and Sammy was playing out in the tractor cemetery, leaving Luc alone.

The fire trucks had left a couple hours before, and now there was just a single cop car parked in his torn-up drive, along with his truck, and the one they'd borrowed from that British bartender. They appeared gaudy among so much colorless devastation. Luc stood, looking at it all, alone with the filthy vestiges of his life.

God, that place—the Church's Center. And the room where they'd hurt Abby... He squeezed his eyes shut, picturing the kids.

He sighed in relief that it was all over and they were safe, but there was pain in his chest for all the wrong that had been done. What a viper's nest that place was. Too much to unravel, even though Clay's task force—which he'd already begun to assemble—had started pouring in. He wondered how long it all would take.

From somewhere behind the barn, he heard the clanging of metal. For a second, he considered telling Sammy not to mess with his things. And then he remembered how pointless it was. Who cared if Sammy screwed the tractor up even more? Who needed a goddamned tractor, after all, if he didn't have vines or even a place to live?

Another loud clang. He should check on Sammy. But still, he waited.

Without leaves on the trees, he could hear everything up here. Especially now, Luc thought, forcing his gaze to take in the charred mountainside, posts and vines and rocks mangled together, with the rare survivor standing intact above the rest. How did those bastards douse it all so fast?

With that amount of accelerant, you'd think the whole thing would be flattened—a clean slate, which would at least have the beauty of potential new beginnings. But no. Instead, it had the carbon-on-snow look of a movie battlefield, grim and gray and a filthy mess to clean up. And no matter how deep he reached, he couldn't find the energy to do it. Part of him wanted to tear the surviving vines down, too—to drown them in gas and burn them with the rest. He might muster up the strength to finish the destruction. Rebuilding, however…

The sound of a vehicle forging up the drive broke through the dead silence of this lifeless hillside. Luc felt no curiosity. Nothing. It could be anyone coming up to see him. Anyone at all, and he had absolutely no more fucks to give. The last of them had been cremated by neighbors he wished he could wipe off the face of the earth.

The car—a pristine, white SUV—swung up the last curve, spitting gravel, and paused at the fork in the drive. Another cop, late to the party? *Don't see me*, he prayed, keeping himself as still as his livelihood's charred remains. When the car started a three-point turn, he thought his wish had been granted, only to be proven wrong when a deputy pointed the driver up here. It reversed and struggled up the steep slope to where he stood beside the winery. The only thing left standing.

The windows were tinted, but suddenly he knew, with a certainty as dead as his vines, who was in that car. Olivier. His half brother, whose impeccable timing proved, once again, that he had worked out a deal with the devil.

How messed up was it that the first thing Luc wanted to do was cry? He turned away, choking back the tears from where they stabbed his sinuses and clogged his throat. Christ, when had he last cried? Ever? Not when his father or *Grandpère* died, or when he'd cut off that stupid finger. Not even last night, as he'd watched his vines burn. No, it took his brother showing up, out of the blue—at exactly this moment—for him to almost shed a tear.

Olivier got out of the car, took off his glasses, and took in the vineyard—not theatrically, the way their mother would have done, but nonchalantly. As if he saw shit like this every day.

And as if he saw Luc every day, Olivier came to stand beside him without a word, looking for all the world like the landowner, the winemaker he was supposed to be. Unlike Luc, who'd always been a peasant.

"Must have some amazing insurance" was all Olivier said.

Luc, expecting a question, an insult—*some* judgment—surprised himself by laughing. "*Insurance? Oh putain, mon vieux.* You have no idea."

"You have some kind of blight? Something you had to burn out?" He raised a brow at Luc.

That sounded about right, didn't it? Luc wasn't sure what would happen to his closest neighbors, but he was fairly sure the blight would leave him alone from here on. Too late, of course.

"*Hein*?" Olivier prompted.

"Not exactly. Neighbors burned me out."

With some satisfaction, Luc watched shock transform his brother's features.

"Someone did this to you? On purpose?"

Luc nodded.

"Jesus. I'll bet it was your winning personality." They stood in silence for a minute. "Nice view. I can see why you picked it."

"Wasn't the view."

"Oh?"

Luc indicated the boulders lurking just above and to the side of them. "Granite."

Olivier's brows were still up, still confused.

Luc shook his head. "Did you ever listen to a damn thing *Grandpère* said? About growing grapes?"

"No. Why should I when we had you for that?"

"You're such an asshole."

Olivier smiled. "Yes. Well, the asshole's here to beg." He paused, eyes on Luc, looking less confident than he ever had. "We need you. Please come back. Your rules."

Luc searched inside himself for some sort of elation or excitement or something victorious. He came up with nothing.

Still, though. Look at this place. Nothing but devastation. Was the universe telling him something? For once, maybe Luc Stanek should listen.

His thoughts flew to Abby, being made to tell her story again, down there with the deputy. Maybe it would be best if he left. For both of them. She'd be better off without him and his special brand of fucked up.

You couldn't ask for a fresher start. For either of them.

"Tell me more," Luc said, leading his brother into the barn to show him the dregs of his American life.

～∞◇～

Abby was exhausted by the time she made it up to the barn, where Luc was talking to a man—handsome, like Luc, but without the rough edges. In fact… She squinted at them and saw the resemblance. It was in the strong line of their noses, the sharp cut of their cheekbones, but where Luc's face was wide, his brother's was long and thin, bony and elegant.

"Abby, this is my brother, Olivier."

"Good to meet you," she said.

"*Enchanté*," Olivier said with a lift of an eyebrow, a kiss to the back of her hand, and a smile that should have dropped her on the spot. "You are…"

"Abby is…my friend," said Luc.

Abby couldn't look at him. Her knees threatened to give out, but she steeled them and forced a smile. Of course. A friend. Just that. "Olivier is trying to get me to go back to France," he went on.

"I'm asking you to come back to your rightful *home*. To take over the vineyard. I'm asking for help."

Abby swallowed, finally turning to Luc, whose eyes burned into hers. "Are you going?"

"He has to," interrupted Olivier. Then, to Luc, "You

were always the heart and soul of the place. I was too blind to see it."

Luc said, "I haven't decided yet," then turned to her. "What do you think I should do?" It was the hope in his eyes that did it. He wanted to go. And now that she'd destroyed his life, he deserved a fresh start. It was what he wanted, wasn't it? When he'd spoken of France, he'd always sounded resentful but also...homesick, maybe?

Blinking back the tears that threatened to push their way out, she said, "You should go."

"Yes?" All was silent except for the sound of Sammy banging on metal out back.

"What's left for you here?" she asked, swallowing hard. And then, to put that final nail in the coffin: "Lord only knows where Sammy and I'll end up. No reason for us to stay here, is there?"

"You'll go away, then?"

"'Course," she lied. "I promised. Besides, it's always been the plan."

Luc asked, "Would you like to come with me?" and Abby almost caved. Almost. But then she remembered this man's sense of responsibility, the way he'd feel obligated to take care of her and Sammy and the dog, and she understood. This was duty speaking.

She forced out a tough laugh. "Me and Sammy? And what, we'd learn French? No, he's got people here." She tried to sound flippant, as if she did this sort of thing every day, and said, "Maybe I'll visit you sometime." Avoiding his eyes, Abby smiled hard and looked between the men. "You couldn't have come at a better time, I'll tell you that, Olivier."

"So I understand," he said with a satisfied smile.

From out back came the rumble of an engine coming to life, and the three of them followed the sound to where Sammy sat atop the ancient tractor.

"Hi, friends!" he yelled cheerily. "Got it fixed!"

Forcing a smile, Abby nodded. "Good job, Sammy-Boy. Good job." She let her eyes meet Luc's and, for just a moment, saw something there that gave her a foolish spark of hope.

Maybe he'll stay, she thought, until his eyes slid to his brother, and she realized exactly what that hope was about—not her, not here, not a stupid, old tractor coming back to life a day too late. No, the hope was for a different kind of second chance. And no matter how hard she tried, she couldn't see herself in that picture. She held it together long enough to grab Sammy, pile into Rory's truck, and drive back into town.

But it wasn't until she and Sammy returned to her tiny, pathetic room above the Nook and she'd taken Le Dog out for a few minutes, that she locked herself into the bathroom and let go with long, hard, silent sobs. Because, while she'd released Luc, giving him a much-deserved second chance at life, there was nothing left for her to do but go on. Even if it meant grieving the loss of the only man she'd ever loved.

~ତ∽

The roots of a grapevine grow down and out. Almost, but not quite, mirroring the branches above. They go deep, and they can spread, although the majority of the roots stay right there, close to the plant.

The best wines don't come easy. You don't plant in wet soil where the roots take hold and grow dense right away. No, you want that plant to struggle, to work hard, to produce fewer grapes. But those grapes… Luc knew from experience that the best wines came from ambitious plants. Plants that overcame obstacles to develop their flavor.

Hardy and sweet. Exactly like Abby Merkley. She'd been given nothing, absolutely nothing in life, and yet she'd reached far and wide for what she'd needed.

Olivier had surprised Luc when he'd offered to stay for a bit and clear away the mess left by the fire. He'd known, somehow, that Luc couldn't leave the place like this—devastated and burned. That whole first day after the fire, the men worked, making plans for a future that Luc couldn't seem to build any excitement around. As they talked, France felt different from before—far away, almost mythical and completely without challenge— drab compared to this place.

As the day drew to an end and Luc thought about spending tonight camped out in front of the tasting-room fire, Olivier approached him, filthier than Luc had ever seen him.

"So, are you going to let me taste it?" his brother asked, handing him a bottle of water.

Luc chugged, wiped his mouth with the back of his hand, and narrowed his eyes dumbly. "What?"

"Your wine, you idiot. All those fucking bottles in there. And the barrels. I'd try one on my own, but that's not really done, is it?" Eyes intense on Luc, he went on. "So, you give me a taste?"

Luc didn't want to give his brother the wine. He didn't want to hear what he'd have to say about it and certainly didn't need the criticism.

But what was the point of refusing? At this point, throwing in the towel meant letting go of all his old anger, didn't it?

With a sigh, he grabbed a couple glasses and the thief. He led Olivier into the barrel room, where the wine worked, if not toward greatness, at least toward something.

He eased the bunghole open and served a good helping into the first glass, because what the fuck difference did it make now anyway, if the barrels weren't topped up?

Trying not to think of that day he'd gone through these same motions with Abby, he went to the other side of the room and served up the second wine for comparison, then handed the glasses to his brother.

"Come on. I want to get a good look at this wine. Can't see a damned thing in here." Olivier led him out into the tasting room, where the last of the day's light illuminated the vintage to a rich, ruby red.

Luc had to force himself to blink and look away as his brother went through the practiced motions of tasting the wine: putting his nose fully in the glass, swirling it, and watching the progression of the legs down the sides.

He heard the sound of slurping as Olivier let his breath float over the liquid in his mouth, humming with what was no doubt disapproval. *Bordel*, why was he this nervous? He'd decided to leave, so what did it matter?

When Olivier finally deigned to speak, he shocked Luc by asking, "Are you planning to say good-bye to your friend?"

"Who?"

"I'm talking about your girlfriend. The one who's

going to keep you in this fucking place as surely as this wine will."

"What are you talking about?"

"I'm talking about you staying here," said Olivier.

Luc started to shake his head and then stopped.

"Wait. You like it?" He flicked his eyes to the glass.

"It's young." His brother's lips turned down in disapproval. God, how very French. "But it's interesting."

"Give me that," Luc demanded. He reached for the glass and took an uncontrolled swig of his own wine.

And it *was* interesting, wasn't it?

Another exploration, slow this time. Luc enjoyed the finish, which was more complex than anything his grandfather had ever managed to produce, and suddenly he couldn't breathe.

Out of the corner of his eye, he spotted a bright splash of color, out of place here in the tasting room. It took a few seconds for him to recognize the blanket—no, quilt—that Abby had given him. He hadn't listened when she'd told him to bring it to the cabin the day she'd thrust it into his hands. The day he'd lost his soul to a kiss.

He barely managed to shove the glass at his brother before bending down, hands on his knees, breath harsh and out of control. On an inhalation so deep it burned his lungs, Luc knew that Olivier was right. *I can't leave.*

The room straightened, and he managed to stand up again, focusing hard on Olivier.

"I'm not leaving," he said, and Olivier just nodded.

Luc saw with crystal clarity how different they were. His brother was the barely rolling hills of Bordeaux, so green and easy, with its neat patchwork of well-behaved vines. But Luc was this place. He was his mountain, wild and rough, its rock belly blown out into the open by tectonic shifts older than human memory. He was broken, splintered, and sullen like this carbonized hillside he'd thought he could leave behind.

Difficult terrain at the best of times, but add in pests, blight, tropical summers—not to mention the neighbors from hell—and you had…a challenge. The thought made him smile, an image of *her* rising up in his mind: the biggest challenge of all.

"I'm staying." His voice came out too loud, and his brother startled.

"I know. Don't worry. We'll survive without you. Somehow." Olivier smirked and then poofed his breath out in that blasé French way that Luc actually missed. "And all for a fucking woman."

"Yeah," breathed Luc, feeling lighter than he had in days or months or ever. "All for a woman."

Olivier handed the glass to him and clinked the second one against it.

"Cheers, my brother," he said, shaking his head. "And good luck."

29

IT WAS THREE DAYS AFTER THE FIRE. THREE DAYS SINCE
they'd seen each other. Three days, and Luc was likely
gone forever. She'd thought he'd come and pick up his
dog. Or at the very least, say good-bye, but she hadn't
heard a peep. With everything else that had happened,
she'd hardly found time to sort things out, much less
worry about the man.

Oh, what a lie. Worry was all she'd done. Aside
from waiting tables, setting up doctor's appointments,
and finding people to help with Sammy, all she'd done
was dwell.

While her life had been turned upside down in more
ways than she could possibly imagine, all she could do
was think about that man.

She still didn't understand what had happened last
night, with the biggest surprise coming in the form of a
lawyer—Hamish's lawyer, to be exact. He'd shown up
out of the blue during last night's shift at the Nook, to
tell her that she, Abigail Merkley, was the sole owner of
the Church of the Apocalyptic Faith. Well, of the land

and its buildings, because she had absolutely no use for the Church itself.

It's my mountain.

She got dizzy at the mere idea.

According to the lawyer, the land had belonged to Hamish all along. He'd started the Church in the eighties, and though Isaiah had tried to usurp the older man, he'd never gotten him to sign over the deed.

It was hers.

And then had come the realization that Isaiah probably wanted her for that reason alone. A puzzle solved.

Standing at the east-facing window, she looked out at the mountain. *Her* mountain.

She should feel triumph. Not this soul-deep sadness. She had saved Sammy and gotten the kids out, broken up the Church that had taken on a life of its own. What was next? Maybe she'd go to college or travel. She'd had this idea, after talking with the Child Protective Services workers, of starting a nonprofit to help people like her, who wanted to start a new life and didn't know how.

None of it felt right, though. Not right or whole. Not the planning or the future or the mountain.

Because she didn't, it turned out, want the mountain without the man.

When the knock came, she imagined more lawyers or police or Rory telling her to get Sammy out of his kitchen, where he'd happily set to work washing dishes the night before. She should have known when Le Dog ran to the door with a very rare *woof* of excitement.

What she hadn't pictured as she opened the door was Luc, holding a small, brown suitcase in one hand and a stack of skinny, wide books in the other.

"Oh" was all she managed to say.

"Can I come in?"

Abby didn't move, at least not on the outside. Inside, though, her body was fizzing and bubbling, full of hope and excitement.

"What's that?" she asked, indicating the suitcase.

"Record player. And records," he answered. "Music."

"Seems rather old-fashioned."

"That's funny, coming from you."

Unable to stop herself, she smiled, feeling her eyebrows rise. "You think we didn't have CDs over there?"

"You did?"

"In the Center. We listened to music. I told you Isaiah always loved music."

"But not dancing." After a pause: "Can I come in, Abby?"

Not quite trusting him—or maybe herself—she backed up one step and then another until he could brush past her. He put down the records and got the player set up while she looked at them. *Jacques Brel, Edith Piaf*—words she could barely make out, much less understand. "These all in French?"

"*Bien sûr.* But of course." He pulled one from the pile, opened it up, and slid out the wide, shiny black disk. "This is how people listened to music once upon a time."

She narrowed her eyes at him. "When you were a kid?"

"No. Before that. These were my grandfather's." Judging by the way he handled the object, he cared about it. "I've bought a few since then, but they're mostly his." He glanced at her. "I never took them out of their box. Left them in the barn. They're the only thing I have left." He paused. "That and a quilt made by an incredible woman."

Oh, why did those words constrict her chest like that? Maybe it was the image of Luc as a little boy, lost and alone with nothing but his grandfather's music to comfort him. Nothing to do with him cherishing her gift.

"I will be back," he said and went outside. A few minutes later, he returned with more electronics, all of which took him some time to set up and turn on before he pushed every stick of furniture away from the center of the room. "First of all, there are things I want, but if you don't want them, then you don't have to say yes."

"What kind of things?"

"I want you in my tasting room, selling the wine."

She suppressed the wave of hope that worked its giddy way out of her heart.

"But first…" When he dropped the needle onto one of the disks, it let out a funny tearing sound, which made her jump slightly, before the notes emerged from two speakers he'd put on the counter.

The music started. Violins swelled, and a man's voice, melodic and crackly, started singing.

Luc looked her in the eye. "May I please have this dance, Abby?"

"What are you—"

"May I have your *first* dance?"

Letting out a hot whoosh of air, she nodded. One of his arms circled her, while his other hand grasped hers— warm and firm—and he twirled her into the center of the room.

It was an entirely different sensation from what she'd experienced with those men encroaching on her downstairs. That had been sexual, sweaty and frenzied in a way she hadn't been comfortable with. This, while still sensual, was...beautiful.

As he led her around the room with nothing but the palm of one hand and the length of his body, Abby felt herself getting more than swept away.

"I danced once before."

"Oh?"

"Downstairs, one night, with George and another friend."

"Did you enjoy it?"

"It was freeing, I suppose."

He smiled.

With a hard sigh that he had to have felt through her chest, she said, "But this, this is better."

"Good." After a few more turns, he asked against her ear, "Do you know what else I want, Abby?"

She shook her head.

"I want to be your first again. From now on, I want to be the one you do new things with. Forever. *Always.*"

She was breathless. "That's...that's sweet, but—"

"I also want to be the last. The last one to touch you and make love to you. I want to be the first and the last. The only one for you. Will you let me? Will you let me be that?"

Abby looked away, her eyes alighting on that mountain through the window before he turned them and it disappeared from view. Goodness, she wanted him. Only him.

A smile lit her face, and she whispered, "Yes."

They danced for another three songs before the heat between them got to be too much. A different heat than what they'd had before. All the shame, the fear, and the doubt was gone, and in its place was a hot, hot tenderness.

Abby felt it in the touch of his lips when he kissed her, in the stroke of his fingers. It was in the brush of his face against hers, his mouth at the crook of her neck, his eyes scorching nerve endings she'd never even realized existed.

"I'm not innocent," she said.

She felt his smile against her skin. "No?"

"I'm a sinner, Luc. I'm a sinner at heart. Isaiah knew it. God's in on it. And now that I've come to terms with it, I want to enjoy it. Can you help me do that?"

"Oh, *ma belle*," he muttered close to the side of her face, his hands moving all the while, stroking, pressing. Good Lord, the man's hands were amazing. Rough and hard, but gentle. Somehow, her shirt was twisted up and away, a bra cup shoved to the side as one of his blunt fingers rasped against her tight nipple. "*Je vais te baiser.*" He smirked. "I want you so badly." His other hand was in her hair, wrapped in it, tugging so she could watch him do these things to her.

No, not to her—*with* her.

She leaned back to shove up his sweater and got lost while admiring the muscles and hair and glorious skin of his chest. This was freedom, wasn't it? It wasn't touching yourself with soap, wrapped in decades of shame, accepting the bad that came crashing in right behind the good.

This was none of the things she'd left behind. This—in this place, with Luc against her—was her choice.

My choice.

The thought sent her forward, pulling down his chin to bite his lip. And he liked that. She could tell he liked it by the grunt that puffed out. Another bite, lower, before drifting to the side, where his skin was soft but smelled so male. *How did I not know what a real man smelled like before Luc? And why does this one smell so* damned *good?*

Freedom had taken on its own smell: woodsmoke and man. Bittersweet until just this minute. It smelled like the mountain, which she'd never expected. No, in her mind, freedom had smelled like sea salt and the unknown of the world's teeming cities. Boat exhaust and city buses. Not this. Not home right here, with him.

"You're my freedom," she said, meaning it.

"And you mine, *mon amour.*"

Another bite as his rough fingers caressed her flesh, left marks she'd have to examine in depth later—marks that would eventually fade and disappear. Nothing like the marks God had left her with.

Isaiah, whispered the voice in her head. *Not God.*

She tugged at his sweater.

"I can't... This keeps sliding down. Can you take it off?" she asked, and he complied. Immediately, gratifyingly.

"You, too. Come on." Oh, his impatience did things to her. To be wanted. Was that what this was? No. No, because the men she'd danced with, the ones who'd touched her, they'd wanted her, too. But *she* hadn't wanted *them* this way.

He struggled with his sweater, and she watched him for a moment, enjoyed the way he stepped back, unabashed, ready. *He's undressing for me.* Again, without a doubt, this was what she wanted. And to undress for him, to give herself.

"What's that mean?"

"What?"

"*Mon amour.* What you said a second ago."

He stopped moving, his eyes meeting hers, so sweet and blue. So different from the day they'd met. "It means my love," he whispered, drawing close once his sweater fell to the floor. He spoke against her ear. "I love you, Abby. More than the vines or the grapes or the dirt or wine. You're my everything. My raison d'être." He swallowed, the sound dry. "You are home. My home."

She hiccupped at those words and the pressure they built in her chest—in her heart, where she'd never expected to feel so full. "And you're mine, Luc."

His lips curved against her ear, smiling what she knew was a handsome, warm smile. Tilting back, she took him in. Happy. He looked *happy.*

I did that, she thought, with the most powerful thrill of her life. *I made this broken man whole.*

And goodness, that did things to her body. She dipped to work at the laces of her boots and the buttons of her shirt, and the thoughts in her head turned to sensations in her body. Heavy and warm, the need settled between her legs. She brimmed with energy. Like syrup or fire or… or wine. Like a bright, thick, strong red wine.

Feeling more blessed than she had ever been, Abby sank into the arms of the man she'd had the pleasure of making whole again and gave thanks.

She must have made a noise as she watched him undress, because he stopped to look at her. She drank him in, knowing with absolute certainty, for the first time since she'd left the Church—maybe the first time in her life—that there was, indeed, something divine smiling down upon her.

Read on for an excerpt from the first book in the Blank Canvas series by Adriana Anders

UNDER HER SKIN

> Old hag in need of live-in helper to abuse. Nothing kinky.

UMA READ THE AD AGAIN.

Jesus. Was she really going to do this?

Yes. Yes, she was. She'd come all the way back to Virginia for the hope its free clinic offered, and if this was the only job she could get while she was in town, she should consider herself lucky to have found it. *Especially*, she thought with a wry smile, *since it's one for which I'm so qualified.*

The smile fell almost immediately. Everything was moving so fast. Not even in town for a day, and here she was, standing on a stranger's front porch. The house, thankfully, wasn't even close to the haunted manor she'd imagined. Then again, who knew what waited behind that chipped red door?

Taking a big, bolstering breath, Uma slipped the newspaper clipping back into her pocket and knocked.

There was a light *thunk* on the other side, followed by what sounded like footsteps, a scuffling, and then nothing. She waited, trying to hear more over the drone of a nearby lawn mower, and thought of all the reasons this was a horrible idea.

Abuse? *Abuse?* How could she possibly take this job in the shape she was in?

But as usual, the desperate reality of her situation pushed all arguments aside. Food, shelter, money. There was no arguing with necessity, even if this place felt off.

And the situation was perfect. No one could find her here. In theory. She was pretty sure her new employer wouldn't be phoning up any references or doing a background check. The woman must be desperate too. She'd practically hired Uma over the phone, for goodness' sake.

Someone should have answered by now.

Uma knocked again. Hard, her hand starting to tremble.

Something moved in her peripheral vision, startling Uma into a gasp. The curtain in the front window?

The cloth twitched a second time. The woman was watching. Making Uma wait out here, overdressed in the unseasonable heat, sweat gathering along her hairline. Okay, fine. She could see how it made sense to check out a stranger before letting her in. She'd give the lady a few more minutes to finish her perusal. If only she could get some air. Just a little air in this stifling heat.

When there was no response to her third knock, Uma panicked. According to the oversize watch on her arm, three minutes had passed. Three minutes spent standing on a porch, enduring the scrutiny of a self-proclaimed *abuser* who represented her only chance at a job. Not the auspicious beginning she had hoped for.

It was all so familiar too. Maybe not the exact

circumstances, but the feelings she lived with on a daily basis—insecurity, worry, fear clawing at her chest, crowding her throat so each inhale was a struggle. Before they could overwhelm her, she shoved them away and walked down the rickety porch stairs and around to the side of the house, where she could gather herself unseen beneath the first-floor windows. She needed to *breathe*.

Uma took a shaky breath in, then out, another in, before biting into the meaty pad of her thumb. The ritual was safe, easy to sink back into, the shape of her teeth already worn into her hand. *Just a little while*, she thought. *Until I sort myself out, and then...* Then she had no idea what. She had nowhere to go, nothing left to aspire to.

One step at a time. That was her life now. No planning, no future.

She was vaguely aware that the lawn mower drew near, no longer background noise, buzzing close and echoing the beat of her heart. She'd have to push off this wall sooner or later, but the warm clapboard was solid against her back, and along with the sharp smell of freshly clipped grass, it kept her right here, present, in her body. A few more breaths and she'd move. Time to decide whether she'd head up to the house to give it another try or cut her losses and take off, find something else.

Yeah, right.

The problem was she wouldn't be cutting her losses by leaving—she'd be compounding them. How on earth could she go back on the road with the gas gauge on *E* and ten bucks to her name?

Strike that. After this morning's breakfast, she had only $6.54.

Uma sank down onto her haunches, the ground

squelching under her heels, and squeezed her eyes shut so hard that black dots floated behind the lids.

She had nothing left—no home, no job, no way of making money, no skills but one…and Joey had destroyed any chance of pursuing her true livelihood when he'd smashed her cameras. Doing that, he'd destroyed *her*. Six months later, she was still trapped.

If she let herself feel it, there'd be no shortage of pain, inside and out. As usual, her wrist under the watch was raw, and her skin itched everywhere. It must be psychosomatic. It couldn't still itch after all this time, could it?

Visualizing his marks on her skin was enough to make her hyperventilate again. And the tightness was there, that constriction that had left her constantly out of breath these past several months. She'd thought the miles would clear the airways, but they hadn't.

And now she was back. Back in Virginia. Shallow breaths succeeded one another, pinching her nostrils and rasping noisily through her throat. Joey was close. Two hours away by car. Way too close for comfort. She swore she could feel him looking for her, closing in on her.

Something cold and wet swiped Uma's hand, snapping her back to the present. She opened her eyes with a start, only to come face-to-face with a *dog*. A black one with a tan face, floppy ears, and pretty brown eyes rimmed in black, like eyeliner. It smiled at her.

It was something else, that dog, with that sweet look on its face. Like it gave a crap. Weird. The expression was so basically human, it pulled back the tunnel vision and let some light seep in. The dog nudged her chest, hard, and pushed its way into her arms in a big, warm tackle-hug. Uma had no choice but to hug back.

Its cold nose against her neck shocked a giggle out of her. "Oh, all right. You got moves, dog."

"She does," said a deep voice from above.

Uma's head snapped back in surprise, sounding a dull *thunk* against the clapboard. Oh God. Where had *he* come from?

"She's a barnacle."

Uma nodded dully, throat clogged with fear. *Stop it*, she berated herself. *You've got to stop freaking out at every guy who says two words to you.* She tried for a friendly smile. It felt like a grimace.

The man just stood there, a few feet away, looking at her. She waited. He waited. He looked like a big, creepy yard worker or something. Tall. Really, *really* tall.

"Gorilla," he said.

"What?"

"My dog, Squeak. She's a guerrilla fighter. Thought about callin' her Shock 'n' Awe."

"Squeak?" She stared up at him, craning her neck with the effort. She was wrong before. To say he was tall was an understatement. The man blocked out the sun. With the light behind him, it was hard to see much, aside from the big, black beard covering half his face and the shaggy mane around it. His voice was deep, gravelly. *Burly.* It went with the hair and the lumberjack shirt. You didn't see guys like him where she came from.

"Wasn't her name originally. She earned it." When he talked, the words emerged as if they hurt, purling out one slow syllable at a time. As if being sociable was an effort. Yet, for some reason—for her—he was trying.

He waited, probably for her to say something in response, but she'd been running too long to be any good at repartee. She'd turned into more of a watch-and-wait kind of girl.

The man finally continued, tilting his chin toward the house she was leaning on. "You her next victim?"

Uma winced, embarrassed. "Guess so."

He lifted his brows in semi-surprise before turning to the side and stuffing his hands deep into the pockets of jeans that had seen better days. They were stained and ratty and littered with what looked like burn holes.

Backlit by the sun, his profile was interesting, despite the bushy lower half of his face. Or maybe because of it. He looked like something you'd see stamped into an ancient coin—hard and noble. The scene came easily into focus: clad in something stained and torn, wading into the thick of battle with his men, sword in hand, face smeared with enemy blood, and teeth bared in a primal war cry. Her hands came to life, itching for a camera.

She blinked and emerged to see him as he was: a filthy redneck with a rug on his face. He was intimidating, to say the least. Not the kind of guy she'd choose to work in *her* yard—not looking all roughed up like he did.

But this new phase of life was about taking back what Joey had stolen. It was about *courage*, and because this guy was so intimidating, Uma decided to face him head-on. Show no fear. Another rule for this new self that she was constantly reinventing: no more letting men intimidate her.

"Help me up?" she asked.

After a brief hesitation, he complied. His grasp was rough and solid, ridged with calluses in places and polished smooth in others. For a moment, after pulling her up to stand, he didn't let go of her hand. Instead, he turned it over and eyed the crescent her teeth had left behind.

She fought the urge to snatch it away.

He raised his brows but finally let her go without a word. Burning with the need to put some distance between them, she took a hurried step back.

"Thanks," she said as he squatted down to scratch Squeak roughly under the chin. The dog's eyes closed in ecstasy.

Forcing herself to steady her nerves, Uma caught his gaze and held it. He was even scarier without the sun behind him, skin marred by a shiny, white scar along his hairline and a dark bruise on a cheek already peppered with errant beard hairs. His nose was crooked and thick, no doubt broken in a barroom brawl or something equally disreputable. She envisioned him in a smoky basement, duking it out for some seedy underground boxing title. Carved squint lines surrounded eyes that were a cool blue.

Or…*oh*. No. She realized with a start that his left eye was blue and the right was dark gold. She was instantly thrown off-kilter. Which one was she supposed to focus on? She blinked and turned aside, uncomfortable with the way he so effortlessly unsettled her.

"I've…" he rumbled, coming up out of the squat to tower over her again. She waited for him to continue.

"You've…?" she finally asked after the silence had stretched too long. She wondered if she was as off-putting to him as he was to her.

"Ive. It's my name. Short for Ivan."

"Oh. I'm Uma." She gave him her real name without thinking. "You mow the lawn here?"

"You could say that." His eyes crinkled. What little she could see of his mouth turned up into a surprisingly warm smile. "Figure I might as well mow her lawn while I'm doin' mine."

She looked at the house behind him. "*That's* your place?"

Her surprise must have been obvious, but he didn't react, just gave a single, brief nod.

"Wow. Nice." The house *was* nice. *Really nice.* Incongruously…civilized. He looked like the kind of guy you'd find chopping wood by his cabin in the boondocks, not maintaining the lawn of his lovely old farmhouse.

It was straight out of *Southern Living*, nicer than some of the places she'd photographed.

The caricature she'd formed in her head of this man melted partially away to reveal something a little softer, less defined. It didn't jibe inside of her, but she'd been running on stereotypes and first impressions and messed-up *wrong* impressions for so long that her instincts clearly needed a reset. Another thing to add to the growing list of upgrades for Uma 2.0.

He nodded, face serious, but she thought she could detect pride beneath the gruff exterior.

She caught sight of a bright-red tricycle in the drive beside a clunky Ford pickup. Kids. Probably a wife. Her perception shifted yet again, and he didn't seem half as scary as he had a moment before. Wow, she couldn't straighten her life out at all, and *this guy* seemed to have his shit together. So much for first impressions.

Acknowledgments

Thank you to my amazing family of beta readers: Radha, Poorna, and Lakshmi Metro, you rock! (I want to see that book, La.) A huge thanks to Callie Russell, whose feedback is always perfectly on point, and to Christine Murray and Corey Jo Lloyd for being my guinea pigs. This would have been a lot harder without my wonderful team of romance buds: Amanda Bouchet, Joanna Bourne, Alleyne Dickens, Chan Cox Elder, Madeline Iva, Wendy La Capra, Kasey Lane, Elizabeth Safleur, and Heather Van Fleet. A huge thank-you to Christine Vrooman of Ankida Ridge Vineyards, who shared her immense knowledge of winemaking with me. Your words are wise and your wine heavenly. All errors are my own.

I owe so much to my editor, Mary Altman, who, along with Laura Costello, helped mold this book into what it is today, along with the rest of the amazing team at Sourcebooks. To Laura Bradford, thank you for being the most efficient, badass agent a woman could want. Finally, thank you to my husband for making this a

priority, to my parents for watching the kids when dead-
lines loomed, and to my babies for spending too many
weekends without your mama.

About the Author

Adriana Anders has acted and sung, slung cocktails and corrected copy. She's worked for start-ups, multinationals, and small nonprofits, but it wasn't until she returned to her first love—writing romance—that she finally felt like she'd come home. Today, she resides with her tall, French husband, two small children, and a fat, French cat in the foothills of the Blue Ridge Mountains, where she writes the dark, emotional love stories of her heart.

Be the first to know about new releases, sales, and more by signing up for Adriana's newsletter at adrianaanders.com/newsletter. Visit Adriana: adrianaanders.com

Like Adriana on Facebook: facebook.com/adrianaandersauthor

Follow Adriana on Twitter: twitter.com/adrianasboudoir